The Angel of Pain

E. F. Benson

The Angel of Pain

ISBN: 978-1-63637-358-4

CONTENTS

FIRST

THE garden lay dozing in the summer sun, a sun, too, that was really hot and luminous, worthy of mid-June, and Philip Home had paid his acknowledgments to its power by twice moving his chair into the shifting shade of the house, which stood with blinds drawn down, as if blinking in the brightness. Somewhere on the lawn below him, but hidden by the flower-beds of the terraced walk, a mowing-machine was making its clicking journeys to and fro, and the sound of it seemed to him to be extraordinarily consonant to the still heat of the afternoon. Entirely in character also with the day was the light hot wind that stirred fitfully among the garden beds as if it had gone to sleep there, and now and then turned over and made the flowers rustle and sigh. Huge Oriental poppies drooped their scarlet heads, late wall-flowers still sent forth their hot, homely odour, peonies blazed and flaunted, purple irises rivalled in their fading glories the budding stars of clematis that swarmed up the stone vases on the terrace, golden rain showered from the laburnums, lilacs stood thick in fragrant clumps and clusters. Canterbury bells raised spires of dry, crinkly blue, and forget-me-nots—nearly over—made a dim blue border to the glorious carpet of the beds. For the warm weather this year had come late but determinedly, spring flowers still lingered, and the later blossoms of early summer had been forced into premature appearance. This fact occupied Philip at this moment quite enormously. What would the garden be like in July? There must come a break somewhere, when the precious summer flowers were over, and before the autumn ones began.

It was not unreasonable of him to be proud of his garden, for any garden-lover would here have recognised a master-hand. Below, in the thick clay that bordered the Thames, were the roses kept apart, with no weed, no other flower to pilfer their rightful monopoly of "richness." A flight of twelve stone steps led up from this garden to the tennis lawn, a sheet of velvet turf, unbordered by any flowers to be trampled by ball-seekers, or to be respected by ball-losers. Above again where he sat now a deep herbaceous border ran round three sides of the gravelled space, in the middle of which a bronze fountain cast water over Nereids and aquatic plants, and behind him rose the dozing house, sun-blinds and rambler rose, jasmine and red bricks.

Certainly at this moment Philip was more than content with life, a very rare but a very enviable condition of affairs. The lines seemed to him to be laid not in pleasant but in ecstatic places, and youth, hard work, a well-earned holiday, keen sensibilities, and being in love combined to form a state of mind which might be envied by the happiest man God ever made. An hour's meditation with a shut book which he had selected at random from the volumes on the drawing-room table had convinced him of this, and the interruption that now came to his solitary thoughts was as delightful in its own way as the thoughts themselves.

Mrs. Home did everything in the way most characteristic of her, and if a Dresden shepherdess could be conceived as sixty years old she might

1

possibly rival the clean, precise delicacy of Philip's mother. She dressed in grey and Quakerish colours, but of an exquisite neatness, and her clothes smelled faintly but fragrantly of lavender and old-fashioned herbs. Even at sixty the china-prettiness of her face gave her pre-eminent charm; and her cheeks, wrinkled with no sharp lines of sudden shock, but with the long pleasant passage of time, were as pink and soft as a girl's. Her hair was perfectly white, but still abundant, and, taken up in rather old-fashioned lines above her temples gave a roundness and youth to her face which was entirely in keeping with her. As she stepped out of the drawing-room window she put up her parasol, and walked quietly over the gravel to where her dark, long-limbed son was sitting.

"Darling, would it not be wise of you to go for a row on the river?" she said. "Your holiday is so short. I want you to make the best of it."

Philip turned in his chair.

"Darling, it would be most unwise," he said. "The best holiday is to do nothing at all. People are so stupid! They think that if your brain, or what does duty for it, is tired, the remedy is to tire your body also."

"But a little walk, perhaps, Philip," said she. "I can explain to your guests when they come. Do you know, I am rather frightened of them. That extraordinary Mr. Merivale, for instance. Will he want to take off all his clothes, and eat cabbages?"

Philip's grave face slowly relaxed into a smile. He hardly ever laughed, but his smile was very complete.

"I shall tell him you said that," he remarked.

Mrs. Home sat down with quite a thump at the horror of the thought.

"Dear Philip," she said, "you mustn't—you really mustn't."

He stretched out his hand to her.

"Oh, mother," he said, "what will cure you of being so indiscreet except threats, and putting those threats into execution if necessary? He will want to take off all his clothes, as we all shall, if it goes on being so hot. Only he won't any more than we shall. He will probably be extremely well-dressed. No, the Hermit is only the Hermit at the Hermitage. Even there he doesn't take off all his clothes, though he lives an outdoor life. You never quite have recognised what a remarkable person he is."

"I should remark him anywhere," said Mrs. Home in self-defence. "And what age is he, Philip? Is he twenty, or thirty, or what?"

Philip considered.

"He must be a year or two older than me," he said. "Yes, I should say he was thirty-one. But it's quite true—he doesn't look any age; he looks ageless. Entirely the result of no clothes and cabbages."

"They always seem to me so tasteless," remarked Mrs. Home. "But they seem to suit him."

"Dear old Hermit!" said Philip. "I haven't seen him for a whole year. It becomes harder and harder to get him away from his beloved forest."

"I can never understand what he does with himself, year in, year out, down there," said Mrs. Home.

"He thinks," said Philip.

"I should call that doing nothing," remarked his mother.

2

"I know; there is that view of it. At the same time, it must be extremely difficult to think all day. I have been thinking for an hour, and I have quite finished. I should have had to begin to read if you hadn't come out. And whom else are you frightened of out of all these terrible people?"

Mrs. Home smoothed her grey gown a little nervously.

"I am frightened of Lady Ellington," she said. "She has so very much—so very much self-possession. She is so practical, too: she always tells me all sorts of ways of managing the house, and suggests all kinds of improvements. It is very kind of her, and she is always quite right. And I think I am a little afraid of Madge."

"Ah, I can't permit that," said Philip, smiling again.

This brought their talk at once into more intimate lands.

"Ah, dear Philip," she said. "I pray God that it may go well with you!"

Philip sat upright in his chair, and the book fell unheeded to the ground.

"How did you guess?" he said. "I suspect you of being a witch, mother; and if we had lived a few hundred years ago, instead of now, it would have been my painful duty to have had you burned. It would have hurt you far more than me, because the sense of duty would have sustained me. I never said a word to you about Madge, yet you knew I was in love with her, I think, almost before I knew it myself."

"Yes, dear. I am sure I did," said Mrs. Home with gentle complacence.

"Well, you dear witch, tell me how you knew."

"Oh, Philip, it was easy to see. You never looked at any girl before like that. I used to be afraid you would never marry. You used to say dreadful things, you know, that really frightened me. Even since you were quite a little boy, you thought women were a bother. You used to say they couldn't play games, and were always in the way, and had headaches, and were without any sense of honour."

"All quite true in the main," said the misogynous Philip.

Mrs. Home held up her hands in protest.

"Dear, when have you known me have a headache, or do anything dishonourable?" she asked pertinently.

"I always excepted you. And I except Madge. She beat me at croquet the other day, and in the middle of the game volunteered the information that she had not moved the ball she croquetted."

"She always would," said his mother gently. "Oh, Philip, good luck to your wooing, my dear!"

There was a long pause; a sparrow in a prodigious bustle alighted on the edge of the fountain, and drank as if it had been a traveller straight from Sahara; the wind woke again in the flower-beds and gave a long, fragrant sigh; the sun-blinds of the drawing-room stirred as it wandered by them, and the pale purple petals of a grape-bunch cluster of wisteria fell on the crimson-striped canvas. The exquisiteness of this midsummer moment struck Philip with a sudden pang of delight, none the less keen because the love with which his soul was full was not yet certain or complete: the pause before completion was his.

3

"Thank you, mother," he said at last. "I shall know very soon, I shall ask her while she is here."

He got up as he spoke.

"I can't sit still any more," he said. "Speaking of it has made me restless. I must go and do something violent. Perhaps I will take your advice and go for a row. They will not be here till nearly seven. Oh, by-the-way, Evelyn Dundas is coming, too. You will have someone to flirt with, mother."

"Dear, you say such dreadful things!" said Mrs. Home. "And if you say them while Lady Ellington is here, I shall feel so awkward."

"Well, Evelyn proposed to elope with you last time he was here," said Philip. "I think I shall commission him to paint your portrait."

"Who wants the picture of an old woman like me?" said Mrs. Home. "But get him to do Madge's."

Philip considered this.

"That's an idea," he said. "He could paint her divinely. Really, mother—if ah! a big 'if.' Do you know, I'm rather uneasy about Evelyn."

"Why? I thought he was getting on so well."

"He is as far as painting goes. They think very highly of him. But the moment he gets a couple of hundred pounds he buys a motor-car or something, and next week his watch is in pawn. Now, when you are twenty-five, it is time to stop doing that."

"I know," said Mrs. Home. "He is dreadful! Last time he was here he gave me a pearl-brooch that must have cost him fifty pounds."

"That was to induce you to run away with him," remarked Philip. "That was quite understood, and I think you behaved rather badly in not doing so."

"Philip, you mustn't!"

"No, nor must you! And now I'm going on the river. If I get drowned it will be your fault for having suggested it."

"Ah, do be careful in those locks," said Mrs. Home. "I get so nervous always when the water goes down and down."

"There's more chance of getting drowned when it goes up and up," said her son, kissing her on the forehead as he passed her chair.

Philip Home at the age of thirty-one was, perhaps, as successful a man of his age as any in the financial world. His father, the head of one of the big South African houses, had died some five years before, and since then the burden of a very large and prosperous house had rested almost entirely on his shoulders, which physically as well as morally were broad. But he combined in an extraordinary degree the dash and initiative of youth with a cool-headedness and sobriety of judgment which, in general is not achieved until something of the fire of the other is lost, and his management was both brilliant and safe. Yet, as must always happen, the habit of mind necessary to the successful conduct of large financial interests, which among other ingredients is made up of incessant watchfulness and a certain hardness in judging and acting, had, it must be confessed, somewhat tinged his whole character, and the world in general was right in its estimate of him as a man who was rather brusque and unsympathetic, a man with an iron hand who did not always even

4

remember to put on the velvet glove. This was a perfectly just conclusion as far as the world in general, that is to say, the world of mere acquaintances, was concerned, and Philip's fine collection of prints was considered to be regarded by him as an investment rather than a joy. They made the same judgment about his garden, thinking that the rarity of plants was a quality more highly-prized by him than their beauty. But where the world in general did him an injustice was that they did not allow for a circle which, though small, was far more intimate and vastly more competent to form the true estimate of the man than they, the circle of friends. These were four in number—his mother, Madge Ellington, namely—and the two men to whom allusion has already been made, namely—the Hermit and Evelyn Dundas. They saw, all four of them, a perfectly different Philip to him who somewhat elbowed his way through the uninteresting ranks of acquaintances, or sat, detached from the real essential man, in his orderly office, harsh-faced, unsmiling and absorbed. And this essential Philip in his own sanctum, where only these four ever came, was, indeed, a very lovable and eager personage; and though the world did not know it, his prints really hung there, and in the windows his flowers blossomed. But few were admitted there, and those only not on business.

So this very efficient person, if we rate efficiency, as seems to be the fashion, by the amount of income-tax annually harvested by the State, left the shade of the house and his mother sitting there, whistled for the two fox-terriers that lay dozing in the shade and went off towards the river. The smile which he wore when in his sanctum of intimates still lingered on his face as he passed down the stone steps to the croquet lawn below, but then it faded. Nor did the gardener who was mowing the lawn smile.

"I gave orders it was to be mown yesterday morning," said Philip; "and it is only half done yet. Did you receive those orders or not?"

The man, a huge young Hercules, touched his cap.

"Yes, sir; at least——"

"There is no 'at least,'" said Philip. "If you can't do as you are told you will have to go."

And he whistled—that Philip who was a parody of himself—to the dogs, and went on.

But before he had got down to the river the official Philip had dispersed, mistlike, in the glorious golden blaze of the summer afternoon, and the man his mother knew (she would scarcely, indeed, have recognised the other) had taken his place again, and as he rowed lazily down the river he gave himself up to mere receptivity of the full-blown beauty that was shed broadcast on sky and land and water. The spring had long been backward and wet, but now the pitiless rains of April bore a glorious and iridescent fruit. Brimful ran the stream from bank to bank, one sheet of untarnished crystal, reflecting the luminous turquoise of the sky. To his right stretched meadows all golden with the flowering of the buttercup; and cattle, knee-deep in the feathery foliage, grazed contentedly, or stood in the shallows of the river to drink, breathing out long soft breaths of kine-fragrance. Between the fields stood elms, stalwart towers of innumerable leaf, and a little way below the red roofs of Pangbourne

5

nestled among red and white flowering thorns. One such tree, a cascade of crimson blossom, grew near the river brink, and Philip paused on his oars a moment as he passed, for the sprays of colour were outlined by the vivid blue of the sky, and on either side stretched the incredible gold of the buttercups. No artist dared have painted that, yet how simple and how triumphantly successful! To the left the sun was just sinking beneath the high lines of wooded hills, and already the tide of clear warm shadow was beginning to advance across the stream. In the woods that covered the hills every shade of green, from the pale milkiness of young beech to the dark velvet of the oak, were mingled together, and glowed as if lit from within with the flakes of sunlight that filtered through the leaves. But that divine restfulness of various green was, somehow less to Philip's mind than the shouting colours of the sunlit fields. For the tides of life, the strong, sweeping currents of vitality, of love, of the work without which the active brain grows hungry and starves, were dashing in headstrong race within him, and rest and tranquility and soft brooding over what has been seemed to him a poor substitute for the eager harvesting of youth. His sickle was in his hand, and he pressed eagerly forward through the ripening corn of life that fell in swathes to his sweeping strokes.

The little party who were assembling at his house that afternoon were to stay with him a week of Whitsuntide. He would, he expected, be probably obliged to go up to London for the inside of the last two days of their stay, but he had managed—chiefly by means of working some sixteen hours out of the twenty-four during the last week—to secure for himself five days of complete holiday. Like a wise man, he had refused to pepper his house with mere acquaintances when friends were there, and with only one out of his four guests did he, like his mother, not feel on terms of intimacy. Her presence, however, as Madge's mother, was a matter of necessity, and Philip did not hide from himself the fact that she certainly favoured his suit. For Lady Ellington, as Mrs. Home had already remarked, was a very practical woman, and it seemed to her, in her own phrasing, that Madge could scarcely "do better." Her practical sense, it may be remarked, was like an all-fitting handle with a smart steel spring which grasped whatever was presented to it in firm tentacles; and the proper way of sweeping carpets, the right board wages for scullery-maids, the correct lead with doubled no trumps at bridge, were as clearly defined in her mind as the desirability of wealth in sons'-in-law. She was, it may be added, extremely generous with advice, being anxious to lay open to all the world the multifarious discoveries of her master-mind.

Lady Ellington was certainly a very handsome woman, and the passage of the glacier of years over her face and her mind had produced hardly any striations either on the one or the other. Her bodily health was superb, and she took the utmost care of it; while, since one of her most constantly applied maxims was to let no sadness or worry weigh on her, her mind had by this time become something like a very hard, bright, polished globe which it was impossible to dint or damage. She had strolled after tea with her hostess and Madge to the croquet lawn, leaving Evelyn Dundas and Tom Merivale to smoke and await Philip's return from the river. The gardener there was still engaged in his belated mowing, and Lady Ellington examined the cutter with a magisterial air.

"Very old-fashioned and heavy," she said. "You should get the new light American type. It does far more work, and a boy with it can get through what it takes a man to do with a heavier machine. How many gardeners do you keep, Mrs. Home."

The poor lady shook her head.

"I don't really know," she said. "How many are there of you, Hawkins?"

Lady Ellington sniffed rather contemptuously.

"The labour-sheet will tell you," she said. "Why are there no flower borders on this lawn?"

"Ah, that is Philip's plan," said his mother, delighted to be able to refer the inquisitor to another source. "He says that they get so trampled by people looking for balls."

"I should have thought wire-netting would have obviated that," said Lady Ellington. "Under the north wall there is an excellent aspect. Personally, I should put bulbs here. And the rose garden is below, is it not? Certainly Mr. Home keeps his garden in fairly good order."

This concession, though not altogether unqualified, was fully appreciated by Mrs. Home.

"I'm sure he spends enough on it," she said.

Lady Ellington laughed.

"That is the surest way of getting satisfactory results," she said. "It is all nonsense to say that flowers do best in the gardens of those that love them, unless that love takes the practical form of spending money on them. And in the latter case, they do equally well if you hate them!"

This was in the best Ellingtonian manner, hard and clean-cut and glittering—there was nothing foggy about it—and it represented very fairly Lady Ellington's method of dealing with life. Love or hatred did not seem to her to matter very particularly; the dinner of herbs, at any rate, in the house of love was markedly less attractive to her than the well-ordered house of hate, and she could do without friends better than without a motor-car. She had had rather a hard tussel with life, and shrewd blows had been given on both sides; she had lost her money and her husband during the last few years, and, being without a son, the title and estates had gone to her husband's nephew, a man for whom for years she had felt, and indeed shown, an extreme dislike. Her jointure was narrow, and she had only got her motor-car by the simple expedient of ordering it but not paying for it. But of the two combatants—life and herself—life was at last beginning to get the worst of it. Certain speculations she had lately indulged in had brought her in money, and if once she could marry her daughter to Philip, she felt that this would be a knock-down blow to life, and her struggles on this side of the grave would be over. What might happen on the other side concerned her very little.

Madge meantime, while this short cross-examination had been going on, strolled a little behind the other two, with a faint smile of amusement in her eyes. She had inherited all her mother's beauty, and dark violet eyes glowed beneath her black lashes. Her nose was a little tip-tilted, as if raised in curiosity about things in general, but her mouth somewhat contradicted that, for it drooped a little at the corners, as if to imply that her curiosity when satisfied proved rather disappointing. Curiosity and a shade of contempt, indeed, were the emotions most strongly in evidence on her face, and the observer—allowing that features may represent the character of their owner rather than that of her ancestry—would perhaps conclude that her habitual view of the world was of the kind that tends to laugh at rather than with that admirable comedy. Otherwise her face was strangely sexless; it was, indeed, more the face of a boy than of a girl. Even among tall women she was tall, and by her side Mrs. Home looked more than ever like a figure of Dresden china.

Lady Ellington after her sympathetic remark about flowers, turned to her daughter.

"Well situated, is it not, Madge?" she said. "And the river is below there. You will be all day on it, I expect, if Mr. Home is kind enough to take you. And who else is here, Mrs. Home?"

"Ah, there is no party at all, I am afraid," said she. "Philip said that acquaintances mix so badly with friends. Only Mr. Dundas and Mr. Merivale."

Lady Ellington thought this over for a moment, and the conclusion apparently was most satisfactory.

"That is charming of him!" she said. "It is always a compliment to be asked to a small party; whereas, if you have a houseful it doesn't matter who is there. Dear me, those roses should be cut much further back, if they are to do any good. But it is quite true; if one asks friends and acquaintances together, the friends always wonder why the acquaintances have been asked, and the acquaintances are disgusted that nobody takes any notice of them. And I particularly want your son's advice on some shares I have lately purchased. Mr. Dundas, too—I am so glad to meet him. They say his portraits are going up in price so. I wonder if he could be induced—just a little sketch—— Ah, there is Mr. Home coming up from the river. I wonder why he wears a dark coat on so hot a day?"

A little curiosity perhaps lingered in Madge's face when she met Philip, and certainly the contempt all vanished. She had a great respect and liking for him, and her whole expression brightened when she saw him. Then after greetings they strolled on, the two elder ladies in front.

"Mother has a great many questions to ask you," she said to him in a gentle, slow, but very audible voice. "She wants to know how many gardeners you have, why you don't cut your roses back and something about South African mines."

Philip's habit of neatness and instinct of gardening led him to stop a moment and nip off a couple of ill-localised buds from a rose. In effect the two others got a little further ahead of them. This may or may not have been intentional.

"All my information is at her service," he said—"particularly on the subject of roses, about which I know more than South African mines."

"And care more!" suggested Madge.

"Infinitely more. Are they not clearly more attractive?"

Madge looked at him curiously.

"I believe you really think so," she said. "And that is so odd. Doesn't the scheming, the calculation, the foresight required in financial things interest you enormously?"

"Certainly; but I scheme just as much over the roses. Whether this one is to have—well, a whisky-and-soda, or whether it is rheumatic and wants a lowering treatment; that is just as interesting in itself as whether South Africans want lowering or screwing up."

"You mean you can do that? You can send things up or down? You can say to us, to mother: 'You shall be poorer to-morrow or richer'?"

Philip laughed.

"I suppose so, to some extent. Pray don't let us talk about it. It sounds rather brutal, and I am afraid it is brutalising. Yet, after all, a landlord may put up the rent of his houses."

Madge Ellington walked on for a few paces without replying.

"How odd of you," she said at length, "not to feel the fascination of power. I don't mean to say that one would necessarily want to use it, but it must be so divine to know it is there. Well, if you wish, I won't talk about it."

Philip turned to her, his brown thin face looking suddenly eager.

"Ah, I would sooner hear you talk about what you please than about what I please," he said.

She laughed.

"Can't I manage to combine the two?" she said. "The river, for instance, I think we both love that. Will you promise to let me live on the river while I am here?"

"I warn you that you will have a good deal of my company, then," said he.

She laughed again.

"But as you are my host I can't decently object," she said. "Oh, tell me, Mr. Home, what is Mr. Dundas like? You are a great friend of his, are you not? He was at tea, and asked a series of the silliest riddles, which somehow made me giggle. Giggle hopelessly, do you understand; they were so stupid. And he is the Mr. Dundas, who paints everybody as if they were so much more interesting than they are?"

"Yes, evidently the same," said Philip. "And what you say is quite true. Yet, again, as you say, his conversation is futile beyond words."

Madge walked on again in silence a little.

"I think that combination is rather charming," she said. "People don't laugh enough, and certainly he makes one laugh. I wish I laughed more, for instance."

"And has Merivale come?" asked Philip.

"Yes; he was at tea, too. What does he do?"

"He doesn't do anything. He just thinks."

"Good heavens! how frightfully fatiguing. All the time, do you mean?"

"Yes, all the time. Have you never met him before? Yet, how should

9

you? He lives in the New Forest, and communes with birds and animals. People think he is mad, but he is the sanest person I know."

"Why?" asked she.

"Because he has had the wit to find out what he likes, and to do it all the time."

"And what is that?" asked the girl.

"He sits by a stream and looks at the water. Then he lies on his back and looks at the sky. Then he whistles, chuckles, what you please to call it, and the thrushes come scudding out of the bushes and chuckle back at him."

"Is that not rather uncanny?" asked Madge.

"Most uncanny. Some day, as I tell him, he will see Pan. And I shall then have to attend a funeral."

The girl's eyebrows wrinkled into a frown.

"Pan?" she said.

"Yes; he is the God of 'Go as you please!' And his temple is a lunatic asylum. But don't be alarmed. The Hermit won't go into a lunatic asylum yet awhile."

"The Hermit?"

"Yes, the Hermit is Merivale. Because he lives quite alone in the New Forest. He never reads, he hardly ever sees anybody, he never does anything. He used to write at one time."

Madge shivered slightly.

"How intensely uncomfortable!" she said. "I think I shall like Mr. Dundas best."

"You are sure to like him."

"Because everybody does? That is the worst of reasons. I always distrust very popular people."

"The judgment of the world is usually wrong, you mean. But occasionally one stumbles on an exception."

The four had turned back towards the house, and as Philip spoke, he and his companion gained the top step of the gravelled square bordered by flower-beds, where he had sat two hours ago with his mother. The shadow of the house had swung over it, and in the gathering dusk the flower-beds glowed with a dim subaqueous radiance. Philip's mother and Lady Ellington had already passed into the open French window of the drawing-room, but on the stout balustrade of the terrace there sat a young man. One long slim leg rested on the gravel, the other was crooked round the lead vase at the head of the steps. His face, extraordinarily boyish, was clean-shaven, or rather so boyish was it, that it looked as if it was still untouched by razor. He held a cigarette in one hand, and the other, long-fingered and white as a woman's, grasped his knee.

"Oh, Philip!" he cried; "how are you? Oddly enough, I am quite well. I always was, like Sydney Smith and his great coat. Isn't there time for a game of croquet before dinner? Let's all be late, and so we shall all be punctual; it is only a question of degree. Miss Ellington, do come and play. Why did the barmaid champagne, and—oh, I asked you that. Stout, porter is rather good though. I do believe you know it, Philip."

SECOND

TOM MERIVALE did not, as Mrs. Home had feared he might, appear without clothes at dinner, nor did he make clamorous demands for cabbage. It is true that he ate no meat of any kind, but he was not of the preaching sort of vegetarians, and did not call attention to his abstinence. Instead, he and Evelyn Dundas between them managed to turn the meal into a ridiculous piece of gaiety by sheer exuberance of animal spirits, and even Lady Ellington forgot to examine the dishes with her usual magisterial air, and really ate and drank without criticising.

There was an extraordinary superficial resemblance in certain ways between the two men. Both, at any rate, were glorious examples of the happiness that springs from health, a happiness which is as inimitable as it is contagious. By health, it must be premised, is not meant the mere absence of definite ailments, but that perfect poise between an active mind and an exuberant body which is so rare.

It was on this very subject that Merivale was speaking now.

"Ah, no, Lady Ellington," he was saying, "to be able to get through the day's work, day after day and year after year, is not health. Perfect health implies practically perfect happiness."

"But how if you have a definite cause of worry?" she said.

"You can't worry when you are well. One knows, for example, that if one is definitely unwell, the same cause produces greater worry and discomfort than if one is not. And my theory is, that if one is absolutely well, if your mind and soul, that is to say, as well as your body, are all in accord with each other and with their environment, worry is impossible."

Lady Ellington, to do her justice, always listened to that were really new to her. She always assumed, by the way, that they were not.

"My theory exactly," she said. "I could scarcely have lived through these last years unless I had made up my mind never to let any anxiety take hold of me."

Evelyn Dundas laughed. Dinner was nearing its end and conversation was general.

"My mind and my body are not in absolute accord this moment," he said, "and I am rather anxious. My body demands some more ice-pudding; my mind tells me it would be extremely unwise. Which am I to listen to, Tom?"

"Give Mr. Dundas some more ice-pudding," remarked Philip to a footman.

"The laws of hospitality compel me to fall in with my host's suggestions," said Evelyn. "Tom, where you are wrong lies in thinking that it is worth while spending all your time in keeping well. He lives in the New Forest, Lady Ellington, and if when you are passing you hear the puffs of a loud steam-engine somewhere near Brockenhurst you will know it is Tom doing deep breathing. He expects in time to become a Ram-jam or something, by breathing himself into Raj-pan-puta."

Tom Merivale laughed.

11

"No, I don't want to become a Ram-jam," he said, "whatever that may be. I want to become myself."

"No clothes," murmured Mrs. Home.

"Become yourself?" asked Lady Ellington.

"Yes, most of us are stunted copies of our real selves," he said. "Imitations of what we might be. And what might one not be?"

The talk had got for him, at any rate, suddenly serious, and he looked up at Lady Ellington with a sparkling eye.

"Explain," she said.

"Well, it seems to me one cripples oneself in so many ways. One allows oneself to be nervous, and to be angry, and to be bound by conventions that are useless and cramping."

"Tall hats, frock-coats?" asked she.

"No, certainly not, because they, at any rate, are perfectly harmless. But, to take an example of what I mean, it seems to me a ridiculous convention that we should all consider ourselves obliged to know what is going on in the world. It does not really do one any good to know that there is war between China and Japan. What does do us good is not to be ill-tempered, and never to be sad. Sadness and pessimism are the worst forms of mental disease I know. And the state will not put sad and pessimistic people in asylums, or isolate them at any rate so that their disease should not spread. Such diseases are so frightfully catching, and they are more fatal than fevers. People die of them, soul and body!"

Lady Ellington felt that Mrs. Home was collecting her eye, and rose.

"What a fascinating theory," she said. "Just what I have always thought. Ah, I have caught my dress under my chair. You should have castors, Mr. Home, on your dining-room chairs."

* * * * * * *

Evelyn moved up next to Tom Merivale after the others had left them.

"Dear old Hermit!" he said. "Now, you've got to give an account of yourself. Neither Phil nor I have seen you for a year. What have you been doing?"

Tom let the port pass him.

"I suppose you would call it nothing," said he.

"Ah, but in real life people don't go and live in the New Forest and do nothing. What have you written in the last year?"

"Not one line. Seriously, I have been doing nothing except a little gardening and carpentering; just manual labour to keep one sane.'"

"Well, it looks as if it suited you. You look well enough, and what is so odd, you look so much younger."

Tom laughed again.

"Ah, that strikes you, does it?" he said. "I suppose it could not have been otherwise, though that wasn't my object in going to live there."

"Well, tell us, then!" said Evelyn, rather impatiently. He had begun to smoke, and smoked in a most characteristic manner; that is to say, that

12

in little more than a minute his cigarette was consumed down one side, and was a peninsula of charred paper down the other, while clouds of smoke ascended from it. Perceiving this, he instantly lit another one.

But Philip rose.

"Tell us afterwards, Tom," he said. "Lady Ellington likes to play bridge, I know, as soon as dinner is over."

Evelyn rose also.

"Ah, she is like me," he said. "She wants to do things not soon, but immediately, Philip, how awfully pretty Miss Ellington is. Why wasn't I told? I should like to paint her."

Philip paused by the door.

"Really, do you mean that?" he said. "And have you got time? I hear you always have more orders than you can ever get through."

Evelyn tossed his head with a quick, petulant gesture.

"You talk as if I was a tailor," he said. "But you suggest to me the advisability of my getting apprentices to paint the uninteresting people for me, and I will sign them. That would satisfy a lot of them. Yes, I have more than I can do. But I could do Miss Ellington remarkably well. Shall I ask her to sit for me?"

"That would be rather original, the first time you saw her."

"A good reason for doing it," said Evelyn, hastily drinking another glass of port.

"But it would certainly give her a good reason for saying 'No,'" remarked Philip.

Madge, it appeared, did not play bridge; her mother, at any rate, said she did not, and Evelyn Dundas, rather to his satisfaction, cut out. That feat happily accomplished, he addressed himself to Madge.

"Fancy a hermit playing bridge!" he said. "Does it not seem to you very inconsistent? Patience is the furthest he has any right to go."

Madge got up.

"Patience, both in cards and in real life, seems to me a very poor affair," she said. "How are we going to amuse ourselves while they play? Will you go out of the room while I think of something, and then you can come in and guess it?"

An amendment occurred to Evelyn.

"We might both go out," he said. "It is deliciously warm; just out on to the terrace."

"And when we come in they can guess where we have been," said Madge.

The night, as he had said, was deliciously warm, and the moon, a day or two only from full, shone with a very clear light. Below them lay the dim, huddled woods, and beyond, shining like a streak of silver, slept the Thames. Somewhere far away a train was panting along its iron road, and to the left scattered lights showed where Pangbourne stood. Odours of flowers were wafted from the beds, and pale-winged moths now and then crossed the illuminated spaces of light thrown by the drawing-room window on to the gravel.

13

"Ah, what a pity to be indoors!" said the girl as they stepped out. "I suppose I must be of Gipsy blood; I always want to go somewhere."

"Where particularly?" asked he.

"That doesn't matter; the going is the point. If you asked me to go to the Black Hole of Calcutta I should probably say 'Yes.' What a pity we can't go on the river!"

"Ah, let us do that!" said he.

Madge laughed.

"It would be quite unheard-of," she said. "I don't live in the New Forest like Mr. Merivale, and cast conventions aside. No, we will walk up and down a little, and then you shall go and play. Do you know, I am really so pleased to have met you I have admired your pictures so. Do you find it a bore having that sort of thing said to you?"

Evelyn thought over this for a moment.

"Well, I think my pictures bore me when they are done," he said, "though the opinion of other people never does. A picture is—is like a cold in the head. It possesses you while it is there, and you have to throw it off. And when it is thrown off, one never thinks of it again. At least, I don't."

They had come to the end of the terrace, and the girl stopped as they turned.

"And then you do another. Ah, how delightful to know that probably to the end of your life you will have things to do!"

"I don't think you would say that if you had to do them," said he. "Yet, I don't know. Of course creating a thing is the biggest fun in the world. But how one tears one's hair over it!"

Madge looked at his thick black thatch.

"You seem to have got some left," she remarked.

"Yes, but I'm looking thinner. Mrs. Home told me so. Oh, look at the moon! What a dreadful thing to say, too! But it really is out of drawing—it is far too big!"

"Perhaps we are far too small," said she.

Evelyn shook his head.

"It is impossible to be small if that occurs to you," he said.

They walked in silence after this for a dozen yards or so, Madge feeling, somehow, strangely attracted by her companion. There was nothing, it is true, particularly brilliant about his conversation; it was boyish rather than brilliant; but she felt, as most people did, that she was in the presence of a personality that was rather unusual. And this personality seemed to her to be very faithfully expressed in his pictures; there was something daringly simple about both him and them. He evidently said whatever came into his head, and her experience was that so many people only talked about such things as were supposed to be of interest. Also, in spite of this moonlight solitude, he evinced not the smallest tendency to notice the fact that she was a very good-looking girl; no hint of it appeared in his talk or his attitude to her. There was not the very slightest suspicion of that even in his desire to go on the river with her. That ridiculous suggestion she felt, with unerring instinct, had been made simply from comrade to comrade; there were two of them together,

14

cut out from a table of bridge, and he had proposed it just as he might have proposed it to a man, instead of a girl, of his own age. And to Madge this was something of an exception in her experience of the other sex, for most unmarried men of her acquaintance had shown a tendency towards tenderness. Her beauty made it perhaps excusable in them, but she found it rather trying. It was a relief, at any rate, to find a young man who took her frankly, who could say "Look at the moon," only to point out that it was out of drawing. For in the matter of emotion Madge was strangely unfeeling, or, at any rate, strangely undeveloped; and if her mother had let any anxiety dwell upon her hard and polished mind, the doubts about Madge's future would, perhaps, have pressed as heavily there as any. As a good mother should, she had brought to her daughter's notice, not to say thrown at her head, a large variety of young men, to none of whom had Madge responded at all satisfactorily. And it was almost intensely pleasing to her at this moment to find someone matrimonially quite impossible to her mother's mind, who was both so attractive to her personally, and who did not show the smallest desire to treat her otherwise than a man should treat a man. He was perfectly natural, in fact, perfectly simple, and quite an exception to her experience of moonlight walkers. And this paragon continued his peerless way.

"Have you met Tom Merivale before?" he asked. "No? Of course he would think it almost profane to say the moon was too large. He takes any fact in nature and then proceeds to fit himself to it. Whatever untutored nature does is right, in his view. I wonder what he would make of slugs eating the faces of pansies slowly away. I shall ask him."

Madge gave a little shriek of horror.

"That is one of the facts of life which I can't get over," she said. "I can't reconcile myself to wanton destruction of beauty. Oh, there is so little in the world."

Now, there is a particular mental sensation which corresponds to the physical sensation of stepping up a step when there is no step there. Evelyn felt this now.

She had gone suddenly into vacancy, with a thump.

"What do you mean?" he said. "I should have thought there was so much there that one was bewildered. Surely almost everything is beautiful."

"Do you really think that?" she asked.

"Why, of course. But the trouble is that one has not wits enough to see it. And all beauty is equal—woman, man, mountain-side, pansy. And probably slug," he added. "But to appreciate that would require a great deal of insight. But Sir John Lubbock says that earwigs are excellent mothers. That opened my eyes to earwigs."

Again Madge walked on in silence for a space.

"Are you ever bored?" she asked at length.

"Bored? No. All that anyone has ever made is at one's disposal to wonder at. And if one can't do that, one can go and make something oneself. No, I hope I shall have the grace to commit suicide before I am bored."

Madge stopped and turned to him. That she was being unwise she knew, but something intimate and indwelling dictated to her.

"I am bored every day of my life!" she said. "And how can I avoid it? Is it very stupid of me?"

Evelyn did not hesitate in his reply.

"Yes, very!" he said. "Because it is such a waste of time to be bored. People don't recollect that."

They had come opposite the drawing-room window, and as they passed Lady Ellington stepped out on to the terrace.

"Is that you, Madge?" she asked.

Even in the darkness Evelyn knew what had happened to Madge's face. The fall of it was reflected in her voice.

"Yes; have you finished your bridge?" she asked.

"We are waiting for Mr.—Mr. Dundas to cut in," she said. "Mr. Home thought he was in the smoking-room, and has gone there."

"Oh, I am not in the smoking-room," said Evelyn.

If one judged by definitions given in dictionaries it would probably be a misuse of language to say that Lady Ellington "played" bridge. Cards were dealt her, and she dealt with them, embarking on commercial transactions. She assessed the value of her hand with far more accuracy than she had ever brought to play on the assessment of her income-tax, and proceeded to deal with her assets with even more acuteness than she was accustomed to dispose on the expenditure of her income. Mrs. Home had silently entreated Philip to allow her to cut out, and Lady Ellington was left to play with three men. This she always enjoyed, because she took full advantage of the slight concessions which were allowed to her sex if no other woman was of the table. But before embarking on the second rubber she turned to Madge.

"I want to speak to you, dearest," she said, "before you go to bed. We shall only play a couple more rubbers. Mr. Home, you really ought to have pneumatic cards; they are a little more expensive, but last so much longer—yes, two more rubbers—I go no trumps—and I will come to your room on my way up. No doubling? Thank you, partner; that is the suit I wanted."

Philip, who was her partner, had exposed two excellent suits, so the imagination of the others might run riot over which particular suit was the desire of Lady Ellington. At any rate she scored a little slam, but was not satisfied, and turned on Evelyn, who, it is idle to remark, had talked during the play.

"I missed a nine," she said. "Mr. Dundas was saying something very amusing."

But as her face had been like flint, Mr. Dundas had to draw the inference that, however amusing, she had not been amused.

Lady Ellington always kept the score herself, and never showed any signs of moving, if she had won, until accounts had been adjusted and paid. To-night affairs had gone prosperously for her; she was gracious in her "good-nights," and even commended the admirable temperature of the hot water, a glass of which she always sipped before going to bed. Madge

16

had gone upstairs, but not long before; and her mother, having locked her winnings into her dressing-case, came to her room and found her sitting by the open window, still not yet preparing to go to bed.

"Do I understand that you walked on the terrace alone with Mr. Dundas?" she asked in a peculiarly chilly voice.

Madge showed no surprise; she had known what was coming.

"Yes, we took a turn or two," she said.

Her mother sat down; Madge had not turned from the window and was still looking out.

"Kindly attend, Madge," she said. "It was very indiscreet, and you know it. I don't think Mr. Home liked it."

Of the girl who had talked so eagerly and naturally to Evelyn on the terrace there was hardly a trace; Madge's face had grown nearly as hard as her mother's.

"I am not bound just yet to do all Mr. Home likes," she said.

"You are bound, if you are a sensible creature, at all events not to run any risks, especially now."

Madge turned away from the window.

"You mean until the bargain is completed. Supposing I refuse?" she said, and there was a little tremor in her voice, partly of contempt, partly of fear.

Lady Ellington, as has been remarked, never let her emotions, however justifiable, run away with her; she never, above all, got hot or angry. Causes which in others would produce anger, produced in her only an additional coldness and dryness, which Madge was, somehow, afraid of with unreasoning nightmare kind of fear.

"I will not suppose anything so absurd!" said her mother. "You are twenty-five years old, and you have never yet fallen in love at all. But as I have pointed out to you before, you will be far happier married than living on into the loneliness and insignificance of being an old maid. Lots of girls never fall in love in the silly, sentimental manner which produces lyrics. You are quite certainly one of them. And as certainly Mr. Home is in love with you."

"We have been into this before," said the girl.

"It is necessary, apparently, to go into it again. Mr. Home, I feel certain, is going to propose to you, and you should not do indiscreet things. With regard to your refusing him, it is out of the question. He is extremely suitable in every way. And you told me yourself you had made up your mind to accept him."

"You made up my mind," said Madge; "but it comes to the same thing."

"Precisely. So please promise me not to do anything which a girl in your position should not do. There is no earthly harm in your walking with any penniless artist in the moonlight, if you were not situated as you are. But at the moment it is indiscreet."

"You are wrong if you suppose that Mr. Dundas said anything to me which could possibly be interpreted into a tender interest," said Madge. "He called attention to the moon merely in order to remark that it was out of drawing."

17

"That never occurred to me," said her mother, "though it would be a matter of total indifference whether he took a tender interest in you or not. I merely want your promise that you will not repeat the indiscretion."

"Oh, certainly," said Madge.

Lady Ellington had put her bedroom candle on Madge's dressing-table. As soon as she had received the assurance she required, she at once rose from her chair and took it up. But with it in her hand she stood silent a moment, then she put it down again.

"You have spoken again of things I thought were settled, Madge," she said, "and I should like your assurance on one point further. We agreed, did we not, that it would be far better for you to marry than remain single. We agreed also that you were not of the sort of nature that falls passionately in love, and we agreed that you had better marry a man whom you thoroughly like and esteem. Mr. Home is such a man. Is that correctly stated?"

"Quite," said Madge. "In fact, I don't know why I suggested that I should refuse him."

"You agree to it all still?"

Madge considered a moment.

"Yes; things being as they are, I agree."

"What do you mean by that exactly?"

Madge got up, and swept across the room to where her mother stood.

"I have long meant to say this to you, mother," she said, "but I never have yet. I mean that at my age one's character to some extent certainly is formed. One has to deal with oneself as that self exists. But my character was formed by education partly and by my upbringing, for which you are responsible. I think you have taught me not to feel—to be hard."

Lady Ellington did not resent this in the slightest; indeed, it was part of her plan of life never to resent what anybody did or said; for going back to first principles, resentment was generally so useless.

"I hope I have taught you to be sensible," she remarked.

"It seems to me I am being very sensible now," said Madge, "and you may certainly take all the credit of that, if you wish. I fully intend to do, at any rate, exactly what you suggest—to accept, that is to say, a man whom I both esteem and respect, and who is thoroughly suitable. For suitable let us say wealthy—because that is what we mean."

Lady Ellington qualified this.

"I should not wish you to marry a cad, however wealthy," she said.

Madge moved softly up and down the room, her dress whispering on the carpet before she replied.

"And it does not strike you that this is rather a cold-blooded proceeding?" she asked.

"It would if you were in love with somebody else. In which case I should not recommend you to marry Mr. Home. But as it is, it is the most sensible thing you can do. I would go further than that; I should say it was your duty."

Again Madge walked up and down without replying at once.

18

"Ah, it is cold-blooded," she said, "and I am doing it because I am cold-blooded."

Then she stopped opposite her mother.

"Mother, when other girls fall in love, do they only feel like this?" she asked. "Is this all? Just to feel that for the rest of one's life one will always have a very pleasant companion in the house, who, I am sure, will always deserve one's liking and esteem?"

Lady Ellington laughed.

"My dear, I can't say what other girls feel. But, as you remark, it is all you feel. You are twenty-five years old, and you have never fallen in love. As you say, you have to take yourself as you are. Good night, dear. It is very late."

She kissed her, left her, and went down the passage to her own room. She was a very consistent woman, and it was not in the slightest degree likely that she should distrust the very sensible train of reasoning which she had indicated to her daughter, which also she had held for years, that a sensible marriage is the best policy in which to invest a daughter's happiness. Lady Ellington's own experience, indeed, supplied her with evidence to support her view, for she herself was an excellent case in point, for her husband had been a man with whom she had never been the least in love, but with whom, on the other hand, she had managed to be very happy in a cast-iron sort of way. She felt, indeed, quite sure, in her reasonable mind, that she was acting wisely for Madge, and it was not in her nature to let an unreasonable doubt trouble her peace. But an unreasonable doubt was there, and it was this, that Madge for the first time, as far as she knew, seemed to have contemplated the possibility of passion coming into her life. There had been in her mind, so her mother felt sure, an unasked question—"What if I do fall in love?"

Lady Ellington turned this over in the well-lit chamber of her brain as she went to bed. But her common-sense came to her aid, and she did not lie awake thinking of it. She had made up her mind that such a thing was unlikely to the verge of impossibility, and she never wasted time or thought over what was impossible. Her imagination, it is true, was continually busy over likely combinations; there were, however, so many of these that things unlikely did not concern her.

The men meantime had gone to the smoking-room, and from there had moved out in general quest of coolness on to the terrace. The moon had risen nearly to the zenith, and no longer offended Evelyn's sense of proportion, and the night, dusky and warm, disposed to personal talk. And since neither Evelyn nor Philip had seen Tom Merivale for a year, it was he who had first to be brought up to date.

"So go on with what you were saying at dinner, Tom," said Evelyn. "Really, people who are friends ought to keep a sort of circulating magazine, in which they write themselves up and send it round to the circle. In any case, you of the three of us are most in arrears. What have you done besides growing so much younger?"

"Do you really want to know?" asked he.

"Yes."

19

Evelyn rose as he spoke and squirted some soda-water into his glass. They were sitting in the square of light illuminated by the lamps of the room inside, and what passed was clearly visible to all of them.

"You must sit quiet then," said Tom, in his low, even-toned voice, "or you will frighten them."

"Them? Whom? Are you going to raise spirits from the vasty deep?" asked Philip.

"Oh, no; though I fancy it would not be so difficult. No, what I am going to show you, if you care to see it—it may take ten minutes—is a thing that requires no confederates. It is not the least exciting either. Only if you wish to see what I have done, as you call it, though personally I should say what I have become, I can give you an example probably. Oh, yes, more than probably, I am sure I can. But please sit still."

The night was very windless and silent. In the woods below a nightingale was singing, but the little wind which had stirred before among the garden beds had completely dropped.

"Have you begun?" asked Evelyn. "Or is that all? Is it that you have been silent for a year?"

"Ah, don't interrupt," said the other.

Again there was silence, except for the bubbling of the nightingale. Four notes it sang, four notes of white sound as pure as flame; then it broke into a liquid bubble of melodious water, all transparent, translucent, the apotheosis of song. Then a thrill of ecstasy possessed it, and cadence followed indescribable cadence, as if the unheard voice of all nature was incarnated. Then quite suddenly the song ceased altogether.

There was a long pause; both Evelyn and Philip sat in absolute silence, waiting. Tom Merivale had always been so sober and literal a fellow that they took his suggestion with the same faith that they took the statements of an almanack—it was sure to be the day that the almanack said it was. But for what they waited—what day it was—neither knew nor guessed.

Then the air was divided by fluttering wings; Tom held his hand out, and on the forefinger there perched a little brown bird.

"Sing, dear," said he.

The bird threw its head back, for nightingales sing with the open throat. And from close at hand they all three heard the authentic love song of the nightingale. The unpremeditated rapture poured from it, wings quivering, throat throbbing, the whole little brown body was alert with melody, instinctive, untaught, the melody of happiness, of love made audible. Then, tired, it stopped.

"Thank you, dear brother," said Tom. "Go home."

Again a flutter of wings whispered in the air, and his forefinger was untenanted.

"That is what I have done," he said. "But that is only the beginning."

Evelyn gave a long sigh.

"Are you mad, or are we?" he asked. "Or was there a bird there? Or are you a hypnotist?"

He got up quickly.

20

"Phil, I swear I saw a bird, and heard it sing," he said excitedly. "It was sitting there, there on his finger. What has happened? Go on, Tom—tell us what it means."

"It means you are the son of a monkey, as Darwin proved," said he, "and the grandson, so to speak, of a potato. That is all. It was a cousin of a kind that sat on my finger. Philip, with his gold and his Stock Exchange and his business generally, does much more curious things than that. But, personally, I do not find them so interesting."

Philip, silent as was his wont when puzzled, instead of rushing into speech, had said nothing. But now he asked a question.

"Of course, it was not a conjuring trick," he said. "That would be futility itself. But you used to have extraordinary hypnotic power, Tom. I only ask—Was that a real nightingale?"

"Quite real."

Evelyn put down his glass untasted.

"I am frightened," he said. "I shall go to bed."

And without more words he bolted into the house.

Philip called good night after him, but there was no response, and he was left alone with the Hermit.

"I am not frightened," he said. "But what on earth does it all mean? Have a drink?"

Tom Merivale laughed quietly.

"It means exactly what I have said," he answered. "Come down to my home sometime, and you shall see. It is all quite simple and quite true. It is all as old as love and as new as love. It is also perfectly commonplace. It must be so. I have only taken the trouble to verify it."

Philip's cool business qualities came to his aid, or his undoing.

"You mean you can convey a message to a bird or a beast?" he asked.

"Oh, yes. Why not? The idea is somehow upsetting to you. Pray don't let it upset you. Nothing that happens can ever be upsetting. It is only the things that don't happen that are such anxieties, for fear they may. But when they have happened they are never alarming."

He pushed his chair back and got up.

"Ah, I have learned one thing in this last year," he said, "and that is to be frightened at nothing. Fear is the one indefensible emotion. You can do nothing at all if you are afraid. You know that yourself in business. But whether you embark on business or on—what shall I call it?—nature-lore, the one thing indispensable is to go ahead. To take your stand firmly on what you know, and deduce from that. Then to test your deduction, and as soon as one will bear your weight to stand on that and deduce again, being quite sure all the time that whatever is true is right. Perhaps sometime the world in general may see, not degradation in the origin of man from animals, but the extraordinary nobility of it. And then perhaps they will go further back—back to Pagan things, to Pan, the God of nature."

"To see whom meant death," remarked Philip.

"Yes, or life. Death is merely an incident in life. And it seems to me now to be rather an unimportant one. One can't help it. Whereas the important events are those which are within one's control; one's powers of thought, for instance."

21

Philip rose also.

"And love," he said. "Is that in one's control?"

Tom took a long breath.

"Love?" he said. "It is not exactly in one's control, because it is oneself. There, the dear bird has got home."

And again from the trees below the bubble of liquid melody sounded.

THIRD

EVELYN DUNDAS was sitting next morning after breakfast on the terrace, where what he alluded to as "the nightingale trick" had been performed the evening before, in company with the conjurer who had performed it. Philip and Madge Ellington had just gone down to the river, Lady Ellington who was to have accompanied them having excused herself at the last moment. But since a mother was in closer and more intimate connection with a girl than a mere chaperone, she had seen not the smallest objection to the two going alone. Indeed she had firmly detained Evelyn by a series of questions which required answers, from joining them, and, though deep in a discussion about art, she had dropped it in its most critical state when she judged that the other two had been given time to get under way. It had required, indeed, all her maternal solicitude to continue it so long, for she cared less for art or Evelyn's theories about it than for a week-old paper.

Like most artists, Evelyn had a somewhat egoistic nature, and since his personality was so graceful and interesting, it followed that many people found his talk equally so, especially when he talked about himself. For his egoism he had an admirably probable explanation, and he was at this moment explaining it to Tom Merivale, who had made the soft impeachment with regard to its undoubted existence.

"Ah, yes," he was saying, "an artist's business is not to put things down as they are, but to put them down as they strike him. Actual truth has nothing to do with the value of a landscape. The point is that the picture should be beautiful. And the same with portraits, only beauty there is unnecessary. You have to put down what you think you see, or what you choose to see."

"That shouldn't lead to egoism," remarked Tom. "It should lead you to the study of other people."

Evelyn shook his head.

"No, no," he said, "it leads you to devote yourself entirely almost to the cultivation of your own faculty of seeing. All fine portraits show a great deal of the artist, and perhaps comparatively little of the sitter. Why are Rembrandts so unmistakable? Not because the type of his sitters

22

themselves was almost identical, but because there is lots of Rembrandt in each. You can't have style unless you are egoistic. In fact, for an artist style means egoism. I have heaps. I don't say or pretend it's good, but there it is. Take it or leave it."

Tom Merivale laughed.

"You are perfectly inimitable," he said. "I love your serious, vivid nonsense. That you are an egoist is quite, quite true. But how much better an artist you would be if you weren't. What you want is deepening. You don't like the deeps, you know. You haven't got any. You don't like what you don't understand; that very simple little affair last night, for instance, frightened you."

Egoists are invariably truthful—according to their lights—about themselves. Evelyn was truthful now.

"Yes, that is so," he said. "I don't pretend to wish to seek out the secrets of the stars. But I know what I like. And I don't like anything that leads into the heart of things. I don't like interiors and symbolism. There is quite enough symbol for me on the surface. What I mean is that the eyebrow itself, the curve of the mouth, will tell you quite as much as one has any use for about the brain that makes the eyebrow frown or the mouth smile. Beauty may be skin deep only, but it is quite deep enough. Skin deep! Why, it is as deep as the sea!"

Tom Merivale was silent a little.

"Do you know, you are an interesting survival of the Pagan spirit?" he said at length.

Evelyn laughed.

"Erect me an altar then at once, and crown me with roses," he remarked. "But what have I said just now that makes you think that?"

"Nothing particular this moment," he answered, "though your remarking that beauty was enough for you is thoroughly Greek in its way. No; what struck me was that never have I seen in you the smallest rudiment or embryo of a conscience or of any moral sense."

Evelyn looked up with real interest at this criticism.

"Oh, that is perfectly true," he said. "Certainly I never have remorse; it must be awful, a sort of moral toothache. All the same, I don't steal or lie, you know."

"Merely because lying and stealing are very inartistic performances," said Tom. "But no idea of morality stands in your way."

Evelyn got up, looking out over the heat-hazed green of the woods below them with his brilliant glance.

"Is that very shocking?" he asked, with perfectly unassumed naïveté.

"I suppose it is. Personally, I am never shocked at anything. But it seems to me very dangerous. You ought to wear a semaphore with a red lamp burning at the end of it."

Evelyn half shut his eyes and put his head on one side.

"I don't think that would compose well," he said.

"That is most consistently spoken," said Tom. "But really, if you are ever in earnest about anything beside your art, you would be a public danger."

Evelyn turned round on this.

23

"You call me a Pagan," he said. "Well, what are you, pray, with your communings with nature and conjuring tricks with nightingales? You belong to quite as early a form of man."

"I know. I am primeval. At least I hope to be before I die."

"What's the object?"

"In order to see Pan. I am getting on. Come down to the New Forest sometime, and you shall see very odd things, I promise you. Really, Evelyn, I wish you would come. It would do you no end of good."

He got up, and taking the arm of the other man, walked with him down the terrace.

"You are brilliant, I grant you," he said; "but you are like a mirror, only reflecting things. What you want is to be lit from within. Who is it who talks of the royalty of inward happiness? That is such a true phrase. All happiness from without is not happiness at all; it is only pleasure. And pleasure is always imperfect. It flickers and goes out, it has scratching nails——"

Evelyn shook himself free.

"Ah, let me be," he said. "I don't want anything else. Besides, as you have told me before, you yourself dislike and detest suffering or pain. But how can you hope to understand Nature at all if you leave all that aside? Why, man, the whole of Nature is one groan, one continuous preying of creature on creature. In your life in the New Forest you leave all that out."

Tom Merivale paused.

"I know I do," he said, "because I want to grasp first, once and for all the huge joy that pervades Nature, which seems to me much more vital in itself than pain. It seems to me that pain may be much more rightly called absence of joy than joy be called absence of pain. What the whole thing starts from, the essential spring of the world is not pain and death, but joy and life."

"Ah, there I am with you. But there is so much joy and life on the surface of things that I don't wish to probe down. Ah, Tom, a day like this now; woven webs of blue heat, hot scents from the flower beds, the faces of our friends. Is that not enough? It is for me. And, talking of faces, Miss Ellington has the most perfectly modelled face I ever saw. The more I look at it, the more it amazes me. I stared at her all breakfast. And the charm of it is its consistent irregularity; not a feature is anything like perfect, but what a whole! I wish I could do her portrait."

Tom laughed.

"There would not be the slightest difficulty about that, I should say," he remarked, "if you promise to present it to her mother."

"Why, of course, I would. How funny it must feel to be hard like that. She is very bruising; I feel that I am being hit in the eye when she talks to me. And she knows how many shillings go to a sovereign."

"Twenty," remarked Tom.

"Ah, that is where you are wrong. She gets twenty-one for each of her sovereigns. And thirteen pence for each of her shillings, and the portrait of her daughter for nothing at all. Oh, Tom, think of it—with a background of something blue, cornflower, forget-me-nots, or lilac, to show how really golden her hair is. There's Mrs. Home."

24

Evelyn whistled with peculiar shrillness on his fingers to the neat little figure on the croquet lawn below them. She started, not violently, for nothing she did was violent, but very completely.

"Ah, it is only you," she said. "I thought it might be an express train loose. Are you not going on the river, dear Evelyn?"

"I was prevented," he said, jumping down the steps in one flying leap. "Dear Philippina——"

"What next? What next?" murmured Mrs. Home. "Oh, do behave, Evelyn."

"Well, Philip is your son, so you are Philippina. But why have prize-fighters in your house?"

"Prize-fighters?"

"Yes. Lady Ellington had my head in Chancery for ten minutes just now. She delivered a series of quick-firing questions. I know why, too; it was to prevent my going on the river. She was perfectly successful—I should think she always was successful; she mowed me down. Now will you tell me the truth or not?"

"No, dear Evelyn," said Mrs. Home rather hastily, guessing what was coming.

"Then you are a very wicked woman; but as I now know you are going to tell an untruth, it will do just as well for my purpose. Now, is Philip engaged to Miss Ellington?"

"No, dear; indeed he is not," said Mrs. Home.

"Oh, why not lie better than that?" said Evelyn.

Mrs. Home clasped her white, delicate little hands together.

"Ah, but it is true," she said. "It really is literally true, as far as I know."

Evelyn shook his head at her.

"But they have been gone half an hour," he said. "You mean—I tell you, you mean that they may be now, for all you know."

Mrs. Home turned her pretty, china-blue eyes on to him, with a sort of diminutive air of dignity.

"Of course you are at liberty to put any construction you please on anything I say," she remarked.

"I am," said he, "and I put that. Now, are you pleased at it?"

"She is charming," said Mrs. Home, hopelessly off her guard.

"That is all I wanted to know," said Evelyn. "But what a tangled web you weave, without deceiving me in the least, you old darling."

Tom Merivale had not joined Evelyn, but strolled along the upper walk through herbaceous borders. He had not stayed away from his home now for the past year, and delighted though he was to see these two old friends of his again, he confessed to himself that he found the call on sociability which a visit tacitly implied rather trying. More than that, he found even the presence of other people in the house with whom he was not on terms of intimacy a thing a little upsetting, for his year of solitude had given some justification to his nickname. For solitude is a habit of extraordinary fascination, and very quick to grow on anyone who has sufficient interest in things not to be bored by the absence of people. And with Tom Merivale, Nature, the unfolding of flowers, the lighting of the

25

stars in the sky, the white splendour of the moon, the hiss of the rain on to cowering shrubs and thirsty grass was much more than an interest; it was a passion which absorbed and devoured him. For Nature, to the true devotee, is a mistress far more exacting and far more infinite in her variety and rewards than was ever human mistress to her adorer. Tom Merivale, at any rate, was faithful and wholly constant, and to him now, after a year spent in solitude in which no man had ever felt less alone, no human tie or affection weighed at all compared to the patient devotion with which he worshipped this ever young mistress of his. To some, indeed, as to Mrs. Home, this cutting of himself off from all other human ties might seem to verge on insanity; to others, as to Philip, it might equally well be construed into an example of perfect sanity. For he had left the world, and cast his moorings loose from society in no embittered or disappointed mood; the severance of his connection with things of human interest had been deliberate and sanely made. He believed, in fact, that what his inner essential self demanded was not to be found among men, or, as he had put it once to Philip, it was to be found there in such small quantities compared to the mass of alloy and undesirable material from which it had to be extracted, that it was false economy to quarry in the world of cities. More than this, too, he had renounced, though this second renunciation had not been deliberate, but had followed, so he found, as a sequel to the other; for he had been a writer of fiction who, though never widely read, had been prized and pored over by a circle of readers whose appreciation was probably far more worth having than that of a wider circle could have been. Then, suddenly, as far as even his most intimate friends knew, he had left London, establishing himself instead in a cottage, of the more comfortable sort of cottages, some mile outside Brockenhurst. In the tea-cup way this had made quite a storm in the set that knew him well, those, in fact, by whom he was valued as an interpreter and a living example of the things of which he wrote. These writings had always been impersonal in note, slightly mystical, and always with the refrain of Nature running through them. But none, when he disappeared as completely as Waring, suspected how vital to himself his disappearance had been. Anything out of the way is labelled, and rightly by the majority, to be insane. By such a verdict Tom Merivale certainly merited Bedlam. He had gone away, in fact, to think, while the majority of those who crowd into the cities do so, not to think, but to be within reach of the distractions that leave no time for thought. For action is always less difficult than thought; a man can act for more hours a day than he can think in a week, and action, being a productive function of the brain, is thus (rightly, also, from the social point of view) considered the more respectable employment.

The subject of this difficult doctrine, however, was more than content; as he had said, he was happy, a state far on the sunward side of the other. He seemed to himself, indeed, to be sitting very much awake and alert on some great sunlit slope of the world, untenanted by man, but peopled with a million natural marvels unconjectured as yet by the world, but which slowly coming into the ken of his wondering and patient eyes. For a year now he had consciously and solely devoted himself to the study and contemplation of life, that eternal and ever-renewed life of Nature, and the joy manifested therein. He had turned his back with the same careful deliberation on all that is painful in Nature, all suffering, all that hinders and mars the fulness of life, on everything, in fact, which is an evidence of imperfection. In this to a large extent he was identically minded with Christian Scientists, but having faced the central idea of Christianity, namely, the suffering which was necessary as atonement for sin, he had confessed himself unable to accept, at present at any rate, the possibility of suffering being ever necessary, and could no longer call himself a Christian. Happiness was his gospel, and the book in which he studied it was Nature, omitting always such chapters as dealt with man. For man, so it seemed to him, had by centuries of evolution built himself into something so widely different from Nature's original design, that the very contemplation of and association with man was a thing to be avoided. Absence of serenity, absence of happiness, seemed the two leading characteristics of the human race, whereas happiness and serenity were the chief of those things for which he sought and for which he lived.

This year's solitude and quest for joy had already produced in him remarkable results. He had been originally himself of a very high-strung, nervous, and irritable temperament; now, however, he could not imagine the event which should disturb his equanimity. For this, as far as it went alone, he was perfectly willing to accept the possible explanation that a year's life in the open air had wrought its simple miracle of healing on his nerves, and, as he had said to Lady Ellington, the perfection of health had eliminated the possibility of discontent.

But other phenomena did not admit of quite so obvious an interpretation; and it was on these that he based his belief that, though all that occurred must necessarily be natural, following, that is to say, laws of nature, he was experiencing the effects of laws which were to the rest of the world occult or unknown. For in a word, youth, with all its vivid vigour, its capacity for growth and expansion, had returned to him in a way unprecedented; his face, as Evelyn had noticed, had grown younger, and in a hundred merely corporeal ways he had stepped back into early manhood. Again, and this was more inexplicable, he had somehow established, without meaning to, a certain communion with birds and beasts, of which the "nightingale trick" had been a small instance, which seemed to him must be a direct and hitherto unknown effect of his conscious absorption of himself in Nature. How far along this unexplored path he would be able to go he had no idea; he guessed, however, that he had at present taken only a few halting steps along a road that was lost in a golden haze of wonder.

He strolled along out through the garden into a solitary upland of bush-besprinkled turf. Wild flowers of downland, the rock-rose, the harebell, orchids, and meadow-sweet carpeted the short grass, and midsummer held festival. But this morning his thoughts were distracted from the Nature-world in which he lived, and he found himself dwelling on the human beings among whom for a few days he would pass his time. It was natural from the attitude of this last year that Evelyn Dundas and Mrs. Home should be of the party in the house the most congenial to him, and the simplicity of them both seemed to him far more interesting than the greater complexity of the others. It would, it is true, be hard to find two examples of simplicity so utterly unlike each other, but serene absence of calculation or scheming brought both under one head. They were both, in a way, children of Nature; Mrs. Home on the one hand having arrived at her inheritance by cheerful, unswerving patience and serenity with events external to herself; while in the case of the other, his huge vitality, coupled with his extreme impressionableness to beauty, brought him, so it seemed to Tom Merivale, into very close connection with the essentials of life. But, as he had told his friend, Evelyn's attitude to life was instinctively Pagan; immoral he was not, for his fastidiousness labelled such a thing ugly, but he had apparently no rudiments even of conscience or sense of moral obligation. And somehow, with that curious sixth sense of prescience, so common in animals, so rare among civilized human beings who, by means of continued calculation and reasoned surmise of the future, which has caused it to wither and atrophize, Tom felt, just as he could feel approaching storms, a vague sense of coming disaster.

The sensation was very undefined, but distinctly unpleasant, and, following his invariable rule to divert his mind from all unpleasantness, he lay down on the short turf and buried his face in a great bed of thyme which grew there. All summer was in that smell, hot, redolent, the very breath of life, and with eyes half-closed and nostrils expanded he breathed it deeply in.

The place he had come to was very remote and solitary, a big clearing in the middle of trees, well known to him in earlier years. No road crossed it, no house lay near it, but the air was resonant with the labouring bees, and the birds called and fluted to each other in the trees. But suddenly, as he lay there, half lost in a stupor of happiness, he heard very faintly another noise, to which at first he paid but little attention. It was the sound apparently of a flute being played at some great distance off, but what soon arrested his attention was the extremely piercing character of the notes. Remote as the sound was, and surrounded as he was by the hundred noises of the summer noon, it yet seemed to him perfectly clear and distinct through them all. Then something further struck him, for phrase after phrase of delicious melody was poured out, yet the same phrase was never repeated, nor did the melody come to an end; on the top of every climax came another; it was a tune unending, eternal, and whether it came from earth or heaven, from above or below, he could not determine, for it seemed to come from everywhere equally; it was as universal as the humming of the bees.

Then suddenly a thought flashed into his mind; he sprang up, and a strange look of fear crossed his face. At the same instant the tune ceased.

FOURTH

IT was not in Lady Ellington's nature to be enthusiastic, since she considered enthusiasm to be as great a waste of the emotional fibres as anger, but she was at least thoroughly satisfied when, two evenings after this, Madge came to her room before dinner after another punting expedition with Philip, and gave her news.

"It is quite charming," said her mother, "and you have shown great good sense. Dear child, I must kiss you. And where is Mr. Home—Philip I must call him now?"

"He is outside," said Madge. "I said I would go down again for a few minutes before dinner."

Lady Ellington got up and kissed her daughter conscientiously, first on one cheek and then on the other.

"I will come down with you," she said, "just to tell him how very much delighted I am. I shall have to have a long talk to him to-morrow morning."

There was no reason whatever why the engagement should not be announced at once, and in consequence congratulations descended within the half hour. Mrs. Home was a little tearful, with tears of loving happiness on behalf of her son, which seemed something of a weakness to Lady Ellington; Tom Merivale was delighted in a sort of faraway manner that other people should be happy; Evelyn Dundas alone, in spite of his previous preparation for the news, felt somehow slightly pulled up. For with his complete and instinctive surrender to every mood of the moment, he had permitted himself to take great pleasure in the contemplation—it was really hardly more than that—of Madge's beauty, and he felt secretly, for no shadow obscured the genuineness of his congratulations, a certain surprise and sense of being ill-used. He was not the least in love with Madge, but even in so short a time they had fallen into ways of comradeship, and her engagement, he felt, curtailed the liberties of that delightful relationship. And again this evening, having cut out of a bridge table, he wandered with her in the perfect dusk. Lady Ellington this time observed their exit, but cheerfully permitted it; no harm could be done now. It received, in fact, her direct and conscious sanction, since Philip had suggested to Madge that Evelyn should paint her portrait. He knew that Evelyn was more than willing to do so, and left the arrangement of sitting to sitter and artist. In point of fact, it was this subject that occupied the two as they went out.

"We shall be in London for the next month, Mr. Dundas," Madge was saying, "and of course I will try to suit your convenience. It is so good of you to say you will begin it at once."

Evelyn's habitual frankness did not desert him.

"Ah, I must confess, then," he said. "It isn't at all good of me. You see, I want to paint you, and I believe I can. And I will write to-morrow to a terrible railway director to say that in consequence of a subsequent engagement I cannot begin the—the delineation of his disgusting features for another month."

29

Madge laughed; as is the way of country-house parties, the advance in intimacy had been very rapid.

"Oh, that would be foolish," she said. "Delineate his disgusting features if you have promised. My disgusting features will wait."

"Ah, but that is just what they won't do," said Evelyn.

"Do you mean they will go bad, like meat in hot weather? Thank you so much."

"My impression will go bad," said he. "No, I must paint you at once. Besides"—and still he was perfectly frank—"besides Philip is, I suppose, my oldest friend. He has asked me to do it, and friendship comes before cheques."

They walked in silence a little while.

"I am rather nervous," said Madge. "I watched you painting this afternoon for a bit."

"Oh, a silly sketch," said he, "flowers, terrace, woods behind; it was only a study for a background."

"Well, it seemed to affect you. You frowned and growled, and stared and bit the ends of your brushes. Am I going to be stuck up on a platform to be growled at and stared at? I don't think I could stand it; I should laugh."

Evelyn nodded his head in strong approval.

"That will be what I want," he said. "I will growl to any extent if it will make you laugh. I shall paint you laughing, laughing at all the ups and downs of the world. I promise you you shall laugh. With sad eyes, too," he added. "Did you know you had sad eyes?"

Madge slightly entrenched herself at this.

"I really haven't studied my own expression," she said. "Women are supposed to use mirrors a good deal, but they use them, I assure you, to see if their hair is tidy."

"Your's never is quite," said he. "And it suits you admirably."

Again the gravel sounded crisply below their feet, without the overscore of human voices.

Then he spoke again.

"And please accept my portrait of you as my wedding present to you—and Philip," he said with boyish abruptness.

Madge for the moment was too utterly surprised to speak.

"But, Mr. Dundas," she said at length, "I can't—I—how can I?"

He laughed.

"Well, I must send it to Philip, then," he said, "if you won't receive it. But—why should you not? You are going to marry my oldest friend. I can't send him an ivory toothbrush."

This reassured her.

"It is too kind of you," said she. "I had forgotten that. So send it to him."

"Certainly. But help me to make it then as good as I can."

"Tell me how?" she asked, feeling inexplicably uneasy.

"Why, laugh," he said. "That is how I see you. You laugh so seldom, and you might laugh so often. Why don't you laugh oftener?"

30

Then an impulse of simple honesty came to her.

"Because I am usually bored," she said.

"Ah, you really mustn't be bored while I am painting you," he said. "I could do nothing with it if you were bored. Besides, it would be so uncharacteristic."

"How is that, when I am bored so often?" she asked.

"Oh, it isn't the things we do often that are characteristic of us," said he. "It is the things we do eagerly, with intention."

She laughed at this.

"Then you are right," she said. "I am never eagerly bored. And to tell you the truth, I don't think I shall be bored when I sit to you. Ah, there is Philip. He does not see us; I wonder whether he will?"

Philip's white-fronted figure had appeared at this moment at the French window leading out of the drawing-room, and his eyes, fresh from the bright light inside, were not yet focussed to the obscurity of the dusk. At that moment Madge found herself suddenly wishing that he would go back again. But as soon as she was conscious she wished that, she resolutely stifled the wish and called to him.

"Evelyn there, too?" he asked. "Evelyn, you've got to go in and take my place."

"And you will take mine," said he with just a shade of discontent in his voice.

"No, my dear fellow," said Philip. "I shall take my own."

He laughed.

"I congratulate you again," he said, and left them.

Philip stood for a moment in silence by the girl, looking at her with a sort of shy, longing wonder.

"Ah, what luck!" he said at length. "What stupendous and perfect luck."

"What is luck, Philip?" she asked.

"Why, this. You and me. Think of the chances against my meeting you in this big world, and think of the chances against your saying 'Yes.' But now—now that it has happened it couldn't have been otherwise."

Some vague, nameless trouble took possession of the girl, and she shivered slightly.

"You are cold, my darling?" he said quickly.

She had been leaning against the stone balustrade of the terrace, but stood upright, close to him.

"No, not in the least," she said.

"What is it, then?" he asked.

"It is nothing. Only I suppose I feel it is strange that in a moment the whole future course of one's life is changed like this."

He took her hands in his, and the authentic fire of love burned in his eyes.

"Strange?" he said. "Is it not the most wonderful of miracles? I never knew anything so wonderful could happen. It makes all the rest of my life seem dim. There is just this one huge beacon of light. All the rest is in shadow."

She raised her face to him half imploringly.

31

"Oh, Philip, is it all that to you?" she asked. "I—I am afraid."

"Because you have made me the happiest man alive?"

A sudden, inevitable impulse of honesty prompted Madge to speak out.

"No, but because I have perhaps meddled with great forces about which I know nothing. I like you immensely; I have never liked anyone so much. I esteem you and respect you. I am quite willing to lead the rest of my life with you; I want nothing different. But will that do? Is that enough? I have never loved as I believe you love me. I do not think it is possible to me. There, I have told you."

Philip raised her hands to his lips and kissed them.

"Ah, my dearest, you give me all you have and are, and yet you say, 'Is that enough?'" he whispered. "What more is possible?"

She looked at him a moment, the trouble not yet quite gone from her face. Then she raised it to his.

"Then take it," she said.

The night was very warm and windless, and for some time longer they walked up and down, or stood resting against the terrace wall looking down over the hushed woods. A nightingale, the same perhaps that had been charmed to Tom's finger two evenings ago, poured out liquid melody, and the moon began to rise in the East. Gradually their talk veered to other subjects, and Madge mentioned that Evelyn was willing to do her portrait.

"He will begin at once," she said, "because it appears his impression of me isn't a thing that will keep. He is putting off another order for it."

"That is dreadfully immoral," said Philip, "but I am delighted to hear it."

"Oh, and another thing. He gives it us—to you and me I think he said—as a wedding present."

"Ah, I can't have that," said Philip quickly. "That is Evelyn all over. There never was such an unthinking, generous fellow. But it is quite impossible. Why, it would mean a sixth part of his year's income."

"I know; I felt that."

Philip laughed rather perplexedly.

"I really don't know what is to be done with him," he said. "Last year he gave my mother a beautiful pearl brooch. That sort of thing is so embarrassing. And if she had not accepted it, he would have been quite capable of throwing it into the Thames. Indeed he threatened to do so. And he will be equally capable of throwing his cheque into the fire."

"All the same, I like it enormously," she said; "his impulse, I mean."

"I know, but it offends my instincts as a man of business. I might just as well refuse to charge interest on loans. However, I will see what I can do."

They went in again soon after this, for it was growing late, and found Lady Ellington preparing to leave the table of her very complete conquests. It had fallen to Evelyn to provide her with a no-trump hand containing four aces, and she was disposed to be gracious. The news, furthermore, that he would begin her daughter's portrait at once was gratifying to her, and she was anxious that the sittings should begin at once. As both they and he would be in town for the next month, the matter was easily settled, and it was arranged that the thing should be put in hand immediately.

Philip followed Evelyn to the billiard-room as soon as the women went upstairs, and found him alone there.

"The Hermit has gone to commune with Nature," he said. "He will die of natural causes if he doesn't look out. He called me a Pagan this morning, Philip. Wasn't it rude? And the fact that it is true seems to me to make it ruder."

Philip lit his cigarette.

"I'm going to be rude too, old chap," said he. "Evelyn, you really mustn't make a present of the portrait to Madge and me. It is awfully good of you, and just like you, but I simply couldn't accept it."

Evelyn shrugged his shoulders.

"Then there will be no portrait at all," he said shortly. "I tell you I won't paint it as an order."

Philip held out his hand.

"I appreciate it tremendously," he said. "It is most awfully good of you. But it's your profession. Hullo, here's the Hermit back."

Tom Merivale entered at this moment.

"Aren't we going to sit out to-night?" he said.

Evelyn rose.

"Yes, let's go out," he said. "Well, Philip, not a line will I draw unless you take it. Or I'll give it to Miss Ellington and not you."

"You really musn't," said Philip.

"But don't you see I want to paint her? I said so to you only the other day. Hang it all, I tell you that I do it for pleasure. I shall also be the vast gainer artistically. I've got an idea about her, in fact, and if you don't let me paint her I shall do it from memory, in which case it will not be so good."

An idea struck Philip.

"Well, paint me as well," he said, "and let me pay you for that."

Evelyn followed Tom out.

"Oh, I can't haggle," he said. "Yes, I'll paint you if you like. But I will paint Miss Ellington first. In fact, you shall be painted when I've nothing else to do. Well, Hermit, seen Pan to-day?"

"No, you scoffer," said Tom.

"Call me when you do. I should like to see him, too. Let's see, he was a man with goat's legs; sort of things you see in Barnum's."

Tom shifted in his chair.

"Some day, perhaps, you may think it serious," he said.

"I daresay; a man with goat's legs is not to be taken lightly," said Evelyn. "And he sits by the roadside, doesn't he, or so Browning says, playing the pipes? What pipes, I wonder? Bagpipes, do you suppose?"

Tom laughed; his equanimity was quite undisturbed even by chaff upon what was to him the most serious subject in the world.

"Ah, who was frightened at a nightingale coming to sit on my finger a few nights ago? Evelyn, if you are not serious, I'll frighten you again."

"Well, but is it bagpipes?" asked he.

Tom suddenly got grave.

33

"No, it sounded more like a glass flute very far off," he said. "No explanations are forthcoming, because I haven't got any."

Evelyn was silent a moment.

"And when did you hear this glass flute very far off?" he asked.

"Two mornings ago, up above the house in that big clearing in the woods," he answered. "I know nothing more about it. It frightened me rather, and then it stopped."

"What did it play?" asked Philip.

"A world-without-end tune," he said. "The catechising is now over. I shall go to bed, I think. I must leave to-morrow, Philip."

"I hoped you would stop a day or two longer. Must you really go?"

"I must, I find."

"Appointment with Pan in the New Forest," remarked Evelyn, dodging the cushion that was thrown at him.

Philip had to spend the inside of the next day in London, and left with Tom Merivale by an early train, leaving Evelyn alone with his mother, Lady Ellington, and Madge. It came about very naturally that Lady Ellington gravitated to Mrs. Home, and Evelyn, finishing his background sketch in front of a great clump of purple clematis, found Madge on the terrace when he went out, with an unopened book on her lap.

The book had lain there, indeed, in the same state for half an hour before he came, for Madge had been very fully occupied with her own thoughts. She had had a talk to her mother the night before, which this morning seemed to her to be more revealing of herself than even her own confession to Philip in their stroll on the terrace had been. She had told her just what she had told him, namely, that she gave him very willingly all that she knew of herself, liking, esteem, respect, adding out of Philip's mouth that this more than contented him. But then Lady Ellington, for the first time perhaps for many years, had made a strategical error, allowing her emotion, not her reason, to dictate to her, and had said—

"Ah, Madge, how clever of you."

She had seen her mistake a moment afterwards, and just a moment too late, for Madge had asked the very simple question "Why?" And the unsatisfactory nature of her mother's reply had given her food for thought.

For Lady Ellington had applauded as clever what was to her the very rudiment of honour, and she had supposed that her mother would say "How very stupid of you." Clearly, then, while extremely uncalculating to herself, Madge had succeeded in giving the impression of calculation to one who, she well knew, calculated. What, then, she asked herself, was the secret of this love of which she was ignorant, that rendered her confession of ignorance so satisfactory a reply?

Effusive pleasure on her mother's part at the termination of this recital had not consoled her. Somehow, according to Lady Ellington's view, an almost quixotic honesty appeared clever. And it was over this riddle that she was puzzling when Evelyn appeared, with brilliance, so to speak, streaming from him. Brilliance certainly streamed from his half-finished sketch, and brilliance marked his exposition of it.

"Oh, I lead a dog's life," he said, as he planted his easel down on the gravel. "Do you know Lady Taverner, for whom this is to be a background?

34

No? I congratulate you. She is pink, simply pink, like a phlox, with butter-coloured hair, probably acquired. Well, put a pat of butter and a phlox on a purple plate, and you will see that the phlox is pinker than ever and the butter more buttery. Therefore, since I really am very thorough, I make a sketch of clematis to see how the flowers really grow, and shall plaster her with them—masses behind her, sapphires round her neck; and a pink Jewess in the middle," he added, in a tone of extraordinary irritation.

Madge let her book slide to the ground.

"Do you want to be talked to or not?" she asked. "If you don't, say so, and I will go away."

Evelyn looked up from his purple clematis.

"I lead a dog's life," he said, "but sometimes somebody throws me a bone. So throw me one."

"You seem to growl over it," said she.

"I know I do. That is because, though I lead a dog's life, nobody shall take my bone from me."

He bit the end of his brush.

"And the filthy thing casts purple shadows upwards," he said. "At least the sun shines on the purple, and reflects the purple on leaves that overhang it. I wish I had been born without any sense of colour. I should have made such ripping etchings."

Madge had no immediate reply to this, and he painted for some ten minutes in silence. She had picked up her book again, and read the words of it—reading it could not be called.

"You haven't given me many bones," said he at length.

Madge looked up.

"I know I haven't," she said; "but seriously I considered if I had got anything to say, and found I hadn't. So I decided to say nothing."

Evelyn dabbed in a purple star.

"But surely one has always something in one's mind," he said. "One can't help that, so why not say it? A penny for your thoughts now."

Madge laughed.

"No, they are worth far more. In fact, they are not in the market," she said.

Evelyn grew portentously grave.

"Mrs. Gummidge," he said.

"Oh, what do you mean?" she asked.

"You've been thinking of the old one," said Evelyn. "Philip."

"Quite true, I was," she said. "He is such a dear."

"So glad you like him," muttered Evelyn, again frowning and biting his brushes. "Lord love us, what a blue world it is this morning! There, I can't paint any more just now."

"That's rather sudden, isn't it?"

"Oh, I always stop like that," said Evelyn. "I go on painting and painting, and then suddenly somebody turns a tap off in my head, and I've finished. I can't see any more, and I couldn't paint if I did. I suppose the day will come when the tap will be turned permanently off. Shortly afterwards I shall be seen to jump off Westminster Bridge. I only hope nobody will succeed in rescuing me."

35

"I will try to remember if I happen to be there," said she.

Evelyn put his sketch to dry in the shadow of the terrace wall.

"The law is so ridiculous," he said. "They punish you if you don't succeed in committing suicide when you try to, and say you are temporarily insane if you do. Whereas the bungler is probably far more deranged than the man who does the job properly."

"I shall never commit suicide," said Madge with conviction.

"Ah, wait till you care about anything as much as I care about painting," said Evelyn, "and then contemplate living without it. Why, I should cease without it. The world would be no longer possible; it wouldn't, so to speak, hold water."

"Ah, do you really feel about it like that?" said she. "Tell me what it's like, that feeling."

Evelyn laughed.

"You ought to know," he said, "because I imagine it's like being permanently in love."

Here was as random an arrow as was ever let fly; he had been unconscious of even drawing his bow, but to his unutterable surprise it went full and straight to its mark. The girl's face went suddenly expressionless, as if a lamp within had been turned out, and she rose quickly, with a half-stifled exclamation.

"Ah, what nonsense we are talking," she said quickly.

Evelyn looked at her in genuine distress at having unwittingly caused her pain.

"Why, of course we are," he said. "How people can talk sense all day beats me. They must live at such high pressure. Personally I preserve any precious grains of sense I may have, and put them into my pictures. Some of my pictures simply bristle with sense."

The startled pain had not died out of Madge's eyes, but she laughed, and Evelyn, looking at her, gave a little staccato exclamation.

"And what is it now?" she asked.

"Why, you—you laughed with sad eyes. You were extraordinarily like what my picture will be at that moment."

The girl glanced away. That sudden, unexplained little stab of pain she had experienced had left her nervous. Her whole nature had winced under it, and, like a man who feels some sudden moment of internal agony for the first time, she was frightened; she did not know what it meant.

"I expect that is nonsense, too," she said. "At least, it is either nonsense or very obvious, for I suppose when anyone laughs, however fully he laughs, there is always something tragic behind. Ah, how nice to laugh entirely just once from your hair to your heels."

"Can't you do that ever?" asked Evelyn sympathetically.

"No, never, nor can most people, I think. We are all haunted houses; there is always a ghost of some kind tapping at the door or lurking in the dusk. Only a few people have no ghosts. I should think your's were infinitesimal. You are much to be envied."

Evelyn listened with all his ears to this; partly because he and Madge were already such good friends, and anything new about her was interesting; partly because, though, as he had said, surface was enough for him—it bore so very directly on his coming portrait of her.

"Yes, I expect that is true," he said; "most people certainly have their ghosts. But it is wise to wall up one's haunted room, is it not?"

Madge shook her head.

"Yes, but it is still there," she said.

She got up from the low chair in which she was sitting with an air of dismissing the subject of their talk.

"Come, ask me some more of those very silly riddles," she said. "I think they are admirable in laying ghosts. So, too, are you, Mr. Dundas. I am sure you will not resent it when I say it is because you are so frightfully silly. Ghosts cannot stand silliness."

Evelyn laughed.

"It is so recuperative to be silly," he said, "because it requires no effort to a person of silly disposition, that is to say. One has to be oneself. How easy!"

She opened her eyes at this.

"That means you find it easy to be natural," she said. "Why, I should have thought that was almost the most difficult thing in the world to be. Now a pose is easy; it is like acting; you have got to be somebody else. But to be oneself! One has to know what one is, first of all, one has to know what one likes."

Evelyn laughed again.

"Not at all. You just have to shut your eyes, take a long breath, and begin talking. Whatever you say is you."

The girl shook her head.

"Ah, you don't understand," she said. "You, you, I, everybody, are really all sorts of people put into one envelope. Am I to say what one piece of me is prompting me to say or what another is thinking about? And it's just the same with one's actions; one hardly ever does a thing which every part of one wants to do; one's actions, just like one's words, are a sort of compromise between the desires of one's different components."

She paused a moment, and, with a woman's quickness of intuition provided against that which might possibly be in his mind.

"Of course, when a big choice comes," she said, "one's whole being has to consent. But one only has half a dozen of those in one's life, I expect."

She had guessed quite rightly, for the idea of her marriage had inevitably suggested itself to Evelyn when she said "one hardly ever does a thing which every part of one wants to do." But in the addition she had made to her speech there was even a more direct allusion to it, which necessarily cancelled from his mind the first impression. He was bound, in fact, to accept her last word. But he fenced a little longer.

"I don't see that one choice can really be considered bigger than another," he said. "The smallest choice may have the hugest consequences which one could never have foretold, because they are completely outside one's own control. I may, for instance, settle to go up to London to-morrow by the morning train or the later one. Well, that seems a small enough choice, but supposing one train has a frightful accident? What we can

37

control is so infinitesimal compared to what lies outside us—engine-drivers, bullets, anything that may kill."

The girl shuddered slightly.

"It is all so awful," she said, "that. An ounce of lead, a fall, and one is extinguished. It is so illogical, too."

"Ah, anything that happens to one's body, or mind either, is that," said Evelyn.

"How? Surely one is responsible for what happens to one's mind."

"Yes, in the way of learning ancient history, if we choose, or having drawing-lessons. But all the big things that can happen to one are outside one's control. Love, hate, falling in love particularly is, I imagine, completely independent of one's will."

The girl gave a short, rather scornful laugh.

"But one sees a determined effort to marry someone," she said, "often productive of a very passable imitation of falling in love."

Had she boxed his ears, Evelyn could not have been more astonished. If this was an example of shutting the eyes; drawing a long breath and being natural, he felt that there was after all something to be said for the artificialities in which we are most of us wont to clothe ourselves. There was a very Marah of bitterness in the girl's tone; he felt, too, as if all the time she had concealed her hand, so to speak, behind her back, and suddenly thrown a squib at him, an explosive that cracked and jumped and jerked in a thoroughly disconcerting manner. And she read the blankness of his face aright, and hastened to correct the impression she had made.

"Did you ever get behind a door when you were a child," she asked, "and jump out calling 'Bo!'? That is what I did just then, and it was a complete success."

He looked at her a moment with his head on one side, as if studying an effect.

"But it was you who jumped out?" he asked rather pertinently.

"Ah, I wouldn't even say that," said she. "I think it was only a turnip-ghost that I had stuck behind the door."

Evelyn gave a sort of triumphant shout of laughter.

"Well, for the moment it took me in," he said. "I really thought it was you."

FIFTH

THE season in London this year had been particularly amusing; there had been a quite unusually large number of balls, the opera had been one perpetual coruscation of evening stars that sang together, the conduct of May and early June from a meteorological point of view had been impeccable, and in consequence when the world in general came back after Whitsuntide they came for the most part with a pleasurable sense of returning for the second act of a play of which the first had been really enchanting. Like taking one's seat again for a play was the sense that various unfinished situations which had been left in an interesting stage would now move forward to their dramatic climaxes. One, however—this was rather unfair—had developed itself to a happy close in the country, and Madge Ellington's engagement to Philip was generally pronounced to be very nice indeed. On both sides, indeed, it was very nice; for it had not been seemly that a millionaire should be unmarried so long, and on the other hand it had not been seemly that Madge should be unmarried so long. But now they had both seen the error of their ways, and had agreed to marry each other.

And above all, it was very nice for Lady Ellington, about whom it was generally known that she had made a considerable sum in speculation lately. To do that was universally recognised as being an assured advance towards the bankruptcy court, but to have captured a wealthy son-in-law who was a magnate in the South African market turned her steps, or might be hoped to turn them, away from the direction of the courts, and point instead towards the waters of comfort and cash. Another thing that excited to some extent the attention and applause of the world was a certain change of demeanor in Madge, which was very noticeable after her return to London from the Whitsuntide holiday. She had always been rather given to put her head in the air, and appear not to notice people; but her engagement had brought to her an added geniality. Hitherto she had been something of "a maid on yonder mountain height," but the shepherd, Philip Home, had, it appeared, convinced her that "love was of the valley," and she had quite distinctly come down. This, at any rate, was the conclusion at which Gladys Ellington, the present Lady Ellington, arrived within two minutes of the time when she met Madge next.

She was of about Madge's own age, and the two, in spite of old Lady Ellington's rooted dislike to her nephew, had always been friends. Gladys was charmingly pretty, most successful in all she did, and universally liked. This was only fair, for she took immense trouble to be liked, and never did an ill-natured thing to anyone, unless it was quite certain that she would not be found out. She had come to tea on the afternoon succeeding Madge's return to London, and, though she professed regrets at the absence of Madge's mother, was really delighted to find her friend alone. She had a perfect passion for finding things out, and her method of doing so was to talk with extreme volubility herself, so that no one could possibly conjecture that she had any object of the sort in her mind. But her pauses were well calculated, and her questions few, while with regard to these, she always gave the appearance of not attending to the answers, which further disarmed suspicion. She was, however, a little afraid of Madge's mother, who always gave her the idea of seeing through her. This made her volubility a little threadbare at times, and consequently she bore her absence with more than equanimity.

"Darling, I think it is too charming," she was saying, "and I always hoped that you would do just this. Mr. Home is perfectly adorable, I think,

39

and though it sounds horribly worldly to say so, it is an advantage, you know, to marry a very rich man. We're as poor as mice, you see, and so I know. Yes, please—a cup of tea, though we're told now that a cup of tea is the most unwholesome thing in the world. And you had a nice party? Mrs. Home, too, just like a piece of china scented with lavender. And who else was there?"

"Only two more men," said Madge, "Mr. Merivale and Mr. Evelyn Dundas."

"The Hermit of the New Forest!" cried Gladys, directing her remarks to him because she wished to hear more of the other. "How too exciting! He lives on cherry jam and brown bread, does he not, and whistles to the cows, who lay their heads on his shoulder and purr. I used to know him in the old days before he was a hermit at all. And Mr. Dundas, too! Do you like him?"

"Yes, very much, very much indeed," said Madge gravely. "He is such a child, you know, and he makes one laugh because he is so silly. He is going to do my portrait, by the way; mine and Philip's."

"How delightful! He ought to make a really wonderful thing of you, dear Madge. Do tell me, how much does he charge? I'm dying to be painted by him, but he is so frightfully expensive, is he not? And you liked him; what a good thing, as you are going to sit to him. It must be awful being painted by a man who irritates you."

Madge laughed.

"He doesn't irritate me in the slightest," she said. "In fact, I don't think I ever got to know a man so quickly. I don't know how it is; somehow he is like clear water. You can see straight to the bottom."

Gladys regarded her rather closely as she nibbled with rather a bird-like movement at a sugared bun.

"Madge, you've quite changed," she said. "You are actually beginning to take an interest in your fellow-creatures. That is so wise of you. Of course Evelyn Dundas is adorable; I'm hopelessly in love with him myself, but I should have thought he was just the sort of man who would not have interested you in the least. Nor would he have a few weeks ago. Dearest, you've stepped down from your pedestal, where you really used to be rather a statue, you know, like Galatea, and it does improve you so. I saw it the moment I came into the room. And just falling in love has done it all."

A sudden look of pain came over Madge's face, and her companion, with a well-chosen pause, waited for her to express it in words.

"Ah, Gladys, are you sure you are right?" she said. "Because I think I must tell you this even as I told Philip—I don't feel as if I had fallen in love. I like him, I esteem and respect him, but—but it isn't what I expected. I'm not—I hate the word—but I'm not thrilled."

Gladys rustled sympathetically, and Madge went on:

"I had it all out with my mother, too," she said, "who very sensibly said that as I had lived twenty-five years without falling in love in that sort of sense, I was very unlikely to begin now. On the other hand, she said that it was much better that I should be married than remain single. And so I am going to marry Philip Home."

40

Again Gladys rustled sympathetically, and gave a murmured "Yes," for Madge evidently had more to say.

"Anyhow, I have been honest with him," she said, "and I have told him that. And he seems to think that it can easily form the basis for happiness, and accepts it. But tell me, am I frightfully cold-blooded? And have I any right to marry him?"

Gladys' quick little brain had hopped over a dozen aspects of this question, and pecked, so to speak, at a dozen different fruits, while Madge was speaking; but with a whirr of wings she was back again, up to time as usual.

"No, not the least cold-blooded, and you have every right to marry him," she said. "For you may be quite sure that you soon will be in love with him, because I assure you that already it has made an enormous difference in you. How do I know that? I can't possibly tell you, any more than you can tell exactly why a person looks ill. You say her face looks drawn. What's drawn? Why, the same as ill. You've woke up, dearest; you've come to life. Life! there's nothing in the world so good as that."

Madge leaned forward, and spoke more eagerly.

"Yes, you're right," she said, "though I don't know that your reason is right I have somehow come to life. But it puzzles me a little to know how it has happened, or why."

Gladys nodded her head with an air of wisdom, and got up. At this time of the year she seldom spent more than an hour in any one place, and still more seldom with only one person, and both Madge and Madge's house had now enjoyed their full share of her time.

"Ah, I am very bad at riddles," she said, "and, besides, none of us know 'why' about anything, and, on the whole, reasons and motives matter very little. Things that happen are so numerous and so interesting that one has literally not time to probe into them and ask how and why. And after all, dear, when anything so very nice has happened as your engagement, which too has brought such a gain to you in yourself, I am more than content, and so should you be, to accept that as it is. Now, I must simply fly; I am dining out and going to the opera, and to a dance afterwards. What a pity there are not forty-eight hours in every day."

This regret was subsequently shared by Madge herself, who found that the life of a young woman who is going to be married in six weeks' time, for the wedding had been fixed for the end of July, implies a full engagement book. And in addition to the ordinary calls on her time, hours were further claimed from her by Evelyn Dundas, who apparently had insisted to another sitter on the prior rights of this subsequent engagement, and announced himself free to begin her portrait at once, to give her sittings whenever she could sit, and finish it as quickly as his powers of brush would permit him. His impetuousness, as usual, swept away all difficulties, and before a fortnight had elapsed, Madge had already given him four sittings, and the picture itself was beginning to live and breathe on his canvas.

These sittings, or rather the artist's manners and moods during them, were strangely various. Sometimes for half-an-hour, as Madge complained, he would do nothing but stare at her, grunting to himself, and

41

biting the ends of his brushes. Then in a moment all would be changed, and instead of staring and grunting with idle hands, he would glance at her and record, record and glance again, absorbed in the passion of his creation, whistling sometimes gently to himself, or at other times silent, but with a smiling mouth. Then that wind of inspiration that bloweth where it listeth would leave him again, and he would declare roundly that he did not know what she was like, or what his picture was like, but that the only thing quite certain was that his picture was not like her. Then, even while these gloomy announcements were on his lips, even in the middle of a sentence, he would murmur to himself, "Oh, I see," and the swish of the happy brush would alone break the silence. At other times there was no silence to break, and from the time she stepped up on to the platform till when she left it, he would pour out a perfect flood of inconsequent nonsense. Or, again, the hours passed in unbroken conversation between the two, the talk sometimes flitting like a butterfly over all the open flowers of life, but at other times, as it had done once or twice at Philip's house, dropping suddenly into the heart of things, finding sometimes honey there, but sometimes shadows only.

A sitting of this latter kind had just come to an end, and Evelyn, after seeing his sitter into her carriage, had returned to his studio, still palette in hand, meaning to work for an hour at the background. Certainly in this short space of time he had made admirable progress, and he knew within himself that this was to be a landmark of his work, and up to the present, at any rate, his high-water mark. He had drawn the girl standing very upright, as was her wont, but with head a little thrown back, and her face, eyes, and mouth alike laughed. It was a daring conception, but the happiness of the execution was worthy of it, and the fore-shortening of the face owing to the throw-back of the head, the drawing, too, of the open mouth and of the half-closed eyes was a triumph. Her figure was shown in white evening dress, with hands locked together, carrying a feather fan, and arms at full length in front of her; over her shoulders, half thrown back, was a scarlet opera cloak, the one note of high colour in all the scheme. Behind her, on the wall, he had introduced, by one of those daring feats that were labelled by detractors as "cheeky," but by any who estimated fairly the excellence of the execution, a round gilt-framed mirror, with a convex glass in it, on which was distortedly reflected the room itself and the back of the girl's figure. It was at this that he had returned to work now.

Evelyn's studio, like all rooms much used by anyone who has at all a vivid personality, had caught much of the character of its owner. He had made it out of the top floor in his house in the King's Road, by throwing all the attics into one big room. Often for a whole day he would not stir from it till it was too dark to paint, having a tray of lunch brought him which sometimes he would savagely devour, at other times leave untouched till he was literally faint with hunger. It was easy to see, too, how the room had grown, so to speak, how it had picked up his characteristics. The big divan, for instance, in the window, piled with brightly-coloured cushions, had evidently been of the early furniture, a remnant of imperishable childhood; so, too, no doubt, was the open Dutch-tiled fireplace, the Chippendale

42

table, the few big chairs that stood about, and the Japanese screen by the door. After that, however, all sorts of various tastes showed themselves. A heap of dry modelling clay in one corner recorded a fit of despair, when he had asserted that the only real form of art was form itself, not colour; a violin with two strings missing denoted that after hearing Sarasate he was convinced, for several hours at least, that the music of strings was alone the flower worth plucking, and showed also a delightful conviction that it was never too late to learn, though the broken strings might imply that it was now too late to mend. A set of Punch, complete from the beginning, lay like a heap of morraine stones round the sofa, a bag of rusty golf-clubs stood in a corner, and behind the Japanese screen leaned a bicycle on which dust had collected, an evidence of its being, for the time at any rate, out of date far as its owner was concerned. But three months before or three months afterwards a visitor might scarcely have recognised the room again. A portrait might have been finished, and with disengaged eyes Evelyn would survey what he would certainly call his pigsty. The bicycle would be sent to the cellar with the golf clubs slung on to it, the heap of modelling clay be dumped on the dustheap, the Japanese screen banished to the kitchen, because for the moment Japanese art was a parody and a profanation, and the violin, perhaps, have its strings mended. Or again, instead of the Japanese screen being banished, Japan might have flooded the whole studio as its armies flood Manchuria, and an equally certain and uncompromising gospel pronounce that it alone was good.

It was then to this temple of contradictions that Evelyn returned, three steps to a stride, after seeing Madge off. The figure was right; he felt sure of that, but the tone of the background somehow was not yet quite attuned to it. Above all, the mirror must be bright burnished gold, not dull, for the flame of the cloak, if it was the only note of high colour in the picture, consumed itself, burned away ineffectually, and it was with a heart that beat fast, not only from his gallop upstairs, but from excitement in this creation that was his, that he again stood before the picture. Yes, that was it; another high light was necessary.

For a moment he looked at the laughing face on his canvas, almost laughing himself. Then all on a sudden his laughter died, the need of his picture for another high light died too, for though his eyes were looking on his own presentment of Madge, it was Madge herself that his soul saw. And even as his eyes loved the work of his hands, so he knew in a burning flash of self-revelation that his soul loved her. Up till now, up till this very moment, he had not known that this was so; that it was possible he had long since recognised, that the possibility was reaching its tentacles out into regions of the probable he had recognised, so to speak, out of the corner of his eye, had recognised, but cut it, and now came the knowledge.

Evelyn gave a great sigh, raising his hands, one with the palette on the thumb, the other with the brush it held, to full stretch, and let them fall again, and stood still in front of his own inimitable portrait, drinking in no longer with the artist's eye only, but with the eye of the lover, the incomparable beauty of his beloved. That rush of sudden knowledge, so impetuous, so overwhelming, for the moment drowned all else; it did not enter his head to consider "What next?" The present moment was so blindingly bright that everything that lay outside it was in impenetrable shadow. The intimate relations into which he was thrown with the girl, by reason of this portrait; the fact that she was engaged, and that to his best friend, did not at first have any existence in his mind; he but looked at this one fact, that he loved her to the exclusion of all else. Then, as must always happen, came reaction from the ecstatic moment, and in the train of reaction, like some grey ghost, thought. But even thought for the time was gilded by the light of that central sun, and it was long before he could frame the situation in the bounding lines of life and conduct. For love is a force which is impatient of opposition, and against opposition it will hurl itself, like a wild bird against the wires of its cage, careless of whether it is dashed to pieces, knowing only the overwhelming instinct and need of liberty, to gain which death is but the snap of a careless finger.

Then, almost with a laugh at himself, came that most important factor that he had overlooked. For a couple of minutes his egoism had run away with him, taking the bit in its teeth, and the thought that he loved her, that he needed her, had not only been uppermost, but alone in his mind. But what of her? She was engaged to Philip, and shortly to be married to him, and he himself was merely to be relegated to that somewhat populous class of "odd man out." That ebb from the full flood of his passion was swift; it came in a moment, as swiftly as the other had come. So that was all that was left of him, all that was possible; that he should just stand aside while the other two went on their way, not daring even to touch the hem of her garment, for she would most surely draw it away from him. That clearly was the logical outcome, but logical as it was, not a single fibre of his inmost self accepted it. That, the one thing which to the reasonable mind must assuredly happen was to him the one thing which could not possibly happen. The very strength of his newly-awakened love was the insuperable bar to it; it could not be, for what—and the question seemed to himself at that moment perfectly unanswerable—what on earth was to happen to him in that case? Here was the Pagan, the interesting survival, as Tom Merivale had called him, most unmistakably surviving, shouting, as it were, that its own happiness, its own need, was the one thing which the rest of the world must accept and respect. And, since the only way in which due acceptation could be secured for it was conditional on Madge's loving him, that had to happen also. Yes, nothing else would do; she had to love him.

This reasoning, if one can call by so deliberate a word these leaping conclusions, was not any act of reflecting egoism. His emotions, his whole being, had been suddenly stirred, and there necessarily rose to the surface the sediment, so to speak, of that which dwelt in its depths. The whole course and habit of his past life no doubt was responsible for what was there, but he was no more responsible at this particular moment for the thoughts and conclusions that leaped in fire into his mind than is a man who is suddenly startled responsible for starting; his nerves have acted without the dictation of his brains. But with Evelyn, as the minutes passed, and he still sat there with heightened colour and flashing eyes, looking at his unfinished picture, he ceased to be comparable to a suddenly startled man; the thoughts that had sprung unbidden to his mind were not put

44

away; they remained there, and they grew in brightness. His conscious reflections endorsed the first instinctive impulse.

It so happened that he had arranged to go down that afternoon to spend a couple of nights in the New Forest with the Hermit, but when this engagement was again remembered by him, it seemed to him at first impossible to go. What he had learned in this last hour was a thing so staggering that he felt as if all the affairs of life, social intercourse, the discussion of this subject or of that, as if any subject but one contained even the germ or protoplasm of importance, had become impossible. But go or stay, everything was impossible except to win Madge's love. Then another impossibility, bigger perhaps than any, made its appearance, for the most impossible thing of all was to be alone, anything was more endurable than that; and side by side with that rose another, namely, the impossibility of keeping his knowledge to himself. He must, he felt, tell somebody, and of all people in the world the Hermit was the person whom it would be most easy to tell.

Then a sort of pale image of Philip came into his mind. He was conscious of no disloyalty to him, because he was incapable of thinking of him at all, except as of somebody, a vague somebody, who dwelt among the shadows outside the light. Mrs. Home was no more, nobody was anything more than a dweller in these shadows. Nor, indeed, had he been able to think of Philip directly, concentratedly, would he have accused himself of disloyalty; either Madge would never love himself, in which case no harm was done to anyone, or she would do so, in which case her marriage with Philip was an impossibility—an impossibility, too, the existence of which had better be found out before it was legally confirmed. Yet all this but quivered through his mind and was gone again, he caught but as passing a glimpse of the world of life and conduct as he caught of the stations that his train thundered through in its westerly course; they but brushed by his inward eye, and had passed before they had ever been focussed or seen with anything like clearness.

The Hermit had once told him, it may be remembered, that he wanted deepening, and Evelyn on that occasion had enunciated the general principle that he had no use for deeps, the surface being sufficient for his needs. And even now, though his egotism was so all-embracing, it was in no sense whatever profound. He did not probe himself, it was of the glittering surface alone on which shone this sun of love that he was conscious. Deeps, perhaps, might lie beneath, but they were unexplored; life like a pleasure boat with shallow-dipping oars went gaily across him. Indeed it was probable that before the depth—if depths were there—could be sounded the sun, so to speak, would have to go in, for with that dazzle on the water it was impossible to see what lay below.

Tom Merivale's cottage, which had begun life as two cottages, stood very solitary some mile or two outside Brockenhurst, and though the high road passed within a few hundred yards of it, it was impossible to conceive a place that more partook of the essential nature of a hermitage. Between it and the high road lay a field, with only a rough track across it; beyond that, and nearer to the house, an orchard, while a huge box-hedge, compact and homogeneous with the growth and careful clipping of many years, was to

45

any who wished to be shut off from the outer world a bar as impenetrable as a ring of fire. Immediately beyond this stood the cottage itself, looking away from the road; in front a strip of garden led down to the little river Fawn, and across the river lay a great open expanse of heath, through which, like a wedge, came down a big triangular wood of beech-trees. It was this way, over the garden and the open forest, that the cottage looked; not a house of any kind was in sight, and one might watch, like a ship-wrecked mariner for a sail, for any sign of human life, and yet in a long summer day perhaps the watcher would see nothing to tell him that he was not alone as far as humankind went in this woodland world. Tom had built out a long deep verandah that ran the whole length of the cottage on the garden front; brick pillars at the two corners supported a wooden roof, and a couple of steps led down into the garden. Down the centre of that ran a pergola, over which climbed in tangled luxuriance the long-limbed tribes of climbing roses. Ramblers spilt their crimson clusters over it, or lay in streaks and balls of white and yellow foam, while carmine pillar seemed to struggle in their embrace, and honeysuckle cast loving tendrils round them both and kissed them promiscuously. And though a gardener might have deplored this untended riot of vegetation, yet even the most orderly of his fraternity could not have failed to admire. Nature and this fruitful soil and the warm, soft air to which frost was a stranger, had taken matters into their own hands, and the result, though as fortuitous apparently as the splashed glories of a sunset, had yet a sunset's lavishness and generosity of colour. On each side of this pergola lay a small lawn of well-tended turf, and a shrubbery on one side of lilacs and syringa and on the other a tall brick wall with a deep garden bed below it gave a fragrant frame to the whole. The Hermit's avowal, indeed, that for the last year he had done nothing except carpentering and gardening implied a good deal of the latter, for the turf, as has been stated, was beautifully rolled and cut, and the beds showed evidence of seed-time and weeding, and had that indefinable but unmistakable air of being zealously cared for. But since such operations were concerned with plants, no principle was broken.

Evelyn arrived here soon after six, and found himself in undisturbed possession. Mr. Merivale, so said his servant, had gone off soon after breakfast that morning and had not yet returned. His guest, however, had been expected, and he himself would be sure to be in before long. Indeed in a few minutes his cry of welcome to Evelyn sounded from the lower end of the garden, and he left his long chair in the verandah and went down through the pergola to meet him.

"Ah, my dear fellow," said Tom, "it is delightful to see you. You have come from London, have you not, where there are so many people and so few things. I have been thinking about London, and you have no idea how remote it seems. And how is the picture getting on—Miss Ellington's, I mean?"

Evelyn looked at him with his direct, luminous gaze. Though he had come down here with the object of telling his friend what had happened, he found that at this first moment of meeting him, he was incapable of making his tongue go on its errand.

"Ah, the portrait," he said; "it really is getting on well. Up to this morning, at any rate, I have put there what I have meant to put there, and, which is rarer with me, I have not put there anything which I did not mean. Do you see how vastly more important that is?"

The Hermit had passed his day in the open merely in shirt and trousers, but his coat was lying in a hammock slung between two pillars of the pergola, and he put it on.

"Why, of course," he said, "a thing which ought not to be there poisons the rest; anything put in which should be left out sets the whole thing jarring. That's exactly why I left the world you live in. There was so much that shouldn't have been there, from my point of view at least."

Evelyn laughed.

"But if we all left out all that each of us thinks shouldn't be there, there would be precious little left in the world," he said. "For instance, I should leave out Lady Ellington without the slightest question."

He paused a moment.

"And when the portrait is finished she, no doubt, would leave out me," he added, with charming candour.

"Quite so," said Merivale; "and since I, not being an uncontrolled despot, could not 'leave out' people, which I suppose is a soft way of saying terminate their existence, I went away instead to a place where they were naturally left out, where for me their existence was terminated. It is all part of the simplifying process."

They had established themselves in the verandah again, where a silent-footed man was laying the table for dinner; and it struck Evelyn for the moment as an inconsistency that the tablecloth should be so fine and the silver so resplendent.

"But in your simplification," said Evelyn, indicating the table, "you don't leave out that sort of thing."

"No, because if I once opened the question of whether I should live on the bare necessities of life, or allow myself, so to speak, a little dripping on my bread, the rest of my life would be spent in settling infinitesimal points which I really don't think much matter. I could no doubt sell my silver and realize a few hundred pounds, and give that away. But I don't think it matters much."

"All the same, it is inconsistent."

"In details that does not seem to me to matter either," said Merivale. "For instance, I don't eat meat partly because I think that it is better not to take life if you can avoid it. But when a midge settles on my hand and bites me, if possible I kill it."

"Well, anyhow your inconsistencies make up a very charming whole," said the other, looking round. "It is all charming."

"I'm glad, and you think you can pass a day or two here without missing the—the complications you live among? I wish Philip could have come down, too; but he is buried in work, it appears, and we know how his leisure is occupied just now."

Evelyn moved suddenly in his chair.

"Ah, do you know, I am rather glad Philip isn't here," he said. "I

47

don't think——" and he broke off again. "And as soon as I've finished this portrait, I'm going to do his," he added.

He was silent a moment, feeling somehow that he never would do Philip's portrait. He would not be able to see him, he would not be able to paint him; something, no shadow, but something so bright would stand between him and the canvas that he would be unable to see beyond or through it.

But Merivale did not seem to notice the check. His eyes were looking out over the glowing garden, where all colours were turned to flame in the almost level rays of the sun as it drew near to its setting. The wall behind the deep garden bed glowed as if the bricks themselves were luminous, light seemed to exude from the grass, the flowers were bells and cups of fire.

"Ah, this is the best moment of all the day," he said, "when sunset comes like this. The whole of the sunshine of the hours seem distilled into it, it is the very essence of light."

He rose from his chair, and went to the edge of the verandah, stretching his arms wide and breathing deeply of the warm, fragrant air. Then he turned again to his companion.

"That, too, I hope is what death will be like," he said. "All the sunlight of life will be concentrated into that moment, until one's mere body can hold no more of the glow that impregnates it, and is shattered. Look at those clusters of rambler; a little more and they must burst with the colour."

Evelyn got up too.

"Don't be so uncomfortable, Tom," he cried, in a sort of boyish petulance. "I could go mad when I think of death. It is horrible, frightening. I don't want to die, and I don't want to get old. I want to be young always, to feel as I feel to-day, and never a jot less keenly. That's what you must tell me while I am here; how am I to remain young? You seem to have solved it; you are much younger than when I knew you first."

Tom laughed.

"And another proof of my youth is that I feel as I do about death," he said. "The more you are conscious of your own life, the more absurd the notion that one can die becomes. Why, even one's body won't die; it will make life, it will be grass on one's grave, just as the dead leaves that fall from the tree make the leaf-mould which feeds that tree or another tree or the grass. It doesn't in the least matter which, it is all one, it is all life."

Evelyn shivered slightly.

"Yes, quite true, and not the least consoling," he said; "for what is the use of being alive if one loses one's individuality? It doesn't make death the least less terrible to me, even if I know that I am going to become a piece of groundsel and be pecked at by your canary. I don't want to be groundsel, I don't want to be pecked at, and I don't want to become your canary. Great heavens, fancy being a bit of a canary!"

"Ah, but only your body," said the other.

Evelyn got up.

"Yes, and what happens to the rest? You tell me that a piece of me, for my body is a piece of me, becomes a canary, and you don't know about the rest. Indeed it is not a cheerful prospect. If some—some bird pecks my eyes out, is it a consolation to me, who becomes blind, to learn that a bird has had dinner?"

Merivale looked at him; even as Gladys had seen that some change had come in Madge, so he saw that something had happened to Evelyn, and he registered that impression in his mind. But the change, whatever it was, was not permanent—it was a phase, a mood only, for next moment Evelyn had broken out into a perfectly natural laugh.

"You shan't make me think of melancholy subjects any more," he cried. "Indeed you may try, but you won't be able to do it. I have never been more full of the joy of life than to-day. That was why I was so glad to come down here, as you are a sort of apostle of joy. But it's true that I also want to talk to you some time about something quite serious. Not now though, but after dinner. Also you will have to show me all the bag of conjuring tricks, the mechanical nightingale, the disappearing omelette—I could do that, by the way—and the Pan pipes. Now, I'm going upstairs to change; I've got London things on, and my artistic eye is offended. Where shall I find you?"

"I shall go down to bathe. Won't you come?" said Merivale.

Evelyn wrinkled up his nose.

"No, I've not been hot enough. Besides, one is inferior to the frog in the water, which is humiliating. Any frog swims so much better!"

SIXTH

MERIVALE had scooped out a long bathing-pool at the bottom of the garden, and when Evelyn left him, he took his towel and walked down to it. A little higher up was a weir, and from this he plunged into a soda water of vivifying bubble, and floated down as the woven ropes of water willed to take him till he grounded on the beds of yellow, shining gravel at the tail of the pool, laughing with joy at the cool touch of the stream. The day had been very hot, and since breakfast he had been on the move, now under the shadow of the trees, but as often as not grilled by the great blaze of the sun on the open heaths, and it was with an extraordinary sense of renewed life and of kinship with this beautiful creature that was poured from the weir in never-ending volumes that he gave himself up to the clean, sensuous thrill of the moment. It seemed to him that the strong flood that bore him, with waves and eddies just tipped with the gold and crimson of the sun, entirely interpenetrated and possessed him. He was not more himself than was the stream, the stream was not more itself than it was he. The blue vault overhead with its fleeces of cloud beginning to flush rosily was part of the same thing, the beech-trees with leaves a-quiver in the evening breeze were but a hand or an eyebrow of himself.

Then, with the briskness of his renewed vigour, he set himself to swim against this piece of himself, as if right hand should wrestle with left, breasting the river with vigorous strokes, yet scarcely moving against the press of the running stream, while like a frill the water stood up bubbling round his neck. Then again, with limbs deliciously tired with the struggle, he turned on his back and floated down again, with arms widespread, to increase the surface of contact. Though this sense of unity with the life of Nature was never absent from him, so that it was his last waking thought at night and stood by him while he slept, ready to awake him again, water somehow, live, running water with the sun on its surface, or the rain beating on to it, with its lucent depths and waving water-weeds that the current combed, gave it him more than anything else. Nothing else had quite that certainty of everlasting life about it; it was continually outpoured, yet not diminished; it mingled with the sea, and sprang to heaven in all the forms and iridescent colours of mist and cloud, to return again to the earth in the rain that made the grass to grow and fed the springs. And this envelopment of himself in it was a sort of outward symbol of his own absorption in Nature, the outward and visible sign of it. Every day the mystery and the wonder of it all increased; all cleansing, all renewal was contained here, for even as the water cleansed and renewed him, so through the countless ages it cleansed and renewed itself. And here alone the intermediary step, death, out of which came new life, was omitted. To water there was no death; it was eternally young, and the ages brought no abatement of its vigour.

Then in the bright twilight of the sun just set he dressed and walked back to the house to find that he had been nearly an hour gone, and that it was close on dinner-time.

During the earlier part, anyhow, of that meal Evelyn showed no return of his disquietude, but, as was his wont, poured out floods of surprising stuff. He talked shop quite unashamed, and this evening the drawbacks of an artist's life supplied his text.

"Yes, everyone is for ever insisting," he said, "that the artist's life is its own reward, because his work is creative; but there are times when I would sooner be the man who puts bristles in toothbrushes. Those folk don't allow for the days when you sit in front of a blank canvas, or a canvas half-finished, and look at it in an absolute stupor of helplessness. I suppose they would say 'Go on, put down what you see,' and they are so wooden-headed as not to realise that on such occasions, unfortunately numerous, one doesn't see anything, and one couldn't put it down if one did. There is a blank wall in front of one. And it is then I say with Mr. Micawber, 'No one is without a friend who is possessed of shaving materials'—yet I don't kill myself. Oh, hang it, here we are talking about death again! Give me some more fish."

Merivale performed this hospitable duty.

"Ah, but what do you expect?" he asked. "Surely you can't think it's possible that a man can live all the time in the full blaze of imaginative vision? You might as well expect him to run at full speed from the day he was born to the day of his—well, all the time, as you dislike the word."

Evelyn drummed the table with his fingers.

"But it's just that I want," he cried. "Whose fault is it that I can't do what I feel is inside me all the time? If I have what you call the imaginative vision at all, who has got any business to put a cap like the cap of a camera lens over it, so that I can see nothing whatever? Oh, the pity of it! Sitters, too! Sitters can be so antipathetic that I feel when I look at them that the imaginative vision is oozing out of me, like sawdust when you clip a doll's leg, and that in another moment I shall be just a heap of collapsed rags on the floor, with a silly waxen head and shoulders on the top. If only people would come to me to paint their caricatures I could do some rippers. The next woman I've got to paint when these two are finished is a pink young thing of sixty, with a face that has exactly the expression of a pansy. Lord! Lord!"

This was so completely the normal Evelyn Dundas that Merivale, if not reassured, for there was no need for that, at any rate thought that he had been mistaken in his idea that some change had come to him. He was just the same vivid, eager boy that he had always been, blessed with one supreme talent, which, vampire-like, seemed to suck the blood out of all the other possibilities and dormant energies of his nature, and suck, too, all sense of responsibility from him.

"Refuse them then," he said; "say 'I won't paint you; you sap my faculties.'"

Evelyn burst out into a great shout of laughter.

"'Mr. Dundas presents his compliments to Lady What's-hername,'" he said, "'and regrets, on inspection, that he is unable to paint her portrait, owing to the fact that a prolonged contemplation of her charms would sap his artistic powers, which he feels himself unwilling to part with.' What would be this rising young painter's position in a year's time, eh? His studio would be as empty as the New Forest. You might then come and live there, Tom."

Evelyn finished his wine and lit a cigarette all in one breath.

"Now, strange though it may seem to you," he said, "I feel that I've talked enough about myself for the moment, though I propose to go on afterwards. So, by way of transition, we will talk about you. As I dressed a number of frightful posers came into my head about you, and I want categorical answers. Now you've been here how long? More than a year, isn't it? What can you show for it? Number two: What's it all about? Number three: How can you call yourself a student of Nature when you deliberately shut your eyes to all the suffering, all the death, all the sacrifice that goes on eternally in Nature? I might as well call myself an artist and refuse to use blue and red in my pictures. I remember asking you something of this sort before, and your answer was eminently unsatisfactory. Besides, I have forgotten it."

Merivale moved sideways to the table, and crossed one leg over the other.

"Does it really at all interest you?" he said.

"It does, or I should not ask. Another thing, too: I have been looking at you all dinner, and I could swear you look much younger than you did five years ago. Indeed, if I saw you now for the first time I should say you were not much more than twenty. Also you used to be a touchy, irritable

51

sort of devil, and you look now as if nothing in the world had the power to make you cease smiling. Did you know, by the way, that you are always smiling a little?"

Tom laughed.

"No, not consciously," he said; "but now you mention it, it seems impossible that I should not."

"Well, begin," said Evelyn, with his usual impatience. "Tell me all about it, and attempt to answer all those very pertinent questions. Smoke, too; I listen better to a person who is smoking, because I feel that he is more comfortable."

A sudden wind stirred in the garden, blowing towards them in the verandah the sleeping fragrance of the beds and the wandering noises of the night, which, all together make up what we call the silence of the night, even as the mixture of primary colours makes white.

"Smoke? No, I don't smoke now," said Merivale; "but if you really want to know, I will tell you all I can tell you. The conjuring tricks, as you call them, I suppose you will take for granted?"

Evelyn, comfortable with his coffee and liqueur, assented.

"Yes, leave them out," he said. "Here beginneth the gospel."

He tried in these words to be slightly offensive; the offensiveness, however, went wide of the mark, and he was sorry. For the Hermit, as he had known him in the world, was singularly liable to take offence, to be irritable, impatient, to be stamping and speechifying on an extremely human platform. But no vibration of any such impatience was in Merivale's voice, and in his words there was no backhander to answer it. So the gospel began.

"It is all so simple," he said, "yet I suppose that to complicated people simplicity is as difficult to understand as is complexity to simple people. But here it is, anyhow, and make the best or the worst of it; that is entirely your concern."

"There is God," he said, "there is also Nature, which I take to be the visible, tangible, audible expression of Him. There is also man—of which you and I are specimens, and whether we are above or below the average doesn't matter in the least—and man by a dreadful process called civilisation has worked himself back into a correspondingly dreadful condition. If he were either fish, flesh, or fowl one would know where to put him, but he is none of those. He seems, at any rate to me, to be a peculiar product of his own making, and instead of being a creature compounded of life and joy, which should be his ingredients and also his study, he has become a creature who is mated with sorrow and at the end with death. He has become rotten without ever being ripe, the flower to which he should have attained has been cankered in the bud. Now, all this it has been my deliberate aim to leave behind me and to forget, and to go straight back to that huge expression of the joy of God, which man has been unable to spoil or render sorrowful, to the great hymn of Nature. Listen to that for a moment—and for the more moments you listen to it the more unmistakable will its tenour be—and you will hear that the whole impression is one of life and of joy. There is, it is true, throughout Nature

52

the sound of death, of cruelty, and of one creature preying on another; but the net result is not death, it is ever-increasing life. And so when I went to Nature I shut my ears and eyes to that minor undercurrent of sound. Of the result I was sure; day after day there is more life in the world, in spite of the death that day after day goes on. All the death goes to form fresh life. In the same way with the joy and sorrow of Nature; for every animal that suffers there are two that are glad, for every tree that dies there are two in the full vigour of the joy of life. And that joy and that life is my constant study. I soak myself in it, and shall so do until I am utterly impregnated with it. And when that day comes, when there is no tiny or obscure fibre in my being that does not completely realise it, then, with a flash of revelation, so I take it, I shall 'grasp the scheme of things entire.' Whether by life or by death, I shall truly realise that I and that moth flitting by, and the odours of the garden and the river are indivisibly one, just an expression of the spirit of life, which is God."

He paused a moment.

"There were two other questions you asked me," he said. "What have I got to show for the years I have spent here? I shrug my shoulders at that; it is I who am being shown. The second concerns my personal appearance, for you say I look younger. That is probably quite true and quite inevitable, for the contemplation of the eternal youth of the world I suppose must make one younger, body and soul alike. And that is all, I think."

Evelyn was listening with extreme attention; he did not look in the least uninterested.

"My word, you've got a perfectly sober plan at the bottom of it all," he said, "and I thought half of it was moonshine and the other half imagination. There is one more question—two more. What if the whole of the suffering and the cruelty and the death in Nature is made clear to you in a flash, if it is that which will come to make you grasp the scheme of things entire?"

Merivale smiled still, rocking forward in his chair with his hands clasped round his knee.

"That is possible," he said, "and I recognise that. But I don't think I am frightened at it If it is to be so, it is to be so. Though I suppose one won't live after it. Well?"

"And the second question. You think, then, it is our duty to seek happiness and joy and forget the sorrow of the world?"

"I think it is so for me," said he, "though I do think that there are many people, most, I suppose, that realise themselves through sorrow and suffering. I can only say that I believe I am not one of those. The way does not lie for me there."

Evelyn got up, and stood leaning on the balustrade of the verandah. This was beginning to touch him more closely now; his own threads were beginning to interweave in the scheme Merivale drew.

"And for me," he said. "What is your diagnosis of me? Am I one of those who will find themselves through sorrow or through joy?"

Merivale turned to him with almost the same eagerness in his face as Evelyn himself showed.

"Ah, how can I tell you that?" he said, "beyond telling you at least that in my opinion, which after all is only my opinion, it is in joy that you, almost above everyone I know, will ripen and bear fruit. Sorrow, asceticism is the road by which some approach happiness, but I do not see you on that road. Renunciation for you——"

Evelyn got up and came a step closer.

"Yes? Yes?" he cried.

Merivale answered him by another question.

"Something has happened to you," he said. "What is it?"

"I have fallen in love," said the other. "I only knew it to-day. Yes, her, Madge Ellington. Good God, man, I love her! And I am painting her—I see her nearly daily alone; it is my business to study her face and get to know her——"

His voice dropped suddenly.

"What am I to do?" he said after a moment. "Philip, the whole thing——"

"Ah, you can't go on," said Merivale quickly. "You must see that. Wherever our paths lie, there is honour——"

"Honour?" cried Evelyn almost savagely. "Have I not as good a right to love her as Philip has? You can't tie one down like that! Besides, how can I help loving her? Night and day are not less in my control. Besides, I have no reason to suppose that she loves me, so what harm is done? But if she does or should——"

Again he stopped, for there was no need to go on; the conclusion of the sentence was not less clear because it was unspoken. After a moment he continued.

"And what was your view just now about renunciation for me?" he asked.

Merivale got up.

"I don't know what to say to you," he said. "What do you propose, you yourself?"

"I propose to tell her what I know—that I love her," said he.

There was a long pause; Merivale was looking out over the dusky garden, and his lips moved as if he was trying to frame some sentence, yet no words came. In the East the moon was soon to rise behind the wedge of beech-wood which came diagonally across the heath, and though it was not yet visible, the sky was changing from the dark velvet blue which had succeeded sunset to the mysterious dove colour which heralds the moon. A night breeze stirred among the shrubs, and the scent of the stocks was wafted into the verandah, twined, as it were, with the swooning fragrance of the syringa. But for once Merivale was unconscious of the witchery of the hour; in spite of himself, the interests, the problems, the suffering and renunciation of human life, from which he had thought he had weaned himself, claimed him again. He had tried, and in great measure succeeded, in detaching himself from them, but he had not completely broken away from them yet. He had enlisted under the banner of joy, but now from the opposing hosts there came a cry to him, and he could not shut his ears to it. Here was the necessity for suffering, it could not but be that of these two friends of his, suffering poignant and cruel lay before one of them, though

54

which that one should be he did not know. But the necessity was dragged before his notice.

Then from the garden his eyes rested on Evelyn again, as he stood close to him with his keen, beautiful face, his eyes in which burned the wonder of his love, his long, slim limbs and hands that trembled, all so astonishingly alive, and all so instinct with the raptures and the rewards of living, and he could not say "Your duty lies here," even had he been certain that it was so, so grey and toneless, so utterly at variance with the whole gospel of his own life would the advice have been. Yet neither, for his detachment from human affairs was not, nor could it be, complete, could he say to him "Yes, all the joy you can lay hands on is yours," for on the other side stood Philip. But his sympathies were not there.

He spread out his hands with a sort of hopeless gesture.

"I don't know what to say: I don't even know what I think," he said. "It is one of those things that is without solution, or rather there are two solutions, both of which are inevitably right, and utterly opposed. But you have as yet no reason to think that she loves you; all goes to show otherwise."

"Yes, all," said Evelyn softly, "but somehow I don't believe it. I can't help that either."

Then suddenly he took hold of Merivale's shoulders with both hands.

"Ah, you don't understand," he said. "You were saying just now that you and the river were indivisibly one. That is a mere figure of speech, though I understand what you mean by it. But with me it is sober truth; I am Madge. I have no existence apart from her. Some door has been opened, I have passed through it into her. Half oneself! Someone says man alone is only half himself. What nonsense! Till he loves he is complete in himself, but then he ceases to be himself at all."

Wild as were his words, so utterly was he in the grip of his newly-awakened passion that possessed him, there was something convincing to Merivale about it. He might as well have tied a piece of string across a line to stop a runaway locomotive as hope to influence Evelyn by words or advice, especially since he at heart pulled in the opposite way to the advice he might thus give. The matter was beyond control; it must work itself out to its inevitable end.

"And when will you tell her?" he asked.

"I don't know. The moment I see she loves me, if that moment comes."

"And if it does not?"

Again his passion shook him like some great wave combing the weeds of the sea.

"It must," he said.

That clearly was the last word on the subject, and even as he spoke the rim of the moon a week from full topped the beech-wood, and flooded the garden with silver, and both watched in silence till the three-quarter circle swung clear of the trees. Just a month ago Evelyn had watched it rising with Madge on the terrace of Philip's house, and the sight of it now made the last month pass in review before him like some scene that moved behind the actors, as in the first act in Parsifal. The light it shed to-day seemed to flash back and illumine the whole of those weeks, and showed him how in darkness that plant had grown which to-day had flowered rose-coloured and perfect. Every day since then, when the seed had first been planted in his soul, had it shot up towards the light; there had been no day, so he felt now, on which the growth had stood still; it had been uninterrupted from the first germination to this its full flower. But the last word had been spoken, and when the moon had cleared the tree-tops, Merivale turned to him.

"I seldom sleep in the house," he said, "and I certainly shall not to-night."

"Where then?" asked the other.

"Oh, anywhere, often in several places. In fact, I seldom wake in the morning where I go to bed in the evening."

"Sleep-walking?" suggested Evelyn.

"Oh, dear no! But you know all animals wake in the night and turn over, or get up for a few moments and take a mouthful of grass. Well, the same thing happens to me. I always wake about three in the morning, and walk about a little, and, as I say, usually go to sleep again somewhere else. But I suppose the dignity of man asserts itself, and I often go further than animals. For instance, I shall probably go to sleep in the hammock in the garden, and walk up into the beech-wood when I wake for the first time."

"Ah, that does sound rather nice," said Evelyn appreciatively.

"Well, come and sleep out too. It will do you all the good in the world. You can have the hammock; I'll lie on the grass. I always have a rug."

But Evelyn's appreciation was not of the practical sort.

"Heaven forbid!" he said. "My bedroom is good enough for me."

It was already late, and he took a candle and went upstairs, Merivale following him to see he had all he wanted. His servant, however, had arranged the utmost requirements in the most convenient way, and the sight suddenly suggested a new criticism to Evelyn.

"Keeping a servant, too," he said. "Is not that frightfully inconsistent?"

Merivale laughed.

"You don't suppose I keep a servant when I am alone?" he asked. "But I find I am so bad at looking after the requirements of my guests that I hire one if anyone happens to be here. He is a man from the hotel at Brockenhurst."

"I apologise," said the other. "But do dismiss him to-morrow. For I didn't want to come to an hotel; I wanted to see how the Hermit really lived."

"Stop over to-morrow then, and you will see," said Merivale. "But I keep a woman in the house, who cooks."

"That also is inconsistent."

"No, I don't think so. It takes longer than you would imagine to do all the housework yourself. I tried it last winter and found it not worth

56

while. Besides, dusting and cleaning are so absorbing. I could think of nothing else."

"But doesn't she find it absorbing?"

Merivale laughed.

"I feel sure she doesn't," he said, "or she would do it better. But when I dusted for myself, nothing short of perfection would content me. I was dusting all day long."

Evelyn looked doubtfully at his bed.

"Shall I have to make it—whatever 'making' means?" he asked, "if I sleep in it? If so, I really don't think it would be worth while. Besides, I know I shan't sleep, and if I don't sleep I am a wreck."

Merivale raised his eyebrows.

"Surely you sleep when you want sleep just as you eat when you are hungry," he said, "or is that an exploded superstition?"

"Quite exploded. I shan't sleep a wink," said Evelyn, beginning to undress. "Oh, how can I?" he cried.

"And you really want to?"

"Why, of course. I'm as cross as two sticks if I don't."

Merivale shook his head.

"I'll make you sleep if you wish," he said. "Get into bed. I must go and turn out the lights. I'll be back in two minutes."

He left the room, and Evelyn undressed quickly.

All that had happened to-day ran like a mill-race in his head, and, arguing from previous experience, he knew perhaps the tithe of what awaited him when the light was out. For often before, when a picture, not as now the original of it, occupied him, misshapen parodies of rest had been his till cock-crow. First of all would come a sense of satisfaction at being alone, at being able to let his thoughts take their natural course uninterrupted; he would feast his eyes on the untenanted blackness, letting his imagination paint there all that it had been so intensely occupied with during the day. But then as the brain wearied, in place of the ideal he had been striving for would come distorted reflections of it, seen as if in some bloated mirror, and still awake he would see his thoughts translated into some horrible grotesque that would startle him into sitting-up in bed, just for the grasping of the bed-post, or the feeling of the wall, to bring himself back into the realm of concrete things. Otherwise the grotesques would grow into dancing, shapeless horrors, and in a moment he would have to wrench himself free from the clutches of nightmare and start up, with dripping brow and quivering throat that could not scream, into reality again. But to-night he feared no nightmare; he knew simply that sleep could not come to him, his excitement had invaded and conquered the drowsy lands, and though he felt now that he would be content to think and think and love till morning, morning, he knew, would, like an obsequious waiter, present the bill for the sleepless night. Consequently, when Merivale again entered, he welcomed him.

"I demand a conjuring-trick," he said, "I know I shan't sleep at all, unless you have some charm for me. Good God, how can I sleep? And, after all, why should I want to? Isn't waking good enough?"

57

Merivale paused; waking and sleeping seemed to him no more matters for concern than they seem to an animal which sleeps when it is sleepy, and wakes when its sleepiness has gone.

"That is entirely for you to settle," he said. "If you want to sleep I can make you; if you don't, I shall go to sleep myself. I shall do that in any case," he added.

Evelyn was already overwrought with the events of the day, and he spoke petulantly.

"Oh, make me sleep, then!" he said. "There is to-morrow coming. I can do nothing to-night, so let's get it over."

"Lie down, then," said the Hermit, "and look at me, look at my eyes, I mean."

He sat down on the edge of Evelyn's bed, and spoke low and slow.

"The wind is asleep," he said, "it sleeps among the trees of the forest, for the time of sleep has come, and everything sleeps, your love sleeps too. Lie still;" he said, as Evelyn moved, "the trees of the forest sleep; and their leaves sleep, and high in the branches the birds sleep. Everything sleeps, the tired even and the weary sleep, and those who are strong sleep, and those who are weak."

Evelyn's eyelids quivered, shut a moment, then half-opened again.

"The flowers sleep," said Merivale, "and the eyelids of their petals are closed, as your eyelids are closing. Sleep, the black soft wing, has shut over them, as the wings of birds shut over their heads. The earth sleeps, the very stones of her sleep; she will not stir till morning, or if she stirs it will be but to sleep again. The sad and the happy sleep, the very sea sleeps and is hushed, and the tides of the sea are asleep. Sleep, too," he said, slightly raising his voice, "sleep till they wake—sleep till I wake you."

He waited a moment, but Evelyn's eyelids did not even quiver again. Then he blew out the light and left the room.

Merivale stepped softly down the stairs, and went out on to the verandah, where they had dined a few hours before. At the touch of the soft night-air all the trouble that during this evening had been his was evaporated and vanished. The sum of his consciousness was contained in the bracket, that he was alive, and that he was part of life. It was like stepping into an ocean that received him and bore him on its surface, or took him to its depths; which mattered not at all—the thing embraced and encompassed him. He went back again to it from the fretful trivialities that had arrested him as the midge on his wrist could for the moment arrest him, trivially and momentarily causing him some infinitesimal annoyance. But that was over; the huge sky was above him, the world was asleep, and was his possession. It—the material part of it—was but a dream, the spirit of it all suffused him. There was life everywhere, life in its myriad forms, its myriad beauties. The sleepy voice of the river was part of him, the moon was he, the utmost twinkle of a star was he also. Yet no less the smallest blade of grass was he; there was no atom of the universe with which he did not claim identity.

Yes, there was one, the fretting of the human spirit, whereas his own did not fret. What he could interpret existence into was to him satisfying.

For himself he longed and wished for nothing, except to hold himself open, as he indeed held himself, for the moods of Nature to play upon. Yet in that bedroom upstairs he had left one, asleep indeed by the mere exercise of a stronger will on his, who would to-morrow awake and combat and perhaps succumb to forces that were stronger than he. For himself, he combatted with no force; he but yielded in welcome to what to him was irresistible. But Evelyn, who slept now, would awake to try his strength against another. Which was right?

SEVENTH

GLADYS ELLINGTON, as has been remarked, was not in the least ill-natured, and never even hinted ill-natured things against anybody unless she was certain to be undiscovered. So, as all the world knew, since she was not "quite devoted," a phrase of her's, to her mother-in-law, the merest elements of wisdom demanded of her that she should be unreserved in her commendation of Madge's engagement. Unreserved, in consequence, she was, even to her own husband. He also was quite unreserved, but his unreserve was whiskered and red-faced like himself, and bore not the slightest resemblance to his wife's voluble raptures.

"Seems to me," he said, "that Madge has married him for his money. Don't believe she loves him. Cold-blooded fish like that. Don't tell me. Hate a girl marrying for money. American and so on. Good love match, like you and me, Gladys. I hadn't a sou, you hadn't a penny. Same sort of thing, eh?"

Lord Ellington usually ended his sentences with "Eh?" If he did not end them with "Eh?" he ended them with "What?" The effect in either case was the same, for, like Pilate, he did not wait for an answer. "Eh?" or "what," in fact, meant that he had not finished; if he had finished, he ended up his period with "Don't tell me." As a consequence, perhaps, nobody told him anything. All worked together for good here, because he would not have understood it if they had. He was fond of his wife, and slightly fonder of his dinner. Why she had married him was a mystery; but there are so many mysteries of this kind that it is best to leave them alone.

Gladys, on this occasion (a speech which had given rise to his, in so far as any speech or connected thought would account for what Lord Ellington would say next), had merely remarked that the engagement was very, very nice.

"You seem to object to him," she said, "because he is rich. That is very feeble. I never knew riches to be a bar to anything except the kingdom of heaven, with which you, Ellington, are not immediately concerned. But you are much more immediately concerned with South African mines. Now, he is dining here to-night, and so is Madge. If you can't get

59

something out of him between the time we leave the room and you join us, I really shall despair of you."

A heavy, jocular look came into Lord Ellington's face.

"You don't despair of me yet, Gladys?" he said.

"No, not quite. Very nearly, but not quite. Oh, Ellington, do wake up for once to-night! Philip Home moves a finger in that dreadful office of his in the City, somewhere E.C., and you and I are beggars, even worse than now, or comparatively opulent. Ask him which finger he moves. If only I were you, I could do it in two minutes. So I'll allow you ten. Not more than that, because we've got the Reeves' box at the opera, and Melba is singing."

"Lot of squawking," said he. "Why not sit at home? Who wants to hear squawking? All in Italian too. Don't understand a word, nor do you. And you don't know one note from another, nor do I. Don't tell me."

Gladys required all her tact, which is the polite word for evasion, sometimes, in getting her way with her husband, and all her diplomacy, which is the polite word for lying. If he got a notion into his head it required something like the Lisbon earthquake to get it out; if, on the other hand, a thing commoner with him, he had not a notion in his head, it required a flash of lightning, followed by the steady application of a steam-hammer to get it in. Also in talking to him it was almost as difficult to concentrate one's own attention as it was to command his, for the fact that he was being talked to produced in him, unless he was dining, an irresistible tendency to make a quarter-deck of the room he was in, up and down which he shuffled. When this became intolerable, Gladys told him not to quarter-deck, but this she only did as a last resort, because he attended rather more when he was quarter-decking than when not.

"Never mind about the opera then," she said, "you needn't go unless you like. But what is important is that since Madge is going to marry Philip Home, we should reap all the advantages we can. Perhaps there is only one, apart from having another very comfortable house to stay in, but that is a big one. He can make some money for us."

This was only the second time she had mentioned this, and in consequence she was rather agreeably surprised to find that her husband grasped it. He even appeared to think about it, and suggested an amendment, though the process required, it seemed to Gladys, miles of quarter-decking.

"Eh, what?" he said. "Something South African? Put in twopence and get out fourpence, with a dividend in the interim? By Gad, yes! But you'd better get it out of him, Gladys, not I. Lovely woman, you know; a man tells everything to lovely woman. Don't tell me."

This had never occurred to Gladys, and she always respected anyone to whom things occurred before they occurred to her.

"How very simple," she said, "and much better than my suggestion. I suppose it was so simple that it never occurred to me."

Ellington chuckled, and as the conversation was over, sat down again to read the evening paper, which had just come in. He read the morning paper all the morning, and talked of it at lunch, and the evening paper all evening, and talked of it at dinner; these two supplied him with his mental daily bread. All the same, he never seemed well-informed even about current events; he managed somehow to miss the point of all the news he read, and could never distinguish between Kuroki and Kuropatkin.

Three days had passed since Madge had had her last sitting for her portrait, and those three days had passed for her in a sort of dream of disquietude which was not wholly pain. She had not seen Evelyn since, and scarcely Philip, for he had been harder worked than usual, and last night, when he was to have dined with them, had sent word that he could not possibly get there in time. They were to go to the theatre afterwards, and he said he would join them there. She had upbraided him laughingly for his desertion of them, telling him that he put the pleasure of business higher than the pleasure of her society. For retort he had the fact that when he was not at work he was never anywhere else but in her society, whereas two days ago, when he was free one morning, she refused to ride with him because she was to give a sitting to Evelyn. But the moment he had said this he was sorry for it, for Madge had flushed, and turned from him, biting her lip. But though he was sorry for the undesigned pain he had apparently given her, his heart could not but sing to him. She could not bear such a word from him even in jest.

But this had not been the cause of Madge's disquietude; Philip's remark indeed had, so far as it alone was concerned, gone in at one ear but to come out at the other. In its passage through it had touched something that made her wince with sudden pain. But the pain passed, and a warmth, a glow of some secret kind, remained. Disquieting it was, but not painful, except that at intervals a sort of pity and remorse would stab her, and at other times her heart, like Philip's, could not but sing to her for the splendour of love which was beginning to dawn. She could not help that dawn coming, and she could not help glorying in its light.

Of what should be the practical issue she did not at once think. It was but three weeks ago that she had promised to marry Philip, and then her honesty had made her tell him that she gave him liking, esteem, affection, all that she was conscious that it was in her power to give. And now, when she knew that she was possessed of more than these, and that the new possession was not hers to give him, a long day of indecision, this day on which in the evening they were to dine together with Gladys Ellington, had been hers. But gradually, slowly, with painful gropings after light, she had made up her mind.

She had no choice—her choice was already made, and all duty, all obedience, all honour, called her to fulfil the promise she had made, to fulfil it, too, in no niggardly lip-service sense of the word, but to fulfil it loyally. She must turn her back to the dawn which had come too late, she must never look there, she must for ever avert her eyes from it. Above all, she must do all that lay in her power to prevent that brightness growing. She must, in fact, not see Evelyn again of her own free will.

Then the difficulties, each to be met and overcome, began to swarm thick about her. First and foremost there was the portrait, for which she was engaged to give him a sitting to-morrow. That, at any rate, as far as this particular sitting was concerned, was easily managed, a note of three lines expressing regret did that. This, however, was only a temporary measure, it but put off for this one occasion the necessity of meeting what lay before her. For she knew she must not sit to him again; she dared not risk that, she must not give this strange new rapture in her heart the food that would make it grow. Yet, again, she must not act like a mad-woman, and what reasonable cause could she give for so strange a freak? Perhaps if she went there with Philip, or if she took her mother with her.

Yet that did not dispose of the question. Evelyn was one of her future husband's warmest friends. In the ordinary course of things they must often meet, but till she had conquered herself, made sure of herself, such meetings were impossible. And how could she ever be sure of herself, to whom had come this utterly unlooked for thing, a thing so unlooked for that only a few weeks before she had consented to its being dismissed as a practical impossibility?

Then came a thought which, for the very shame of it, was bracing. Not by word or look or sign had Evelyn ever showed that he regarded her with the faintest feeling that answered hers. She remembered well the rise of the full moon on the terrace of Philip's house above Pangbourne, how he had called attention to it, merely to point out that it was not in drawing, how she herself on that occasion had noticed how different he was to the ordinary moonlight-walker. No hint of sentiment, no sign of the vaguest desire towards the most harmless flirtation had appeared in him then, nor had any appeared since. While she was sitting to him, half the time he scowled at her, the other half he bubbled with boyish nonsense. For very shame she must turn her back on the dawn.

Dinner was to be early to-night, as the objective was Melba and the opera, and her maid came in to tell her that dressing-time was already overstepped. She got up, but paused for a moment at the window, looking out from Buckingham Gate over the blue haze that overhung St. James' Park, driving her resolution home. She half-pitied, half-spurned herself, telling herself at one moment that it was hard that she had to suffer thus, at another that she was despicable for thinking of suffering when her road was so clearly marked for her. If what had happened was not her fault, still less should there be any fault of hers in what should happen. Clearly the future was in her own control; of the future she could make what she would.

Her mother was not coming with her to-night; indeed, she seldom wasted the golden evening hours at the opera, when there was a rubber of bridge so certainly at her command, and Madge went into the drawing-room to wish her good-night before she set off. Prosperity—and the last three weeks seemed to Lady Ellington to be most prosperous—had always a softening effect on her, and she was particularly gracious to her daughter, since Madge was responsible for so large a part of these auspicious events.

"So you're just off, dear," she said. "Dear me, you are rather late, and I mustn't keep you. But give my love to Philip, and let him see you home, and if I am in—you can ask them at the door—bring him in for a few minutes. And don't forget your sitting with Mr. Dundas to-morrow."

"Ah, I have put that off," said Madge, "I am rather busy!"

"A pity, surely."

"Well, I have sent the note, I am afraid. Good-night, mother, in case I am in first."

Philip had already arrived when she got to her cousin's house, and they went down to dinner. Lord Ellington had got the news of the evening feverishly mixed up in his head, and was disposed to mingle fragments of Stock Exchange with it, forgetful, apparently, that this had been relegated to his wife. But his natural incoherence redeemed the situation, and when dinner was over it was already time to start for the opera. While Gladys got her cloak, however, the two lovers had a few private minutes, as the master of the house remained in the dining-room when they went out. Philip had sent her that day a diamond pendant which she was wearing now.

"It is too good of you, Philip," she said, "and I can't tell you how I value it. It is most beautiful. But why should you always be sending me things?"

Philip was usually serious, and always sincere.

"Because I can't help it," he said. "I must give you signs of what I feel, and even these clumsy, material signs are something."

That sincerity touched the girl.

"I know what you feel," she said. "I want to have it never absent from my mind. I want to think of nothing else but that."

This was sincere too, the outcome of this long day of thought. But Philip came a little closer to her, and his voice vibrated as he spoke.

"That contents me utterly," he said—"that and the gift of yourself that you made me."

She gave a long sigh.

"Oh, Philip!" she began. But the voice of Gladys called to her from the passage outside the drawing-room.

"Come, Madge. Come, Mr. Home," she cried. "We are already so late, and I can't bear to miss a note of Bohême."

Apparently to be present in the opera-house when Bohême was going on was sufficient for Gladys, and constituted not missing a note, for she spent that small portion of the first act which still remained to be performed after their arrival in an absorbed examination of the occupants of the other boxes, and whispered communications as to the result of her investigations to Madge. The fall of the curtain had the effect of rendering these more audible.

"Yes, absolutely everybody is here; so good of you, dear Mr. Home, to ask us to-night. Of course, it is the last night Melba sings, is it not? How wonderful, is she not? That long last note quite thrilled me. So sad, too, the last act, it always makes me cry! Oh! there is Madame Odintseff, dearest Madge, did you ever see such ropes of pearls—cables you might call them. Who is that she is talking to? I know her face quite well. That's her daughter, yes, the sandy-coloured thing, rather like a rabbit. They say she's engaged to Lord Hitchin, but I don't believe it. Dear Madge, is it not brilliant? You look so well, dear, to-night. If only Mr. Dundas could paint you as you are looking now! By the way, how is the portrait getting on?"

63

Philip also had risen when the act ended, and was looking out over the house. Here he joined in.

"Evelyn was absolutely jubilant when I saw him a few days ago," he said. "And though he is usually jubilant over the last thing, I saw he thought there was something extra-special about this. By-the-way, Madge, you are sitting to him to-morrow afternoon, are you not? I shall try to look in; my spate of work is over, I hope."

"Oh! I'm afraid I have had to put it off," said she. "I couldn't manage it to-morrow."

She fingered her fan nervously for a moment.

"In fact, Philip," she said, "I am so dreadfully full of engagements for the next week or two that I don't see how I can squeeze in another sitting. I am so ashamed of myself, but I can't help it. I wish you would go down to Mr. Dundas' studio to-morrow and tell him so."

Philip looked at her a moment in blank surprise.

"Ah, but you can't do that," he said; "a painter isn't like a tailor to whom you say, 'I am not coming to try on; send it home as it is.'"

Madge lost her head a little; the burden of the hours of this day pressed heavily on her.

"Ah! but that is what I want him to do," she cried. "It is a wonderful portrait; he said so himself. There is a little background that must be put in, but I needn't be there for that."

Gladys Ellington had turned her attention again to the house, and, with her opera-glasses glued to her eyes, was spying and observing in all directions. Philip cast one glance at her, and rightly considered himself alone with Madge, for the other was blind and deaf to them.

"Madge, is anything wrong?" he asked gently.

"No, nothing is wrong," she said, recovering herself a little. "But I ask you to do as I say. I can't bear sitting for that portrait any more, and Mr. Dundas—he bores me."

That got said, also she managed to smile at him naturally.

"That is all, dear Philip," she added. "Pray don't let us talk of it any more."

"And you wish me to tell Evelyn what you say?" he asked.

"Yes, anything, anything," she said. "I don't want to sit to him again. But make it natural, if you can. Look at the portrait; tell him you don't want it touched any more. Believe me, that is best."

She paused a moment.

"I am excited and rather overwrought to-night somehow," she said, "and you mustn't indeed think that there is anything the matter. Indeed, there is nothing. Tell me you believe that?"

"Why, dear, of course, if you tell me so," he said.

"I do tell you so."

As has been mentioned before, there were two Philips; one known only to the four people who knew him best, the other the Philip who showed a sterner and harder face to the world. And though, since he was with Madge, the Philip of the inner sanctum, where only the intimates were admitted, was in possession, yet the door of the sanctum, as it were,

64

opened for a moment, and the other Philip, quick as a lizard, glanced in. His appearance was of the most momentary duration, but he did look in.

She laid her hand on his arm as she said these last words, then left the back of the box, where they had been standing, and took a chair next Lady Ellington.

"How full it is!" she said. "Look at the stalls too; they are like an ant-heap, covered with brilliant, crawling ants. How hard it is to recognise people if one is above them. I'm sure there are a hundred people I know, but the tops of heads are like nothing except the tops of heads. How many bald heads too! What a blessing we don't go bald like men. Who is that walking up the gangway now? I'm sure I know him. Ah! it's Mr. Dundas."

The sudden stream of her talk stopped, as if a tap had been turned on. Her eyes left the stalls and gazed vacantly over the boxes opposite. She was conscious of wondering what would happen next—whether she would speak, or her companion, or whether Philip would say something. Then it seemed to her nobody would say anything any more; there was to be this dreadful silence for ever. That possibility, at any rate, was soon averted, for Gladys signalled violently to Evelyn, and spoke.

"Yes, he sees us," she said. "Mr. Home, do put the door of the box open, it is so stuffy. And Mr. Dundas I am sure is coming up. He's such a darling, isn't he?"

The greater part of her speech was justified by realities. Evelyn had seen them; the heat was undeniable; also, in answer to the violent signalling he had received, mere politeness, to say nothing of inclination, would have made him come. But he had seen too who sat in profile by Lady Ellington, and he took two and three steps in the stride as he mounted the staircases. And before Madge had time to put into execution her very unwise idea of asking Philip not to let him in, he was at the door of the box.

"You lordly box-holder," he said to him, "just let me in. How are you, Lady Ellington? Yes, I'm just back from the Hermitage, to-night only, from three days in the forest with Merivale. How are you, Miss Ellington? I had to come up to-night, or I shouldn't have been able to keep the appointment to-morrow."

A sense of utter helplessness seized Madge; she could not even respond by a word to his greeting, for his presence merely was the only thing that mattered, the only thing she loved and dreaded. And he continued:

"Half-past two, isn't it?" he said. "I could have come up to-morrow, of course, but it was necessary for me to have a morning's work at the background before I troubled you again."

Then Gladys broke in.

"Too wonderful, isn't it?" she said, "the portrait, I mean. But, Mr. Dundas, who is that just opposite with rubies? I'm sure you've painted her. That great pink thing there, who must have come from the west coast of Asia Minor. How naughty of me!"

But Evelyn apparently condoned the naughtiness; he mentioned the name of the great pink thing, and turned to Madge again.

"But by half-past two I shall be ready," he said. "Please, if it is not an

65

impossible request, please be punctual. Art takes so long, you know. Not that life is short. Nobody ever died too soon."

She turned to him, the diamond pendant that Philip had sent her that day glittering on the smooth whiteness of her bosom.

"I am so sorry," she said, "and I know I ought to have let you know before, Mr. Dundas. But I can't come to-morrow. I wrote you this evening only, I did not know you were out of town, explaining—at least saying—I could not come."

Philip—the real, intimate Philip—heard this. And it was he only, the lover of this girl, who spoke in reply.

"We have settled that I shall come instead," he said. "So your time won't be wasted, Evelyn. You have to paint me too, you know, and if you want it to be characteristic, make a study of a telephone and a tape-machine. Half-past two, I think you said."

There came a sudden hush over the crowded house as the lights went down. Philip laid his hand on Evelyn's shoulder, as he sat in the front of the box between the two ladies.

"Half-past two, then, to-morrow," he repeated.

The hint was plain enough, and Evelyn took it, and stumbled his way out of the box to regain his seat in the stalls. What had happened, what this all meant, he did not and could not know; he knew only what he was left with, namely, that Madge for some reason would not sit to him to-morrow. In his eager way he searched for a hundred motives, yet none satisfied him, and he was forced to fall back on the obvious and simple one, that she was busy. Nothing in the world could be more likely, his whole practical self assured him of that; but he felt somehow as if someone had leaned out of the window when he called at a house and had shouted stentoriously to the servant who opened the door, "I am not at home." He was bound to accept a thing which he did not believe.

Then he questioned himself as to whether the fault was his. Yet that was scarcely possible, for it was not till after he had last seen her that the knowledge of his love for her had dawned on him. It was impossible that he could have made that betrayal of himself, for until she had gone he had not known that there was anything to betray. He and she had always been on terms of the frankest comradeship, yet to-night her manner had somehow been subtly yet essentially different. All the good comradeship had gone from it, the indefinable feeling of "being friends" was no longer there. Was it that the "being friends" was no longer sufficient for him, and did the change really lie in himself? He felt sure it did not; Madge was different.

Evelyn was not of an analytical mind; his inferences were based usually on instinct rather than reason, and reason was powerless to help him here and his instinct drew no inference whatever. However, Philip was coming to take her hour to-morrow, and he would try to find out something about this. Indeed, perhaps there was nothing to find, for he knew that now and for ever his own view of Madge would be coloured by the super-sensitiveness of love. Then a suspicion altogether unworthy crossed his mind. Was it possible that Philip had.... But, to do him justice, he instantly dismissed it.

Gladys, like the stag at eve, had drunk her fill of the occupants of the boxes, and turned her attention to the stage during the second act. Her mind was rather like a sparrow, it hopped about with such extraordinary briskness, and apparently found something to pick up everywhere. The things it picked up, it is true, were of no particular consequence, but they were things of a sort, and at the end of the act she announced them.

"Opera is really the best way of carrying on life," she said. "You always sing, and at any crisis you sing a tune—a real tune. And if the crisis is really frightful, you make it the end of the act, pull the curtain down, and have some slight refreshment in privacy, and put on another frock. Mr. Home, is that Mrs. Israels there—that woman bound in green? How nice to have a husband who is a magnate of South African affairs! You can even afford to be bound in green; it doesn't matter how you look if you are rich enough."

Philip looked where she pointed; it certainly was Mrs. Israels.

"Yes, that is she," he said; "but I had no idea they were as rich as her appearance indicates."

Lady Ellington gave a little gasp of horror.

"Good gracious, I forgot you were a magnate too!" she cried. "How rude of me! But, really, you are so unlike Mrs. Israels."

Then she sank her voice to a confidential whisper.

"Dear Mr. Home," she said, with all the brilliance of unpremeditated invention, "do talk shop with me for one minute. Ellington told me he had got a little sum of money—you know the sort of thing, not big enough to be of any real use—ah, you mustn't tell him I asked you. He would be furious, quite furious. Yes, and if you could just casually mention some investment which might eventually cause it to be of some use——"

Philip—she could not see him, as he was sitting behind her, with his arm on the back of her chair—could not help frowning. He was delighted to be of any use to his friends, but sometimes, as now, his help was asked in a sideways, hole-and-corner manner. Why shouldn't her husband know? He did not like intrigue at any time; purposeless intrigue was even more tiresome. But he expunged the frown from his voice anyhow when he answered:

"Yes, I can certainly recommend you an investment or two," he said, "but I can promise you no certainty. I can only say that I hold a stake in them myself. I suppose, as you have this—this sum of money, you will take up your shares—pay for them, I mean!"

She gave a little laugh of surprise.

"You are too delicious!" she said. "You mean we can buy them without paying for them, like a bill?"

He laughed.

"Well, I don't recommend that," he said. "But it can be done. However, that is not my concern, as I'm not a broker. I will send you a note in the morning."

"Too good of you!" she said. "And you won't tell my husband I asked you?"

"Certainly not," said he, "though I really can't imagine why not."

The unreal Philip—the one, that is to say, that Madge did not know—had had the door slammed pretty smartly in his face, and when the real Philip went to Evelyn's studio the next afternoon he had not attempted to put in another appearance. Evelyn, when he arrived, was working at the background of Madge's portrait, and he yelled to the other to keep his eyes off it.

"You musn't see it till it's done!" he cried. "Just turn your back, there's a good chap, till I put it with its face to the wall. I had no idea till I looked at it to-day how nearly it is finished. I do wish Miss Ellington could have come this afternoon instead of you—which sounds polite, but isn't— and I really think I might have made it the last sitting. That sounds polite too. By the way, what an ass I am; I never made another appointment with her last night!"

This was all sufficiently frank, for Evelyn had managed, with the healthy optimism of which she had so much, to reason himself out of his fantastic forebodings of the evening before. It was left, therefore, for Philip, a task which was not at all to his taste, to put them all neatly back again.

"I really doubt if she could have given you an appointment off-hand," he said, still fencing a little. "She is really so frightfully busy I hardly set eyes on her. Apparently, when you are to be married, you have to buy as many things as if you were going to live on a desert island for the rest of your life."

Evelyn checked for a moment at this; the healthy optimism weakened a little.

"I must write and ask her," he said, "or go and try to find her in. I must have the sitting soon; the thing won't be half so good if I have to wait. It is all ready; it just wants her for an hour or two."

Philip was conscious of a most heartfelt wish that Madge had not entrusted him with this errand, and he cudgelled his head to think how least offensively to perform it. Then Madge's own suggestion came to his aid.

"I wish you would let me see it," he said. "Pray do; I really mean it."

Evelyn hesitated; though he had been so peremptory in its removal before, the impulse, he knew, was rather childish, it being but the desire to let the finished thing be the first thing seen. Yet, on the other hand, he so intensely believed in the portrait himself that he now felt disinclined to defer the pleasure of showing it.

"Well, you mustn't criticise at all," he said, "not one word of that, or I may begin to take your criticism into consideration, and I want to do this just exactly as I see it, not as anybody else does. Do you promise?"

"Certainly."

"Very well; stand back about three yards—three yards is about its focus. Now!"

He turned the easel back into the room again, where it stood fronting Philip. And the latter did not want to criticise at all; he felt not the smallest temptation to do so. Indeed, it was idle to do so; the picture was Madge, Madge seen by an unerring eye and recorded by an unerring brush. It stood altogether away from criticism; a man might conceivably reject the

68

whole of it, if he happened not to care about Evelyn's art, but he could not reject a part. As Evelyn had said to Merivale, he had put there what he meant to put there, but nothing that he did not. It was brilliant, superb, a master-work.

Philip looked at it a long minute in silence.

"It is your best," he said.

Evelyn laughed.

"It is my only picture," he said.

Then Philip saw an opportunity, which was as welcome as it was unexpected.

"I beg you not to touch Madge's figure or face again," he said. "It is absolutely finished; there is nothing more to be done to it. Please!"

Evelyn gave a snort of disgust.

"That is criticism," he said.

"Not at all; there is nothing to criticise. I mean it, really."

Now Philip was no bad judge, and Evelyn was well aware of that. He had been as he painted, intensely anxious that Philip should like it, and Philip more than liked it. The great pleasure that that knowledge gave him was sufficient for the time to banish the forebodings that had begun to creep back, and were in a way confirmed by Philip's wish that it should not be touched.

"Oh, Philip, is it really good?" he said. "I feel that I know it is, but I want so much that both you and she should think so."

"I can answer for myself," said the other.

With that the whole subject was dismissed for the time. Evelyn had given no promise that he would not touch the figure again, but Philip on his side was wise enough to dwell on that point no more, for he saw quite well that a certain inkling of the true state of things had been present, however dimly, to the other, and any further allusion would but tend to disperse that dimness and make things clearer. So the new canvas was produced, and Philip was put into pose after pose without satisfying the artist.

"No, no," he cried; "if you stand like that, you look like an elderly St. Sebastian, and, with your hand on the table, you look like a railway director. Look here, walk out of the room, come in whistling, and sit down. I am not going to paint you portrait, you are not going to be photographed. Just pretend I'm not here."

This went better, and soon, with inarticulate gruntings, Evelyn began to put in the lines of the figure with charcoal. At first he laboured, but before long things began to go more smoothly; his own knitted brow uncreased itself, and his hand began to work of itself. Then came a half hour in which he talked, telling his sitter of his visit to the Hermit, and the really charming days he had spent in the Forest. But that again suggested a train of thought which caused silence again and a renewal of the creased brow. But it was not at his sketch that he frowned.

Eventually he laid his tools down.

"I can't go on any more," he said. "Thanks very much! It's all right."

He wandered to the chimney-piece, lit a cigarette, and came back again.

69

"You mean Miss Ellington doesn't want to give me any more sittings, don't you?" he said. "For it is childish to expect me to believe that she can't spare one hour between now and the end of the month."

The childishness of that struck Philip too.

"But I ask you not to touch it any more, except of course the background," he said. "Won't that content you?"

"Not in the least. It is not the real reason."

Philip was cornered, and knew it.

"It is a true one," he said rather lamely. "After seeing the picture, I should have said it, I believe, in any case."

"But it's not the real reason," repeated Evelyn. "Of course, you need not tell me the real reason, but you can't prevent my guessing. And you can't prevent my guessing right."

"Ah, is this necessary?" asked Philip.

Evelyn flashed out at this.

"And is it fair on me?" he cried. "I disagree with you; I want another sitting, and she really has no right to treat me like this. I'm not a tradesman. She can't leave me because she chooses, like that, without giving a reason."

Philip did not reply.

"Or perhaps she has given a reason," said Evelyn, with peculiarly annoying penetration.

Indeed, these grown-up children, boys and girls still, except in years, are wonderfully embarrassing, so Philip reflected—people who will ask childish questions, who are yet sufficiently men and women to be able to detect a faltering voice, an equivocation. Tact does not seem to exist for them; if they want to know a thing they ask it straight out before everybody. And, indeed, it is sometimes less embarrassing if there are plenty of people there; one out of a number may begin talking, and with the buzz of conversation drown the absence of a reply. But alone— tactlessness in a tête-à-tête is to fire at a large target; it cannot help hitting.

This certainly had hit, and Philip knew it was useless to pretend otherwise. And, as the just reply to tactlessness is truth, also tactless, he let Evelyn have it.

"Yes, she gave a reason," he said, "since you will have it so. She said she was bored with the sittings. And you may tell her I told you," he added.

Evelyn had put his head a little on one side, an action common with him when he was trying to catch an effect. He showed no symptom whatever of annoyance, his face expressed only slightly amused incredulity.

"Bored with the sittings, or bored with me?" he asked.

Philip's exasperation increased. People in ordinary life did not ask such questions. But since, such a question was asked, it deserved its answer.

"Bored with you," he said. "I am sorry, but there it is; bored with you."

"Thanks," said Evelyn. "And now, if you won't be bored with me, do get back and stand for ten minutes more. I won't ask for longer than that. I just want—ah, that's right, stop like that."

70

Philip, as recommended, "stopped like that," with a mixture of amusement and annoyance in his mind. Evelyn was the most unaccountable fellow; sometimes, if you but just rapped him on the knuckles, he would call out that you had dealt a deathstroke at him; at other times, as now, you might give him the most violent slap in the face, and he would treat it like a piece of thistledown that floated by him. Of one thing, anyhow, one could be certain, he would never pretend to feel an emotion that he did not feel; he would, that is to say, never pump up indignation, and, on the other hand, if he felt anything keenly, he might be trusted to scream. Philip, therefore, as he "stopped like that," had the choice of two conclusions open to him. The one was that Evelyn felt the same antipathy to Madge as Madge apparently felt for him. The other was that he did not believe Madge had said what he had reported her to have said. But neither conclusion was very consoling; the second because, though all men are liars, they do not like the recognition of this fact, especially if they have spoken truly.

Yet the other choice was even less satisfactory, for he himself did not believe that Evelyn was bored by Madge; nor, if he pressed the matter home, did he really believe that Madge was bored by Evelyn. She had said so, it is true, and he had therefore accepted it. But it did not seem somehow likely; down at Pangbourne they had been the best of friends, and they had been the best of friends, too, since. Yet—and here the door was again slammed on the unreal Philip—yet she had said it, and that was enough.

EIGHTH

A WAVE—such waves are tidal-periodic, and after they have passed leave the sea quite calm again—a wave of interest in the simplification of life swept over London towards the end of this season. A Duchess gave up meat and took to deep-breathing instead; somebody else had lunch on lentils only and drank hot water, and said she felt better already; some half-dozen took a walk in the Park in the very early morning without hats, and met half-a-dozen more who wore sandals; and they all agreed that it made the whole difference, and so the movement was started. Simplification of life: that was the real thing to be aimed at; it made you happy, and also made any search for pleasure unnecessary, for you only sought for pleasure—so ran the gospel, which was very swiftly and simply formulated—because you were looking for happiness, and mistakenly grasped at pleasure. But with the simplification of life, happiness came quite of its own accord. You breathed deeply, you ate lentils, you wore no hat (especially if there was nobody about), and under the same condition you wore sandals and walked in the wet grass, to reward you for which happiness came to you, and you ceased to worry. Indeed, in a few days, for London flies on the wings of a dove to any new thing, the gospel was so entrancing and so popular that hatless folk were seen in the Park at far more fashionable hours, and Gladys Ellington actually refused to go to a ball for fear of not getting her proper supply of oxygen. She, it may be remarked, was never quite among the first to take up any new thing, but was always among the foremost of the second.

The other Lady Ellington, it appeared, had known it "all along." It was she, in fact, so the legend soon ran, who had suggested the simplification of life to Tom Merivale, who now lived in the New Forest, ate asparagus in season, but otherwise only cabbage, and had got so closely into touch with Nature that all sorts of things perched on his finger and sang. The devotees, therefore, of the doctrine were intent on things perching on their fingers and singing, and wanted to go down to the New Forest to see how it was done. But while they wanted, Lady Ellington went. If the simplification of life were to come in, it was always best to be the first to simplify; in addition, it would save her so much money in her autumn parties. And she could always have a chop upstairs.

Her expedition to the New Forest took place a couple of days after Philip had given his first sitting to Evelyn Dundas. Madge at this time was looking rather pale and tired, so her mother thought, and, in consequence, she proposed to Madge that she should come with her. This pallor and lassitude, as a matter of fact, was a reasonable excuse enough, though had Madge looked bright and fresh it would not have stood in her way, since in the latter case the reason would have been that Madge enjoyed the country so much, and had the "country-look" in her eyes. In any case Lady Ellington meant that Madge should go with her, and if she meant a thing, that thing usually occurred.

To say that she was anxious about Madge would be over-stating the condition of her mind with regard to her, for it was a rule of her life, with excellent authority to back it, to be anxious about nothing. To say also that she thought there was any reason for anxiety would be still over-stating her view of her daughter, since if there had been any reason for it, though she would still not have been anxious, she would have cleared the matter up in some way. But her hard, polished mind, a sort of crystal billiard-ball, admitted no such reason; merely she meant to keep her daughter under her eye till she, another billiard-ball, it was to be hoped, went into her appointed pocket. Then the man who held the cue might do what he chose—she defied him to hurt her.

Yet Lady Ellington knew quite well what, though not the cause of any anxiety on her part, was the reason why she kept Madge under her eye, and that reason was the existence of an artist. Madge had cancelled an appointment she had made with him; the day after he had called, while she and her daughter were having tea alone together, and Madge had sent down word, insisted indeed on doing so, that they were not at home. She had at once explained this to her mother, saying that she had a headache, and meant to go to her room immediately she had had a cup of tea, and was thus unwilling to leave the guest on Lady Ellington's hands. That excuse had, of course, passed unchallenged, for Lady Ellington never challenged anything till it really assumed a threatening attitude. She reserved to herself, however, the right of drawing conclusions on the subject of headaches.

The idea, however, of the expedition to the New Forest Madge had hailed with enthusiasm. They were to go down there in the morning, lunch with the Hermit on lentils—she had particularly begged in her letter, otherwise rather magisterial, that they might see his ordinary mode of life—spend the afternoon in the forest, sleep at Brockenhurst, returning to London next day. His reply was cordial enough, though as a matter of fact Lady Ellington would not have cared however little cordial it was, and they travelled down third-class because there were fewer cushions in the third-class, and, in consequence, far fewer bacteria. The avoidance of bacteria just now was of consequence, hence the windows also were both wide open, and there would have been acrimonious discussion between Lady Ellington and another passenger in the same carriage, who had a severe cold in the head, had she not refused to discuss altogether.

The simplification of life had not at present in Lady Ellington's case gone so far as to dispense with the presence of a maid. She was sent on to the inn to engage rooms for them, and a separate table at dinner that evening, and the two took their seats in the cab that Merivale had ordered to meet them. He had not been at the station himself, and though Lady Ellington was secretly inclined to resent this, as somewhat wanting in respect, she had self-control enough to say nothing about it. Indeed, her own polished mind excused it; "physical exercises for the morning," she said to herself, probably detained him.

But the Hermit proved somehow unnaturally natural. He did not give them lentils to eat, but he gave them cauliflower au gratin and brown bread and cheese, and to drink, water. Somehow he was not, to Lady Ellington's mind, the least apostolic, for these viands were indeed excellent, and, what was worse, he made neither an apology nor a confession of faith over them. It was all perfectly natural, as indeed she had begged it should be. Therefore the leanness of her desire went deep. After lunch, too, cigarettes were offered them, and she wanted one so much that she took one. True, he did all the waiting himself, but he did it so deftly that one really did not notice the absence of servants. Then, worst of all, when lunch was over, he put his elbow on the table, and was serious.

"What did you come down into the wilderness for to see, Lady Ellington?" he asked. "It is only a reed shaken by the wind. There is really nothing more. I cannot say how charming it is to me to see you and Miss Ellington. But I can't tell you anything. You wanted to see a bit of my life, how I live it. This is how. Now, what else can I do for you? I am sure you will excuse me, but I am certain you came here to see something. Do tell me what you want to see."

This was quite sufficient.

"Ah, if there happened to be a bird of some kind," said Lady Ellington.

Merivale laughed.

73

"What Evelyn called a conjuring trick?" he asked. "Why, certainly. But you must sit still."

On the lawn some twenty yards off a thrush was scudding about the grass. It had found a snail, and was looking, it appeared, for a suitable stone on which to make those somewhat gruesome preparations for its meal, which it performs with such vigorous gusto. But suddenly, as Merivale looked at it, it paused, even though at that very moment it had discovered on the path below the pergola an anvil divinely adapted to its purpose. Then, with quick, bird-like motion, it dropped the snail, looked once or twice from side to side, and then, half-flying, half-running, came and perched on the balustrade of the verandah. Then very gently Merivale held out his hand, and next moment the bird was perched on it.

"Sing, then," he said, as he had said to the nightingale, and from furry, trembling throat the bird poured out its liquid store of repeated phrases.

"Thank you, dear," said he, when it paused. "Go back to your dinner and eat well."

Again there was a flutter of wings and the scud across the grass, and in a few moments the sharp tapping of the shell on the stone began. On the verandah for a little while there was silence, then the Hermit laughed.

"But there is one thing I must ask you, Lady Ellington," he said, "though I need not say how charmed I am to be able to show you that, since it interests you; it is that I shall not be made a sort of show. Evelyn Dundas was down here a few days ago, and he told me that all London was going in for the simplification of life. Of course it seems to me that they could not do better, but I really must refuse to pose as a prophet, however minor."

Lady Ellington gave no direct promise; indeed from the Hermit's point of view her next speech was far from reassuring.

"It is too wonderful," she said, "and now I can say that I have seen it myself. But do you think, Mr. Merivale, that you have any right to shut up yourself and your powers like that when there are so many of us anxious to learn? Could you not—ah, well, it is the end of the season now, but perhaps later in the autumn when people come to London again, could you not give us a little class, just once a week, and tell us about the new philosophy? I'm sure I know a dozen people who would love to come. Of course we would come down here"—this was a great concession—"not expect you to come up to London. You would charge, of course; you might make quite a good thing out of it."

Merivale tried to put in a word, but she swept on.

"Of course that is a minor point," she said, "but what is, I think, really important, is that one should always try to help others who want to learn. There is quite a movement going on in London; people deep-breathe and don't touch meat; the Duchess of Essex, for instance—perhaps you know her——"

Here he got a word in.

"I am so sorry," he said, "but it is absolutely out of the question. To begin with, I have nothing to tell you."

74

"Ah, but that thrush now," said she. "How did you do it? That is all I want to know."

He laughed.

"But that is exactly what I can't tell you," he said, "any more than you can tell me how it is that when you want to speak your tongue frames words. I ask it to come and sit on my finger—hardly even that. I know no more how I get it to come than it knows, the dear, why it comes."

"And what else can you do?" continued Lady Ellington, abandoning for the present the idea of a class.

Merivale got up without the least sign of impatience or ruffling of his good-humour.

"I can show you over the house," he said, "or walk with you in the forest, as you are so kind as to take an interest in what I do and how I live, and, if you like, I will talk about the simple life and what we may call the approach to Nature. But I must warn you there is nothing in the least startling or sensational about it. Above all, as far as I know, it is not possible to make short cuts; one has to tune oneself slowly to it."

This was better than nothing, for Lady Ellington had an excellent memory, and could recount all the things which Merivale told her as if she had suggested them to him and he had agreed. Also, if there was to be no simplification class, it would at least be in her power to say that he saw absolutely no one, but had been too charming in allowing Madge and her to come down and spend the day with him. Indeed, after a little reflection, she was not sure whether this was the more distinguished rôle, to be the medium between the Hermit and the rest of aspiring London. Thus it was with close attention that she made the tour of the cottage, and afterwards they walked up through the beech-wood on the other side of the stream on to the open heath beyond, to spend the afternoon on these huge, breezy uplands.

Now, it so happened that on this morning Evelyn, after rather a sleepless, tossing night, had gone up to his studio after breakfast to find there that, when he tried to paint, he could not. Somebody, as he had said once before, had turned the tap off; no water came through, only a remote empty gurgling; the imaginative vision was out of gear. There were three or four pictures in his studio over which he might have spent a profitable morning, but he could do nothing with any of them. He had only the afternoon before thought out a background for the picture he was doing of Philip, thought it out, too, with considerable care and precision, and all he had to do was to set a few pieces of furniture, arrange his light as he wished it over the corner which was to be represented, and put it in. Yet he could not do anything with it; his eye was wrong, and his colours were harsh, crude, or merely woolly and unconvincing. He could not see things right; it seemed to him that what he painted was in the shadow, or as if something had come between him and his canvas.

There was still one picture at which he could work, which he had not looked at yet, nor even turned its easel round from the wall, and he stood for some time in front of it, unable apparently to make up his mind as to whether he would touch it or not. Then suddenly, with a sharp, ill-humoured sort of tug, he wheeled it round. Yes, this was why he could not touch Philip's portrait; here in front of him, dazzling and brilliant, stood that which came between him and it. And as he looked his eye cleared; it was as if a film, some material film, had been drawn away from over it, and he examined his work with eager, critical attention. Though ten minutes ago he could not paint, now he could not help painting. He starved for the palette; his hands ached for the slimy resistance of the paint dragged over the canvas. On the convex mirror, which was to be on the wall behind the girl, reflecting her back and the scarlet shimmering of her cloak, he had, like a child saving the butteriest bit of toast till the end, reserved for the end the big touches of light on the gilt frame. The more difficult, technical painting of the mirror itself he had finished, putting the reflections in rather more strongly than he wished them eventually to appear, for he knew, with the artist's prescience, exactly how the lights on the gold frame would tone them down. And it was with a smile of well-earned satisfaction that he put these in now; he almost laughed to see how accurately he had anticipated the result. Then, after some half-hour of ecstatic pleasure—for at this stage every stroke told—he stepped back and looked at it. Yes, that too was as he meant it—that too was finished.

Slowly his eye dwelt next on the figure of the girl. Was Philip right after all? Did it indeed need nothing more? He felt uncertain himself. In ninety-nine other cases out of a hundred, if he had really not been certain, there was no one's judgment which he would have more willingly have deferred to than Philip's; but here he could not help connecting his insistence that nothing more should be done with the subsequent revelation that Madge did not wish to sit again to him. It was impossible to disconnect the two; coincidences of that sort did not happen.

Then the whole world of colour, of drawing, of his own inimitable art, went grey and dead, and from its ashes rose, so to speak, the thought that filled the universe for him, Madge herself. What, in heaven's name, did it all mean? What had he done that she should treat him like this? Search as he might, his conscience could find no accusation against him; yet he could not either believe that this was a mere wilful freak on her part. Then, again, he had called two days ago at an hour when she was almost always in, and the man had not given him a "Not at home" direct; he had gone upstairs. He felt absolutely certain that she had been in and had refused to see him.

For another hour he sat idle in his studio; he lay on his divan and took a volume from the morraine of old Punches, but found the wit flat and unprofitable; he took the violin, played a dozen notes, and put it down again; he leaned out of the window, and remarked that it was an extremely fine day. But as to painting any more, he could as soon have swum through the air over the roofs of the sea of houses below him. The studio was intolerable; his thoughts, with their dismal circle that ended exactly where it began and went on tracing the same circle again and again, were intolerable also; his own company was equally so. But from that there was no relief; good or bad, it would be with him to the grave.

Then suddenly an idea occurred to him which held out certain promise of relief at least, in that he could communicate his trouble, and he thought of the Hermit Merivale had always an astonishingly cooling effect on him; it was a pleasure in itself, especially to a feverish, excitable mind like his, to see anyone, and that a friend, who, with great intellectual and moral activity, was so wonderfully capable of resting, of not worrying; restful, too, would be the glades of the immemorial forest. And no sooner had the idea struck him than his mind was made up; a telegram to the Hermit, a hurried glance at a railway guide, and a bag into which he threw the requisites of a night, were all that was required. He had just time to eat a hurried lunch, and then started for Waterloo.

The day had been hot and sunny when he left London, and promised an exquisite summer afternoon in the country, where the freshness would tone down a heat that in town was rather oppressive. But this pleasant probability, as the train threw the suburbs over its shoulder, did not seem likely to be fulfilled, for the air, instead of getting fresher, seemed to gather sultriness with every mile. Evelyn was himself much of a slave to climatic conditions, and this windless calm, portending thunder, seemed to press down on his head with dreadful weight. Even the draught made by the flying train had no life in it; it was a hot buffet of air as if from a furnace mouth. Then, as he neared his destination, the sky began to be overcast, lumps of dark-coloured cloud, with hard, angry edges of a coppery tinge began to mount in the sky, coming up in some mysterious manner against what wind there was. This, too, when he got out at Brockenhurst, was blowing in fitful, ominous gusts, now raising a pillar of dust along the high road, then dying again to an absolute calm. Directly to the south the clouds were most threatening, and the very leaves of the trees looked pale and milky against the black masses of the imminent storm. Yet it was some vague consolation, though he hated thunder anywhere, to know how much more intolerable this would be in London, and he arrived at the cottage glad that he had come.

It was about four when he got there, and the first thing he saw on entering was a telegram on the table in the hall, still unopened, which he rightly conjectured to be the one he had himself sent. In this case clearly the Hermit was out when it arrived, and had not yet returned; so, leaving his bag at the foot of the stairs, he passed out on to the verandah. There, looking out over the garden, and alone, sat Madge. She turned on the sound of his step, and, whether it was that the dreadful colour of the day played some trick with his eyes or not, Evelyn thought she went suddenly white.

She rose and came towards him with a miserable semblance of a smile, not with that smile with which, in the portrait, she laughed at the worries of the world and all its ups and downs. She was not laughing at them now; her smile did not rise from within. Her voice, too, was a little strange; it faltered. And it was clear that speaking at all was an effort to her. "This is quite unexpected, Mr. Dundas," she said. "I had no idea, nor, I think, had Mr. Merivale, that you were coming."

Evelyn said nothing; he did not even hold out his hand in answer to hers; he but looked at her, but looked with an unquenchable thirst. But then he found speech and a sort of manners.

77

"I did not know either till this morning," he said; "but then I telegraphed. I fancy Tom has not received it—not opened it anyhow; there is a telegram for him at least on the table inside, which I guess is mine. I did not know you were here either."

Then his voice rose a little.

"Indeed, I did not," he said.

The girl passed her hand wearily over her brow, brushing back her hair. She was hatless—her hat lay on the table, where still the platters of their frugal lunch remained, since they had started on their tour of inspection as soon as that meal was over.

"Oh, no, I believe you!" she said. "Why should you assert it like that? But there is a storm coming. I hate thunder. And I was alone."

Certainly the dreadful tension of the atmosphere had communicated itself to these two. Madge was, at any rate, frightfully aware that her speech was not wise. But wisdom had gone to the vanishing point. This meeting had been so unthinkably unexpected. In a way it stunned her, just as the approaching storm made her unnormal, unlike herself. But she had wits enough left to laugh—the conventional laugh merely, that is like the inverted commas to a written speech.

"I suppose I had better explain myself and my presence here," she said. "My mother asked Mr. Merivale if we might come down and see the simplification of life on its native heath. So we came and lunched here. Then we all three went for a walk, but I was tired and headachy, and turned back. They went on. I knew a storm was coming, though when we set out it was quite clear. I told them so. And in the last ten minutes it has come up like the stroke of a black wing. Ah!"

She shut her eyes for a moment as a violent flicker of lightning cut its way down from the clouds in the south, and waited, still with shut eyes, for the thunder.

"It is still a long way off," said Evelyn, as the remote growl answered.

"I know, but if you had seen the sky an hour ago. It was one turquoise. And I daren't go back to Brockenhurst. I must stop here and wait for them."

"May I take you back?" asked Evelyn.

"No; what good would that do? I may as well be terrified here as on the road. Also I can keep dry here."

Again she winced as the lightning furrowed its zig-zag path through the clouds. This time the remoteness of the thunder was less reassuring; there was an angry, choking clap, which suggested that it meant business.

By this time Evelyn had recovered himself from the first stabbing surprise of finding Madge alone here. Her terror, too, of the approaching storm had drowned his dislike of it; also, for the moment, at any rate, his ordinary, natural instinct of alleviating the mere physical fear of this girl drowned the more intimate sense of what she was to him. If only she might become thoroughly frightened and cling to him—for this outrageous possibility did cross his mind—how he would rejoice in the necessity that such an accident would force on him the necessity, since he knew that he would be unable to offer resistance, of saying that which he had told

78

Merivale only a few days before he felt he could not help saying! But to do him justice, he dismissed such a possibility altogether; that it had passed through his mind he could not help, but all his conscious self rejected it.

Then, at the moment of the angry answering thunder, a few big splashes of rain began to star the dry gravel-path below them, hot, splashing drops, like bullets. They fell with separate, distinct reports on the leaves of the lilacs and on the path; they hissed on the grass, they whispered in the yielding foliage of the roses of the pergola, and were like spirit-rappings on the roof of the verandah.

And Madge's voice rose in suppressed terror:

"Oh, where are they?" she cried. "Why don't they come back? He can't make the lightning just sit on his finger like the thrush. Shall we go to meet them? Oh, go to meet them, Mr. Dundas!"

"And leave you alone?" he asked.

Madge's wits had thoroughly deserted her.

"No, don't do that," she cried. "Let's go indoors, and pull down the blinds and do something. What was that game you suggested once, that you should go out of the room while I thought of something, and that then you should come back and try to guess it. Anything, draughts, chess, surely there is something."

Evelyn felt strangely master of himself. At least, he knew so well what was master of him that it came to the same thing. He had certainty anyhow on his side.

"Yes, let us come indoors," he said. "I know my way about the house. There is a room on the other side; we shall see less of it there; I hate thunder too. But you need have no earthly anxiety about Lady Ellington. They may get wet, but that is all. There then, stop yours ears; you will hear it less."

But he had hardly time to get the words out before the reverberation came. Again clearly, business was meant, immediate business too; the thunder followed nervously close on the flash. And at that Madge fairly ran into the house, stumbling through the darkness in the little narrow hall, and nearly falling over the bag that Evelyn had left there. True though it was that she disliked thunder, she did not dislike it to this point of utterly losing her head in a storm. But, just as her nerves were physically upset, so, too, her whole mind and being was troubled and storm-tossed by this unexpected meeting with Evelyn, and the two disorderments reacted and played upon one another. Had there been no thunderstorm she would have faced Evelyn's appearance with greater equanimity; had he not appeared she would have minded the thunderstorm less. But she braced herself with a great effort, determined not to lose control completely over herself. And the effort demanded a loan from heroism—physical fear, the fear that weakens the knees and makes the hands cold, is hard enough in itself to fight against, but to fight not only against it but against a moral fear, too, demands a thrice braver front.

She, too, remembered in their tour over the house the room of which Evelyn had spoken. It looked out, as he said, in the other direction, and she would, at any rate, not see here the swift uprush of the storm. It was very dark, not only from the portentous sootiness of the sky, but because the big box hedge stood scarcely a dozen yards from the window. Here Evelyn followed her, and, striking a match, lit a couple of candles. He also had by now got a firmer hand over himself, but at the sight of Madge sitting there, a sort of vision of desolateness, his need for her, the need too that she at this moment had for comfort, almost mastered him, and his voice was not wholly steady.

"There, you'll be better here," he said, "and candles are always reassuring, are they not? You will laugh at me, but I assure you that if I am alone in a storm I turn on all the electric light, shut the shutters, and ransack the house for candles and lamps. Then I feel secure."

Madge laughed rather dismally.

"Yes, thanks, that makes me feel a little better," she said. "It is something anyhow to know one has a companion in one's unreasonableness. I don't know what it is in a thunderstorm that agitates me; I think it is the knowledge of the proximity of some frightful force entirely outside the control of man, that may explode any moment."

Evelyn had turned to shut the door as she spoke, but at this a sort of convulsive jerk went through him, and involuntarily he slammed it to. There was something of deadly appropriateness in the girl's words; indeed, there was a force in proximity to her outside her control. He could not even feel certain that it was within his own, whether he was able to stop the explosion. But her previous conduct to him, her refusal to sit again, her saying that he bored her, her refusal even to see him when he paid an ordinary call, were all counter-explosions, so to speak.

The noise of the door that he had banged startled him not less than her.

"I beg your pardon," he said. "I don't know how I did that. It flew out of my fingers, as servants say when they break something."

The first slow, hot drops of rain that had been the leaking of the sluices of heaven, had given place to a downpour of amazing volume and heaviness. In the windless air the rain fell in perpendicular lines of solid water, as if from a million inexhaustible squirts, rattling on the roof like some devil's tattoo, and hissing loud in the hedge outside. The gurgling of the house gutters had increased to a roar, and every now and then they splashed over, the pipes being unable to carry away the water. But for the last few minutes there had been no return of the lightning, and the air was already a little cooler and fresher, the tenseness of its oppression was a little relieved. And in proportion to this Madge again rather recovered herself.

"I really am most grateful to you, Mr. Dundas," she said, "for your arrival. I don't know what I should have done here alone. Did you come down from London this morning?"

Evelyn drew a chair near her and sat down.

"Yes, I settled to come quite suddenly," he said. "I had meant to work all day, and I did for half an hour or so, but everything else looked ugly, I could not see either colour or form properly...."

"Everything else?" said Madge unsuspectingly; his phrase was ambiguous; she did not even distantly guess what he meant.

"Yes, everything else, except my portrait of you," he said shortly.

There was a pause of unrivalled awkwardness, and the longer it lasted the more inevitable did the sequel become.

"I must ask you something," said Evelyn at length. "I ask it only in common justice. Do you think you are treating me quite fairly in refusing to sit for me again? For I tell you plainly, you cheat me of doing my best. And when one happens to be an artist of whatever class, that is rather a serious thing for anybody to do. It means a lot to me."

His words, he knew, were rather brutal; it was rather brutal too to take advantage of this enforced tête-à-tête. But he could not pause to think of that; he knew only that unless he said these things he could not trust himself not to say things less brutal, indeed, but harder for her to hear. He could not quite tell how far he had himself in control. She had put out one hand as he began, as if to ward off his question; but as he went on it fell again, and she sat merely receiving what he said, sitting under it without shelter.

"You have no right to treat me like that," he continued. "We part at my door, as far as I know, perfectly good friends one day, two days afterwards I am told that you cannot sit to me again. What can I have done? Have I done anything? Is it my fault in any way?"

She looked at him once imploringly.

"Please, please don't go on asking me," she said.

But she could not stop him now; his own bare rights justified his questions, and there was that behind which urged him more strongly than they.

"Is it my fault in any way?" he repeated.

Then a sort of despairing courage seized the girl; she would nerve herself to the defence of her secret whatever happened.

"No, it is not your fault," she said.

"Then when you told Philip that it was because I bored you——"

"Did he tell you that?" she asked.

"Yes, he told me. It was not his fault. I made him practically. He could not have refused me."

She thought intently for a moment, unable to see where her answer would lead her, or, indeed, what answer to give. In that perplexity she took the simplest way out, and told the truth.

"Yes, I said that," she said. "But it was not true."

"Then, again, I ask you why?" said he.

She felt that she must break if he went on, and made one more appeal.

"Ah, I beg of you not to question me," she cried. "You talk of justice too—is it fair on me that you use the accident of finding me alone here in this way? I can't go away, you know that, there is no one here to protect me. But if you by a single other question take advantage of it, I shall leave the house, just as I am, in this deluge, and walk back to the hotel. I must remind you that I am an unprotected girl, and you, I must remind you, are a gentleman."

She rose with flashing eyes; it had taxed all her bravery to get this out, but it had come out triumphant.

81

But the moment had come; all the force that had been gathering up was unable to contain itself in him any longer. One terrific second of calm preceded the explosion, and, as if Nature was following the lines of this human drama, for that second the downpour of the blinding rain outside was stayed. Inside and out there was a moment's silence.

"I know all that," he said quietly, "but I can't help myself. It is not for the picture—that doesn't matter. It is for me. Because I love you."

Madge threw her arms wide, then brought them together in front of her as if keeping him off, and a sort of cry of triumph that had begun to burst from her lips ended in a long moan. Then the room for a moment was so suddenly illuminated by some hellish glare that the candle burned dim, and simultaneously a crack of thunder so appalling shattered the stillness that both leaped apart.

"Oh, something is struck!" she cried. "It was as if it was in the very room: Is it me? Is it you? Oh, I am frightened!"

But Evelyn hardly seemed to notice it.

"That is why—because I love you," he said again.

For the moment Madge could neither speak nor move. That sudden double shock, the utter surprise of it all, and, deep down in her heart, the tumult of joy, stunned her. Then she raised her eyes and looked at him.

"You must go away at once, or I," she said. "We can't sit in the same room."

"But you don't hate me, you don't hate me for what I have said?" cried he.

"Hate you?" she said. "No, no, I"—and a sob for the moment choked her—"no, you must not think I hate you."

Just then the sound of a footfall outside and a voice in the hall struck in upon them, and Madge's name was called. In another moment the door opened and Lady Ellington entered, followed by Merivale.

"Ah, there you are, Madge!" she said. "Has it not been appalling? A tree was struck close to—— Mr. Dundas?" she said, breaking off.

Evelyn came a step forward. By a difficult, but on the whole a merciful arrangement, whatever private crisis we pass through, it is essential that the ordinary forms of life be observed. The solid wood may be rent and shattered, but the veneer must remain intact. This is merciful because our thoughts are necessarily occupied in this way with trivial things, whereas if they were suffered to dwell entirely within, no brain could stand the strain.

"Yes, I got here just before the storm began," he said, "and Miss Ellington and I have been keeping each other company. We both hate thunder."

Madge, too, played at trivialities.

"Ah, mother, you are drenched, soaking!" she cried. "What will you do?"

"I really urge you not to wait," said Merivale. "Let me show you a room; get your things off and wrap up in blankets till your maid can come from Brockenhurst with some clothes. I will send a boy in with a note at once."

Madge went upstairs with her mother to assist her, and Merivale came down again to rejoin Evelyn.

"I've only just seen your telegram," he said, "but I'm delighted you have come. That's a brave woman, that Lady Ellington. A tree was struck only a few yards from us, and she merely remarked that it was a great waste of electricity. But I'm glad it was wasted on the tree and not me."

He scribbled a few lines and addressed them to Lady Ellington's maid, and went off to get somebody to take the note into Brockenhurst. Then he came back to Evelyn.

The latter had not gone back to the room where he and Madge had sat during the storm, but was out on the verandah. Just opposite, on the other side of the river, was the tree that had been struck, not a hundred yards distant. One branch, as if in a burst of infernal anger on the part of the lightning, had been torn off, as a spider tears off the wing of a fly, and down the center of the trunk from top to bottom was scored a white mark, where the wood showed through the torn bark. But the tree stood still, no uprooting had taken place; but even now, in this windless calm, its leaves were falling—green, vigorous leaves, that seemed to know that the trunk and the sap that sustained them were dead. They fell in showers, a continuous rain of leaves, until the ground beneath was thick with them. All the pride of the beech's summer glory was done; in an hour or two the tree would be as leafless as when the gales of December whistled through it. What mysterious telegraphy of this murderous disaster had passed through the huge trunk, that had sent the message to the uttermost foliage like this; some message which each leaf knew to be terribly true, so that it did not wait for the dismantlement of the autumn, but even now, in full vigour of green growth, just fell and died? Somehow that seemed to Evelyn very awful and very inevitable; the citadel had fallen, struck by a bolt from above, and in the uttermost outworks the denizens laid down their arms. Something, too, of the sort had happened to himself in the last hour; he had told Madge the secret of his life, that which made every artery fill and throb with swift electrical pulsation of rapturous blood, and it had all passed into nothingness. She had said she did not hate him; that was all. His recollection, indeed, of what had happened after he had told her was still rather dim and hazy; there had been a terrific clap of thunder, she had said she did not hate him; then her mother and Merivale came in.

Then, as the falling leaves from the tree might be gathered and put in a heap, at any rate, the shattered fragments of the afternoon began to piece themselves together again. She had confessed that she had said he bored her, she had confessed also that that was not true. What did that mean? She had said she did not hate him. What did that mean? And was her utter disorderment of mind, that hopeless, appealing agitation which had been so present in her manner throughout, merely the result of the thunderous air? Or was there something else that agitated her, his presence, the knowledge that she had behaved inexplicably? And—was it possible that the tree should live again after that rending furrow had been scored on it?

Merivale soon returned, still smilingly unruffled, and still in soaking

83

clothes. But he seemed to be unconscious of them, and sat down in the verandah by Evelyn. Since that terrific clap there had been no return of the thunder, but the rain was beginning to fall again, slow, steady, and sullen from the low and dripping sky. He saw at once that something had happened to Evelyn; he was trembling like some startled animal. But since he held that to force or even suggest a confidence was a form of highway robbery, he forbore from any questioning.

"So you were with Miss Ellington during the storm," he said. "How I love that superb violence of elements! It is such a relief to know that there are still forces in the world which are quite untamable, and that by no possibility can Lady Ellington divert the lightning into accumulators, which will light our houses."

Evelyn turned on him a perfectly vacant face; he seemed not to have heard even.

"What did Lady Ellington do?" he asked.

"She attended when I talked to her," said the Hermit, with pardonable severity.

Evelyn pulled himself together.

"Look here, something's happened," he said briefly. "It's—I've told her that I love her. And that's all; it's a rope dangling in the air, nothing more happened. She just said I had better go to another room. She made no direct answer at all; she wasn't even shocked."

Then the tiny details began to be gathered in his mind, as if a man swept the fallen leaves from the stricken tree into a heap.

"She gave a sort of cry," he said, "but at the end it was a moan. She threw her arms wide, and then held them to keep me off. What does it mean? What does it all mean?"

He got up quickly and began walking up and down the verandah.

"Where is she?" he said. "I must see her again. I must say what I said again, and tell her she must answer me."

The Hermit, for all his inhuman life, had some glimmerings of sense.

"You must do nothing of the sort," he said. "You don't seem to realise what you have done already. Why, she is engaged to Philip, to your friend, and you have told her you love her. Good gracious, is not that enough to make her moan?"

"I told you I should a week ago," said Evelyn.

"Yes, but you told me that conditionally. You said you would do so when you saw she loved you. Instead—— Good heavens! Evelyn, you must be unaware of what you have done. You were left with the girl during a thunderstorm, a thing that excites you and terrifies her, and you took advantage of your excitement and her terror to say this. It's ugly; it's beastly. But I can say it isn't like you."

Evelyn showed no sign of resenting this. As far as the mere criticism of what he had done was concerned, he appeared merely to feel a speculator's interest in how it all struck another spectator. Even Lady Ellington's hard, polished mind could not have presented a surface more impervious to scratches.

84

"You speak as if I did it all intentionally," he remarked. "But I never intended anything less. It had nothing to do with what I could control. I had no more power over it than I had over the thunderstorm. After all, you don't blame your thrush for eating worms. If one acts instinctively, nobody has any right to blame me. Besides, I don't want your moral judgment. I just want to know what it means. You have called me a Pagan before now, and I did not deny it. But there I am. I don't happen to like the colour of your hair, but I accept it. It seems to me buttery, if you want to know. And I seem to you Pagan, without conscience, you think I have acted uglily. Very well."

Merivale hesitated a moment; he had no desire to say hard things because they were hard. On the other hand, he felt that the game must be played, rules had to be observed, or human life broke up in confusion, as if the fielders in a game of cricket would not run after the ball or the bowler bowl. He himself did not go in for cricket, he deliberately stood aside, but the rules were binding on those who played. Yet it was no use trying to convince a person who fundamentally disagreed.

"Well, you asked me," he said, "and I have given you my opinion. That's all. Nobody's opinion is binding on anyone else. But I do ask you to think it over."

Evelyn gave a little click of impatience.

"Think it over!" he said. "What else do you suppose I should be thinking about, or what else have I thought about for days?"

Merivale shook his head.

"Try to get outside yourself, I mean, and look at what you have done from any other standpoint than your own. You say you couldn't help telling her. Well, there are certain things one has got to help, else——"

He stopped; it was no use talking. But Evelyn wanted to hear.

"Else?" he suggested.

"Else you had better not mix with other people at all," said Merivale. "You have better reason for turning hermit than I. You have told a girl who is engaged to your friend that you love her. Think over that!"

NINTH

IN spite of her wetting Lady Ellington felt she had had a most interesting day, when, an hour later, she drove back with Madge and her maid to Brockenhurst. She was not in the least afraid of having caught cold, because her physical constitution was, it may almost be said, as impervious to external conditions as her mind. That frightful flash of lightning, too, which had shattered the now leafless tree, had also, as we have seen, been powerless to upset the even balance of her nerves, and had only evoked a passing regret that so much electric force should be wasted.

She could, therefore, observe with her customary clearness that something had occurred to agitate Madge, and though the thunderstorm alone might easily account for this—where Madge had got her nerves from she could not conjecture, there was nothing hereditary about them, at any rate, as far as her mother was concerned—yet it required no great exercise of constructive imagination to connect Evelyn's sudden appearance with this agitation. She remembered also Madge's refusal to see him the other day, and her rather unaccountable postponement of the sitting. A few well-chosen questions, however, would soon settle this, and these she delivered that evening after dinner, firing them off like well-directed shots at a broad target. She did not, to continue the metaphor, want to make bull's eyes at once, a few outers would show her the range sufficiently well.

She had first, however, committed to writing on half-a-dozen sheets of the hotel paper her impressions of the day and the conversation of Mr. Merivale, in so far as it bore upon the simplification of life, and was pleased to find how considerable a harvest she had gathered in. Lady Ellington's literary style had in perfection those qualities of clearness and sharp outline that distinguished her mind, and her document might have been a report for an academy of science, so well arranged and precise was it. There were no reflections of her own upon the matter; it was merely a chronicle of facts and conversation. This having been written, revised, and read aloud to Madge, she then marched with her gun to her position in front of the target.

"It was odd that Mr. Dundas should have appeared so unexpectedly, Madge," she said. "You must have had some considerable time with him if he arrived before the storm began."

Madge had been rather expecting this, and she winced under her mother's firm, hard touch.

"Yes, he had been there about an hour before you came in," she said. "I think your account is quite excellent, mother."

This, if we consider it as an attempt to draw Lady Ellington off the subject of Evelyn, was quite futile. She did not even seem to notice that such an attempt had been made.

"And did you arrange about your further sittings?" she asked.

"I don't think any more will be necessary," replied Madge. "Philip agrees with me too."

"And Mr. Dundas?"

"I don't think he will ask me for any more either."

Lady Ellington considered this a moment.

"But surely you had settled to have one more," she said, "the one which you postponed."

"Yes, but I think we all agree now that as far as I am concerned the picture is finished."

Lady Ellington was not exactly puzzled; it would be fairer to say that though she did not quite know where this led, she was quite certain it led somewhere. It was not a puzzle; it was rather a clue. So she got behind a bush, as it were, and continued firing from there.

"He is a great friend of Philip's, is he not?" she said. "I suppose you will see a good deal of him after your marriage?"

This sharp-shooting was frightfully trying to Madge's nerves; she never knew where the next shot might be coming from. But in that it was now quite clear to her that shooting was going on, it was the part of wisdom to defend herself.

"Oh! I hope so," she said, "he is charming. I expect he will be constantly with us."

This was a little disconcerting; Madge had distinctly had the best of that exchange. But she was in the beleaguered position; she felt that at any moment she might have to give in. She had a wild desire simply to leave the room, for she wanted to be alone, and to think over all that she now knew, but the clock inexorably pointed to half-past nine only, and to say she was going to bed would simply strengthen whatever idea it was in Lady Ellington's mind that prompted her questions. Maternal anxiety and solicitude, though the point of view of the mother was perhaps a little predominant, were the moving causes of them, if they were referred back to primary motives; to put it more bluntly yet, Lady Ellington merely wished for a guarantee that nothing of any sort had occurred which might, however remotely, influence the matrimonial design for her daughter which she had formed and Madge had agreed to carry out. That she had fears that things were running otherwise than smoothly—by smoothly being meant that the marriage would take place on the twenty-eighth of the month—would be an overstatement of the idea that prompted these questions, but she certainly wished for some convincing word that she need have none.

Now, in the art of conversation as generally expounded, provision is not made for one very important and common contingency. Of the two conversationalists one may be willing to talk of anything in the world except one subject, the other may for the time wish to talk about no other than that, and thus conversation becomes difficult. But it would often be a tactical error—a thing of which Lady Ellington was seldom guilty—for the person who wishes to speak of one subject only to batter the other with too many questions on it. It is often better to sit quietly down and wait, refusing with what politeness there may be handy to talk of anything else, and simply let silence do its stealthy work—for awkward silences are wearing, and the wearing effect is inevitably felt by the side which is willing to talk of any but the one subject. Lady Ellington perhaps had never formulated this in all its naked simplicity, but she had often before now put the theory into practice with masterly effect, and she did so now. There was, so to speak, but one gate through which the beleaguered garrison could make a sortie: round that she concentrated her forces. The beleaguered garrison knowing that, tried to make a sortie through every other gate first.

A long silence.

"That was a terrible storm this afternoon," said Madge. "The rain fell in bucketsfull. I saw there were quite deep channels across the road along which we drove back here, which it had made."

"I did not notice them," said Lady Ellington.

Silence.

87

"Fancy Mr. Merivale cooking for himself and doing all the housework," said Madge.

"Fancy!" said Lady Ellington.

Silence.

"Shall we go up after breakfast to-morrow?" asked Madge.

"Unless you would like to go before," said her mother.

There is a terrible little proverb about being cruel only to be kind, and this benignant sort of torture exactly describes the procedure of Lady Ellington. Should there be—and she was quite sure there was—something going on in Madge's mind with regard to Evelyn she was quite convinced that it would be better in every way that she should know about it. That was the ulterior kindness; the immediate cruelty was apparent—for Madge was on the edge of a crisis of nerves; a very little push might send her sprawling. If that then was the case, Lady Ellington distinctly wished that she should sprawl; if, on the other hand, there was nothing critical or agitating in her outlook, the little push would do no harm whatever, for a mind at peace does not have its tranquility upset by vague suggestions and indefinite suspicions.

But since poor Madge was far from owning just now that inestimable possession of a tranquil mind, in the silence that followed her third fiasco in making general conversation, she began to get restless and fidgetty. She opened a book and looked blankly at a page, and shut it again; she fingered the ornaments on the mantlepiece; she went to the open window and looked out for a considerable time into the hot, wet blackness, for the slow, steady rain was again falling, and the heavens wept from a sullen sky. The ridge of the forest below which stood Merivale's house was directly opposite the window—she had seen that before night fell—and, like the thrush that came to his voiceless call, so now her spirit sped there to one who called for her. That sudden flash of lightning had not been more unexpected than Evelyn's declaration to her that afternoon, nor had the thunder that followed it come quicker in response than she had come. And now she wondered, half with dread, half with a wild, secret hope, whether he had noticed that momentary self-betrayal that she had made. She knew that before she could think or control herself, a cry had been on her lips, her arms had flung themselves wide. True, as soon as her conscious brain could work, she had revoked and contradicted what she had done. But had he seen? How terrible if he had seen! How terrible if he had not!

What had become, she asked herself, of all her sober and sane conclusions of a week ago? She knew then that she loved him, that that which had been a stranger to her all her life, no pleasant domestic affection, but something wild, unbarred, almost brutal, yet how essential now to life itself, had dropped into her heart, as a stone drops into the sea, going down and down to depths unplumbable, yet still going down until the bottom—the limits of her soul—was reached. And he? Was she to him another such stone? Was she really sinking down and down in his heart, so steadily and inevitably that all the tides of all the seas might strive, yet could never cast that stone up again? It was such a little thing, yet no power on earth, unless the laws that govern the earth were revised and made ineffectual, could ever stay its course, if it moved under the same command as she. Each had to settle in the depths of the other. Once the surface was broken by the little splash, down that would go which made the splash, and whether in a wayside puddle or in the depths of mid-Atlantic, it would rest only where it touched bottom. Such was the sum of her wide-eyed staring into the blackness of the rain-ruled night. Then, still restless, she turned back again into the room, and faced not the world of dreams and solitary imaginings, of what must theoretically be the case, but the material side of it all, which indubitably had its word to say. On the table was the letter she had received an hour before dinner, forwarded from London, and expressing the pleasure of the donor in sending a wedding present; there too was her own answer of neatly-worded thanks, and, above all, there was her mother, patiently adamant. And the beleaguered garrison, though it knew that the enemy—that friendly enemy—awaited it, went out on a sortie too forlorn to call a hope through the only available gate.

Madge sat down in the chair she had occupied before.

"You have been asking me a lot of questions, mother," she said, "which bear on Mr. Dundas. I suppose you think or have guessed that something has happened. You are quite right; I think you are always right. He told me this afternoon that he was in love with me."

Lady Ellington hardly knew whether she had expected this or not; at any rate she showed no sign of surprise.

"What very bad taste," she said, "his telling you, I mean."

Madge had given a sudden hopeless giggle of laughter at the first four words of this, before the explanation came. Lady Ellington waited till she had finished.

"What did you say to him?" she asked.

"I hardly know. I think I said that one or other of us must leave the room."

"Very proper; and he?"

"He—he asked me whether I hated him for it. And I told him I did not."

Then she broke; whether or no it was wiser to be silent she did not pause to consider, for she could not be silent. There must be a crash; a situation of this kind could not adjust itself in passivity, it was mere temporising not to speak at once.

"Because I don't hate him," she said, now speaking quickly as if in fear of interruption. "I love him. Oh! I have done my best; if he had never spoken, never let me know that he loved me, I could have gone on, I think, and done what it has been arranged for me to do. Philip knew, you see, that I did not love him like that. I had told him. But I did not know what it was. I almost wish I had never known. But I know; I can't help that now."

Whatever Lady Ellington's gospel as regards the best plan on which to conduct life was worth, if weighed as a moral principle, it is quite certain that she acted up to it. She put a paper-knife into the book she had taken up during Madge's aimless wanderings about the room to mark the page of her perusal, and spoke with perfect calmness.

"And what do you propose to do?" she asked.

Madge had not up till that moment proposed to do anything; she had not, in other words, considered the practical interpretation of this bewildering discovery. The fact that her silent, secret love—a love which she was determined to lock up forever in her own breast—was returned, was so emotionally overwhelming that as from some blinding light she could only turn a dazzled eye elsewhere. Her first instinct, at the moment at which that was declared to her, was of rapturous acceptance of it, but almost as instinctive (not quite so instinctive, since it had come second) was a shrinking from all that it implied—her rupture with Philip, his inevitable suffering, the pressure that she knew would be brought to bear on her. Yet the thing had to be faced; it was no use shrinking from it, and Lady Ellington's question reminded her of the obvious necessity for choice. Her choice indeed was made; it was time to think of what action that choice implied. But she answered quietly enough.

"No, I have not yet thought of what I mean to do," she said. "I suppose we had better talk about it."

Then Lady Ellington unmasked all her batteries. It was quite clear that Madge already seriously contemplated breaking off her engagement with Philip and marrying this artist.

"Indeed, we had better talk about it," she said. "But I want to ask you one question first. Has Mr. Dundas the slightest notion that his feeling for you is reciprocated?"

Madge thought over this a moment.

"He has no right to think so," she said. "I—I have told you what occurred. The whole thing was but a few seconds."

"There are various ways of spending a few seconds," said her mother. "But you think you spent them discreetly."

Madge looked up with a sort of weary patience.

"You mustn't badger me," she said. "It is no use. I did my best to conceal it."

Then the bombardment began.

"Very good; we take it that he does not know. Now let us consider what you are going to do. Do you mean to write a note to him saying, 'Dear Mr. Dundas, I love you?' If that is your intention, you had better do it at once. There is no kind of reason for delay. But if it is not your intention, taking that in its broadest sense to mean that you will not make known to him that you love him, dismiss that possibility altogether. Pray give me your whole attention, Madge; nothing that can occur to you in the whole of your life is likely to matter more than this."

"But I love him," pleaded Madge, "and he loves me. Is not that enough? Must not something happen?"

"I ask you whether you intend to do anything; that implies now that you, without further action on his part, will show him that you love him. The question just requires 'Yes' or 'No.'"

"And supposing I decline to answer you?" asked Madge, suddenly flashing out.

"I don't think you can do that. You see I am your mother; as such, I think I have a right to know what you propose to do."

Madge covered her eyes with her hand for a moment. The question had to be answered; she knew that, and she knew also that unless Evelyn made a further sign she could do nothing. If his love for her, as she doubted not at all, was real, he must approach her again. Here then were all the data for her answer.

"No," she said. "I shall do nothing, because there is no need. He must——" And she broke off. Then she got up with a sudden swift movement.

"You put it coarsely, you make cast-iron of it all, mother," she said, "when you ask me if I intend to write to him and tell him. Of course I do not."

"Nor see him?" pursued Lady Ellington.

"If he asks to see me I shall see him," said she. "And if his object is to say again what he said to-day, I shall tell him."

Now to get news, even if it is not very satisfactory, is better than not getting news. In uncertainty there is no means of telling how to act, and whatever the contingency—a contingency known is like a danger known—it can perhaps be guarded against, and it can certainly be faced. How to guard against this Lady Ellington did not at the moment see, but she knew that danger lay here.

"And from that moment you will break off your engagement with Philip?" she asked.

There was no need here of any reply, and Lady Ellington continued:

"Now consider exactly how Mr. Dundas stands," she said. "He knows you are engaged to a friend of his, that you will be married in a few weeks, and he allows himself, left alone with you by accident, to make this declaration to you. Does that seem to you to be an honourable action?"

Then once again Madge flashed out.

"Ah, who cares?" she cried. "What does that matter?"

Lady Ellington rose.

"You have also promised to marry Philip," she said. "I suppose that does not matter either? Or do I wrong you?"

"He would not wish me to marry him if he knew," said Madge.

Lady Ellington poured out her glass of hot water, and sipped it in silence. She knew well that many words may easily spoil the effect of few, and her few, she thought, on the whole had been well chosen. So just as before she had refused to talk on any subject but one, so now, since she had said really just what she meant to say, she refused any longer to talk on it, but was agreeably willing, as Madge had been some ten minutes before, to talk about anything else.

"I think there will be more rain before morning," she said.

Then Madge came close to her and knelt by her chair.

"Are you not even sorry for me, mother?" she said.

"I shall be if you act unwisely," replied the other, and Madge, there was nothing else to be done, got up again.

There was a slightly chalybeate taste in Lady Ellington's hot water to-night, and she remarked on it; this was more noticeable if the water was hot than if it was cold, but the taste was not unpleasant. Then the question of their train up to town the next day was debated, and it was settled to leave that till to-morrow. Indeed, it was rather a pity to come down into the country for so few hours, and their afternoon to-day had really been spoiled by the rain. Another walk in the forest—it would look beautifully fresh and green after the storm—would be very pleasant to-morrow morning, if it was fine.

All this, delivered in her cool, well-bred voice, had a sort of paralytic effect on Madge; she felt as if coils were being wound round her that hampered her power of movement. She could scarcely picture herself as in active opposition to her mother's will, and the picture of herself triumphant over it was even more unthinkable. But, as usual, she kissed her mother when she said "Good night" to her, and her mother offered her bromide if she thought that the excitement and agitation caused by the thunderstorm would be likely to prevent her sleeping.

Lady Ellington did not propose taking any bromide herself to make her sleep; she did not, on the other hand, propose to attempt to go to sleep just yet, for she had matters to weigh and consider, and perhaps take steps consequent on her consideration, before she went to sleep. Like all practical and successful people, she believed intensely in prompt action; it was better in most cases to decide wrongly than not to decide at all, and she intended before she slept to-night both to decide, and, as far as the lateness of the hour permitted, to act on her decision. The proposition, the thesis of her decision, was very soon rehearsed; indeed, that was the thing that she took for granted, but had now to prove and demonstrate. There was a house, so to speak, which she was under contract to build and have ready in a few weeks, it was her bricks and mortar she had to procure, and have the house solidly built and ready by the required date. And the house to be built, it is almost superfluous to remark, was the house which Madge and Philip would occupy together.

Now, according to her lights, little lights, they may have been, "much like a shade," she was convinced that Madge would be extremely happy in the house she had to build, for she was a woman of sense, and fully believed that everything that was sensible, even a sensible marriage, was ipso facto better than its corresponding equivalent with the sense left out. Philip was in every way a suitable match; he was a gentleman, he had all those solid qualities, the qualities that wear well, which are so supremely important if they have to wear for the remainder of mortal existence, and he was much devoted to Madge. Madge on her side was much attached to him, and was quite certainly unemotional. It was therefore only reasonable to suppose that her sudden ascent into these aerial regions which had culminated in this evening's crisis were but a Daedalus-flight; her wings, or the fastenings of them, would melt, and she would, if she pursued the unwise course, come to earth with a most uncomfortable and shattering bump. Evelyn, no doubt, possessed for her something which she missed in Philip, or would have missed if she had looked for it. But she had not looked for it, she had told him that she brought him affection, esteem, respect, and he had been content. He was content still, and Madge must be content too.

Browning says that it is "a ticklish matter to play with souls," but Lady Ellington did not stand convicted over this. She did not play with them at all; with a firm, cool hand, she shoved them into their places. For weeks Madge had accepted, if not with rapture, at any rate with a very sincere welcome, the future that had been planned for her, and it was an insanity now to revoke that for the sake of what might easily be a moment's freak. That there was something very attractive about this irresponsible boy with his brilliant talent and his graceful presence, Lady Ellington did not for a moment deny, even when she was quite by herself. But to plan a lifetime that merely rested on these foundations was to build a house upon sand. Madge had fallen in love with externals; it was impossible that she should be allowed to make her blunder—for so her mother regarded it— irreparable, and it was the means whereby this should be rendered impossible that Lady Ellington had now to determine. And since she was quite firmly convinced of the desirability of this end, she did not, it must be confessed, feel particularly scrupulous with regard to means.

All this time Lady Ellington's mind had not been only formulating but also constructing, and her construction was now complete. Late though it was, she drew her chair to the small writing-table, so conveniently placed under the electric light, and wrote:

> Dear Mr. Dundas.—My daughter has told me, as indeed she was bound to do, what took place this afternoon when you arrived unexpectedly at Mr. Merivale's house and found yourself alone with her. I feel of course convinced that you must be already sorry for having allowed yourself to take advantage of my girl's accidental loneliness in this way, but since I gather from her that Mr. Merivale and I returned almost at that moment, I am willing to believe that you would not have——

Lady Ellington paused a moment; she wished to put things strongly.

> —have continued to obtrude your presence and your speech on one to whom it was so unwelcome.
>
> I have no desire to add to the reproaches I am sure you must be heaping on yourself, and I will say no more on this subject. It is of course impossible that my daughter should sit to you again, it is equally impossible that you should write to her or attempt to see her, since you cannot possibly have anything to say except to reiterate your regrets for what you have done. These it is better to take for granted, as I am perfectly willing to do. We both of us forgive you—I can answer for her as completely as I can answer for myself—with all our hearts, and will maintain, you may rest assured, the strictest silence on the subject.
>
> I should like to have one line from you in acknowledgment of the receipt of this.—Yours very truly,
>
> Margaret Ellington.

93

This note was written with but few erasures, for it was Lady Ellington's invariable custom to think her thoughts with some precision before she committed them to paper. Yet, late as it had grown, she copied it out afresh, put it in an envelope and directed it, and placed it on a small table by the head of her bed, so that when her tea was brought in the morning, it would be patent to the eyes of her maid. But, rather uncharacteristically, she thought over what she had said in it as she continued her undressing. Yet it was all for the good, likewise there was no word in it that was not true. And she slept with a conscience that was hard and clear and quite satisfied. For if one was doing one's best for people, nothing further could be demanded from one. And that she was doing her best she had no kind of doubt. Thus her mind was soon at leisure to observe that it was impossible to put out the electric light after getting into bed. It was necessary to light a candle first, and she made a mental note to refuse to pay for candles in case they were charged in the bill.

Lady Ellington's postponement of the settling of the train by which she and Madge should go up to town next day was due, as the reader will have guessed, to her desire to get Evelyn's answer to her note before she went. A glorious morning of flooding sunshine and a world washed and renewed by the torrents of the day before succeeded the storm, and at breakfast her plan of spending the morning in the forest, and going up to London after lunch was accepted by Madge if not with enthusiasm, at any rate with complete acquiescence. She of course must not know that her mother had written to Evelyn; it was wiser also, in case she was familiar with his handwriting, that there should be no risk run of her seeing the envelope addressed by him in reply. A very little strategy, however, would affect all this, and in obedience to orders, as soon as Lady Ellington and Madge had started on their ramble this morning, her maid took a cab to the Hermitage, bearing this note, the answer to which she would wait for, and give it to her mistress privately. This seemed to provide for all contingencies anyhow that could arise from this note itself. Indeed, though there were dangers and contingencies to be avoided or provided for before Madge would be safely Home—Lady Ellington thought this rather neat— she felt herself quite competent to tackle with them. Madge had declared she would take no step without the initiative on the part of Evelyn, and after the really very carefully worded note which he would receive this morning, it was not easy to see what he could do. Luck, of course, that blind goddess who upsets all our plans as a mischievous child upsets a chess-board on which the most delicate problem is in course of solution, might bring in the unforeseen to wreck everything, but Lady Ellington's experience was that Luck chiefly interfered with careless people who did not lay their plans well. She could not accuse herself of belonging to that class, nor in fact would her enemies, if, as was highly probable, she had enemies, have done so.

It was therefore in a state of reasonable calm and absence of apprehension that she came back from her long stroll in the forest with Madge just before lunch. She had had a really delightful walk, and they had talked over, without any allusion to the subject that really occupied them both, the gospel of the simple life, as practised by Merivale. Madge had not slept well; indeed, it would be truer to say she had scarcely slept at all, and her face bore traces of the weary hours of the night. But she too, like her mother, though for different reasons, had no temptation to re-open the subject, simply because she felt she could not stand any more just then, and it was something of a relief to devote even the superficial activity of her mind to other topics. Not for a moment did she doubt that Evelyn would write to her asking to see her; he must indeed do that for his own sake no less than hers, and though the waiting was hard enough, yet at the end of it there shone so bright a light that even the waiting had a sort of luminous rapture about it. So comforting herself thus, she responded to her mother's bright, agile talk, and indeed took her fair share of conversation.

The answer had arrived when Lady Ellington reached home, and her maid gave it her in her bedroom. It acknowledged the receipt of her note, as she had asked, and which indeed was all she had asked. She should, therefore, have been perfectly satisfied. Yet she was not quite; she did not feel as secure as she could have wished.

TENTH

IT was some ten days after the events of the thunderstorm, and Evelyn, who had returned to London the day after, was in his studio working at the portrait of Philip. The last ten days had passed for him like an evil dream—a dream, too, unfortunately from which there was no prospect whatever of waking. Indeed, as the dream went on it seemed to gain in its ghastly vividness; every day that passed repeated the effect of it, and stamped its reality deeper. But with good sense that did him credit, instead of brooding desolately over his lot, or driving himself half-mad with the thought of Madge, he turned with a sort of demented fury to his work, and day after day painted till he could no longer see, not leaving off till his brain was dull and almost incapable of further thought. But though nervous, excitable and highly-strung, he was luckily also very strong, and believed that he was capable, at any rate, of going on at this frightful high pressure anyhow till the marriage had taken place. When that was accomplished, he felt that the tension of the suspense would be lightened; he might himself, it is true, drop like a stone in the sea, but the struggle would then be over, he would not battle any longer to try to keep afloat. In the inside pocket of his coat he kept the note that he had received from Lady Ellington; it was soiled and wilted with much handling and re-reading, and simple and straightforward (from a literary point of view) as it was, he had tried fifty interpretations on each of those very intelligible sentences. But not one contained a grain of comfort for him.

But though the whole fibre of his spiritual being was in so great and agonising a state of unrest, he found that his eye and his hand had lost not one particle of their powers of vision and execution. Sometimes, it is true, it was rather hard to get to work; it seemed scarcely worth while putting in a light or a shadow, but when once he had begun there was no abatement in the brilliance of his skill, and though he only felt a vague, far-away satisfaction in what he was doing, he brought all his keenness of observation, all his dexterity of handling to his work. Again, when his sitters were there, there was the same merciful necessity of normal behaviour, and probably there was only one person who saw him during these days who suspected that there was anything wrong. This was Philip. But of what was wrong he had not the faintest inkling.

Philip himself, so said the world in general, had become wonderfully softened since his engagement. He had gained enormously in geniality, a quality of which the world had not considered him particularly lavish before, and he did not in these new days take himself quite so seriously as he had been used to. Why he had fallen in love with Madge originally nobody quite knew, for there was no very obvious common ground between them. But the ways of love are past finding out, and even as when two tiny carbon poles of an electric battery are brought near to each other a light altogether disproportionate to their size illuminates the night, so it was with Philip. And certainly now the miracle was easier of explanation; there apparently had been in him the germ of a quite different Philip to that which he showed the world—a Philip admirably kind and gentle, the very man who would so easily fall in love with anyone possessed of half Madge's perfectly obvious attractions. All this was said in general talk, but in whispers it had begun to be said that Madge was not so desperately in love with him, and for this Gladys Ellington was not, as a matter of fact, directly responsible, though no doubt she would have been if she had thought she would not be found out. It was rather Madge's own manner which suggested it. She too, like Philip, had been much humanised, coincidentally anyhow, with their engagement; but later, during these last ten days in fact, she really seemed to have hired a snail-shell and curled herself up in it. Her trousseau—this alone was immaterial—did not seem to give her the smallest pleasure, and yet her indifference to that was not the indifference which might have been the fruit of her private intense happiness, which could conceivably have made even these confections seem tasteless. In fact, it was not only the trousseau that she appeared to find tasteless; she found everything tasteless, and really, to judge from her mode of behaviour when she was with Philip, you would have thought that she was an icicle just being introduced to an eligible snowflake.

Philip on this particular day had sat for Evelyn for nearly a couple of hours, grumbling at the length of his detention, but in a manner that did not suggest active discontent. He intended, in fact, to give Madge the picture on their wedding day, if it could be finished, and to further that desirable object he was willing really to sit for as long as Evelyn required. The latter, various and numerous as were the moods to which he usually treated his sitters, seemed to-day to have gone through them all; he was, in fact, more like himself than Philip had lately seen him.

96

"Until one really looks at a man's face," he had been saying, "one never knows how ugly he is. I always used to think you passably good-looking. But you are awful, do you know? Men's faces generally are like chests of drawers—square, don't you know, and covered with knobs that suggest handles. And you are balder than when I began to paint you."

"I am sure I apologise. And do you really think you can finish it by the twenty-eighth? I shall be immensely grateful if you can."

"The twenty-eighth? Ah! yes, the happy day."

Thereat another mood came over him, and for the spate of surprising remarks which he had been pouring forth there was exchanged a frowning, brush-biting silence. This lasted another twenty minutes, and Philip, as thanks for his offerings on the altar of conversation, got only grunts, and once a laboriously polite request to stand still. But eventually he hit on a subject that produced a response.

"And Madge's portrait?" he said. "Have you decided to yield to our ignorance perhaps, but anyhow our desire, and consider it finished?"

Evelyn stopped dead in the middle of a stroke, and a new and frightfully disconcerting mood suddenly appeared to possess him.

"How can you ask me if I yield," he said hotly, "when you have told me I can't have any more sittings? I yield as a man yields who is pinioned and hung. I only yield to force. As for the portrait, it is there, face to the wall. I will not send it to you, but you may fetch it away without opposition on my part. I never want to see it again. Oh! I make one condition—it must never be exhibited."

"Ah! my dear fellow," said Philip, "I cannot take it if you feel like that about it."

"Leave it then."

Philip was very deeply hurt somehow by this. Evelyn's absolute insistence on his taking it as a present from him had much touched him, though he had tried to combat it. But this ending of the affair was intolerable. He could not leave matters like this. And now while he was debating what to do, Evelyn spoke again, resuming his painting with rapid, unerring strokes.

"I must say this, too," he said. "I had an inspiration for that portrait quite unlike any I have ever had before. It is, even as it stands, my masterpiece, but you—you and Miss Ellington anyhow—have prevented me from completing what is my best, and would have been far better. Far better? It would have been on a different plane altogether. I am sorry if this hurts you, but it is only right you should know. I don't say it is your fault; I don't say it is anybody's fault. But there the picture stands; I give it you with all the completeness with which I originally gave it you, and with all—all the best wishes."

He paused a moment.

"But I won't send it you," he said, "since I don't think it ought to be sent. Yet take it with my love, my best love, Philip. And I should be obliged if you would say no more at all about it. Turn your face a bit more to the left, there's a good fellow; you have shifted slightly."

He painted on for some little time in silence, and Philip, complying

97

with his request that nothing more should be said about it, answered his next question, some common topic, and himself introduced another. But all the time his thoughts were busy enough on the tabooed subject. For a second time, as at the opera a few nights ago, the vague suspicion crossed his mind that Evelyn was in love with Madge, and had somehow betrayed this to her; but now, as then, he formulated this thought only to give it instant dismissal. That being so, he was morally bound to do Evelyn justice, to accept without either comment or reservation the fact that he really required another sitting from Madge, and to do his utmost, whatever her unwillingness and whatever the cause of it, to make her sit to him again. Both the Philip known to the few intimates and the Philip so much respected by the world at large had a very strong sense of fairness, and the fair thing quite certainly was this. It was impossible to deny an artist another sitting if he felt like this about it; it was doubly impossible to deny it to a friend. Even if the picture had been an order, a commission, it would have been but shabby treatment, now that he knew how Evelyn felt about it, not to do his very utmost to get Madge to give him another sitting; but the picture was not that, it was a present, given too, as he had said, "with his love." He could not really doubt that when it was put to Madge like this, she would see it as he himself did.

The task itself of talking to her on the subject, it was distasteful to him, for she had been mysteriously indeed, but unmistakably in earnest, about it a few nights ago at the opera. Whatever the cause (and he consciously turned back from even conjecturing at the cause), she had, so she thought, at any rate, an adequate reason for not wishing to continue the sittings, even when the artist's point of view was presented to her, and he foresaw that he might find himself in an opposition to her that would be painful to both of them. Nor had the change in her, which the world compared to the action of a snail retiring into its shell, escaped him. She had been for the last ten days or so reserved, silent, and apt to be startled. More than once he had asked her if anything was wrong, and the vehemence of her assertion that nothing was wrong had rather surprised him. But here, again, he had to pull himself up, and studiously refrain from conjecturing that Evelyn was in any way connected with any private worry of hers. Besides she had said that nothing was wrong; he was bound to accept that. For this reason he rejected the notion of consulting Lady Ellington about it; that would imply a distrust of the girl herself.

He was going to see her as soon as this sitting was over, and since he had thoroughly made up his mind that he must do his best to persuade her to do as he desired about the portrait, he determined not to put it off, but to speak to her to-day. But he judged it better not to tell Evelyn what he was going to do, because on the one hand his mission might fail of success, and on the other because he had been asked to allude no further to the question. So for the remainder of the sitting they talked, neither quite naturally, since both were thinking of the one subject that could not be talked about, on strictly public topics. But every minute was an age of discomfort, and Philip, at any rate, was heartily glad when it was over, and he was out again in the hot, sunny streets.

98

Madge scarcely knew how the days had passed since that afternoon in the New Forest, for it seemed to her that all the values of life were altered, as if a totally new scheme of things must be made, for that which existed at present was not possible. Day after day, too, brought the twenty-eighth nearer—that date before which something which would upset and reverse her whole world must assuredly occur. For she was pledged then to do that which she knew she could not do, the impossibility of which was every hour more vividly impressed on her. She had herself promised her mother to do nothing whatever, unless Evelyn made some further advance; what she did not know was how very skilfully he had been debarred from that. But already the promise she had herself given had begun to lose for her its moral validity, it was only in a second-hand sort of way that she considered it binding, for one thing only she felt was really binding on her, and that the impossibility of fulfilling her pledge to Philip. That was outside her power; by what step she would make that known, she did not yet consider. A way must be found; what the way was seemed to her, if she considered it at all, very immaterial.

For side by side with that impossibility, and not less securely throned, was another certainty, namely, that Evelyn must repeat what he had said before; no man could leave it like that. And in those days she knew what it was to start and change colour when the door-bell rang, to frame any excuse, or no excuse, to go downstairs and see what the post had brought, to watch at balls and parties the arrival of fresh-comers, and glance across the crowded rooms in a sort of yearning certainty that now at last she would see one face among the crowd, which would come slowly closer and closer through the throng, until it was by her. Then—even the trivial, commonplace little details were imagined by her—he would ask her for a dance, or take her out to some unfrequented room. Philip at the time would probably be with her; he would certainly smile and nod at Evelyn, and resign her to him for "just ten minutes." But the days went on, and none of these visions were realised; he appeared no more at houses where she had often seen him. Often, too, people asked her about the progress of her portrait, and to these she replied that it was finished. Finished! These moments were lit with a certainty and a sure hope, but there were others, black ones. What if he had spoken without thought, excitedly, carried away by some moment's passion, bitterly regretted since? Supposing he did not really love her, supposing it had been just the flame and the blaze of a moment.

There was no preparation possible for the crash that was inevitable. No gradual estrangement from Philip, ending in a quarrel, was to be thought of; she could not scheme and soften things; the granite of the bouleversement could not be kneaded into dough. More than once he had asked her if anything was the matter, and on the last occasion, as we have seen, she had denied it with vehemence—the vehemence of one who is sick with a deadly, devouring sickness, whose instinct, feverish and irresistible, is to hold on to the last, affirming her health. But her own vehemence had startled not only him, but herself, and she had vowed to show more self-control, and exhibit that self-control in its most difficult demonstration—

merely that of appearing quite normal, and not exercising or, indeed, needing any self-control at all. More especially was this difficult when she was alone with him—the half-hinted caress, the look of love in those honest eyes, had to be somehow telegraphed back; some resemblance that would pass muster as a response had to be sent by her. It was all so mean, and the only comfort, and that cold, was that it could not now last long. For the one supreme impossibility remained—she could not be at his side on the twenty-eighth. Some thing, Fate or her own action dictated by it, would interfere with that, but about it she felt a sort of cold irresponsibility. Meantime, since responsibility was not as yet definitely fallen on her, the need for normal behaviour was paramount.

To-day Philip was coming to tea; he was going to return to dinner, and they, with her mother, were going to the theatre. After that there was a dance; from the hours between five and the small hours of the next day she would scarcely be alone a moment. And it was in loneliness that she could best bear the hopeless tangle—that tangle which, so it seemed to her now, could never be unravelled, but must be cut with a knife. A small knot more or less no longer made any difference, and it was with apathy almost, certainly without strong feeling of any kind, that she heard from Lady Ellington that she would perhaps be late for tea, and in consequence that Philip and herself would be alone together. An hour or two more of make-believe did not seem to her now to matter much; the hours that there could be of that were definitely limited, and, since limited, it was possible to deal with them. For it is only the endless succession of impossible hours, this knowledge that they will continue as long as life itself, that brings despair. But above all, till the crash came, she must be normal. She must give no sign of the storm that was raging within her, and though the depths and lowest abysses of her nature were upheaved by wild billows yet somehow the surface must be kept calm. It was one of the forces outside her own control which had taken possession of her, and with a sort of shudder she thought of the duck-and-drake discussions she had held with Evelyn about incontrollable forces, making these things of vital import the subject for a jest and an epigram. But she knew now, as she had not known then, what such a force meant.

This dismal drawing-room, with its frippery hanging over the window to hide it from the gaze of the square, its grand piano, its window at the opposite end, which commanded a small sooty yard! A hundred drawing-rooms east and west of it were exactly like it, yet on this had Fate—that cruel, velvet-pawed cat—pounced, selecting it at random, to make it the scene of one of her mean little dramas, at which one cannot laugh for fear of tears, at which one cannot cry because other people laugh. And here Madge sat alone, Lady Ellington not having yet returned, the silver urn occasionally lifting its lid with the infinitesimal pressure of the steam beneath, with all the mocking accessories of comfortable life round her, waiting for the inevitable explosion. It might be to-day, it might be to-morrow, it might be any day up to the twenty-eighth. But by that time it must have come; yet the same carpet would be trodden on, the same pictures would cast incurious eyes on to a human tragedy, the same

100

everything would preserve its mute, inanimate composure. That composure she, too, had now to rival; she must be as suitable as the sofa.

Her greeting of him, anyhow, was good enough.

"At last!" she said. "Philip, it is weeks since I set eyes on you. Where have you been, and what have you done with yourself all this time? Now, don't say it has only been business. I don't believe you do any, and I shall send a detective to get on your track. Ah! you wouldn't like that, I can see it; you gave what novelists call an involuntary shudder."

Then she broke down a little.

"Tea," she asked. "You like it weak, don't you?"

Philip settled himself in the chair she had indicated. He, too, like Madge, was inclined to temporise, though his reasons for so doing were different, for his inevitable errand was unpleasant, and the present so extremely the reverse. Her temporisation on the other hand, was that of postponing the inevitable for the sake of the impossible.

"Well, it is good anyhow to see you again," he said. "Yes, business chiefly has stood in my way. But I won't be dishonest; I spent nearly two hours this afternoon over the portrait."

"What portrait?" asked Madge, with a swiftness that she could not help. But she would gladly have recalled it. For the present, however, it appeared that Philip did not notice her vehemence.

"Mine," he said quietly. "I am sitting to Evelyn, you know. He hopes to have it finished by the twenty-eighth. You shall see it then, but not till then."

"Yes, keep it for then," she said, again bracing herself to keep up some sort of attitude which should be natural in a girl to a man she was shortly going to marry. "It must come as a surprise to me, Philip. But only tell me: it is good, isn't it? I shan't be disappointed?"

Now, this portrait of himself seemed to Philip more magical work than even that of Madge. He knew himself pretty well, but this afternoon, when he was allowed to see it, he felt that Evelyn somehow must have been inside him to have done that. Brilliant as Madge's portrait was (the artist himself indeed considering it quite his high-water mark), it was yet but a mood of Madge that he had caught so correctly and delineated so unerringly—that mood of reassuring laughter at the worries and the sorrows of life. But in his own portrait he felt that he himself was there.

"No, I promise you that you will not be disappointed," he said, "though I daresay it will make you jump. It isn't on the canvas at all, it seems to me; it is stepping right out of it. And there is there," he added, "not only this poor business man, but the man who loves you. He has put that in. My goodness, how could he have known what that was like?"

Madge gave a sudden little start, but recovered herself immediately. She could not meet this seriously; it had to be laughed off.

"Well, I don't know what it is like," she said, "because with all my faults, I've really never loved myself. I never think of myself except as rather a little brute. It's better to do that oneself, isn't it, not to leave it to others. Not that it prevents them doing it also."

Philip had possessed himself of Madge's left hand, the hand that he never ceased to wonder at. It was always cool, never hot, never cold, and

101

the skin of it was like a peach. The fingers were long and tapered to almond-shaped nails, and for all its slimness and delicacy it was yet a strong hand. And mechanically she returned the touch of his, which half unconsciously lingered at the base of the fourth finger as if showing the place where so soon the plain circlet of gold would be.

"Ah! it is always a pity if anybody thinks one a brute," he said. "It often must happen, but I think one should try to make such occasions rare, so long as one does not have to sacrifice principle to them. I mean, if anyone thinks one a brute, and one can convince him of the contrary, it is usually worth while."

For a moment it flashed through Madge's brain what was coming. Considering what her mind was full of, it was not surprising. And it came.

"I want to ask a favour of you, dear," he said. "I call it a favour because it is a real favour—it implies your doing something that I know you don't want to do. It also will make somebody cease to think you a brute, and instead of sacrificing a principle in its performance—you will satisfy one, and that a very good one, the principle of fairness."

Madge had left the sofa where they were sitting together during this, and simply in order to be doing something instead of inertly listening, poured herself out another cup of tea. So her back was turned to Philip when she replied:

"You state it as if I couldn't help saying 'Yes,'" she said, her voice trembling a little. "What is it, Philip?"

"Merely this, that you give Evelyn another sitting," he said. "I had no idea how strongly and keenly he felt about it till this afternoon. Shall I tell you about it?"

"Yes, do."

"Well won't you come and sit here again?"

She did not dare, for she felt too uncertain of herself, and as she poured the milk into her tea, her hand was no longer master of itself, and the saucer was flooded.

"Ah! what a mess," she cried. "Go on, Philip."

"He feels that you are treating him shabbily," he said. "Mind, he never said that; he never would. But it was clear to me. He believes that his portrait of you is the best piece of work he is ever likely to do, and though I may disagree with him, that says nothing against his right to his opinion, which is probably correct. Well, he wants one more sitting——"

"Did he say that this afternoon?"

"No, but he did before, and this afternoon he told me I might fetch it away if I liked, and he would offer no opposition, but that he would not send it. I can't take it like that; neither you nor I can take it if that is his feeling about it. It isn't as if I paid for it; it is a present—a most generous, splendid present. So will you be very kind, Madge, and though he bores you, just go back once? Indeed, it is only fair that you should. After all, it is only for an hour or so, and really, I don't believe he bores you much."

Though in the next moment Madge thought of so much, the pause was not long, for her thoughts flashed lightning-wise through her mind. First came the dramatic wonder that it should be Philip—Philip of all people in the huge world, who should be asking her to do this. If it had been anybody else the thing would not have been so astounding, but it was he. Then came the thought of her mother, and the promise she had given her. Even before this that promise, set in the scales with larger issues, had weighed light: now it just kicked the beam. But then, after that, and stronger than all else, came the sense of solution, of a riddle answered. How often had she puzzled over the manner in which it would turn out that the twenty-eighth should be to her a day without significance. Here was the answer, different from all her imaginings, and told her by Philip himself. And of imaginings and puzzlings she had had enough, and she did not put her brain to the task of imagining what that sitting would be like, how he would speak, what he would say. Simply, she was going to meet him again. And her voice when she answered was perfectly calm, without vibration. She felt indeed now so certain of herself that she came and sat by Philip again.

"Yes, if he feels it like that," she said, "and if you feel it like that, I will do as you wish. As you say, an hour or two doesn't matter much. I will write to him; it had better be as soon as possible—to-morrow if he has time. I have rather an empty day to-morrow."

She got up again.

"I will write now, I think," she said, "because I must eat a little, just a little, humble pie, and as I have no relish for that, I will get it done with as soon as possible. Now, what shall I say? Let me think."

Her pen travelled with remarkable ease over the paper; the humble pie, it appeared, was being consumed without much difficulty. Once only she stopped for a word, then the scream of the quill underlined her own name.

"Will this do?" she asked, and read:

Dear Mr. Dundas.—I feel that I have no right whatever, since you wish me to give you another sitting, to refuse it. This has been pointed out to me quite clearly by Philip, who is with me now, and I see that it is not fair either on you or the portrait. I wonder if to-morrow would suit you? I could come any time between three and six. If three will do, pray do not trouble to answer, and I will assume the affirmative.

Philip's habit of considering business letters led him to pause.

"Yes, that is amende honorable," he said at length. "It will do excellently. But if you are bored, Madge, why not take your mother with you, or I would meet you there?"

"Oh, no, he would think it so odd," she said lightly. "You see, I am accustomed to go alone. And he has told me that he hates other people in the studio while he is painting."

She directed the note and rang the bell.

"There is one thing more, Philip," she said, "and that is that I don't want my mother to know I am going. You see, I told her, too, that I was not going to sit again, and if one goes back on one's word, well, the fewer people who know about it the better. Everyone hates a changeable person who doesn't know her own mind."

Philip willingly gave his assurance on this point, for though it seemed to him rather a superfluous refinement, he was, on the whole, so pleased to have met with no opposition that he was delighted to leave the matter settled without more discussion. Then, since it was already time for him to go home and dress for the early dinner before the theatre, he got up.

"Ah! Madge," he said, lingering a moment. "You don't know, and you can't guess, how divinely happy you make me. In the big things I knew it was so, but in little things it is so also. You are complete all through."

This struck her like a blow. She could scarcely look at him, it was even harder to return his caress.

"Oh, don't think too well of me," she said, "and—and go now, or you will be late."

Then, after he had gone, Madge felt tired as she had never felt tired before. The fact that the tension was over showed her what the tension had been; she had struggled, and while she struggled the need for effort had postponed the effect of weariness which the effort produced. She could go on living her ordinary life, and had not this occurred she could still have gone on, but it was only now, when the need for going on was over, that she knew how utterly weary she was. Yet with the weariness there was given her a draught of wine; it would no longer be "to-morrow and to-morrow and to-morrow," but to-morrow only. She knew as surely as she knew how tired she was, that to-morrow would see her with him, and the rest she was content to leave; no imagination or picturing of hers was necessary. It would be as it would be.

After Philip had left her, there was still half an hour before she need go to dress, but the thought that her solitude might be disturbed here by anyone who called, or by her mother, who would be returning any minute, caused her to go upstairs to her own room, where, till the advent of her maid at dressing-time, she would be alone.

Thus it was scarcely a minute after her lover had gone that she went upstairs. As she mounted the steps to the storey above, she heard the front-door bell ring, congratulated herself on having just escaped, and went more softly, and closed the door of her bedroom very gently behind her.

The ring at the bell which she had heard was her mother returning. The footman who had taken Madge's note, who had also just let Philip out, let her in, having laid down the note in question on the hall table, meaning to put a stamp on it, and drop it into the letter-box. Madge's handwriting was unmistakable; it was brilliantly legible, too, and the address leaped from the envelope.

Now, Lady Ellington, as both her friends and her possible enemies would have at once admitted, was a very thorough woman. She did not, in fact, when she desired or designed anything, neglect any opportunity of furthering that desire or design, or on the other hand, neglect to remove any obstacle which might possibly stand in the way of its realisation. She had excellent eyes, too—eyes not only of good sight, but very quick to observe. Yet even a short-sighted person might easily have involuntarily read the address, so extremely legible was it. And Lady Ellington, with her excellent sight, read it almost before she knew she had read it. The footman in question had meantime just gone out to deliver her order to the chauffeur for the motor this evening, and before he had got back again into the hall, Lady Ellington was half-way upstairs with the note in her hand.

William—the footman—had a week before received a month's warning on the general grounds of carelessness and inattention. Whether justified or not before they were justified now, for on re-entering he thought no more at all about the note he had to post, but stared at himself in a looking-glass, and hoped the next butler might be more agreeable to a sensitive young fellow, than the one he at present served under. He was a student of the drama, and smiled to himself in the glass, detecting in that image a likeness to Mr. George Alexander. So he smiled again. And as befits so vacant-minded a young man, he vanishes from this tale after a short and inglorious career. His career he himself regarded in a different fashion.

Lady Ellington went into the drawing-room on her way upstairs. Philip, she knew, since she had passed him fifty yards from the house had gone, and Madge, so it appeared, had gone too. But the tea was still there. For herself, she had already had tea, but she took the trouble to rinse out a cup, pour a little boiling water into it, and proceeded to lay the note face upwards over it. Thorough in every way, she took the precaution of sitting close to the table, ready at any moment to snatch the note away and be discovered sipping hot water—a practice to which she was known to be addicted, and to which she attributed much of her superlative health and freedom from all digestive trouble. How well founded that belief was may be judged from the fact that she digested without qualms of any kind what she was doing now. The good purpose that lurked behind assimilated apparently any meanness. In fact, the good purpose was of the nature of the strongest acid; the meanness ceased to exist—it was absorbed, utterly eaten away.

She was in no hurry, for there was still plenty of time before she need dress, and she waited till the flap of the envelope began to curl back of its own accord as the gum that fastened it was made fluid again by the steam. This happened very soon, because it was not yet really dry. Then, taking precaution against the sheet inside being touched by it, she drew it out and read. The clear, neat handwriting—she had taken great pains with Madge's early tuition in this art—was as intelligible as print, and she only needed to read it through twice before she placed it back again in its envelope, pressed the flap back, and left it to cool and dry. Yet during this very short process her own ideas were also cool and dry, and the reasoning sound and effective. So she put a stamp on the envelope, and went downstairs herself, and dropped it into the letter-box.

That was necessary, since in her note Madge had stated that she would be at the studio at three unless she heard to the contrary. Therefore there was no object to be gained in merely sequestrating the note, since Madge proposed to go there unless stopped. For Lady Ellington knew well that no plan, however well-founded, could be quite certain of success; uncertainty, the possibly adverse action of Fate might work against it, and thus to let this note go—of which she had mastered the contents—was to

105

provoke an accident the less, since, on her present scheme, she had not stopped it. For the fewer dubious things one does on the whole, the less is the risk. It is the unfortunate accident of guilt which in nine cases out of ten hangs a man. So though she had been guilty—in a way—when she wrote to Evelyn, implying Madge's acquiescence in her letter, she had the more excellent reason now, especially since she had completely mastered the contents of this note, in not taking the more questionable step of stopping it. For she knew for certain, and at the moment did not require to know more, the immediate movements of the enemy; if Madge heard nothing, she would go to the studio to-morrow at three. But no one under any circumstances could prevent her mother making her appearance there too.

Again, it is true, some sort of reply might come. But the fact of a reply coming was equivalent to Evelyn's saying that he could not be there at three to-morrow, which rightly she put down as being a negligible contingency. And in this case again, if Lady Ellington could not keep watch over Madge's movements during the next ten days she felt she would be really ashamed of herself. And as she had never been that yet, she saw no reason why she should begin now. She was probably right—the chances were immensely at this moment in favour of her not beginning to be ashamed of herself. For the beginnings of shame are searchings of the heart; Lady Ellington never searched her heart, she only did her best.

The evening passed in perfect harmony; and though she had a good deal to think about, she could yet spare time to be characteristically critical about the play. That was easy, since it was a very bad one, and the deeper consolations of her brain were devoted all the time to certain contingencies. This note had been posted by half-past seven; it would be received that night. Supposing there was a reply to it, it was almost certain that the answer would come at the second morning post, the one that rapped towards the end of breakfast time. If so, and if that reply was received by Madge, she had merely, in the most natural manner possible, to suggest complete occupations for the day, challenging and inquiring into any other engagement. But she did not seriously expect this—no reply was the almost certain rejoinder. In this case, Lady Ellington would be quite unoccupied after lunch.

The ramifications went further. Madge had consented to give Mr. Dundas another sitting after she had declared she would not take the next step. It was better, therefore, to meet guile with guile, and not suggest a suspicion or possibility of it till the last moment. She would go out to lunch to-morrow herself, with regrets to Madge, leaving her free to spend the afternoon as she chose, without asking questions. She herself, however, would leave lunch early, and manage to be at Mr. Dundas's by three o'clock, five minutes before perhaps; it was always well to be on the safe side.

Lady Ellington's applause at the end of the second act was rather absent-minded. Her thoroughness made her examine her own position a little more closely, and there was one point about it which she did not much like, namely, the fact that she had written to Mr. Dundas from

Brockenhurst, implying Madge's concurrence in what she said. It would be rather awkward if any hint of that ever reached Madge; it really would be difficult to explain. Explanation, in fact, was impossible, since there was none. But it followed from this, as a corollary, that he must not see Madge alone; the chances then were enormous of the whole thing coming out. Yet how again would she be able to explain her own presence at Evelyn's house in the King's Road at three o'clock that afternoon? It was childish to say she happened to be passing. Then a solution occurred to her—one which was extraordinarily simple, and extremely probable—Philip had told her that Madge was sitting again. So probable, indeed, was this, that she could, almost without effort, persuade herself that he had done so.

Lady Ellington was happily unconscious at this moment what an extremely tangled web she was weaving, and how impossible it was for her to disentangle it, for not having had the privilege of overhearing Madge's conversation with Philip, she had, by no fault of hers, no idea that he was pledged to secrecy. True, he had not actually mentioned, a thing which he might be expected to have done, the fact that Madge was going to sit again, but no doubt a little well-turned conversation might make him do so. Madge, at the end of the third act, was talking to a neighbour in the stalls, and she herself turned to Philip.

"A stupid act, rather," she said. "Those two laid their plans so badly."

Then, with a sudden sense of the inward humour of her words:

"It isn't enough to open people's letters," she said, "you must hear their conversations too. I should really have made an excellent villain, if I had studied villainy. I should have hidden behind the curtains, and under the tables, and listened at key holes, for the private conversations of other people, and carefully looked in such places, and hung a handkerchief over the key-hole before indulging in any of my own."

Philip laughed.

"Yes, I think you would be thorough in all you did," he said, "and certainly, whatever your line was, I should 'pick you up' first, as schoolboys say, to be on my side."

"Ah! I am certainly on your side," said she. "Now, what have you done with yourself all day? I like to hear always exactly what people have done. A few weeks of what people have done gives you the complete key to their character."

"Is that why you ask?" said he.

"No, because I know your character. I ask merely from interest in you."

"Well, I rode before breakfast," said he, "and got down to the city about half-past ten. I worked till half-past two, dull work rather—but, by-the-bye, hold on to your East Rand Mining, I think they are going better—then I ate three sandwiches and a piece of cake; then I sat to Evelyn for two hours, then I went round to see Madge, dressed, dined, and didn't think much of the play."

"And your portrait?" asked Lady Ellington. "Is it good?"

"Ah! all he does is good," said Philip. "A man like that cannot do a bad thing. But it is more than good. It's Mary Jane's top-note."

107

"I thought Madge was his top-note," said Lady Ellington.

"Well, I think he has gone a semitone higher," said he. "Of course I am the worst person to judge, but it seems to me that he is even more sure in this than he was in her portrait. Haven't you seen it?"

Lady Ellington was quite quick enough to catch at this.

"No, but I should so much like to," she said. "Do you think he would let me see it?"

"I'm sure he would."

Philip paused a moment.

"Send him a note, or I will," he said. "I shouldn't go to-morrow, if I were you, because I know he is busy."

"Ah! what a pity," said Lady Ellington, lowering her voice a little. "I have nothing to do to-morrow afternoon."

"I know he is busy," repeated Philip. "He told me so."

"And Madge's portrait," she said, "when shall we see that? It is quite finished, is it not?"

Suddenly the preposterous idea occurred to Philip that he was being pumped. No doubt it was only Madge's rather ridiculous request that her mother should not know that she was going to sit again that suggested it, but still it was there. On this point also he had given his promise to her, and he went warily in this time of trouble.

"I fancy he is going to work a little more at it," he said, anxious to tell the truth as far as possible. "Indeed, he told me so to-day. But he said that if I sent for it in a couple of days it would be ready for me to take."

It was quite clear, therefore—indeed, the letter that had so providentially come into her hands told her that—that Philip knew that Madge was going to sit again to-morrow. The letter anyhow had told her that she was going to sit again; Philip's suggestion that she herself should not go to see his portrait to-morrow was quite sufficiently confirmatory of the rest. He had not told her, it is true, that Madge was going to do this, but it would answer her purpose well enough. There was only one thing more to ask.

"I think Madge said she would not sit for him again," she observed.

"Yes, I know she did," said he, "because I was the bearer of that message from her. I thought it was a mistake, I remember, at the time."

It was on the tip of Lady Ellington's tongue to say, "And have told her so since," but she remembered how terribly this would fall below her usually felicitous level of scheming. So, as the curtain went up at this moment, she turned her attention to the stage. Had it not gone up, she would have diverted the talk into other channels; the raising of the curtain was not a deliverance to her.

"Let us see what these second-rate schemers make of it all," she said.

The act was played to a tragic end, and Philip helped her on with her cloak.

"No, they committed an initial fault," she said; "they didn't lay their original schemes well enough."

But though the play was a disappointment, she pondered over it all the way home.

ELEVENTH

MADGE lunched alone next day, a thing that seldom happened to her and a thing that was always in a childish way rather a "treat." For in order to counteract the natural tendency of mankind to gobble over the solitary meal, or else to eat nothing at all, it was her custom to bring some book down with her, prop it up against the mustard-pot, and intend, anyhow, to read slowly and to eat slowly. These sensible results seldom happened, since, as a matter of fact, the result was that she read two pages of her book, and then took a dozen rapid mouthfuls. And to-day not even that result was attained, for she read nothing, not even opening the book she had brought down with her, and ate hardly more. For in spite of all that lay before her, the rupture with Philip, his inevitable pain and sorrow, his natural and justified indignation and contempt of her, all of which were scarcely faceable if she faced them only, in spite, too, of all that her mother would feel and no doubt say, in spite of the fear she felt in the face of that, in spite of all that the world in general would say, she was too happy to read, and too happy to eat. For the birthday of her life, she knew, had come: this afternoon, in an hour or two, she would be face to face with the man who loved her, the man she loved, and in front of that tremendous fact, the fact that swallowed up the rest of the world in a gulp, nothing else could really count for anything. Everything else was like minute type of some kind, while in the middle was just the one sentence, in huge, glowing capitals.

Everything had fallen out so conveniently, too: Lady Ellington had told her at breakfast that she was going to be out for lunch, and engaged after lunch, and she did not inquire into Madge's plans at all. She had received no reply to her note to Evelyn, and the very fact that there was none seemed to bring her into more intimate relations with him. Then after lunch she had to change to her white evening dress, over which she put a long dark cloak, her maid arranged her hair, for it was best to go complete, and she took with her, in case of need, the scarlet opera cloak. And all this preparation was so much joy to her, she felt in her very bones that it was while he was looking at her dressed thus that he first knew he loved her, and thus dressed she would come back to him to-day. Above all, the long riddle of these days was solved now; here was the answer, she was the answer.

Yet though all her heart leaped forward, it did not accelerate her actual movements; the four-wheeler also was rather slow, and it was some ten minutes after three when she arrived at the door of the studio in the King's Road. Just beyond it was drawn up a motor-car, beside which stood a footman. As she stepped out of her cab, he went to the door of the motor and opened it. And within a yard or two of her stood her mother.

Instantly all the passion and love in Madge's heart was transformed into mere resolve, for she knew that a struggle, the matching of her will against her mother's lay in front of her. But all the strength of her love was

109

there; it lost nothing of that. Lady Ellington had crossed the pavement more quickly than she, and stood in front of the door.

"Where are you going to, Madge?" she asked.

Madge turned not to her but to the footman, holding out a florin.

"Pay my cab, please," she said.

Then she turned to her mother.

"I have made an appointment to sit to Mr. Dundas this afternoon," she said. "It is absurd for you to tell me that you didn't know that. But I ask you how you knew?"

"Philip told me," said Lady Ellington.

"Philip!" cried Madge. Then she controlled that sudden ebullition, for every fibre within her knew that her incredulity, which only half-believed this, had done him wrong.

So, calming herself, she spoke again.

"I don't believe that," she said.

That was the declaration of war; quiet, tranquil, but final. The point between the two was vital, it reached downwards into the depths of individuality where compromise cannot live, being unable to breathe in so compressed an atmosphere. And Lady Ellington knew that as well as Madge; there was war. She and her daughter stood in unreconcileable camps, diplomacy was dumb, the clash of arms could alone break the silence. She pointed to the motor-car, for the modernity of setting was inevitable, even though primeval passions were pitted against each other.

"It does not make the slightest difference whether you believe it or not," she said quietly. "Get into the motor, as you have sent your cab away."

Madge seemed hardly to hear this.

"Philip never told you," she repeated, "because he promised me he would not."

Lady Ellington judged that it would be mere waste of energy or ammunition to contest this, for it was now immaterial to her campaign. She realised also that she needed all the energy and ammunition that she possessed to enable her to carry out her main movement. She knew, too, that Madge had long been accustomed to obey her mere voice; the instinct of obedience to that was deeply rooted. But how wholly it was uprooted now she did not yet guess.

"Get into the motor, Madge," she said. "Are we to wait all day here?"

Then Madge came a step nearer.

"Yes, that used to frighten me," she said, "but now it does not. And Philip never told you what you said he did. Who was it, then? Nobody else knew."

Again she took one more step closer.

"Mother, have you been tampering with my letters?" she asked. "For how could you have known otherwise? It is ridiculous to say that Philip told you. What else have you done, I wonder? Now, stand away, please, and let me ring the bell. Or do you propose that you and I, you and I, should fight like fishwives on the pavement?"

The old instinctive right of fighting for one's own, obscured by

110

centuries of what is called civilisation, obscured, too, in Madge's own instance by years of obedience, broke out here. She was herself, and nobody else was she. It did not matter one penny-worth who stood between her and the bell; if all the apostles and prophets had stood there she would have fought them all. And Lady Ellington knew that this particular engagement was lost; the bell would be rung. But her plan was not defeated yet, so far as she knew. What she did not know was that mere scheming, mere brain-wrought work on her part, had no chance at all against its adversary. No clever person can understand that until it is enacted under his eyes, and the cleverer he is, the less he will conceive it possible that his spider-weavings can fail to hold their fly. But when passion comes along, it is a bumble-bee that blunders through them all, without knowing that there has been any opposition.

"I certainly do not resemble a fishwife," she said, "nor have I any intention of acting as one. There is the bell—ring it."

Madge looked at her for a moment in wide-eyed astonishment, feeling sure that by some trick—anyhow, something underhand—her mother had got her knowledge.

"And for my mother to do that!" she said.

Lady Ellington may or may not have felt the depth of the well from which this sprang. In any case it was beside her purpose to waste a volley on what was merely rhetorical. And the faint tinkle of the electric bell was the only response.

A maid-servant opened the door.

"Miss Ellington," said Madge, and passed in. But the door was not so open to the other.

"Mr. Dundas said he was at home only to Miss Ellington, ma'am," said she.

"Then kindly tell Mr. Dundas that Lady Ellington has come with her," said she.

The fight was in grim earnest now. Both Madge and her mother were disposed to fight every yard of ground. But the former had some remnant of duty, of compassion left. Horrible to her as had been the scene on the doorstep, convincing as it had been to her of some breach of faith, of honour, on her mother's part, she did not want to expose that.

"Ah! is it wise of you?" she said. "Had you not better go home? You can do no good, mother."

"We will go upstairs," said Lady Ellington.

The studio was at the top of the house, and two landings had to be passed and three staircases surmounted before it was reached. On the second of these Madge had fallen back behind her mother, throwing the dark cloak which she wore on to a chair. The scarlet opera cloak she had on her arm. The maid had preceded them both, and threw the door of the studio open without announcement of names. Lady Ellington entered first, a moment afterwards came Madge, dressed as for the portrait, with the cloak over her arm.

Now Evelyn had been through an emotional crisis not less vital than that of Madge. Indeed, the changes that had passed for him since he had

111

received her note were wider than was anything that had come to her. She had passed only from the uncertainty as to the manner in which he and she would come face to face again; while he had passed from the certainty that all was over to the certainty that all was yet to come. Yet when the door opened and Lady Ellington appeared, he felt as if death on the white horse was there. But a moment afterwards, before he had even time to greet her, came life with the eyes he loved and the face and form that he loved. And he stood there silent a moment, looking from one to the other.

"I learned that my daughter was going to sit to you again, Mr. Dundas," said Lady Ellington, "and I came with her, met her here rather, in order to forbid it. After what you said to her on that day down in the New Forest, it is not conceivable that she should sit to you again. You must have known that. Yet you allowed her to come here, alone, for all you knew. I only ask you if you think that is the act of a gentleman?"

Evelyn flushed.

"When Miss Ellington proposed it, how could I refuse?" he said quickly. "She had decided to trust me, and from the bottom of my heart I thanked her for it, and I should not have been unworthy of her trust. Ever since you wrote to me from Brockenhurst——"

Madge turned to him.

"My mother wrote to you from Brockenhurst?" she asked.

"Yes; surely you knew—you must have known!" he said.

"I had not the smallest idea of it till this minute. What did she say?"

Lady Ellington lost her head a little.

"The letter I wrote you was private," she said; "it was meant only for your eye."

"It concerns me," said Madge, tapping the table with a nervous, unconscious gesture. "I must know."

Evelyn and she looked at each other, and it was as if each caught some light from the other's eyes.

"Yes, that is true," said he. "Lady Ellington forbade me to write or attempt an interview with you, and I gathered that you acquiesced in this. I gathered, as was natural, that you were deeply offended——"

He stopped, for the light that shone in Madge's face was that which was never yet on sea or land, but only on the face of a woman. And Lady Ellington's presence at that moment was to them less than the fly that buzzed in the window-pane, or the swallows that swooped and circled outside in this world of blue and summer. The secret that was breaking out was to them a barrier impenetrable, that cut off the whole world, a ring of fire through which none might pass. Dimly came the sounds of the outer world to them there that which his eyes were learning, that which her eyes were teaching, absorbed them almost to the exclusion of everything else. Lady Ellington, perhaps, had some inkling of that; but she did not yet know how utterly she had lost, and she manned, so to speak, her second line of defence. The first had been lost; she was quick enough to see that at once.

"So since Madge was going to give you this sitting," she said, "it was only reasonable that I should accompany her, to prevent—to prevent," she repeated, with biting emphasis, "a recurrence of what happened when you, Mr. Dundas, last found yourself alone with my daughter."

Then Madge lifted her head a little and smiled, but she still looked at Evelyn.

"Ask how she knew," she said, "that I was going to sit to you. No, it does not matter. I am ready, Mr. Dundas, if you are."

She turned and mounted the platform where she had stood before.

"The cloak, shall I put that on?" she asked. "It is by you there."

Lady Ellington was at length beginning to feel and realise the sense of her own powerlessness; they did not either of them seem to attend to her remarks, which she still felt were extremely to the point.

"You have not done me the favour to answer me, Mr. Dundas," she said.

Evelyn was already moving the easel into position, and he just raised his eyebrows as if some preposterous riddle had been asked him.

"No, I have no answer," he said. "It all seems to me very just. You came here to prevent a repetition of—of what occurred when I was last alone with Miss Ellington. Was not that it?"

Then suddenly Madge laughed; her head a little back, her eyes half-closed, and Evelyn, looking at her, gave a great triumphant explosion of sound.

"That is it—that is what I have been trying for!" he cried. "I never quite got it. But now I can."

He had been painting before they came in, and he picked up the palette and dashed to the canvas.

"Hold that if you can for half a minute!" he cried. "I don't ask for more. Look at me; your eyes have to be on me. Ah, it is a miracle!"

He looked once and painted; he looked and painted again. Then for the third time he looked, and looked long, but he painted no more.

"I have done it," he said.

There was a long pause; he put his palette down again, and looked at Madge, as she stood there.

"Thank you," he said. "That will do."

Then Lady Ellington spoke.

"It was hardly worth my daughter's while to come here for half a minute," she remarked, "or mine either."

Evelyn turned to her; he was conscious of even a sort of pity for her.

"It was not worth your while," he said, "because your presence here makes no difference. When I said your daughter might have trusted me and come here alone, I did not know what I know now. I love her. Madge, do you hear?"

She gave one long sigh, and the scarlet cloak fell to the ground. But she did not move.

"Oh! Evelyn," she said.

Lady Ellington rustled in her chair, as she might have rustled at a situation in a play that interested her. She knew what had happened, but she had not yet fully realised it. But her cool, quick brain very soon grasped it all, and began forging ahead again. There were a hundred obstacles she could yet throw in the way of this calm, advancing force.

113

"And which of you proposes to tell Philip?" she said.

The effect of this was admirable from her point of view. It brought both of the others back to earth again. Evelyn winced as if he had been struck, and Madge came quickly off the platform.

"Philip?" she cried. "Ah, what have we done? What have we said? Philip must never know. We must never tell him. Ah, but next week!"

The one thought that for this last ten minutes had possessed her, had possessed her to the exclusion of everything else. There had been no Philip, no world, no anything except the one inevitable fact. But Lady Ellington's well-timed and perfectly justifiable observation made everything else, all the sorrows and the bitternesses that must come, reel into sight again. But she turned not to her mother, but to Evelyn.

"Oh, poor Philip!" she cried. "He has always been so good, so content. And Mrs. Home—— Evelyn, what is to be done?"

She laid her hand in appeal on his shoulder; he took it and kissed it.

"Leave it all to me," he said. "I will see that he knows."

"And you will tell him I am sorry?" she said. "You will make him understand how sorry I am, but that I could not help it?"

"Ah, my darling!" he cried, and kissed her.

Now, Lady Ellington had seldom in all her busy and fully-occupied life felt helpless, but she felt helpless now, and two young folk, without a plan in their heads while she was bursting with excellent plans, had brought this paralysis on her. She also had very seldom felt angry, but now it would not be too much to say that she felt furious, and her sense of impotence added to her fury. She got out of her chair and took Madge by the shoulder.

"You ought to be whipped, Madge!" she cried.

The girl held out her hand to her.

"Ah, poor mother!" she said. "I had forgotten about you, because I was so happy myself. I am sorry for you, too. It is awful! But what am I to do?"

"You are to come home with me now," she said.

But Madge no longer looked to her for her orders. It was for this cause, after all, that a woman also should leave her father and mother, and her allegiance was already elsewhere.

"No; you had better wait a little," said Evelyn, as her glance appealed to him. "There are things we must talk about at once, things that you and I must settle."

Madge took this; this came from the authentic source.

"I am not coming home yet," she said to her mother.

Then Lady Ellington used unnecessary violence; the door banged behind her. But again her quick, cool brain was right in deciding not to stop, to wrangle, to expostulate, though a woman more stupid than she might have done so. Had she been less wise, she would have made a scene, have talked about the Fifth Commandment, have practically forced Madge, as she could no doubt have done, to come with her. But she was clever enough to see that there was no use in that. The fat was in the fire, so why pretend it was not? She could no doubt delay the actual frizzling for an hour or a day, but where was the use? If anything could still be done, the scene of the operations was not here. But she did not believe that it was all up yet, though here a stupider woman might, perhaps, have arrived at more correct conclusions. She still clung to her plotting, her planning, as if plans ever made even steerage-way against passion. And even for this forlorn hope she had to think, and think hard, whereas, those she had left behind her in the studio did not have to think at all. But her destination, anyhow, was clear enough; she had to go to see Philip. What exactly she should say to him was another question; that had to be thought out while the motor pursued its noiseless, shifting way through the traffic, steering, as a fish steers upstream, avoiding obstacles by a mere turn of the fin, imperceptible to the eye as was the movement of the steerage-wheel.

But as she went, she thought heavily. Her whole plans up till now had broken down completely. A very short survey of the last hour or two was sufficient to convince her of that, and, once convinced, it was contrary to her whole nature to waste a further ounce of thought on them. The flaws there had been in them she momentarily deplored; they might obviously have been better, else they would not have failed, but to deposit even a regret over them was mere misuse of time. They were discarded, as an old fashion is discarded, and the dressmaker who attempts to revive it is a fool. Lady Ellington certainly was not that, and as the motor hummed eastwards towards the City she cast no thought backwards, since this was throwing good brain-power after bad, but forwards. In half an hour she would be with Philip; what was to be her line? But, puzzle as she might, she could find no line that led anywhere, for at the end of each, ready to meet her on the platform, so to speak, stood Evelyn and Madge together.

Lady Ellington was going through quite a series of new sensations this afternoon, and here was one she had scarcely ever felt before—for in addition to her impotence and her anger, she was feeling flurried and frightened. She could not yet quite believe that this crash was inevitable, but it certainly threatened, and threatened in a toppling, imminent manner. And thus all her thinking powers were reduced to mere miserable apprehension.

She had guessed rightly that Philip would still be in the City, and drove straight to his office. He was engaged at the moment, but sent out word that he would see her as soon as he possibly could. Meantime, she was shown into a room for the reception of clients, and left alone there. In the agitation which was gaining on her she had a morbid sensitiveness to tiny impressions, and the trivial details of the room forced themselves in on her. It was a gloomy sort of little well set in the middle of the big room, with its rows of clerks on high stools with busy pens. The morning's paper lay on the table. There was an empty inkstand there also, and a carafe of water with a glass by it. A weighing machine, with no particular reason to justify its existence, stood in one corner; against the wall was an empty book-case. The Turkey carpet was old and faded, and four or five mahogany chairs stood against the wall. Then, after ten minutes of solitary confinement here, the door opened and Philip came in, looking rather grave as was his wont, but strong and self-reliant—the sort of man whom anyone would be glad to have on his side in any emergency or difficulty. One glance at her was sufficient to tell him that something had happened, no little thing, but something serious; and though he had intended to propose that they should go to his room, he shut the door quickly behind him.

"What is it?" he said. "What has happened? Is it—is it anything about Madge?"

"Oh! Philip, it is too dreadful," she began.

Philip drummed on the table with his fingers.

"Just tell me straight, please," he said, quite quietly. "Is she dead?"

Lady Ellington got up and leaned her elbow on the chimney-piece, turning away from him.

"I have just come from Mr. Dundas's studio," she said. "Ah, don't interrupt me," she added, as Philip made a sudden involuntary exclamation—"let me get through with it. I left Madge with him. They have declared their love for each other."

For a moment or two he did not seem to understand what she said, for he frowned as if puzzled, as if she had spoken to him in some tongue he did not know.

"I beg your pardon?" he asked.

Lady Ellington's own most acute feelings of rage, indignation, disappointment, were for the moment altogether subordinated by her pity for this strong man, who had suddenly been dealt this shattering, paralysing blow. If he had raged and stormed, if he had cursed Madge and threatened to shoot Evelyn, she would have felt less sorry for him. But the quietness with which he received it was more pathetic, all strength had gone from him.

"What do you recommend me to do?" he asked, after a pause.

"Ah, that is what I have been trying to puzzle out all the way here," she said. "Surely you can do something? There must be something to be done. You're not going to sit down under this? Don't tell me that! Go to the studio, anyhow—my motor is outside—storm, rage, threaten. Take her away. Tell him to her face what sort of a thing he has done!"

Philip still exhibited the same terrible quietness, unnatural, so Lady Ellington felt it, though she was not mistaken enough to put it down to want of feeling. The feeling, on the other hand, she knew was like some close-fitting, metal frame; it was the very strength and stricture of it that prevented his moving. Then he spoke again.

"And what has he done?" he asked. "He has fallen in love with her. I'm sure I don't wonder. And what has she done? She has fallen in love with him. And I don't wonder at that either."

Now the minutes were passing, and if there was the slightest chance of saving the situation, it had to be taken now. In a few hours even it might easily be too late.

"Just go there," she said. "I know well how this thing has shattered you, so that you can hardly feel it yet; but perhaps the sight of them together may rouse you. Perhaps the sight of you may stir in Madge some sense of her monstrous behaviour. I would sooner she had died on her very

116

wedding-day than that she should have done this. It is indecent. It is, perhaps, too, only a passing fancy, she——"

But here she stopped, for she could not say to him the rest of her thought, which was the expression of the hope that Madge might return to her quiet, genuine liking for Philip. But she need scarcely have been afraid, for in his mind now, almost with the vividness of a hallucination, was that scene on the terrace of the house at Pangbourne, when she had promised him esteem, affection and respect, all, in fact, that she knew were hers to give. But now she had more to give, only she did not give it to him.

"I am bound to do anything you think can be of use," he said, "and, therefore, if you think it can be of use that I should go there, I will go. I do not myself see of what use it can be."

"It may," said Lady Ellington. "There is a chance, what, I can't tell you. But there is certainly no chance any other way."

Then his brain and his heart began to stir and move again a little, the constriction of the paralysis was passing off.

"But if she only takes me out of pity," he said, "I will not take her on those terms. She shall not be my wife if she knows what love is and knows it for another."

Then the true Lady Ellington, the one who had been a little obscured for the last ten minutes by her pity for Philip, came to the light again.

"Ah, take her on any terms," she cried. "It will be all right. She will love you. I am a woman, and I know what women are. No woman has ever yet made the absolute ideal marriage unless she was a fool. Women marry more or less happily; if Madge marries you, she will marry extremely happily. Take my word for that. Now go."

Through the City the tides of traffic were at their height; all down the Strand also there was no break or calm in the surge of vehicles, and the progress of the motor was slow and constantly interrupted. Sometimes for some fifty or a hundred yards there would be clear running, and his thoughts on the possibilities which might exist would shoot ahead also. Then came a slow down, a check, a stop, and he would tell himself that he might spare his pains in going at all. True, before now it had more than once occurred to him as conceivable that Evelyn was falling in love with Madge, but on every occasion when this happened he had whistled the thought home again, telling himself that he had no business to send it out on this sort of errand. That, however, was absolutely all the preparation he had had for this news, and he had to let it soak in, for at first it stood like a puddle after a heavy storm on the surface of his mind. This was an affair of many minutes, but as it went on he began to realise himself the utter hopelessness of this visit which Lady Ellington had recommended. They might both of them, it was possible, when they saw him, recoil from the bitter wrong they were doing, the one to his friend, the other to her accepted lover; but how could that recoil remain permanent, how could their natural human shrinking from this cruelty possibly breed the rejection of each by the other? However much he himself might suffer, though their pity for him was almost infinite, though they might even, to go to the furthest possible point, settle to part,—yet that voluntary

117

separation, if both agreed to it, would but make each the more noble, the more admirable, to the other. Or Madge again alone, in spite of Evelyn, might say she could not go back on her already plighted troth, and express her willingness to marry him. She might go even further, she might say, and indeed feel, that it was only by keeping her word to him that she could free her own self, her own moral nature, from the sin and stain in which she had steeped it. Loyalty, affection, esteem would certainly all draw her to this, but it was impossible that in her eyes, as they looked their last on Evelyn, there should not be regret and longing and desire. Whether he ever saw it there himself or not, Philip must know it had been there, and that at the least the memory of it must always be there.

How little had he foreseen this or anything remotely resembling it on that moonlight night. She promised to give him then all that she was, all that she knew of in herself, and it was with a thrill of love, exquisite and secret, that he had promised himself to teach her what she did not know. It should be he who would wake in her passion and the fire and the flower of her womanhood, and even as he had already given himself and all he was to her, so she, as the fire awoke, should find that precious gift of herself to him daily grow in worth and wonder. It was that, that last and final gift that she had promised now, but not to him. And with that given elsewhere, he felt he would not, or rather could not, take her, even if it was to deliver her soul from hell itself.

Then (and in justice to him it must be said that this lasted only for a little time), what other people would say weighed on him, and what they would say with regard to his conduct now. And for the same minute's pace he almost envied those myriad many to whom nothing happens, who know nothing of the extremes of joy, such as he had felt, or the extremes of utter abandonment and despair, such as were his now. Assuredly, in the world's view, it was now in his power to do something to right himself, to make himself appear, anyhow, what is called a man of spirit; he could curse her, he could strike him; he could make some explosion or threaten it, which would be hard for either of the two others to face. Madge had sat to Evelyn alone, she had often done that, Evelyn was a friend of his; and here he could blast him, he could make him appear such that the world in general would surely decline the pleasure of his acquaintance. Madge again, if he was minded on vengeance, how execrable, how rightly execrable, he could make her conduct appear. There was no end to the damage, reckoning damage by the opinion of the world, that he could do to both of them. All this he could easily do; the bakemeats for the marriage-table were, so to speak, already hot—they could so naturally furnish the funeral-feast, as far as the world was concerned, of either Evelyn or Madge. The whole thing was indecent.

Step by step, punctuated to the innumerable halts of the motor-car, the idea gained on him. Between them there had been made an attempt to wreck him; wreck he was, yet his wreck might be the derelict in the ocean on which their own pleasure-bark would founder. At that moment the desire for vengeance struck him with hot, fiery buffet, but, as it were, concealed its face the while, so that he should not recognise it was the lust

118

for vengeance that had thus scorched him, and, indeed, it appeared to him that he only demanded justice, the barest, simplest justice, such as a criminal never demands in vain. It was no more than right that Evelyn should reap the natural, inevitable harvest of what he had done, and since Madge had joined herself to him, it must be to her home also that he should bring back the bitter sheaves. Indeed, should Philip himself have mercy, should he at any rate keep his hand from any deed and his tongue from any word that could hurt them, yet that would not prevent the consequences reaching them, for the world assuredly would not treat them tenderly, and would only label him spiritless for so doing. For the world, to tell the truth, is not, in spite of its twenty centuries of Christianity, altogether kind yet, and when buffeted on one cheek does not as a rule turn the other. More especially is this so when one of its social safeguards is threatened; it does not immediately surrender and invite the enemy to enter the next fort. And the jilt—which Madge assuredly was, though perhaps to jilt him was akin to a finer morality than to go through with her arranged marriage—is an enemy of Society. Male or female, the jilt, like the person who cheats at cards, will not do; to such people it is impossible to be kind, for they have transgressed one of Society's precious little maxims, that you really must not do these things, because they lead to so much worry and discomfort. Wedding-presents have to be sent back, arrangements innumerable have to be countermanded, subjects have to be avoided in the presence of the injured parties.

It was the unworthier Philip, as he drove to Chelsea, who let these thoughts find harbourage in his mind. But somewhere deep down in his inner consciousness, he knew that there was something finer to be done, something that the world would deride and laugh at, if he did it. How much better he knew to disregard that, and to be big; to go there, to say that his own engagement to Madge was based on a mistake, a misconception, to accept what had happened, to tell them, as some inner and nobler fibre of his soul told him, that his own personal sorrow weighed nothing as compared with the more essential justice of two who loved each other being absolutely free, however much external circumstances retarded, to marry. He was capable even in this early smart of conceiving that; was he capable of acting up to it?

He was but twenty doors from the studio in King's Road when the finer way became definite in his mind, and he called to the chauffeur to stop, for he literally did not know if he could do this. But he realised that otherwise his visit would be better left unpaid; there was no good in his going there, if he was to do anything else than this. Then he got out of the car.

"You can go home," he said to the chauffeur.

The man touched his cap in acknowledgment of the tip that Philip gave him, waited for a lull in the traffic, and turned. Philip was left alone on the pavement, looking after the yellow-panelled carriage.

Then he turned round quickly; his mind was already made up; he would go there, he would act as all that was truly best in him dictated. But as he hesitated, looking back, two figures had come close to him from a door near, hailing a hansom. When he turned they were close to him.

His eyes blazed suddenly with a hard, angry light; his mouth trembled, the sight of them together roused in him the full sense of the injury he had suffered.

"Ah, there you are!" he cried. "I curse you both; I pray that the misery you have brought on me may return double-fold to you!"

Evelyn had drawn back a step, putting his arm out to shelter Madge, for it seemed as if Philip would strike her. But the next moment he turned on his heel again, and walked away from them.

TWELFTH

MRS. HOME was walking gently up and down the terrace in front of the drawing-room windows at her son's house above Pangbourne. The deep heat of the July afternoon lay heavily on river and land and sky, for the last fortnight, even in the country, had been of scorching sort, and the great thunderstorm which, ten days ago, had been as violent here as in the New Forest, had not sensibly relieved the air. Philip had not been down for nearly a month, and his mother, though she knew nothing about gardening (her ideal of a garden-bed was a row of lobelias, backed by a row of calceolarias, backed by a row of scarlet geraniums), felt vaguely that though she did not at all understand the sort of thing Philip wanted, he would be disappointed about the present result. For to-day she had received a telegram from him—he telegraphed the most iniquitously lengthy and unnecessary communication—saying that he would arrive that evening. Surely a postcard even the day before would have conveyed as much as this telegram, which told her that he was coming down alone, that he wished a reply if anyone was staying with her, and, if so, who, that he was leaving Madge in London, and that Evelyn, who had proposed himself for this last Saturday till Monday in July, was not coming. Also—this was all in the telegram for which a postcard the day before could have done duty—Gladys Ellington and her husband, who were to have spent the three days with them, were unable to come, and he supposed, therefore, that his mother and he would be alone. The little party, in fact, that had been arranged would not take place; he himself would come down there as expected, but nobody else.

To Mrs. Home this was all glad news of a secret kind. She had seen so little of Philip lately, and to her mother's heart it was a warming thing to know that he was to spend the last Sunday of his bachelor life with her, and with nobody else. To say that she had been hurt at his wishing the family into which he was to marry being present on these last days before he definitely left his mother to cleave to his wife would be grossly misinterpreting her feeling; only she was herself glad that she would have him alone just once more. For the two had been not only mother and son, but the most intimate of friends; none had held so close a place to him, and now that Mrs. Home felt, rightly enough, that henceforward she must inevitably stand second in his confidence, she was, selfishly she was afraid but quite indubitably, delighted to know that they were to have one more little time quite alone. All that was to be said between them had already been said, she had for herself no last words, and felt sure that Philip had not either, and she rehearsed in her mind the quiet, ordinary little occupations that should make the days pass so pleasantly, as they had always passed when they two were alone together. Philip would get down by tea-time on Saturday, and was sure to spend a couple of hours in the garden or on the river. Then would follow dinner out on the terrace if this heat continued, and after dinner she would probably play Patience, while Philip watched her as he smoked from a chair beside her observing with vigilant eye any attempt to cheat on her part. Mrs. Home's appetite for cards was indeed somewhat minute, and if after twenty minutes or so Miss Milligan, unlike a growing girl, showed no signs of "coming out," she would, it must be confessed, enable her to do so by means not strictly legitimate. Sometimes one such evasion on her part would pass unnoticed by Philip, which encouraged her, if the laws of chance or her own want of skill still opposed the desired consummation, to cheat again. But this second attempt was scarcely ever successful, she was almost always found out, and Philip demanded a truthful statement as to whether a similar lamentable indiscretion had occurred before. When they were alone, too, Philip always read prayers in the evening, some short piece of the Bible, followed by a few collects. This little ceremony somehow was more intimately woven in with Mrs. Home's conception of "Philip" than anything else. It must be feared, indeed, that the dear little old lady did not pay very much attention either to the chapter he read or the prayers he said, but "Philip reading Prayers" was a very precious and a very integral part of her life. His strong, deep voice, his strong, handsome face vividly illuminated by the lamp he would put close to him, the row of silent servants, the general sense of good and comforting words, if comfort was needed, words, anyhow, that were charged with protection and love, all these things were a very real part of that biggest thing in her life, namely, that she was his mother, and he her son. Her son, bone of her bone, and born of her body, and how dear even he did not guess.

Sunday took up the tale that was so sweet to her. He would be late for breakfast, as he always was, and very likely she would have finished before he came down. But she never missed hearing his foot on the polished boards of the hall, and if he was very late she would have rung for a fresh teapot before he entered the room, since she had a horror, only equalled by her horror of snakes, of tea that had stood long. Often he was so late that his breakfast really had to be curtailed if they were to get to church before the service began, for they always walked there, and her mind was sometimes painfully divided as to whether it would not be better to be late rather than that he should have an insufficient breakfast. She had

121

heard great things of Plasmon, and a year ago had secretly bought a small tin of that highly nutritious though perhaps slightly insipid powder, of which she meant to urge a tablespoonful on Philip if he seemed to her not to have had enough to eat before he started for church, since apparently this would be the equivalent of several mutton chops. But the tin had remained unopened, and only a few weeks ago she had thrown it away, having read some case of tinned-food poisoning in the papers. How dreadful if she meant to give him the equivalent of several mutton chops, and had succeeded only in supplying him with a fatal dose of ptomaine!

Then after the walk back through the pleasant fields there would be lunch, and after lunch in this July heat, long lounging in some sheltered spot in the garden. Tea followed, and after tea Philip's invariable refusal to go to church again, and her own invariable yielding to his wish that she should not go either. That again was an old-established affair, uninteresting and unessential no doubt to those who drive four-in-hand through life, but to this quiet old lady, whose nature had grown so fine through long years of speckless life, a part of herself. He would urge the most absurd reasons; she would be going alone, and would probably be waylaid and robbed for the sake of her red-and-gold Church-service; it threatened rain, and she would catch the most dreadful rheumatism; or life was uncertain at the best, and this might easily be the last Sunday that he would spend here, and how when she had buried him about Wednesday would she like the thought that she had refused his ultimate request? This last appeal was generally successful, and it was left for Mrs. Home to explain to their vicar, who always dined with them on Sunday, her unusual absence. This she did very badly, and Philip never helped her out. It was a point of honour that she should not say that it was he who had induced her to stay away, and his grave face watching her from the other side of the table as she invented the most futile of excuses, seemed to her to add insult to the injury he had already done her in obliging her to invent what would not have deceived a sucking child.

Then on Monday morning he would generally have to leave for town very early, but if this was the case, he always came to her room to wish her good-bye. And her good-bye to him meant what it said. "God be with you, my dear," was it, and she added always, "Come again as soon as you can."

All these things, the memory of those days and hours which were so inexpressibly dear to her, moved gently and evenly in Mrs. Home's mind, even as the shadows drew steadily and slowly across the grass as she walked up and down awaiting his arrival. And if sadness was there at all, it was only the wonderful and beautiful sadness that pervaded the evening hour itself, the hour when shadows lengthen, and the coolness of the sunset tells us that the day, the serene and sunlit day, is drawing to a close. That the day should end was inevitable; the preciousness of sunlit hours was valued because night would follow them, for had they been known to be everlasting, the joy of plucking their sweetness would have vanished. And the same shadowed thought was present in Mrs. Home's mind as she thought how the evening of her particular relationship to Philip was come; all these memories, though dear they would always be, gathered a greater fragrance because in the nature of things they must be temporary and transitory, even as the memory of childish days is dear simply because one is a child no longer. While childhood remained they were uncoloured by romance, the romance the halo of them only begins to glow when it is known that they are soon to be at an end.

Yet Mrs. Home would not have had anything different; that her relation to Philip must fade as the day-star in the light of dawn, she had always known. Even when the day-star was very bright and the dawn not yet hinted in Eastern skies, she knew that, and now when the whole East was suffused with the rosy glow, she would not have delayed the upleap of the resplendent sun by an hour or a minute. For old-age unembittered was her's, and in the completeness and fulness of Philip's manhood, not in keeping him undeveloped and unstung by the sunlight, though through it was flung bitter foam of the sea that breaks forever round this life of man, she realised not herself only but him most fully and best. She would not retain him, even if she could; he had got to live his life, and make it as round and perfect as it could be made. It was her part only to watch from the shore as he put out into the breakers, and wish him God-speed. Yet now, as far as she could forecast, no breakers were there, a calm sunny ocean awaited him; there was but the tide which would bear him smoothly out. How far he would go, whether out of sight of the land, where she strained dim eyes after him, or whether, so to speak, he should anchor close to her, she did not know. He had now to put out; once more they—he and she alone—would play together on the sands, but each would know— he very much more than she, that they played together for the last time. After this he must, as he ought, take another for his playmate. And if at the thought her kind blue eyes were a little dim, it was the flesh only that was weak. With all her soul she bade him push out, and if to herself she said: "Oh, Philip! must you go?" all in herself that she wished to be reckoned by, all that was truly herself, said "God-speed" to him.

The gardeners at Pangbourne Court had been startled into dreadful activity that day. "The master," it was known, would be down for this Sunday, but "the master" by himself was a much more formidable affair than he with a party. As Philip had conjectured at Whitsuntide, there would come a break in the happy life of the garden, and it was quite indubitably here now. The hot and early summer which had produced so glorious an array of blossom in that June week now exacted payment for that; roses which should have flowered into August had exhausted themselves, the blooms of summer were really over, while the autumn plants were still immature. All this was really not the fault of the gardeners, but of the weather; but, as has been said, they were stirred into immense activity by the prospect of Philip's arrival, since if the beds presented a fair show, he would be more likely to be lenient to other deficiencies. But Mrs. Home, as she went up and down the paths waiting for his arrival, saw but too clearly that things were not quite as they should be. A dryness, an arrest of growth, seemed to have laid hands on the beds; it was as if some catastrophe had stricken the vegetable kingdoms that withered and blighted them. The grass of the lawn, too, lacked the vividness of the velvet that so delighted Philip's London-wearied eye—there were patches of brown and withered green everywhere, instead of the "excellent emerald." Yet, perhaps, surely almost, he would not vex himself with that. Three days only intervened between now and the twenty-eighth; he would have no fault to find with anything in the sunlight of life which so streamed on him.

She was passing between two old hedges of yew, compact and thick of growth as a brick wall, and impervious to the vision. Her own path lay over the grass, but on either far side of these hedges was a gravel walk, and half-way up this she heard a footstep sounding crisply. For one moment she thought it was Philip's, and nearly called to him, the next she smiled at herself for having thought so, for it altogether lacked the brisk decision with which he walked, and she made sure it was one of the gardeners. It went parallel with her, however, in the same direction, and when she got to the end of her own yew-girt avenue, she met the owner of the footstep in the little sunk Alpine garden, which was Philip's especial delight. It was he. She had not recognised the footstep, and though when they met, her eyes told her that this certainly was her son, it was someone so different from him whom she knew that she scarcely recognised him.

Misery sat in his face, misery and a hardness as of iron. He often looked stern, often looked tired, but now it seemed as if it was of life that he was tired, and his whole face was inflexible and inexorable. It was not the sort of misery that could break down and sob itself into acquiescence, it was the misery of the soul into which the iron has entered. And mother and son looked at each other long without speaking, he with that face and soul of iron, she with a hundred terrors winnowing her. He had not given her any greeting, nor she him. Then she clasped her hands together in speechless entreaty, and held them out to him. But still he said nothing, and it was she who spoke first.

"Philip, what is it?" she said. "Whatever it is, tell me quickly, my dear. I can bear to know anything. I cannot bear not to."

He looked away from her for a moment, striking the gravel with his stick.

"Madge?" said Mrs. Home. "Is she dead?"

Yet even as she spoke she knew it was not that. That, even that, would not have made Philip like this. He would have come to her to be comforted; it was not comfort that he asked for.

"No, she is not dead," he said. "I wish she was. She has betrayed me and thrown me over. She is probably by this time married to Evelyn Dundas!"

He paused a moment.

"That is what has happened," he said; "and, here to you and now, mother, I curse them both. I met them together yesterday, I cursed them to their faces. There is nothing I will not do that can damage them in any way. I will ruin him if I can, and I will wait long for my vengeance if need be. I tried to forgive them, I tried to go to the house and tell them so, but I could not. I don't forgive them, and if for that reason God does not forgive me what I have done amiss, I don't care. I would forgive them if I could; I

124

can't. If that is wrong I can't help it. It is better you should know this at once. I am sorry if it hurts you, but there is no manner of use in my trying to 'break it' to you, as they call it. Break it! It is I who am broken!"

Then all the tenderness of maternity, all the years of love between her and Philip, the complete confidence which had forged so strong and golden a chain between them, rose in Mrs. Home's mind and sent to her lips the only answer she could make. Sorrow for him, sympathy with him, of course he took for granted; there was no need to speak of things like these.

"Ah, dear Philip, unsay that, unsay that!" she cried. "Whatever happens to one, it is impossible that you should feel that!"

He looked at her with the same glooming face.

"I don't unsay it," he said, "I don't unsay one single word of it. In proportion as both of them were dear to me, so is that which has happened detestable to me. I don't want to talk about it—there is no use in that. I have got to begin my life again; that is what it comes to, and I have to begin it on a basis of hate and utter distrust. Two people who were the friends of my heart, people whom I could have trusted, so I should have thought, to the uttermost verge of eternity, have done this."

Then all his bitterness, and there was much of that, all his resentment and anger, all his love gone sour, rose in his throat.

"For what guarantee have I now," he cried, "that everyone else whom I trusted will not behave to me like that? You, mother, you, what plans and plots may you not have got against me? It is all very well to say that you cannot, that you are my friend. But what is my experience of friends? They are those who know one best, and can thus stab most deeply. God defend me from my friends—I would sooner shake hands with my enemies. Ah! I forgive them, for I might know that they were enemies; but, fool that I was, I never guessed that my friends were but enemies who sat at my table. They ate my food—I wish it had choked them; they drank my wine again and again—I wish I had poisoned it. For they have poisoned me, they have made my life impossible. Ah, don't say I shall get over it! That is silly. How can I get over it? For if I could, I should not say these things to you. I should be silent, I hope, and trust to what is called the healing hand of Time. But there are certain things Time never heals. One of them is the infidelity of those whom one thought were friends."

He was speaking quickly now, the bile of bitterness overflowed.

"Friends!" he said. "Madge and Evelyn and I were friends. But they two have done this accursed thing. And if I have another friend in this world, I shall now expect him to believe the chance word of any lying tongue. Apart from you, I have one friend left, and if Tom Merivale told me to-morrow that I had cheated at cards, and that in consequence he declined the pleasure of my further acquaintance, I should not be surprised. I believe nothing good of my friends, and I believe less harm of my enemies! They, anyhow, can hurt me less. I have had but four friends in my life, and yet even with four, fool that I was, I counted myself rich in them. Two have gone, and there are just two people in this world whom I hate. Till yesterday there were none."

125

Mrs. Home laid her hand timidly on his arm.

"Philip, dear Philip," she said, "is there any good in saying these things? Does it help in any way what has happened, or does it help you?"

"No, it does no good," said he. "I don't want to do any good. I just choose to say what I am saying, and what I say, I assure you, is no exaggeration of what I feel—it does not even do justice to what I feel. One thing I have misstated, or it was but a mood of the moment. I said I was broken; I am nothing of the sort. I never did a better day's work than to-day. But I don't want to say these things again, and I have no intention of doing so. I beg you also never to refer to them. But I choose just this once to say what my feeling towards them is. I tried, indeed I tried my best, to forgive them, but I can't. I can no more now conceive forgiving them than a blind man can conceive the colour of that rose. I loved them both, and in proportion as my love for them was strong, so is my hate for them."

He paused a moment.

"That is all," he said. "I wanted you to know that, and to be under no misconception as to what I felt. Let us never talk of either of them again. I have already given all necessary orders in London, and all I have to do here is to send back all wedding presents. I will do that to-night."

He looked at her a moment as she stood there with hands that trembled and eyes that were dim, pitying him to the bottom of her kind, loving soul, but imploring him, so he felt, not to be like this. And the pity reached and touched him, though the entreaty did not.

"Poor mother," he said. "I am sorry for you, indeed I am that. We have not kissed yet, or shaken hands."

But Mrs. Home, gentle and loving and pitiful as she was, could not do quite as he asked, though her hands and her lips yearned for him.

"No, Philip," she said; "but with whom do I shake hands, and whom do I kiss? You, the Philip who is my son, or the man who has said this? Indeed, dear, I know you well, and it is not you who have spoken."

He looked at her steadily.

"Yes, it is I who have spoken," he said. "This is now your son, the man who has said these things. Do you cast me off, too?"

Unfair, unjust as the words were, she felt no pang of resentment with him, telling herself that he was not himself. And, whatever he was, her relationship to him, she knew, could never be altered. If he was lying in the condemned cell for some brutal murder, whatever he had done or been could never make any difference to that. He knew that, too, his best self knew it, and it was to his best self she spoke.

"You know I can never cast you off," she said, "and those were wild words but they are unsaid. Here is my hand, my darling, and here are my lips. You want me also never to say any more about it. I will not; but I must say this about you—that you will not always feel like this. I know you will not. And when the change comes, tell me. You cannot take that belief away from me."

He kissed her, holding both her hands in his, but his face did not relax.

"Poor mother!" he said again.

126

They walked back towards the house together, down the grassy walk between the yew hedges, where Mrs. Home had first heard his footstep, and Philip, according to contract, began at once to speak of other things. Dismal though this was, it was still perhaps better than silence; whatever had happened, the present was with them, and the present had to be lived through; ordinary human intercourse had got to be continued. Whether in the immediate future he would go abroad, and try by the conventional prescription of travelling to find, if not relief, at any rate the sense of unreality that travelling and change sometimes give, he had not yet determined, though the idea had occurred to him. He was still really incapable of making plans at all, he could not yet face the future, but, so far as he had considered it, he was not disposed to think that he would try it. For idleness to a man accustomed to lead a very busy life, a life, too, which every day demands concentration of thought and decisiveness of action, is in itself irksome, even though the panorama of foreign lands and skies is drawn by before him. To such a mind, even when it is at peace with itself, a holiday is generally only a means of recuperation, and the recuperation effected, such a man frets to be at work again, and to him now, with this dreadful background always with him, the idea of travel appealed very little. He would be better, so he thought, back at work, and the harder and more continuously he worked, the less intolerable, perhaps, would be the burden which he carried about with him. Truly, we make our own heaven and hell, and since the kingdom of God is within us, so also within us are the flames of the nethermost pit.

But in those three minutes as they went back again to the house, Mrs. Home made her resolve. Whatever it cost her, and however difficult each minute might be, however much she might long herself to go and weep, or better still, to weep with him, she would do her very best to act as he had wished, and never in thought or word dwell on the past. A tragedy had happened; but it was necessary to go on, to begin life again, not to sit and bewail; nothing was ever cured, so she told herself, by thinking of what might have been avoided, if things had been different. But things were this way and not otherwise, and that which had not been avoided had already become part of the imperishable past, the hours of which are, indeed, reckoned up, but do not perish, since it is of them that the present is made.

She left him after this to go round the garden; he had already sent for the head-gardener, who was waiting as bidden at the front door, in some trepidation of mind. Mrs. Home hated to have to scold and find fault, she hated also that Philip should do it, and she went indoors instead of accompanying him. There was no sweeter and kinder soul in this world than she, and even now, when her heart bled for her son, no vindictiveness or desire for revenge on those who had made him suffer so had place in her mind. But forgiveness could not be there yet, and it was the most she could do to resolve not to think about either Madge or Evelyn. Philip's sorrow and what faint consolation or palliation she could bring to that was enough to fill her thoughts; the authors of his sorrow she wished as far as was humanly possible to root out from her mind altogether. Resentment would do no good to anybody and only hurt herself, and since she knew that she could not wholly forgive, since there was no sign of sorrow or regret on their parts, the best thing she could cultivate in their regard was oblivion.

She went, therefore, first to the smoking-room, where there hung the little water-colour sketch that Evelyn had once made of her; a photograph of him also stood there, and this she took with her also. The frames were her own, but she took the pictures out of each. Then, going to her bedroom, she unlocked her jewel-case and took from it the pearl brooch he had given her. No anger was in her mind; and even as she handled those dear and familiar things, she detached it from what she was doing. Then making a packet of them, she sealed and directed it to him. There was no need that any word of hers should go with it; indeed, there was no word she could say to him.

But though she had resolved not to think about either of them, that was one of those resolutions which in the very nature of things cannot be kept, and afterwards when this business of returning his gifts was over, and she sat down with her piece of needlework, she could not keep her mind off them. But now, so far from vindictiveness being there, it was rather pity, pity deep and sincere, that filled it. Terrible though the practical result had been, bitter and deadly as was the blow dealt at the man whom she loved better than anyone else in the world, what other course had been open? Madge and Evelyn had found they loved each other, and that being so, how infinitely more wretched must any attempt to disregard or stifle that have proved! The thought of the girl as Philip's wife secretly loving another was a situation which she knew well was far more terrible than this, far more rotten, far more insecure. There the foundation of their lives would be founded on a lie, their house would be built over a volcano which might break out and overwhelm with fire and burning the fabric that was reared upon it. At the best, what happiness could there be in it, and how could it be a home in any true sense? And since they two loved, what essential good was served by their waiting to join themselves together? Convention certainly would be shocked at the suddenness of it all, but Mrs. Home found as she thought about it that she, personally, was not. For what was Madge to do? Go home and continue to live with her mother? She herself knew Lady Ellington fairly well, and she knew that no girl could possibly stand it.

So her resolve not to think about them at all had ended in this, that she thought about them with only pity for what in the inscrutable decrees of God had, so to speak, been forced on them. That necessity she deplored with all her heart, for it was pierced as it had never been pierced before with sorrow for her son, but even in these early hours of her knowledge of the tragedy, she could not blame them. Then, half-ashamed of her infirmity of purpose, she went quietly to the post-box, and took out the package she had just done up, and instead of sending it, locked it up.

She did not see Philip again till dinner-time, and then this ghastly game of make-believe that nothing was wrong began again. She saw well what he felt, that as no words could possibly ameliorate the situation, it was best that no words should pass concerning it, and she guessed also with a woman's intuition that drops unerringly on to the right place, even as a bird drops on to a twig, that any expression of pity or sympathy were, above all, what he could not stand. He could bear no hand, however gentle, to touch the wound, but winced at even the thought of it. So they spoke just of all those things except one, which they would naturally have spoken about, and they said the same things on such subjects as they would naturally have said. The drought, the Japanese war, the irritating particles of dust from wood-pavements, all the topics of the day were there, and there were no silences, not even any racking of the brain on the part of either to think what should be said next. That dreadful mechanical engine of habit was in full work, and just as Philip would have maintained normality though the City was in a depressed and depressing state, and just as Mrs. Home would have been quite herself to her guests though some below-stairs crisis was most critical between domestics, so now when the crisis was such that nothing could have touched her more keenly, it was easy, but dismal, to maintain the ordinary forms of life. Servants certainly, that relentless barometer of local disturbances, saw nothing that night which indicated trouble; no storm-cone was hoisted, the gardeners, too, had come off lightly, and Mr. Philip was pronounced to be at the utmost "rather silent about next week's occurrences." That was the phrase of "the room," which crystallised any vague or fluid speech that might find utterance. "Just a little silent"—so well the prime actors in the dining-room played their parts.

Yet yearning was on one side, the yearning of the mother for the break-down—for it was that it amounted to—of the son, and on the son's side was a harshness which the mother could not yet believe existed. But his implacable speeches had been soberly and literally true, and the strength of his hate was proportionate to what the strength of his love had been. There was no denying the genuineness of that dreadful alchemy; love in a hard nature indeed may undergo that terrible transformation, whereas liking can scarcely be transmuted into anything more deadly than dislike, while it is most hard of all for mere indifference to struggle into the ranks of the more potent lords of the human soul. It is a matter of indifference or at most of reprisal, what are the doings of those who are indifferent to one. Action for damages may ensue, but hate still slumbers in its cave. But it is when those whom a man loves hurt him that the hurt festers and spreads poison through the soul. Indeed, it is only those whom such a man loves who have power to hurt him at all.

After dinner, too, the daily round was continued in all its dismal unreality. Philip even asked, an old and quite uninteresting joke, whether he might smoke in the drawing-room, and on Mrs. Home's saying "No!" threatened to go to the stables. It was never a good joke, or, indeed, anything approaching it, but to-night it came near to move tears on the poor lady's part, for it was like speaking of the odd little ways of some loved one who is dead. Then, again, in the drawing-room the table for cards was placed out, with decorous wax candles burning at the corners, and Mrs. Home sat in her usual seat, and as usual Philip drew a chair sideways near her, so that he could watch without seeming to watch. And his mother announced Miss Milligan, with the usual futile determination

129

not to cheat. So in silence Miss Milligan pursued her abhorred way; and during that silence the tears, the break-down inevitable for all her brave resolves, came close to the surface. Mrs. Home already could not speak, she had to clench her teeth to prevent the sobs coming. Then at last there came a hitch, she cheated, and Philip saw it.

"Black nine," he said; "not red nine."

Mrs. Home's hands were already trembling, and at this they failed, and the cards were scattered over the table.

"Oh, Philip!" she cried, "I can't bear it, I can't bear it. Oh, my darling! put your head on my lap as you used to do when you were a little boy and in trouble, and let me see if I cannot comfort you."

She looked up at him with tear-dimmed eyes, and not till then did she fully know how deep the iron had gone. Not a sign of relenting or softening was there. He got up and spoke in a perfectly hard, dry voice.

"Not one atom can you comfort me," he said. "We have both to bear what has to be borne, and as I have said, it is better to bear in silence. I think now I had better go; I have those matters to arrange to-night which I spoke to you of. Perhaps you would tell the servants that—that everything will go on just as usual here."

Mrs. Home saw the hopelessness of further appeal just now.

"Yes, dear, go and do what you have to," she said. "I will tell them. Will you come back to read prayers, Philip?"

"No," said he.

Then he bent and kissed her, and as he held her hands the first faint sign in the trembling of his lip showed that for her, at any rate, he was not all adamant.

"I am not sorry for myself," he said, "but I am sorry for you, dear mother, that you cannot possibly help me. Breakfast as usual to-morrow? Good night."

THIRTEENTH

BY Monday morning when he returned to town, Philip had quite made up his mind that all thought of travel by way of distraction was futile, and had determined to find in work, the hardest and most continuous, a succession of hours of forgetfulness, so far as he could secure it, of this blow that had fallen on him. Forgetfulness itself, he knew well he could not hope to secure, but by hard application of the brain to work, he hoped that for this hour and for that he would be able to put that which had so stricken and embittered him on a second and more remote plane of consciousness. True, at any relaxation, at any interval in which his brain was not actively employed, it would start out again like the writing on the wall; but for the working hours of the day, and these he determined should be long and fully filled, he believed he could to some extent crush the other out of his consciousness. In work, at any rate, he believed his best chance lay, and the attempt, though perhaps desperate, was one which none but a strong man could have made.

He occupied at present while in London a flat in Jermyn Street, modest in dimensions, but containing all he wanted. There was a spare room there which his mother always used on her rather rare visits to town, but otherwise it held only the necessary accommodation for two servants and himself. He had already given his landlord notice that he was going to quit, but to-day he went to the estate office to ask if he could renew his tenancy since his bachelor days were not yet over. All this was horribly uncomfortable; he felt that the clerk in the office knew what had happened, and would, after his departure, talk it and him over with the other clerks, and though their criticism and comments could not possibly matter to him, he felt that some deformity, some malformation or scar of his own body was being publicly shown the world, and he hated the world for looking at it. Then also he had to say that he should not require the house for which he was in contract in Berkeley Square, to complete which nothing really remained except the signing of the lease. It was all a business so unexpectedly disagreeable that he wished he had conducted it by letter.

To-day promised to be very busy; he was to have dined that night with Lady Ellington, but that engagement was automatically cancelled, and he left word at his flat that he would be there that night, and would dine alone. That done, he drove straight down to the City, where he expected that there would be awaiting him a report of an agent of his with regard to certain South African mining properties on which he held an extremely large option which he must take up before the end of the week, when it expired. He had not been able to make his mind up about it hitherto, and had wired for the report, putting off his decision until the last possible minute.

The report in question had arrived, and, without further delay, he proceeded to master it. The problems it contained were of a complicated order; the dip and depth of the reef, the assay value of it, the cost of working, the reduction which might be obtained in this by the use of Chinese labour, all these were things which had to be considered. Should he not exercise his option, the right, that is, of buying his shares at the figure agreed on, he would lose, of course, what he had spent in purchasing that right. It was by a careful study of this rather voluminous report on the property that he had to make up his mind whether he would exercise it or not.

Now the problems of finance, that extraordinary and ubiquitous game in which the most acute brains in the world are pitted against each other for the acquisition of those little yellow metal counters, which in this present world are so undeniably potent to procure for their owner a comfortable journey through it, had at all times an immense attraction for Philip, and he found that even to-day they were no less absorbing than they had ever been. He found, too, that, in spite of the frightful shock that he had undergone, his reasoning and deductive faculties had not been shaken or dulled, and he felt himself as capable as ever of weighing the evidence which should decide his course. The report itself was fairly satisfactory, and he was inclined to believe that the shares which he could call up were worth the price, which to-day stood steady at the figure which he would have to pay for them. His money, which ran into six figures, would perhaps be locked up for a time, but he did not particularly object to that. On the other hand, supposing he bought, the effect on the market would certainly be to send the value of the shares up, so that he could probably, if he wished, clear out again, realising a small profit. This was all plain sailing enough; the report was good enough to justify his exercising his option. But the market altogether, as he well knew, was, in consequence of the Russo-Japanese war, in a rather excitable and nervous state, and the more difficult problem must claim his attention—what would be the effect on it if he did not buy? It was known, of course, that his option was a considerable one, and dealers in these shares were awaiting any news as to his movements with some anxiety.

The report had fallen rustling to the ground, and Philip sat there staring in front of him, with his elbows on the table and eyes fixed intently on nothing. Every now and then some clerk came in with a paper for his signature, or a letter for his consideration; every now and then he was rung up on the telephone that stood by his elbow. But he had that rarest of gifts, a mind that can detach itself from one thing and attach itself in its entirety to another, and he gave his whole attention to these interruptions when they occurred, and transferred it all back to the problem he was digging at when he had dealt with them. The way he pursued was narrow and winding, but step by step he traced it out.

It took him not less than an hour of hard thinking to make up his mind definitely on the point: there were so many things to consider, for, as he always held, there was hardly an event that took place in the world which did not have its definite and certain effect on the money-market; and the sole and only office of the financier was to be able, on the basis of what had happened before, to conjecture what was going to happen now (for things followed an invariable rule), and estimate what the effect of his conjectured events would be. And nothing in the world was more engrossing than that; there was no bit of knowledge a man might possess concerning human nature, however fragmentary and hard to fit in, that did not have its place in the puzzle he had to put together. Above all, Philip did not believe in chance in these affairs; it might, indeed, be chance whether he himself correctly estimated how future events would shape themselves, but the element of luck here was only, if one ran it to the ground, his own ignorance; for if his knowledge of the past could be complete, so also would his knowledge of the future be, for in the City of all places is it most true that the future is only the past entered through another door.

His mind, then, was made up, but once more he ran through the data upon which his conclusion was based. These goldfields of Metiekull on which he held an option, were a company that had aroused a good deal of comment when brought out, and it had been held in level-headed quarters that the shares which had been run up to 4 had reached that

132

figure without there having been produced any guarantee that they were worth half that. But, as is the inscrutable way of the Stock Exchange, they had, for no particular reason, been turned into a gambling counter, and there was no venture which enjoyed a freer or more fluctuating market. Things, however, had steadied down when it was known that Philip Home had bought this option of 30,000 shares, and just at this moment, as has been stated, there was considerable interest felt in the question of whether he would exercise it or not. If he did not, it meant a loss to him of about £7,000; whereas if he did, it might be regarded as certain that the shares, since gambling in them was just now, like bridge, a favourite method of losing money, would enjoy a very substantial rise, and, as usual, it was highly likely that Philip would reap a profit worth reaping, should he choose to sell during this.

So much, of course, all the world could see, but Philip saw a little further. He took into consideration the excitable state of the South African market, the uncertainty with regard to the Japanese war which would certainly make French speculators nervous, and French speculators, as he knew, had been very busy over the goldfields of Metiekull. Then came in the question of the report which he had been reading; on the whole it was good, and his sober opinion was that the shares were worth buying at the price. Yet he proposed not to take up his option, but to lose at once £7,000. But he would also let it be freely known that he had received a detailed report from his agent on the spot.

He decided, therefore—so the market would say—to abandon his option after the receipt of this report. What was the inference? That the report was unfavourable. Then all the other factors he had been considering added their weight to the scale; there was a nervous market, there was likely to be stringency of money, there was the vast hovering thundercloud of war in the East. If he knew anything about the ways of the City, it was an absolute certainty that there would be a slump in Metiekull. He would let it slump; he would even, by selling, assist it to slump; a hundred little bears—Philip detested the small operator—would sell, and when they had committed themselves pretty deeply, he would buy not only the original 30,000 shares of his option, but somewhere near twice that number; for there was no question as to the value of the property, and he would be picking up his shares at something like rubbish price.

The chain of reasoning was complete, he took his elbows off the table, and turned to light a cigarette. Then suddenly his heart sank, he felt sick and empty, for the concentration of thought was relaxed, and from a thousand spouting weir-gates the thought from which he had obtained an hour's respite flooded his whole soul. Forgetfulness of that? It was as if he had just slept in his chair for an hour, and awoke again in full consciousness of the horror of life. It was no slow awakening, it was a stab that made a deep and dreadful wound out of which flowed the black blood of his hatred and resentment, not against those two alone, but against the world. To this hatred he gave himself up with a hideous sort of luxury in the overpowering intensity of it. He suffered himself, by no fault of his; well, others should suffer, too, and if by his manipulation of the market, which was according to the principles which governed it perfectly legitimate, others were ruined, it was not his fault but theirs for competing with him.

Then a thought blacker than these, because it was more direct, more personally full of revenge, entered his mind. Surely not so long ago someone had consulted him as to an investment. Yes, it was Evelyn—Evelyn, in a sudden burst of prudence—who had decided not to buy a motor-car, but to put away a big cheque that had just been paid him. Philip had refused to give him advice professionally, since he was not a broker, but had told him that he had himself bought a large option in Metiekull. He remembered the interview perfectly, and knew that he had recommended Evelyn not to dabble, since he did not know the game, but to put his money into something safe. What he had eventually done with it Philip did not know. But for a week afterwards his studio had been littered with financial papers, and he talked the most absurd nonsense about giving up the artistic career and taking offices in the City, since he felt sure that his real chance of brilliant achievement lay there.

Now, bitter suffering like that which Philip was now undergoing cannot but have a very distinct effect on the sufferer. And in such a nature as his, the particular kind of suffering he had to bear could scarcely have had any effect but that of the worst. His circle of friends, those to whom he showed all that was best in him, was but small, and numbered four only. By two of these he had been betrayed, and that impulse which at the first moment of his knowledge did just flicker within him, the impulse of generosity, of taking the big and sky-high line of which for the moment he had been capable when he dismissed the motor three days ago near Evelyn's studio, had been crushed, if not out of life, at any rate into impotence and unconsciousness by the ingrained hardness of his nature shown to the world at large. That hardness covered him now and indurated him; he could feel neither pity nor softening for any, least of all for one who had so bitterly injured him. His power of hurting, it is true, might be small compared to the hurt that had been done him, but such as it was, he would use it. He was hurt himself, but he would not scream, he would just strike back where and when he could.

London meantime was busy with its thousand tongues in discussing what had happened, and, as was to be expected, it took a very decided line over it all. This sort of thing was really impossible, and not to be tolerated. Why, even the bridesmaids had received their presents, and everybody's plans, for everybody had settled to go to the wedding, were absolutely upset. Besides, the whole thing was an insult hurled at the sacred image of Society, a bomb-shell which had exploded in the very middle of the temple. And though Gladys Ellington had only one, not a thousand tongues, she used that one to the aforesaid effect so continuously that it really seemed impossible that flesh and blood could stand the wear and strain. She was using it now to Lady Taverner, to whom she always told things in confidence when she wanted them repeated. Lady Taverner, it may be remarked, was the pink and butter-coloured lady, to emphasize whose charms Evelyn had studied purple clematis.

"Of course, dear Alice," she was saying, "I can say these things to you, because I know you won't repeat them, and, of course, we all want it talked about as little as possible. But Madge has really behaved too abominably; it's all very well to say you must follow the dictates of your own heart, but if your heart tells you to commit really an indecency, as this is, I should say it was better not to follow it. But Madge is so odd: it is only a few weeks ago that she told me how devoted she was to Philip—esteem, affection, and all that. Well, what sort of esteem and affection has she shown? My dear, three days before the wedding."

Lady Taverner sighed.

"Of course, I won't talk about it," she said, "but I shall never speak to Madge again. And my portrait was being done by Mr. Dundas, which makes it very awkward. Of course, I want it finished, but how can I go to sit to him again?"

This was a new light which Gladys had not yet considered.

"Of course, he has ruined himself," she said cheerfully. "Nobody will go to be painted by him now. And consider his relation to Philip! Why, he was his best friend. I haven't dared to see Madge's mother yet, but I understand she is mad with rage, and I'm sure I don't wonder. And they were married, I hear, on Saturday, and have left London. How can people be such fools!"

This last remark was a genuine cri du cœur, for Gladys was absolutely unable to perceive how any interior impulse could possibly prove too strong for discretion, for savoir faire—she was fond of scraps of French—for any rending of or throwing out of window those social pads and cushions which alone ensure a passage through life that will be free from succession of bumps and jars. That was why she was almost universally considered so charming: she always said the pleasant thing, and did the agreeable one (for everybody had to assist the pads and cushions), unless she was quite safe from detection. Then, it is true, the sheathed claws occasionally popped out, when it was quite dark, but before the return of light they were always sheathed again, and the velvet touch was in evidence.

"Imagine the marriage!" she went on. "A sexton and a sextoness were probably the witnesses, and they probably came—the happy pair, I mean—in a hansom and went away in a four-wheeler. Such nonsense to wreck your life like that. And a wreck is a crime; it is a danger to other shipping unless it is blown up."

Now what Gladys said so directly, all London was thinking, if not with the same precision, at any rate with the same general trend. There had been a violation of its social codes, flagrant and open, and for the time, at any rate, it was disposed to visit the offence with the full severity of its displeasure. As Gladys had remarked: "How could they be such fools!" and the children of this world, being wiser in their generation than the children of light, are the first to punish folly. And it is very foolish to openly break the rules which Society has laid down if you wish to continue to occupy your usual arm-chair in that charming club. For the rules are so few, and so very easy to remember, and Evelyn and Madge had quite distinctly

135

broken one of the most elementary of them. And Society, however accommodating in many lines, never forgives, at once anyhow, any such open violation of its laws as this. But just at present neither of the sinners cared nearly so much for all these laws as they cared for a single moment of this blue, fresh-winded day.

They had been married, as Gladys had said, on a Saturday, and had left England that same afternoon to spend a fortnight on the coast of Normandy, and there at this moment they were, on the very coast itself, with the blue, crisp ripples of the English Channel hissing gently on the sand. Evelyn had spent most of the morning constructing a huge sand-castle of Gothic design, but the rising tide half an hour ago had driven him from the last of its fortifications, and he was now sitting on the sand with Madge by his side. All this week he had been in the most irresponsible, irrepressible spirits, which any thought of the unhappiness that had been caused seemed powerless to dull; any suggestion of it passed in a moment like breath off a mirror. With the huge egotism of his nature he had determined quite satisfactorily to himself that what had happened was inevitable. He knew how ardent was his own love for Madge, he knew it was returned, he knew too, for she had told him how different was this from the quiet, sober affection she felt for Philip. Her marriage with him could not have taken place: she felt that herself, whereas nothing in the world was strong enough to pull them apart. And with the great good sense that so often characterises egotism, Evelyn, though he was very sorry for Philip, could not either be ashamed of himself, or on the other hand be sorry for Philip long. He faded from his mind almost the moment he thought of him. He could not bring his mind to bear on Philip when Madge was with him.

He had been wading during the building and the subsequent occupation of the Gothic sand-castle, and his feet were still bare, and his flannel trousers rolled up to his knees. Also a dead bee had been washed ashore in the foam of the ripples, and search must be made for a suitable coffin, since burial with all possible honour must be given to a honey-maker from those on the honey-moon. A pink bivalve shell was eventually discovered, which he considered worthy of containing the honoured corpse. Its grave was dug above high-water mark, a mound of sand in pyramid form raised over it, and the sides of this decorated with concentric circles of pebbles. A small passage constructed of shell, and flat stones led to the tomb-chamber itself, and the door of this was hermetically sealed. In front a small stone altar was raised, and offerings of sea-weed laid on it.

"And so," said Evelyn, in conclusion of the short panegyric which, in capacity of preacher as well as architect, undertaker, and mason, he pronounced when the rites were over, "we commit to rest this follower of the fragrant life, who made his living among the flowers, and extracted honey and nothing less sweet than that from the summer of his days. My brethren, may we constantly follow this example of the perfect life. Amen. Say 'Amen,' Madge."

Madge laughed.

"I don't think I ever saw anyone so ridiculous," she said; "and it appears you can go on being ridiculous all the time."

136

"All the time I am happy," said he.

"And you're happy now?" she asked.

"Absolutely. I want nothing more. All this week I could have said to every moment: 'Stay, thou art fair.' And, oh! how fair you are, Madge. Smile, please—no, not the sad smile with all the sorrows of the world behind it."

Madge ceased smiling altogether.

"Oh, Evelyn, I am so happy, too!" she said. "But I can't forget all the scaffolding, as it were, in which our house of love was built, which now lies scattered about in bits."

Evelyn sat up quickly, demolishing the altar he had made with such care.

"Ah! don't think of that," he said. "We agreed that what has happened had to happen. Now pity and sorrow when you can't help in any way seems to me a wasted thing."

"But if you can't help pitying and being sorry?" she asked.

Evelyn gave a little click of impatience.

"You must go on trying till you do help it," he said. "Of course, if one dwells on the matter, one is sorry for Philip; I am awfully sorry for Philip when I think of him. I hate the idea of anybody being wounded and hurt as he must have been, and since he was my friend, it is the more distressing. Only it is an effort for me to think of him at all. I can only think of one person, and of one thing—you and my love for you."

This time Madge's smile was more satisfactory, and with his bright eager eyes he looked at her as the eagle to the sun.

"Ah, you are absolutely adorable!" he cried.

The wind, such as there was of it, had veered round at the time of high tide, and blew no longer off the sea, but breathed gently from the land. A mile away on the right were the tall, dun-coloured houses of Paris-plage, perched at the edge of the sea, and the sands there were dotted with the costumes of the bathers, like polychromatic ants who crawled about the beach. The sea itself was full of shifting greens and blues, and far out a fleet of boats like grey-winged gulls hovered, fishing. Even the shrill ecstasies of the bathers of Paris-plage, whose bathing appeared to be of a partial description, but who made up for that by dancing in the ripples, and splashing each other with inimitable French gaiety, were inaudible here; nothing stirred but the light, noiseless wind, warm with its passage over the sand-dunes, and faintly aromatic with the pungent scent of the fir-woods over which its pleasant path had lain. All things paused in this hour of the glory of the fulfilled noontide, that seemed equally remote from both past and future, so splendid and so real was the one present moment. If there had been hurricane in the morning, it was forgotten now; if there was to be a tempest to-night, it would be time to think about tempests when the winds began to blow, and it was mere futility to waste a moment of what was so perfect in contemplation, whether retrospective or anticipatory, of what had been or yet might be. There was just the hushed murmur of blue, breaking ripples, their sh-sh as they were poured out on to the golden sand, white gulls hung in the air, white boats drifted over the

137

sea. And by Madge's side sat her lover, the man whom her whole nature hailed as its complement, its completion. Whatever he did, whatever he said, she felt that she had herself dreamed that in remote days. Various and unexpected as were his moods, they were all fiery; the sand-castle as it first stood triumphant against the incoming tide had been to him a monument of more than national import, its gradual fall a tragedy that beggared Euripides. The bee, too—if he had been burying her he could not have shown a tenderer interest. But she was not so sure that she agreed with the sermon that had been preached over the grave. And in spite of the completeness of the noonday, she could not help going back to it.

"Evelyn," she said, "were you really serious when you said that the honey-gatherer, who looked only for what was sweet, was the example of our lives? Something like that you said, anyhow."

But he continued just looking at her, as he looked when he said: "You are adorable," with eyes gleaming and mouth a little open. He did not even seem to hear that she had asked him a question. But she repeated it.

"I don't know," he said. "How am I to know whether I am serious or not? I suppose one says a hundred stupid things that are based on something one believes. I am only serious about one thing in the world."

She did not affect not to know his meaning.

"I know—we love each other," she said. "But we have breakfast and lunch just the same."

He looked doubtful.

"Do we?" he asked. "But they don't matter!"

Suddenly to Madge the hush of the noonday and the arrest of "before and after" ceased. It was as if she had been asleep and was suddenly awakened from a dream by a hand that shook her. The dream was still there, but also, dimly, there was the wall-paper, a brass knob at the end of the bed, a counterpane.

"Ah! with all my heart I wish they didn't matter. I wish nothing mattered, I ask for nothing better than to sit here with you, to go on living as we have lived this last week. But the time must come when we shall have to consider what we shall do next. Are we going back to London, or what?"

"It is August," said he. "London in August——"

"What then? Shall we stop here?"

Then Evelyn was puerile.

"Of course, if you are tired of this," he began.

But she let the puerilities go no further.

"Oh, don't be a baby," she said. "Ah, such a dear baby, I grant you! But, Evelyn, it is life we are living."

Evelyn stroked his chin with a hugely pompous air.

"'Life is real,'" he said, "'life is earnest.' Now, Madge, Poet Longfellow said that, therefore he must be right."

"And so Painter Dundas agrees with him?" she said.

"Oh, certainly! Life is undoubtedly real and earnest, but what then? Am I never to talk nonsense any more? Shall we unbury the bee? Dear me, the unburial of the bee. How unspeakable pathetic and terrible! But what I have buried I have buried. So I shall draw your profile in the sand with one finger and all my heart."

But she still remained serious.

"Tell me when you have finished," she said.

Evelyn was already absorbed.

"With a helmet on," he remarked, "because she has to meet and defeat the realities of life, and the corners of her mouth turned down because life is earnest, and just winking with the other eye; the one you see, in fact, because she wants to signal to her friend, which is me, that it's all a huge joke really, only she mustn't talk in church."

There was a compelling fascination for her in the nimble finger that traced a big outline so deftly in the sand, and since she was upside down to it, where she sat, it followed that she got up, and went round to see what manner of a caricature this was. Hopelessly funny she found it, and hopelessly like, so much so that she danced a war-dance all over the outline, and sat down again on the middle of her own face.

"Now attend!" she said to her husband.

"After you have ruined the picture of my life," said he. "It was more like you than anything. You are being consumed with moral responsibility for me. I object to that, you know; you can be consumed by your own moral responsibility, or you can consume it, like you consume your own smoke, but mine is mine."

"Evelyn, am I your wife?" she asked.

"I have reason to believe so. I was told so in church."

"Very well—your conscience is kept in the kitchen; when I go to order dinner I look at it—I order more if we are likely to run short. So give me the cheque, please, there is a bill for conscience owing, and we must have a fresh supply."

"I don't understand one word," said Evelyn, rubbing the sand off his legs preparatory to turning his trousers down again. "Not one word. Does it matter?"

Madge's face grew quite grave again; smiles had spurted as with explosions from eyes and mouth when she saw his sand-sketch of her, but these had ceased.

"Yes, it does matter," she said, "for unless you propose that we should remain at Le Touquet quite indefinitely, it will be necessary some day to become definite. I suggest that we should become definite now. Everything," and she dug impatiently in the sand with scooping fingers— "everything has been left at a tag-end. We can't forever leave things frayed like that——"

Evelyn interrupted her.

"Oh, I know so well!" he exclaimed; "the metal thing comes off the end of a lace, and you have to push it through the holes; a little piece only comes through, and what does not come through gets thicker and won't follow. Then one has to take it out and begin again."

Madge leaned forward.

"Yes, it is exactly that," she said. "That has happened to us. When that happens, what do you do?"

"I take off the boot in question," said Evelyn gravely, "and ring the bell. When answered, I tell them to take away the boot and put in another lace. That is done: then I put the boot on. But I don't wrestle with laces which have not tags. You are wrestling, you know."

For the second time this morning a feeling as if she was dealing with a child seized Madge. The child was a very highly-developed man, too. This was a handicap to her; a heavier handicap was that she loved him. Even now, as he sat most undignifiedly wiping the sand from his feet, preparatory to getting his socks on again, she felt this immensely.

"The sand will be rubbed through the skin, and cause mortification," he remarked to himself.

Madge turned on him with some indignation.

"Ah, can't you see," she cried, "that I am serious? And you talk about the sand between your toes! You are rather trying."

Evelyn paused in his toilet.

"Dearest, I am sorry," he said. "I thought we were still playing the fool! But we are not—you, at any rate, are not. What is it then?"

This completeness of surrender was in itself disarming, and her tone was gentle.

"It is just this," she said—"that you and I are lost in a golden dream. But the dream can't go on forever. What are we to do? Shall we go back to London? Will you go on painting just as usual? People, perhaps, will be rather horrid to us, you know."

Everything now, even to him, had become serious.

"Do you mind that?" he asked.

"No, of course not, if you don't," she said. "But I have been wondering, dear, whether if by your marriage with me you have hurt your career."

"You mean that pink Jewesses who want to be fashionable won't come to ask me to paint their portraits any more?" he said.

"No, not that, of course. What does that matter?"

Evelyn finished putting his shoes and socks on.

"Then, really, I don't understand what you do mean," he said, "by my career, if you don't refer to the class of person who thinks it a sort of cachet to be painted by me—though Heaven knows why she can think that. What are we talking about? How otherwise can my career, which is only my sense of form and colour, be touched?"

Madge's eyes dreamed over the sea for a little at this.

"No, I was wrong," she said. "Taken like that, it can't matter. But we must (though I was wrong there, I am right here)—we must settle what we are going to do. We must go back some time; you must begin working again."

Evelyn finished tying the last lace.

"Romney painted Lady Hamilton forty-three times," he said. "I could paint forty Madges of the last hour. You never look the same for two minutes together, and I could paint all of you. Let's have an exhibition next spring called 'Some Aspects of the Honourable Mrs. Dundas. Artist—her husband.'"

140

"They would all come," said Madge.

There was no more discussion on this present occasion about the future. Evelyn being again properly clothed, they went back by a short cut across the sand-dunes to the clearing in the forest behind, which was known as Le Touquet. For a space of their way, after they had got out of the pitiless sun on the sand, their path led through the primeval pine forest, where the air was redolent and aromatic, and the footfall went softly over the carpet of brown needles. Then other growths began, the white poplar of France shook tremulous leaves in fear of the wind that might be coming, young oak-trees stood sturdy and defiant where poplars trembled, and away from the pines the bare earth showed a carpet of excellent green. Then, as they approached the hotel, neat white boards with black arrows displayed signs in all directions, and a rustic bridge over a pond, by which stretched a green sward of lawn on which it was 'defended to circulate,' led to the gravel sweep in front of the hotel.

A broad verandah in the admirable French style sheltered those who lunched there from the sun; small tables were dotted about it, and from the glare of the gravel sweep it was refreshment to be shielded from the heat. Their table was ready spread for them, and the obsequious smile of the head-waiter hailed them.

But for the first time Madge was not content. Evelyn still sat opposite her; all was as it had been during the last week. Yet when he said: "Oh, how delicious, I am so hungry!" she felt she was hungry, too, but not in the way he meant. She was hungry, as women always are and must be, for the sense of largeness in the man, and she asked herself, but quenched the question before it had flamed, if she had given herself to just a boy. Yet how she loved him! She loved even his airy irresponsibility, though at times, as this morning, she had found it rather trying. She had lived so much in a world that schemed and planned, and was for ever wondering what the effect of doing this or avoiding that would be, that his utter want of calculation, of considering the interpretation that might be placed on his acts, was as refreshing as the breath of cool night air on one who leaves the crowded ball-room. And for very shame she could not go on just now pressing him to make decisions; she would return to that again to-morrow, for to-day seemed so made for him and his huge delight in all that was sunny and honey-gathering. To-morrow, also, she would have to mention another question that demanded consideration, namely, that of money. They were living here, with their big sitting-room and the motor-car they had hired—and, as a matter-of-fact, did not use—on a scale that she knew must be beyond their means; and since she was perfectly certain that Evelyn had never given a thought to this question of expense, any more than the price of the wine which he chose to drink concerned him, it was clearly time to remind him that things had to be paid for. He had loaded her, too, with presents; she felt that if she had expressed a desire for the moon, he would have ordered the longest ladder that the world had ever seen in order, anyhow, to make preliminary investigations with regard to the possibility of securing it. He apparently had not the slightest notion of the value of money, no ideas of his were connected with it, and though this argued a certain defective apparatus in this money-seeking world, as if a

141

man went out to walk in a place full of revolver-armed burglars with no more equipment than a penny cane, she could not help liking his insouciance. Once she taxed him with his imprudence, and he had told her, with great indignation, how he had read nothing but financial papers for a whole week earlier in the summer, and at the end, instead of spending a couple of thousand pounds in various delightful ways, he had invested it in some South African company in which—well, a man who was very acute in such matters was much interested. And yet she called him imprudent!

After lunch they strolled across to the lawn where circulation was forbidden.

"We won't be breaking any rules," said he, "unless the word applies to the currents of the blood, because we will sit under a tree and probably sleep. I can think of nothing which so little resembles circulation as that."

Letters and papers had arrived during lunch, and Evelyn gave a great laugh of amusement as he opened one from Lady Taverner, asking if he would be in London during October, and could resume—this was diplomatic—the sittings that had been interrupted.

"Even that branch of my career hasn't suffered," he observed.

There was nothing more of epistolary interest, and he opened the paper. There, too, the world seemed to be standing still. There had been a skirmish between Russian and Japanese outposts at a place called something like Pingpong, fiscalitis seemed to be spreading a little, but otherwise news was meagre.

"Is there nothing?" asked Madge, when he had read out these headings.

"No, not a birth or death even. Oh, by-the-way, you called me imprudent the other day! Now we'll find the money-market, and see what my two thousand pounds is worth. Great Scott, what names they deal in—Metiekull, that's it."

There was a long silence. Then Evelyn laughed, a sudden little, bitter laugh, which was new to Madge's ears.

"Yes, I bought them at 4," he said. "They are now 2. That was a grand piece of information Philip gave me."

He got up.

"Oh, Evelyn, how horrible!" she cried. "Where are you going?"

"Just to telegraph to them to sell out," he said. "I can't afford to lose any more. I'll be back in a minute. And when I come back, dear, please don't allude to this again. It is unpleasant; and that is an excellent reason for ceasing to think about it. In fact, it is the best reason."

FOURTEENTH

IT was perhaps lucky as regards the future of Madge and her husband that this debacle had taken place so near to the end of the season. Many people, indeed, had waited in London only for the marriage, for the season was already over, and for the last three days there had been nothing but this to detain them. Genuine sympathy was at first felt for Philip, but it very soon was known that he was at his office again every day and all day, worked just as hard if not harder than usual, and was supposed, by way of signalising his own disappointment, to have made some great coup over a South African company, thereby inflicting a quantity of very smart disappointments on the gentlemen of the Stock Exchange. He had dealt these blows out with an impartial hand; first there had been some staggering smacks which had sent the bulls flying like ninepins, while the bears stood round and grinned, and profited by the experience of their fraternal enemies. Then Philip, it seemed, had seen them grinning, and had done the same for them.

In other words, things had come off in exactly the way he had anticipated. The knowledge that he had bought a very large option had induced many operators less substantial than he to buy also, and the sudden news that he had received a detailed report from the spot, and had subsequently not exercised his option, landed many of these buyers in awkward places. Then, as was natural, the bears saw their opportunity, sold largely, on the strength of the inference that Philip's report was highly unfavourable, bringing prices down with a run. Then, with the same suddenness with which he had decided not to take up his option, he bought at this very much lower price a vastly increased number of shares, and within a week of the original slump Metiekull was considerably higher than it had ever been. The £7,000 he had forfeited over not taking up his option was but a bagatelle to his subsequent gains, and the market generally at this conclusion remarked, among other things not worth repeating, that there was a good deal to be said in favour of long spoons; while that not inconsiderable part of more westerly London which is always burning its fingers in this City fire of the Stock Exchange, said with a somewhat cynical smile that since Philip could still hit so hard, he had not, perhaps, been so hard hit himself. Perhaps, in fact, Madge had not made such a very terrible mistake, after all, for Mr. Dundas was undeniably the most fascinating person, whereas Philip, so it appeared, did not let the most dreadful affair of the heart interfere in the slightest with the stuffing of the money-box.

But in this they utterly mistook him, for this steady, concentrated application to work was, perhaps, the only thing in the world which could have prevented him breaking down or losing his mental balance altogether. Even as it was, it partook only, as far as he could see, of the nature of a temporary alleviation, for in the very nature of things he could not go on working like this indefinitely. And what would happen to him when he relaxed he could not imagine, he only knew that the hours when he was not at the office were like some nightmare repeated and again repeated. Nor did they lose, at present, the slightest edge of the intensity of their horror. This week was as bad as last week; last week was no better than the week before, all through this hot August when he remained in town, not leaving it even for his usual week end on the river, but seeing its pavements grow hotter and dustier and emptier as more and more of its toiling crowds escaped for a week or two to the sands or the moors.

The worst time of all was the early morning, for though he usually went to sleep from sheer weariness when he went to bed, he began to wake early, while still Jermyn Street was dusky and dewy, and as yet the sparrows in the plane trees opposite his window had not begun to tune up for the day. Morning by morning he would watch "the casement slowly grow a glimmering square," or if it was, as often, absolutely unbearable to lie in bed, he would get up and go into his sitting-room, where the wan light but brought back to him the dreadful hours he had passed there the evening before. The glass from which he had drunk stood on the little table by the sofa, and by it lay the unread evening paper. The beloved Reynolds prints, Mrs. Carnac, Lady Halliday, Lady Stanhope, Lady Crosbie, all first impressions, smiled meaninglessly on the wall, for all the things he had loved and studied had lost their beauty, and were blackened like dahlias in the first autumn frosts. Sometimes a piece of music stood on the piano, from which he had played a bar or two the night before, but had then stopped, for it, too, conveyed nothing to him; it was but a jangle of senseless chords. Sometimes in these dreadful morning hours he would doze a little on the sofa, but not often; and once he had poured out into the glass a stiff dose of whisky, feeling that even an alcohol-purchased oblivion would be better than more of this wakefulness. But he had the sense left not to take to that; if he did that to-day he would do it to-morrow, and if he admitted the legitimacy of such relief, he knew he would find less and less reason every day for not letting himself sink in that slough. Besides, he had to keep himself clear-headed and alert for the work of the day.

Two passions, to analyse a little further, except when he was at work, entirely possessed him, one his passion for Madge, of which not one jot, in spite of what had happened, was abated. It was not, nor ever had been, of the feverish or demonstrative sort, it did not flicker or flare, it burned steadily with a flame that was as essential a part of his life as breathing or the heart-beat. And the other, existing strangely and coincidently with it, was the passion of hate—hatred for her, hatred for Evelyn, a red flame which shed its light on all else, so that in the glare of it he hated the whole world. Two people only stood outside of it—his mother and Tom Merivale; for these he did not feel hate, but he no longer felt love; he was incapable of feeling that any longer except for Madge. But he did not object to them, he thought of them without resentment, but that was all.

Then, as his nerves began to suffer under this daily torture, the hours of enforced idleness became full of alarm. What he feared he did not know, he only knew that he was apprehensive of some further blow that might be dealt him from a quarter as unexpected as that from which this had come. Everything had been so utterly serene when this bolt from the blue struck him, he could not have conjectured it; and now he could not conjecture what he expected next.

But all this London did not know: it only knew that this very keen man of business was as acute as ever, to judge by the Metiekull episode, and began to reason that since he was so callous to what had happened, Madge had really not behaved so outrageously as had been supposed. She had found—this was the more human and kindly view induced by the cessation of the late London hours, and the substitution of a great deal of open air for the stifling ballroom of town—she had found that she really was in love with Mr. Dundas, and that Philip on closer acquaintance was what he had proved himself to be, business man first, lover afterwards. And really Mr. Dundas's pictures this year had been stupefyingly clever. They made one just gasp. Surely it would be silly to get somebody else to "do" one instead of him, just because Madge had found out her mistake in time, and he had assisted at the correction of it. He was certain to have heaps of orders in any case, so it would be just as well to be painted by him as soon as possible. Of course that implied that one accepted his marriage in a sort of way, but, after all, why not? Besides—here the world's tongue just tended to approach the cheek—it would be a kindness to old Lady Ellington to smooth things over as much as possible, and that dear little thing, Gladys, whom everybody liked so much, would be so pleased to find that Madge was not hardly thought of. Yes, quite so, and has the dressing-gong sounded already? And Tom killed a stag, and they had a good day among the grouse, and Jack killed a salmon, so there will be fish for dinner. What a blessing!

One of these mornings which saw Philip in the gloaming of dawn hearing the sparrows beginning their chirruping in the plane-trees, saw Tom Merivale also, not only hearing but listening to the twitter of half-awakened birds in his garden. He had slept in the hammock slung in the pergola, and after the coolness of the clear night following on the intense heat of the day before, the dew had been heavy. His blanket was shimmering with the seed-pearls of the moisture, his hair also was wet with it, and on the brick of the pergola path it lay like the condensation of the breath of the spirit of woodland itself. The cleanness and purity of this hour of dawn was a thing that every morning more astounded him. Whether a clear and dove-coloured sky brooded as now overhead, or whether morning came wrapped in rain-clouds, it always brought to one who slept with the sky for a roof a sense of renewal and freshness which it was impossible to get used to. Everything was rested and cleaned, ready to begin again on the hundred joyful businesses of day.

Just as a stone falling through the air moves with a speed that is accelerated each moment by double the acceleration of the last, so Merivale felt that every day his communion with and absorption in Nature made progress out of all proportion to what he had achieved before. It was so few months ago that he had himself wondered at the mysterious and silent telepathy that ran through all Nature, the telepathy that warns birds and beasts of coming storm, that makes the bats wake and begin their eerie flittings even at the hour when sunset is brightest, knowing that the

145

darkness is imminent, that connects man, too, as he had proved, if man only will be quiet and simple instead of fretful and complicated, with birds and beasts, so that they know he is their brother and will come to his silent call to them. But of late that had become such a commonplace to him that he only wondered how it could ever have been otherwise than obvious. He remembered, too, how so few weeks ago he had for the first time heard the sound of the glass flute in the woods above Philip's house at Pangbourne, but now not a day passed, often not an hour, in which that unending melody, the eternal and joyful hymn of Nature and of life, was not audible to him. Whether what he heard was really a phenomenon external to himself or only the internal expression, so to speak, of those thoughts which filled his entire consciousness, both waking and sleeping, he did not care to ask himself, for it did not in the least seem to him to matter. Wherever that melody came from, whether it was born in his own brain and telegraphed from there to his ears, or whether it was really some actual setting of the joy of life to song, external to him, and heard just as a railway whistle or the bleat of a sheep is heard and conveyed from his ears to his brain, he did not even wish to know, for wherever coined, it was of royal minting, the secret and the voice of Life itself was there.

The woods of Pangbourne—Philip. He had heard from Mrs. Home of the catastrophe, and in answer to a further letter of his he had learned that Philip remained in London slaving all day at the office, seeing no one but his clerks, silent, alone, giving no sign even to her. This letter had come only last night, and ended with an imploring cry that if Tom thought he could help him in any way, his mother besought him to do what he could. Philip had been down to see her once only, immediately after his engagement was broken off, and he had been utterly unlike himself—hard, terrible, unforgiving. Could Merivale not do something? Philip had never had but four friends in the world, two of these had turned enemies (Mrs. Home had crossed out in a thin, neat line the last two words and substituted "ceased to be friends"), and there were left only himself and she. And she had tried, and could do nothing.

Tom Merivale thought over all this as the twitter of birds grew more coherent in the bushes, passing from the sound like the tuning-up of an orchestra into actual song. The resemblance, indeed, was curiously complete, for after the tuning-up had ceased, while it was still very faintly light, there was a period of silence before song began, just such a silence as ensued when the strings of a band had found the four perfect fifths, and there was the hush and pause over singers and audience alike until the conductor took his place. Day was the conductor here, and to-day it would be the sun who would conduct his great symphony in person at dawn, the approach of which to Philip but meant the hard outlining of the square of window, but to Tom all the joy of another day, a string of round and perfect pearls of hours. The East was already in the secret, for high above the spot where dawn would break rosy fleeces of clouds had caught the light, while nearer to the horizon the nameless green of dawn, that lies between the yellow of the immediate horizon itself and the blue of the zenith, was beginning to melt into blue. Then, how well he knew it, the skeins of mist along the stream below would dissolve, the tintless, hueless, darknesses of clear shadow that lay beneath the trees would grow green from the sun striking through the leaves. These things were enough to fill this hour with ecstasy, and every hour to him brought its own. There would be the meal prepared by himself, the work in the garden, claiming fellowship and friendship every moment with the green things of the earth, the mid-day bathe, when he was one with the imperishable water, the long communing with eyes half-shut on the sunny heather, where even the stealthy adder was no longer a thing of aversion, and then for the sake "of his sister, the body," as the old Saint said, a walk that might cover twenty miles before he returned at dusk. Oh, how unutterably good, and how unutterably better each day!

A wind came with the dawn itself, that scattered more dew on to him from the rose-sprays overhead, and he slid out of the hammock to go into the house to make his breakfast, stretching himself once or twice before he went in to feel his muscles, the rigging of the ship of the body, all twang sound and taut. Nor did it seem to him in any way unworthy that even this physical fitness of his should give him such joy: it would, indeed, have been a disgrace if it had been otherwise. For all the sensations and functions of life were on one plane, and whether the sweat poured from him as he dug the garden, or his teeth crushed a nuthusk, or the great thigh-muscles strained as he mounted a hill, or his ear was ravished with the fluting of a bush-bowered thrush, it was all one; each was a function of life, and the sum of them was just joy.

But Philip; this morning he could not get Philip out of his head, for detached from the world of men and women as he was, he could not help pitying the blind, meaningless suffering of his old friend. For all suffering to him was meaningless, he did not in himself believe that any good could come out of it considered merely as suffering: much more good, that is to say, would have come out of joy; this was withheld by suffering, a thing almost criminal to his view. But he could realise, and did, that all that Philip loved best had gone from him; it was as if in his own case the sun and the moon had been plucked from the sky, or water had ceased to flow, as if something vital in the scheme of things was dead.

It seemed to him, then, with his mind full of Philip, very natural that there should be a letter from him when the post came in that morning. It ran thus:

> Dear Tom,—I had rather an unpleasant experience yesterday, for suddenly in the middle of the morning I fainted dead off. It seemed sensible to see a doctor, who of course said the usual thing—overwork, overworry, go and rest completely for a time. He was a sensible man, I've known him for years, and so I have decided to do as he tells me.
>
> Now you are such an old friend that I trust you to say "No" quite frankly if you don't want me. I therefore ask you if I may come down and stay with you a bit. I thought of going home, but I should be alone there, as my mother is away just now, or on the

147

point of going, and I don't want to bring her back, and I really think I should go crazy if I was alone. You seem to have found the secret of happiness, and perhaps it might do me good to watch you. All this is absolutely subject to your saying "No" quite frankly. Just send it or the affirmative by telegram, will you, and I will arrive or not arrive this evening. But I warn you I am not a cheerful companion.—Yours,

Philip Home.

For any sake don't say a word or give a look of pity or sympathy. I shall bring a servant—may I?—who will look after me. I don't want to give you trouble, and I intend to take none myself. Mind, I trust you to telegraph "No" quite simply if you don't want me.

There was only one reply possible to this, and, indeed, Merivale had no inclination to give any other. Of course Philip was welcome; he would very likely have proposed this himself had not this letter come so opportunely, and the telegram in reply was genuinely cordial. Poor old Philip, who used to be so happy in the way in which probably a locomotive engine is happy, groomed and cared for, and only required to do exactly that which it loves doing, namely, being strong and efficient, and exercising its strength and speed. Yet though Tom's welcome of him was so genuine, he shrank inwardly, though he did not confess this even to himself, from what lay before him, for he hated misery and unhappiness— hated the sight or proximity of it, he even thought that it was bad for anybody to see it, but if on this point his attitude was inconsistent with the warmth of his telegram, the inconsistency was wholly human and amiable.

On the other hand, though he was by no means of a proselytising nature, there was here, almost forced upon him, a fine test case. He believed himself very strongly in the infectious character of human emotions; fear seemed to him more catching than the smallpox, and worry ran through a household even as does an epidemic of influenza. And if this which he so profoundly believed was true, that truth must hold also about the opposite of all these bad things; they, too, must be infectious also, unless one chose to draw the unthinkable conclusion that evil was contagious, whereas good was not communicable by the same processes. That could not be, the spiritual microbes must, as far as theory or deduction could be trusted to supply an almost certain analogy, correspond to the microbes of the material world; there must in fact be in the spiritual world, if these microbes of suffering and misery were there, much vaster armies of microbes that produced in man all the things that made life worth living; battalions of happiness-germs must be there, of germs that were forever spreading and swarming in their ceaseless activity of building-up and regenerating man, of battling with the other legions whose work was to destroy and depress and kill. And if there was anything in his belief—a belief on which he would gladly have staked his life—that joy, health, life were ever gaining ground and triumphing over their lethal foes, then it followed that the germs of all things that were good were more potent than those that were evil if their armies were mobilised.

148

How mysterious and how profoundly true this transference of emotion was, or, in terms of the present analogy, these invasions of spiritual microbes! For what caused panic to spread through a crowd? Not danger itself, but fear, fear which ran like an electric current through the ranks of its quivering victims. Serenity, therefore, must be equally contagious, and if one could isolate one of those fear-ridden folk for a moment in a ring of men who were not afraid, it could not be doubted that their fearlessness would triumph. No reassuring word or gesture need be spoken or made, the very fact of the atmosphere of calm must inevitably quiet the panic-stricken. Worry, too, would stifle if isolated in serenity, just as serenity would vanish if the hosts of its enemy hemmed it in. And here, to take the case in point, was Philip, possessed and infected by the poisonous microbes of unhappiness, which blackened his soul and darkened the sun for him. What was the remedy? Not, as he had been trying to do, to drug himself into unconsciousness over work, while they continued their ravages unchecked and unchallenged, but to steep himself as in some antiseptic bath in an atmosphere that was charged with their bitterest foes. It was happiness, the atmosphere of happiness, that alone could combat his disease. And of the eventual result of that treatment Merivale did not entertain the slightest doubt; there would, of course, be war between happiness and the misery of his friend, but he felt within himself that it was impossible that Philip's misery could be so strong as the armies on his own side. Think of the allies, too, that surrounded him: his light-armed skirmishers, the birds and bees, with their staccato artillery of joy forever playing on the object of their detestation; the huge guns of the great beech forest forever pouring their sonorous discharge on to the enemy; the flying cavalry of the river, the heather-fragrant wind which encompassed and outflanked him in each direction.

Thus though, as has been said, his first impulse was one of shrinking from this proximity to what was unhappy and suffering, how splendid a demonstration of all that on which he so largely based his theory of life was here offered him. He did not seek after a sign, no demonstration could deepen his belief, yet he rejoiced that a sign was offered him, even as one who utterly believes in the omnipotence of God may yet look on the shining of the starry-kirtled night, and glow at the reminder he is given of what he believes. Well he knows the glory of God, but it does his heart good to behold it.

The work of the house took him, as a rule, but an hour or so to get through every morning; but to-day there were further preparations to be made for his friend's arrival; linen had to be brought out for his bed, water to be fetched for his jug, and his room to be dusted and made ready. But these menial occupations seemed to Merivale to be in no way mean; nothing that was necessary for the ordinary simple needs of life could possibly be derogatory for the wisest or busiest or wealthiest of mankind to perform for himself, though to pass a lifetime in performing them for others was a mean matter both for employer and employed. But such things were not to him even tedious, any more than breathing or washing were tedious, and to find them tedious but meant that one was out of tune with the great symphony of life. Everyone, so ran his theory, ought ideally to be so simple in his needs that he could minister to his own necessities, without any sense that his time was wasted; one washed one's hands, and brushed the hair. For this was part of the true simplification of life—to need but little, and provide that little oneself. Yet inasmuch as most of the world did not yet take his view (and Philip was one of them), he was accustomed to hire help, and intended to do so now, for a friend's visit.

He moved quickly and deftly enough about his work; pausing to think for a moment as to the making of the bed, for all this summer he had scarcely once slept in one, while in winter a mattress and a rug comprised his own needs. Then the work of dusting brought him to the dressing-table, and for a moment he looked at himself in the glass with a sort of pang of delight, though in his delight there was neither self-consciousness nor vanity that this was he. For he was now several years past thirty, a time of life when on every face there begin to appear the marks of years; but from the glass there looked back into his eyes the face of a youth just standing on the threshold of manhood. The strength of manhood was there, but it was a strength in which the electric vigour of boyhood still quivered like a steel spring; not a sign of slack or wrinkled skin appeared there, and his hair, with its close-cropped curls, was thick and shining with health. But looking at this image of perfect and vigorous youth, he thought, after the first inevitable delight in the knowledge that this was he, not at all of himself, only of the fact that to any who lived his life this must be the certain and logical consequence. For the body was but the visible sign of the spirit: it was the soul of man that made his body, as a snail its shell; it was worry and discontent assuredly that drew lines and wrinkles on the face and brought fatigue and sloth to the muscles, not the passage of the years; it was just as surely serenity and the passionate acceptance and absorption of the joy of life that made a man young, and would keep him so body and soul alike.

But never before had he so fully realised this change that had come to him, and when, after his work in the house was over, he walked into Brockenhurst to engage a servant for the cooking which Philip's visit would involve, he found himself wondering with a more than usually vivid curiosity to what further knowledge and illumination his undeviating quest should lead him. For he felt he was getting nearer every day, and very quickly nearer to the full realisation of his creed, namely, that all life was indivisibly one, and that the purport of all life was joy. And when his knowledge of this was made perfect, how would the revelation come, and what would be the effect? Would life eternal lived here and now be his, or would that light be too great for him to bear, so that this tabernacle of flesh and blood, hereditarily weakened by centuries of sin and shame, could not stand it? Was it life or seeming death that awaited him? He scarcely cared.

The tree that had been struck by lightning at the end of the garden he had felled soon after, and part of his daily work now was to cut up the branches into faggots and sticks of firewood for the winter. That dreadful stroke from the skies which had dealt death to this beautiful tree in the prime of its strength and luxuriance of its summer had often seemed to

Merivale to involve a difficult question, for it was intimately bound up with all those things on which he had deliberately turned his back. Death did exist in the world, and though, as he had once said to Evelyn, out of death invariably came life, yet the fact of death was there, just as beyond all possibility of denial, pain and disease and sorrow were in the world also. These, however, were largely of man's making, yet here, in the case of this poor stricken tree, it was Nature herself who deliberately attacked and slew part of herself. One animal, it is true, preyed on another, and by its death sustained its own life: that was far easier to understand. But there was something senseless and brutal in the fact of this weapon of the storm, a thing as inanimate as a rifle-bullet, striking at life. It was wanton destruction. Nothing came of it (and here he smiled, though not believing he had guessed the riddle), except firewood for him.

The morning was intensely hot, and as he worked hatless under the blaze of the sun, the wholesome sweat of toil poured from him. How good that was; how good, too, to feel the strong resistance of the wood against the blade of his axe, to feel the sinews of his arms alternately tighten and slacken themselves in the swiping strokes, to stand straight up a moment to rest his back, and wipe the moisture from his face and draw in two or three long, satisfying breaths of summer air. It was as if the song of the birds, too, entered into his very lungs, and the hum of the bees, and the murmur of the forest, which was beginning to be hushed a little at the hour when even the cicala sleeps. One thing alone would not be hushed, and that the liquid voice of the river, in which he would soon be plunged. No length of drought in this wonderful year seemed to diminish the wealth of its outpouring; it was as high between its fern-fringed banks now as it had been in April. But first there was the carrying of the aromatic, fresh-cut logs to the house to be done, and he almost regretted how near completion was the stack that filled the wood-shed, for there was something about the hardness of this particular toil that was intimately delightful. It required the exercise of strength and vigour, the full use of supple and well-hardened muscles; it was very typical of the splendid struggle for life in which the struggle itself, the fact of work, was a thing ecstatic. He had cut more than usual this morning, and it was with a boyish sense of playing some game against a rigid and inflexible opponent that he determined not to make two journeys of it, but carry all he had cut in one. And underneath this staggering burden which he loved he toiled to the wood-shed.

Merivale had just come up from his bathe in the evening when Philip arrived, and he met him halfway up the garden. That extraordinary change which he had himself seen in the glass that morning struck his friend, too.

"It was awfully good of you to let me come, Tom," he said. "And what has been happening to you? If I had not known you ten years ago, I should scarcely have recognised you now."

Tom laughed.

"And in ten days you won't recognise yourself," he said. "You look pulled down, and no wonder, if you've been working in London all August. Anyhow, this isn't the least like London, and you are going to do no work.

151

You are going to sit in the garden, and go for immense slow walks, and listen to my practically incessant and wholly fatuous conversation."

But it was difficult for him to conceal the shock that Philip's appearance gave him. He looked so horribly tired and so old. The suffering of this last month had made him haggard and heavy-eyed, and what was worse, the hatred that had been his soul's guest had made his face hard and bitter, and yet for all the hardness it was strangely enfeebled: it had lost the look of strength and life that had always been so characteristic of it. The vital principle had been withdrawn from it; all that it expressed was lethal, negative.

Philip's weary eyes looked round on the garden and the low, thatched house where dinner was already being laid in the verandah.

"So this is the Hermitage," he said. "Dear God, you have found peace."

Then he broke off suddenly, and began again in a different voice, a voice that was like his face, bitter and hard and old.

"Yes, I've been overworking," he said, "and as I told you, yesterday I suddenly collapsed. I think my work has got on my brain too much; I didn't sleep well. London was dreadfully hot and stuffy, too. But I've made a pot of money this month. Those fools on the Stock Exchange say that August is a slack month. Of course it is if you are slack. But certainly from a business point of view I've had an all-round time. I brought some of them back, too, from their deer-forests and fishings in double-quick time. And they were mostly too late even then. Good joke, too, my going off suddenly like this, and leaving them grilling in London."

Merivale could not quite let this pass; besides, he must answer somehow. He laughed.

"I don't altogether agree with your idea of humour," he said. "Was it really—from a humorous point of view—worth while?"

Philip's face did not relax.

"It was from a business point of view," he said.

Then his gardener's eye was suddenly arrested by a perle des jardins that was ramping beyond all bounds.

"I used to know about roses," he said, "and I'll cut that back for you to-morrow. You are not getting half the roses out of it."

"I know, but it's enjoying itself so enormously," said Merivale.

Philip considered this as an abstract question on to which he had not previously turned his mind.

"And you think that ought to be taken into consideration when one deals with the destinies even of rose-trees?" he asked with a terrible air of being in earnest.

Merivale smiled.

"Decidedly London has not been good for you," he said. "I think your words were 'the destinies even of rose-trees.' Now what destiny matters more than that? Not mine, I am sure, and I doubt if yours. Besides, the destinies of your rose-trees used to be of extraordinary importance, not only to them, but to you."

Philip was silent a moment. Then for the first time, at the sense of

152

peace that was here so predominant a note, or at the sight of Tom himself, in all the vigour and freshness of a youth that measured by years was already past, some faint gleam, or if not a gleam, the sense that light was possible to him, broke through the dismal darkness of his soul. For one short moment he laid his hand on his friend's arm.

"Make allowance for me, Tom," he said.

In spite of his long aloofness from the fretful race of men and the ways of them, Merivale had not forgotten—indeed it is as impossible for one who has ever known it to forget it as it is to forget how to swim—that divine gift of tact. Indeed, it is probable that his long sojournings alone had, if anything, made more sensitive those surfaces which come into contact with others and which others insensibly feel (for this is tact) to be smooth and warm and wise. And it was a fine touch that he did not respond, however remotely, to Philip's appeal, for Philip had told him that pity and sympathy were exactly what he could not stand. Consequently he let this cry be the voice of one in the desert; it wanted silence, not audible answer. He, like the trees in the garden and the stream, must be dumb to it.

This silence was the key to several days that followed: there was, in fact, no intimate conversation of any sort between the two friends. Philip would sit for hours in the garden, stung sometimes into spasmodic activity, during which he would send off a dozen telegrams to his office on monetary affairs, but for the most part with an unread paper on his knees, or a book that tumbled unheeded on to the grass. But soon during this frosty and strictured time, Merivale thought he saw, as birds know the hour of sunrise before the faintest dawn illuminates the sky, that there were signs that this frost was less binding than it had been. Philip would take a pruning-knife sometimes, and with his deft and practised hand reduce a rose to reasonable dimensions. Sometimes half-way through the operation he would let the knife fall from his fingers, as if his labours, like everything else, were not worth while; but often afterwards he would resume his labours, and enable the tree to do justice to itself. By degrees, too, these outbursts of City activity grew rarer and more spasmodic, becoming, as it were, but the echoes of a habit rather than demonstrations of the habit itself. He did not join Merivale in his long tramps over the forest, but he began to wait for his return, and if he knew from what point of the compass he was likely to return, he sometimes set out to meet him. Once Merivale was very late: his tramp had taken him further than usual, and night, falling cloudy and moonless, had surprised him in a wood where even one who knew the forest as well as he might miss his way. On this occasion he found Philip pacing up and down the garden in some agitation.

"Ah, there you are," he cried in a tone of obvious relief when his white-flannelled figure appeared against the deep dusk of the bushes that lined the stream. "I was getting anxious, and I did not know what to do. I should have come out to look for you, but I did not know where you might be coming from."

And that little touch of anxiety was perhaps the first sign that he had shown since he had abandoned himself to bitterness that his heart was not

153

dead: never before had the faintest spark of the sense of human comradeship or its solicitudes appeared.

Then Merivale knew that the fortnight that Philip had already spent here had not been utterly wasted, and before going to bed that night he wrote one line of hope to Mrs. Home.

FIFTEENTH

A COUPLE of days after this the weather suddenly broke, and for the unclouded and azure skies they had a day of low, weeping heavens, with an air of dead and stifling dampness. Never for a moment through the hours of daylight did the sullen downpour relax; the trees stood with listless, drooping branches, from which under the drenching rain a few early autumn leaves kept falling, though the time of the fall of the leaf was not yet. In the garden beds the plants had given up all attempts to look gay or to stand up, and bent drearily enough beneath the rain that scattered their petals and dragged their foliage in the muddy earth. The birds, too, were silent; only the hiss of the rain was heard, and towards afternoon the voice of the river grew a little louder. Merivale, however, was undeterred and quite undepressed by these almost amphibious conditions, and, as usual, went off after breakfast for one of those long rambles of his in the forest, leaving Philip alone. There was no hint of unfriendliness taken in this; indeed, Philip had exacted a promise from his host on the evening of arrival that his normal course of life should be undisturbed.

That first little token that he had given two days before that his heart was not dead had more than once repeated itself since then, and he was perhaps faintly conscious of some change in himself. He was not, so far as he knew, less unhappy, but that frightful hardness was beginning to break down, the surface of its ice was damped with thawed water, his hatred of all the world, his deep resentment at the scheme of things—if any scheme underlay the wantonness of what had happened—was less pronounced. It might, indeed, be only that he was utterly broken, that his spirit of rebellion could no longer raise its banner of revolt, yet he did not feel as if he had surrendered, he did not in the least fold his hands and wait mutely for whatever the Powers that be might choose to do with him. He was conscious, indeed, of the opposite, of a certain sense of dawning willpower; and though his life, so to speak, lay shattered round him, he knew that subconsciously somehow he was beginning to regard the pieces with some slight curiosity that was new to him, wondering if this bit would fit on to that. In a way he had plunged into business again with that feverish rush which had taken him through August with some such idea; his immediate salvation, at any rate, he had believed to lie in concentrated occupation; yet there had been nothing constructive about that; it was a palliative

154

measure, to relieve pain, rather than a course that would go to the root of the disease. Also, such as it was, it had failed, his health had given way: he could for the present take no more of that opiate.

In another respect also it had failed, for to-day by the mid-day post there had come for him communications of the greatest importance from the City, information which was valuable, provided only he acted on it without delay. There was no difficulty about it, the question had no complications; he himself had only to send off instructions which ten minutes' thought could easily frame. Yet he sat with paper and pens in front of him, doing nothing, for he had asked himself a very simple question instead. "Is it all worth while?" was what he said to himself. And apparently it was not.

Now, if this had happened a month ago, it would have been equivalent to a surrender; it would have been a confession that he was beaten. But now the whole nature of his doubt was changed. Work, it is true, had done something for him; it had got him through a month in which he was incapable of anything else, it had got him, in fact, to the point which was indicated two days ago by his little anxiety about Merivale. And had he known it, that was much the most important things that had happened to him for weeks. Something within him had instinctively claimed kinship again with mankind.

How hollow and objectless to-day seemed the results of the last month! "Home's August," as it was already ruefully known on the Stock Exchange, had plentifully enriched Home, but though the gold had poured in like a fountain, yet, mixed with it, indissolubly knitted into the success, had come a leanness. What did it all amount to? And lean above all was his paltry triumph over Evelyn, who, as he had since ascertained, had sold out Metiekull when things were at their very worst, only to realise that if he had left it alone, he would have made a handsome profit. But what then? What good did that pin-prick of a vengeance do? What gratification had it brought to Philip's most revengeful and hating mood? The wedding-tour had been cut short: Evelyn and Madge had come back to London, but that to-day gave him not the smallest feeling of satisfaction in that, however feebly, he had hit back at them. It was all so useless: the futility and childishness of his revenge made him feel sick. If he had a similar chance to-day, he would not have stirred a finger.

But all this emptiness, and the intolerable depression that still enveloped him, was, somehow, of different character to what it had been before. It was all bad and hopeless enough, but his eyes, so to speak, had begun to veer round; they were no longer drearily fixed on the storms and wreckage of the past, but were beginning, however, ineffectually as yet, to peer into the mists of the future. It was exactly this which was indicative of the change that had come, and the indication was as significant as the slow shifting of a weather-cock that tells that the blackening east wind is over, and a kindlier air is breathing, one that perhaps in due time shall call up from the roots below the earth the sap that shall again burst out in mist and spray of young green leaf, and put into the heart of the birds that mating-time has come again. And that first hint of change, though lisped

155

about while yet the darkness before dawn was most black, is better than all the gold that had poured in through the hours of the night.

Not all day nor when night fell did the rain cease, but the air was very warm, and the two dined out as usual in the verandah. The candles burned steadily in the windless air, casting squares of uncertain light on to the thick curtain of the night which was hung round them. Merivale, it appeared, had passed a day of high festival even for him; the rain of which the thirsty earth was drinking so deeply suited him no less.

"Ah, there is no mood of Nature," he cried, "which I do not love. This hot, soaking rain falling windlessly, which other people find so depressing, is so wonderful. The earth lies beneath it, drinking like a child at its mother's breast. The trees stand with drooping leaves, relaxing themselves, making no effort, just drinking, recuperating. The moths and winged things creep close into crevices in their bark—I saw a dozen such to-day— or cling to the underside of the leaves, where they are dry and cool. Everything is sleeping to-day, and to watch the earth sleep is like watching a child sleep: however lovely and winsome it is when it is awake, yet its sleep is even more beautiful. There is not a wrinkle on its face: it is as young as love, and with closed eyes and mouth half-open it rests."

Philip was looking at him with a sort of dumb envy, which at length found voice.

"I would give all I have for just one day of your life," he said, pushing back his plate and putting his elbows on the table, a characteristic movement when he wanted to talk, as Merivale knew.

"Ah, my dear fellow," he cried, "it is something very substantial gained already, if you wish that. To want to be happy is a very sensible step towards it."

"It is true that a fortnight ago I don't think I even wanted to be happy," said Philip.

"I know. But you have made the first step. Also, I can say it now, you look very much better than when you came."

"I am not more happy," said Philip.

"No, but you conceive it distantly possible that one day you may be. That has only just begun to occur to you."

Philip established his elbows more firmly yet.

"You are a living miracle, Tom!" he said. "I believe you are happier than any man on this earth has ever been, since, at any rate, man began to grow complicated and want things. You want nothing, I suppose, do you? And is it that which has made you a boy again, while wanting and not getting, and being robbed of what was mine, has made an old man of me?"

Tom smiled, showing his white even teeth.

"Ah, I want," he said, "I want passionately, but I feel sure I shall get what I want. It is the old story, I have told it you before: what I want is the full realisation of the oneness of all life, and of the joy that pervades everything."

"What would I not give to realise one millionth-part of that?" said Philip.

He paused a moment and then broke out suddenly.

156

"Ah, it is the very intensity and completeness with which I loved her that makes it all so bitter," he said. "A little love would only have meant a little bitterness. But my love was not little, and so also is not my bitterness. And afterwards, I did the best thing I could think of. I worked, using work as a drug. As you know, I took too much of that drug, and nearly broke down in consequence. And, oddly enough, now, so far from finding myself a slave to it, the thought of it is rather distasteful than otherwise. I might have made quite a lot of money to-day, if I had only taken the trouble to write a telegram, which would have been done in ten minutes and have cost me ten shillings. But I thought: 'Is it worth while?' And when one thinks that, it is certainly not worth while: only things that are quite indubitably worth while are worth while at all. And then I thought over what I had done to Evelyn, and that seemed not worth while either. I should not do it again if I had the chance."

"What was that?" asked Merivale.

Philip told him in a few words the history of Metiekull.

"It was designed to hurt Madge, too," he said, "which again doesn't seem worth while. I don't care whether she is hurt or not. And I thought I was so strong, so unbending."

He paused a moment, but the need of confiding, of laying his heart open, was strong upon him. It had long been dammed up, now the flood-water had at last begun to make a breach in the banks.

"I love her still," he said, "and I loved her all the time when I would have done anything to hurt her. I wonder if you understand that. It is true at all events. I would like, or rather I would have liked, to hurt her and go on hurting till she writhed with pain, and all the time I should have been longing to kiss her tears away. But now I don't want to hurt her any more. It does not seem worth while. And besides, I can't hurt her; only one person in the world can really hurt her, because she loves him. I am an object of indifference to her, and therefore I have no power to hurt her. My God, by what diabolical trick is it that only those we love have the power to hurt us? That was a cruel trick God played on us when he made us so. It is infamous!"

His hands, which were supporting his head, trembled, and for the first time his eyes grew soft with unshed tears. Never until this moment had he felt the slightest desire to weep; now the tears were ready to come. But he repressed them and went on.

"My house is in ruins," he said, "and perhaps I have been looking at the ruins too long. It has done no good in any case: looking at them has brought me no nearer to laying the first stone again. I have just the sense left to see that. One has to build, to begin again, not count over the destruction that has been wrought. Yet my house was so beautiful, the house that was already built, and waited only for one to enter."

Again he paused, for his voice trembled, too.

"But as there is no such futile fool as the pathetic fool," said he, "I will not go on about that. I want, and I want you to help me in this, to look the other way, forward. I think you have vitality enough, or call it what you will, to resuscitate a man who is all but drowned, over whose head the

157

billows have gone. There is something infectious about you, I think; you somehow shine on one, and I feel as if I was sickening, so to speak, by being with you, for the disease of life. Work, anyhow, did me no good; it only ended in my breaking down. But mere idling here has done something for me. I feel as if I could acquiesce in continuing idle here, whereas before the thought of continuing to do either anything or nothing was intolerable. I could but just get through the present dreadful moment. Through all these weeks the next moment, the next hour, the next day, might easily have proved to be impossible. For, look here—you know I am not melodramatic!"

He took from his pocket a little surgical lancet, and stroked the side of his throat with his thumb.

"I tried to get prussic acid," he said, "but I suppose I asked for it badly, and they did not believe some foolish tale about a dog which I wanted to put out of the way. So I bought this. One little incision—I took the trouble to learn the right place, for it is dreadfully foolish to make a mess, over and above the mess that must be made, about such simple things. I don't really know why I have not used it before; I can only say it was not from cowardice. But now I want it no longer; I am beginning to be able to look forward. So it goes."

With a jerk of his wrist he flung it among the shrubs to the right of the lawn, where it fell with a little splutter of applause, as it were, from the leaves, as if they, too, were glad to assist in the disposal and forgetting of it.

But Merivale looked neither shocked nor surprised; it was as if but a very commonplace thing had been told him.

"Yes, my dear chap," he said, "of course I don't put it down to cowardice, the fact, I mean, that you did not use that abominable little knife. Why, if you were a coward, you would have done so. Of course it must have been much easier for you to die than to live all this time. But I'm glad you weren't a coward, Philip. I don't think a coward can be much good for anything. A man who won't meet what is in front of him, and prefers to run away somewhere, he doesn't know where, is a poor sort of being. Of course, we all have our fears; life is full of terror. All we can do is to say we are not afraid, and to behave as if we were not. And since you have thrown that knife away, I may say that I think suicide is one of the most abject species of cowardice. Of course you were not yourself when you contemplated it, however vaguely. Now that you are a little better, you throw the thing away."

His tone was so extremely matter-of-fact that its very normalness arrested Philip. As he had said, it was perfectly true that nothing was further from his thoughts than melodrama, and the interest he felt in Tom's attitude, as thus revealed, towards life and death and fear was a fresh sign, and he himself felt it to be such, of his reawakening interests. Hitherto it had not, however remotely, concerned him as to what anyone else might think of it all.

"You talk of fears," he said; "what do you know of them? Surely you, at any rate, are free from fear. Oh, talk, Tom, interest me in anything; talk about yourself, or birds, or beasts. You have given me so much: give me

158

more. Give me the foundation of my new house, since it is you—yes, you, you dear fellow—who have made me turn my back upon the ruins. I have got to begin again; I have nothing to begin with. I am bankrupt. I beg you to give me a bit of that which you have so abundantly."

His voice again half-failed him, but he recovered it in a moment.

"We were talking about fear," he said; "what have you got to fear? You don't depend on men and women; you don't love. There is nothing in the world to be afraid of except love. I have found that out. Yet people seek it, the fools. They call it by sweet names: they say it is love that makes life worth living. My God, I should be so content if I had never known what it was. Damn her! I could have lived exactly like you—no, that is not true; I could never have been even remotely happy without loving her, just as, if I had never loved her, I should never have known what misery was. But you among your birds and beasts and trees, what on earth have you to fear? You won't fall in love with a beach-tree and find that it elopes with an elm. Tell me about your bloodless Paradise, and how the serpent, which is fear, can enter into it."

Tom Merivale had grown rather grave during this sudden outburst. Nothing in the world, so he believed, had power to ruffle his temper: only it was difficult to explain to such a child as Philip had shown himself to be. But before the pause was on his side the other spoke again.

"I am sorry," he said, "but it was a sort of baffled ignorance that spoke. I don't understand you; and for that reason I had no business to call your happiness, which is maddeningly real to me, a bloodless Paradise. But, for God's sake, show me anything approaching Paradise, at the door of which there is not an angel with a sword, not flaming, but cold and convincing. And where, above all, is your fear? How can fear exist for you? What is there to be afraid of unless you love and can be betrayed?"

Philip's servant came out from the house, bringing a tray with glasses and bottles. He paused by his master a moment.

"What time will you be called, sir?" he asked.

"Usual time; you can go to bed."

The pause lasted till the man had entered the house again. Then Merivale spoke.

"I fear all I have not learned," he said. "I fear the revelation of what people suffer, of what you have suffered, of what Christ suffered. I fear that all suffering, in its degree, is atonement. I don't believe it, mind you, but I am afraid it may be true, and that somehow I shall have to believe it. I am not a Christian, and so I put it that a man who was as infinitely above the rest of mankind as Shakespeare is above the child which is idiotic from its birth and has never felt the warmth of the slightest spark of reason, found it necessary to die, and believed that his death atoned for the sins of the whole world. Ah, if I only believed that he was right, how instinctively I should believe that he was God. No one but God could have thought of that."

He paused a moment.

"But I am beginning to think that I shall not die without believing it," he said. "I don't think that even the death of the body could come to

159

this body of mine unless I became convinced of the necessity for suffering and for death. Why am I beginning to think that? I can't possibly say; there is never any reason for one's believing anything, except the conviction that it must be so. Evelyn, I remember, once talked to me about it. At that time I was satisfied with my own reasoning; now I am not. I said to him then that my métier was the realisation of joy. Well, at present I know nothing that invalidates that belief. But I see clearly now the possibility that he was right, in which case it is possible that my fears, about which you asked, are right also. Mind, I am not afraid in any case. I would sooner see all the sorrows of the world, and realise them, as far as I am able, than turn aside. But my fear is that I may be called upon to realise them. I shall not like it, but if that is to be, I can assure you that I shall not attempt to turn back. Not one step of the way which I have gone along would I retrace. I will meet them all, I will realise them all. And, in my own language, that means that I shall see Pan, the god of all Nature, of the suffering and sorrow of Nature as well as the illimitable life and joy of her. And to tell you the truth, I think it quite probable that I may have to do so."

The rain had stopped, and a sudden sough of the wind in the bushes sounded as if some animal had strayed there. Twigs creaked as if broken; small branches swayed. Also, so it seemed to Philip, the wind brought with it some faint, indefinable aroma, evoked no doubt by this rain from some shrub in the garden. But for all his horticultural knowledge, he could not give a name to it; it was pungent, of an animal flavour to the nostrils, and reminded him, with the instantaneous evoking of memory which scent possesses above all the other senses, of a châlet in which he had once taken refuge from a sudden mountain storm in some Alp above Zermatt. Tom, too, just then threw back his head, and seemed to sniff for a moment in the air. But he made no comment, and continued—

"Yes, it was Evelyn who suggested that to me," he said. "His idea, I think, was that somehow and somewhere the balance is struck, that if one is overloaded with joy, some compensating pain has got to be put in before one is complete. It may come in a moment, so I conjecture, or one may have to suffer the agony of months and years, but of this I am sure, that the balance is in favour of joy. If I have to suffer, my suffering will be quite certainly less than the joy I have had. If the sorrows of death come upon me, they will weigh—I am certain of this—less than the ecstasies of life that have been mine. But, dear God, I have a long bill to settle."

The mention of Evelyn had roused black blood again.

"He too will have a bill to pay," said Philip.

Merivale took this quite impersonally.

"Yes, Evelyn is extraordinarily happy," he said. "I have scarcely ever known him otherwise. If he is right about me, he will have to be right about himself. Poor chap! What a good thing it is that neither you nor I have to be his judges, or have to apportion to him the dose of misery which will suit him. How could one tell when a man has had enough to make him whole, complete?"

He got up quickly and looked out into the night.

"Ah, we have all got to be made perfect," he cried. "I take it that no man in his senses can have any doubt of that. The thing which is you, that

160

essential, vital flame, has got now or at some future time to burn its best. I have to do the same; we shall all be strung up to perfection either through joy, or, perhaps, if we are approaching it from the other side, through some blinding pain. We all have to attempt to approach perfection to the best of our abilities. Our abilities may make a mistake; very likely they do. But I, when I attempt to approach the best of me through the pleasant ways of joy and simplicity, I would not go back one step to save myself from the pangs that may follow. I am very likely blind, but, as far as I know, I do my best. Perhaps—who knows, since my life has been an extraordinarily useless one, as the world counts 'use,' the world may be right, and I shall have to embark on a career of work in an office. But I don't think that is likely."

Again he paused a moment, taking a deep breath of the night air into his lungs. Then he turned round.

"You told me not to pity you," he said, "and I tacitly agreed not to, and fully intended not to. But the time has come when my pity cannot hurt you. For I pity you from the same plane as that on which I perhaps some day may be glad of your pity. You have suffered, and you are suffering. Well, I pity you, as God pities you, supposing that suffering does happen to be necessary. I would not spare you one pang of it, if this is so, but I just put out my hand to you, saying that I am there, and watching and worshipping, I may say, for if suffering is necessary it is certainly sacred. I don't know that it is necessary; but if it is, there am I, if that will do you any good, and there also are all those who have suffered, watching you with the pity that cannot help healing a little, and the sympathy that lightens. But if I were convinced, even for the winking of an eye, and to save a woodlouse from the absence of its dinner, that suffering must be, I should accept it all, and take not only my share of it, but the share of anybody else who would be so good as to shoulder me with it, for it is impossible to have enough or too much of anything that is right. At present I have not seen—so as to know—the necessity of it, though I have long known that all Nature groans under it. Everything preys on something else—you prey on the animals you eat, and the folk you make fools of on the Stock Exchange. And Evelyn preys on you. Yes, yes. And I—I try to prey on nobody, but perhaps this law of preying will some day be brought home to me. My joy, which so weighs down the scale, may have its compensating burden of suffering given to it. And whatever blackness of horror awaits me, I won't turn back. My way of approach is this: to others there is the rough-and-tumble of the world, to others the ascetic life. But I believe that joy and life are the predominant factors; that is why I have chosen them, it has been my business to get acquainted anyhow with them. But what I absolutely refuse is the horrible mean, where one makes no ventures, and but paddles on the shore of the eternal sea. Let the breakers leave me high and dry and smashed on the shingle, or let me steer through them and see the unimagined islands of myth and fable. But I will not just pull my shoes and stockings off, and shriek when the water comes up to my knee. Something, whatever it is, must infallibly be so much better than nothing."

He walked up and down the verandah once or twice with his long, smooth step, moving with that peculiar grace and ease which denotes great

161

physical strength. He had forgotten about Philip, and Philip for the first time had forgotten about Philip too.

"But during these last years," he went on, "I have consciously and deliberately turned my back on pain, because it is hideous, because it is a foe to joy, and because I have not and do not now realise its necessity. All I can say is, with Oliver Cromwell, it is just possible I may be mistaken, and in that case I am sure I shall have to—ah, no, be allowed to—learn my mistake. A child crying seems to me a dreadful thing, a beggar by the wayside with a broken tobacco-pipe, and not a penny to get another, the shriek of the rabbit when the stoat's teeth fasten in its throat; they are all dreadful, and enemies to joy. But I am no longer convinced, as I used to be, that pain is unnecessary; I am beginning, as I said, to hold an open mind on the subject, and only say that I believe I can realise myself best and bring myself best into harmony with Nature, with the whole design, by avoiding it. Yet for me also pain and suffering may be necessary. If so, let them come; I am quite ready. I only hope that it will be soon over, that it will be so frightful that I can't stand it. I should prefer that, some blinding, dreadful flash of revelation, to any slow, remorseless grinding of the truth into me. That, however, is not in my hands."

Philip's mind had gone back again on to himself.

"But how can it possibly be any good that those two should have behaved like this to me?" he cried, speaking directly for the first time. "What monstrous image do you make of the controller of the world and all our destinies, if it is by his will that this is done to me which turns all that may have been good in me into hatred and bitterness? Is that the lesson that I am meant to learn—that those whom one loves best are one's bitterest foes, and will hurt one most?"

Tom stopped in his walk and sat down on the edge of the table by Philip.

"My dear fellow," he said, "Oliver Cromwell will help us again. Is it not just possible that you too are mistaken when you assume that your trouble was sent you in order that your love might be turned into hate? That it should have happened so may (just possibly again) be in some measure your fault. Could you not have done otherwise, and done better? I don't want to preach, you know."

Philip sat silent, but his face hardened again.

"If I could have done better, it would not have been I," he said. "It would have been altogether another man."

Tom got down off the table.

"Ah, you repudiate moral responsibility for your own acts," he said.

"Not exactly that. I say that there may be circumstances under which one's will is crumpled up like a piece of waste paper, and one's powers of resistance are paralysed. Don't you believe that?"

Merivale shook his head.

"No, I don't believe that the power of choice is ever taken away from one while one remains sane," he said. "The moment one cannot choose, the doors of Bedlam are opened."

Philip got up.

162

"They are still ajar for me," he said. "But they were more widely open when I came here. For pity's sake, Tom, go on helping me. It is only you, I think, who can get them closed for me."

He paused a moment, looking out into the still blackness of the garden, and again something stirred and creaked in the bushes, and the drowsy wind was tainted with some sharp smell. He turned to Tom—

"I wonder if all that you have been saying is a fairy tale," he said, "and whether I have been taking it literally, so that I imagine that things which are only, and can only be, allegorical and mythical are true."

"You mean the Pan-pipes, for instance, which I heard for the first time at Pangbourne, and which I hear so often now?" asked Merivale.

"Yes, that among other things. Pan himself, too. I begin to think of Pan as a real being, the incarnation of all the terror and fear and sorrow of the world. The crying child you spoke of is part of Pan, the shriek of the rabbit is part of him. All these things, as you say, you have turned your back on. What if they should all be shown you suddenly, they and the huge significance and universality of them?"

Merivale looked quite grave; anyhow it was no fairy story to him, whatever it might be to others.

"Yes, that is all possible," he said, "and that will mean that I shall see Pan. What a wonderful mode of expression that is of the Greeks. For Pan means 'everything,' and to see everything would be clearly more than one could stand. And so to see Pan means death."

Once again the strange, pungent odour was noticeable.

"Where are you going to sleep to-night?" asked Philip suddenly.

"Oh, in the hammock," said Tom. "I hardly ever sleep in the house."

Then a more definite, though utterly fantastic, fear seized Philip.

"No, sleep in the house to-night," he said, feeling that his fear was too childish to be allowed utterance.

At that Merivale laughed; there was no need for Philip to utter his thought, for he knew perfectly well what it was.

"I know what you mean," he said, "but do you think that if Pan is going to visit me he will only come into the garden, and not into the house? You are mixing up the fear of Pan with the general sense of insecurity about sleeping out of doors, which comes from unfamiliarity with that delightful way of spending the night. And I know another thing you felt; you heard an odd rustling in the bushes, as I often hear it, and you smelt a rather queer smell, something rather pungent, and it reminded you of a goat. Of course Pan used to appear, so the Greek myth said, in goat form, and your inference was that Pan was in those bushes. But he is just as much in this verandah, and, for that matter, in Piccadilly, poor thing! There is quite certainly no getting away from him; I am as safe here as I should be if I was locked into the strong-room in the Bank of England. For it is not just to this place or that that he comes, but to this person or that."

They parted after this, Philip going upstairs to his bedroom, while Tom, after changing into a sleeping suit, went out with a rug over his arm into the dusky halls of the night. Sleep, when the time for sleep had come, visited him as quickly as it visits every healthy animal; and if it kept aloof,

163

he no more worried about it, or tried to woo it, than he would take appetising scraps of caviare or olives to make him hungry. And to-night he lay for some time, not tossing or turning in his hammock, but with eyes wide open, looking through the tracery of briar and leaf above him into the sombre darkness of the clouds overhead. So dark was it that the foliage was only just blacker than the sky, and to right and left the trees were shapeless blots against it. But all that mattered was that sky and clouds and trees were all round him, and that he could sink and merge himself in the spirit and the life with which they were impregnated. He lay open to it; just as his lungs were filled with the open air and his body vivified by it, so his soul and spirit drank in and breathed that open, essential life that ran through all things, the life that day by day he more fully realised to be One thing, expressing itself in the myriad forms of tree and beast and man. And though still that curious rustle and stir went on in the bushes, and though once he thought he heard the tap as of some hoofed thing upon the brick path of the pergola, he did not stir, nor did any sense of dismay or fear come to him. He had followed the path which he believed was his, striving to make himself one with the eternal harmony of Nature, and if the revelation of her discords was to come to him, come it would; the matter was not in his hands. But in whoever's hands it was, he was content to leave it there.

Philip meantime fared less easily in his bed indoors. The talk this evening had brought back to him with a terrible vividness all he had been through, the bitterness and hatred of his own heart all blossomed poisonously again, now that Merivale had gone, and he was left alone in the darkness and quiet of the night. That there was some subtle and very powerful influence which surrounded the Hermit like an atmosphere of his own he felt fully; in his company he knew how strong a sense of healing and serenity was abroad, but to-night, at any rate, all his foes, which he had almost dared to hope were being vanquished and left for dead, were rising about him again in ghostly battalions. He had, so he dimly hoped, begun to slay them, but it seemed for the moment that he had been but smiting at shadows that took no hurt from his blows. For a little while he had been able to set his face forward, to fancy that he was beginning really to make way, but now, as he glanced back over his shoulder, the enemy pursued undiminished after him. Again he felt his lips were quivering with sheer hatred of those who had so hurt him, and his hands were clenched in passionate desire to strike. And thus for hours he tossed and turned, until his window again, as in Jermyn Street, began to "grow a glimmering square," and the tentative notes of birds to flute in the bushes, and he was back again in those darkest hours he had ever known.

Then his bed became intolerable, and he rose from it and walked about the room, until the huelessness of the earliest dawn began to be touched with colour. Never since the blow had fallen upon him had he been able to pray; his bitterness and hatred had come like the figure of Satan himself between him and prayer.

Philip suddenly paused; another dawn was beginning to break, a dawn yet remote and far off in the Eastern skies, but a faint, dim streak of

164

light was there. It was indeed true; it was his own hatred, his own bitterness, not what others had done to him, which had stood in his way, and, as Merivale had said, the power of choice was in possession of every man who was fit to move about the world. He had accepted that when it was stated to him; he knew it to be true, and thus choice was still his. He had to choose, and to choose now. Did he want to hate and be bitter? Did he deliberately, in so far as he could choose, choose that?

So, though no word crossed his lips or was even formed in his brain, he prayed.

SIXTEENTH

THE elder Lady Ellington had never yet in the whole course of her combative life been knocked out of time by the blows of adverse circumstances, and she did not intend to begin being knocked out now. That Madge's marriage was a frightful disaster she did not deny or seek to conceal, but her admirable habits of self-control and her invariable custom of never letting anything dwell on her mind or make her worry, served her in good stead now. She considered that Madge and Evelyn had both behaved quite unpardonably, and though she had no thought of pardoning either of them, she had no thought of dwelling on the matter. When the thing was done, it was done, and, like David, she, so to speak, proposed to go and oil herself—in other words, to pay her customary round of summer and autumn visits, carrying with her all her old inflexible firmness and readiness to advise. For Philip, finally, she hardly felt pity at all; a man really must be a fool if he could lose his wife like that at the eleventh hour. It was impossible to acquit him altogether of blame, though it would have puzzled her who had so nearly been his mother-in-law to say exactly where the blame lay. General incapacity to keep what was morally one's own perhaps covered it, and incapacity of all kinds she detested.

These visits took her up to Scotland about the middle of August, since this was on the whole the easiest way of not getting out of touch with people. Scotland, if one went to the right houses, she considered to be a sort of barometer as to the way people would behave, and the general trend of affairs go, when the gatherings began for the autumn parties in England and people came up to London in the spring; and though she could not have been considered exactly a conventional woman, she very much wanted to know what kind of line society in general would take about Madge. For with all her hard shrewdness, she had not what we may call a sensitive social touch. When Society beat time she could follow it with scrupulous exactitude, but she was not capable of conducting herself. And this concerted piece was rather complex, and though Society had been so unanimous in its condemnation at the time, Lady Ellington, knowing it

165

pretty well, did not feel at all sure that the sentence it passed on July 28th would not be reprieved, whether, in fact, Society would not say that there had been a miscarriage of justice, and that Madge—and Evelyn, for that matter—were entirely innocent and even laudable. For if Philip had wealth, which he undoubtedly had, and Madge had thrown that overboard, she had at any rate picked up, as one picks up a pilot, a man with extraordinary charm and extraordinary gifts, about whom Society was even now on the point of losing its head. Evelyn, in fact, if he continued to be as gay as he always was, to enjoy himself as thoroughly, and also continued to paint pictures which really furnished Society with conversation to quite a remarkable degree, promised well to be as desirable a husband as the other. Also Philip's stern attention to business during the month of August had done his cause, as has been mentioned, no inconsiderable damage. Indeed if he had married old Lady Ellington instead it perhaps would have been more suitable. But having failed to secure the rose, he had not shown any inclination to be near it, and had gone to the City instead.

It was all this which Lady Ellington hoped to pick up in Scotland. She wanted, in fact, to know what would be her most correct attitude towards Madge. Her own personal attitude she knew well enough; she was still quite furious with her. But (she put it to herself almost piously) it is better sometimes to sink the personal feeling in the deep waters of the public good, just as you drown a superfluous kitten. However she felt privately, it might be kinder and wiser to conceal and even eradicate that personal grudge. She went, in fact, in order to see whether Society was possibly taking a more Christian line about her daughter than her daughter's mother really was. Strange as the fact may sound, this was the fact, for it would never do that Madge's mother should on the one hand be estranged from her daughter, while all the world embraced her; nor, on the other, that Madge's mother should continue to embrace her daughter while all the world discreetly looked the other way and said "That minx!"

Now, as has already been briefly stated, the country verdict about Madge, the verdict, that is to say, of London gone into the country, had reaped the benefit of country air and early hours. The personal inconvenience and the necessary incidental chatter had died down; nobody really cared about it; the stern condemnation originally made was felt to be but a hollow voice, and Society, which, whatever may be said about it, is really rather indulgent, just as it hopes individually for indulgence, in that most unlikely contingency of indulgence being desirable, was already, without the slightest sign of embarrassment, executing a volte-face. For if the volte-face is general, the only embarrassment arises from not executing it. And Lady Dover's house, which, so to speak, kept social Greenwich time without error, was the first place that Lady Ellington visited.

It was only this strong sense of duty—duty towards Madge—that drew her there; otherwise nothing would have induced her to go. There was a night in the train and a day in the train, and at the end of that a thirty-mile drive starting from a spot called Golspie. Her experience of Golspie was that it rained, and that an endless road stretched over mile after mile of moor, where it rained worse than in Golspie. But in Scotland it is officially supposed never to rain; the utmost that can happen in the way of moisture is that it should be "saft." She arrived at Golspie, an open motor-car was waiting for her, and it was "saft." Also the motor could not take all her luggage; that was to follow in a cart. The cart, so she mentally calculated, if it did not stick in a bog (not a wet one, only a "saft" one) might arrive about midnight. Another passenger also alighted at Golspie; the present bearer of her husband's title. He too was going to Lady Dover's, and the motor was to take them both. He hazarded that this was "awfully jolly," but he seemed not to have said the right thing.

The softness grew softer as they breasted the hills, and Lady Ellington really wondered whether this was worth while. But the conclusion must have been that it was, otherwise she would have had no hesitation in turning back even now and sleeping at Golspie, if sleep could be obtained in so outlandish a spot. She knew well too what her week there would be; a Scotch breakfast, the departure of the male sex to the hills, with fishing "in the burn" probably for those who remained; the return of the male sex about six, their instant dispersal to baths and their own rooms; dinner, no bridge, but conversation, and the final dispersal of everybody about half-past ten. Yet it was worth it; from here, goodness knew why, ticked out the "correct attitude." Lady Dover's opinion, not because she was clever, so said her guest to herself, but because she was completely ordinary, would be an infallible sign as to what the rest of the world would think about Madge. Assembled at her house too would be those who, right and left, would endorse Lady Dover's opinion, not because she had intimated it to them, but because they would naturally think as she did. It was, in fact, the bourgeois conclusion of the upper class that she sought.

Bourgeois conclusions of all sorts she got on her drive.

"Devilish evening, eh?" said Lord Ellington. "Makes one wonder if it's worth while. Thirty miles of this, isn't it, shofer?"

"Yes, my lord; thirty-two miles."

"Well, let's get on a bit; don't you think so, Lady Ellington? Put your foot down on some of those pedals, and turn some of those handles, eh? And how's all going, Lady Ellington? Rum thing; there'll be two Lady Ellingtons in the house. Gladys arrived three days ago. I couldn't. Detained, don't you know. I always say detained, eh?"

All this anyhow was a kind of olive branch. It continued with but short replies on her part, to wave in the wind.

"Awful smash, wasn't it?" continued he. "Gladys and I were very sorry. Good fellow, Home, he put her—me—up to an investment or two that turned out well. But there's no telling about girls; kittle cattle, you know, eh? I daresay she's awfully happy—what? And of course the man doesn't matter. Men are meant to go to the wall. Lord, how it rains!"

Lady Ellington did not really mind rain; she knew too that even this man, whom she detested, had his vote in public opinion, and, what was more, he reflected public opinion, like some newspaper. What he said other people would say. She did not in the least want the vote of bohemian circles, any more than she wanted the vote of bishops; what she wanted to

167

know was the general opinion of her class. A most elusive thing it was, and one on which it was intensely rash to risk a prophecy. For one person would be found with a stolen halter in her hand, and yet no one would say that the halter was dishonestly come by; another would but look over a hedge, and the whole world would say that the design was to steal horse and halter too. To which class did Madge, with her calm eyes, belong in the world's opinion?

"Yes, of course, it has been terrible," she said. "My poor girl has gone so utterly astray. What could have been nicer than the marriage that was arranged?"

"Well, she seems to have found something she thought nicer," said her companion.

"Yes, but from the sensible point of view. Supposing you fell in love with a match girl——"

Lord Ellington gave a loud, hoarse laugh.

"Trust Gladys for hoofing her out of it in double quick time," he remarked.

Yet this, too, was what Lady Ellington sought; vulgar, hopeless as the man was, he yet reflected the opinion of the average person, which it was her purpose to learn. For the votes of the "Moliere's housemaids" will always swamp those of the most enlightened critics, and the popularity of the play depends on them. And Lady Dover's house was a sort of central agency for such opinions; smart, respectable, and rich people congregated there, who were utterly conventional, not because they feared Mrs. Grundy, but because they were Mrs. Grundy—she herself, and no coloured imitation of her. The good old home-brewed, national, typical, English upper-class view of life might here really be said to have its fountain head, and to have stayed in the house was a sort of certificate that you were all right. Scandal might, just possibly, twitter afterwards about some one of Lady Dover's guests; but these twitterings would be harmless, for the knowledge that he or she about whom it twittered had stayed at Glen Callan would convince all right-minded people that there was nothing in it.

It was after eight when they arrived, and when they emerged into the light and warmth of the hall, hung round, as was suitable in the Highlands, with rows of stags' heads and sporting prints, dinner had already begun. But Lady Dover came out of the dining-room with her husband to welcome them.

"Dear Lady Ellington," she said, "what a dreadful drive you must have had. But no one minds rain in Scotland, do they? How are you, Lord Ellington? So nice that you could come together! Gladys arrived two days ago. Mr. Osborne calls her the fishmonger, because she really supplies us all with fish; we are now eating the grilse she caught this afternoon. Take Lord Ellington to his room, will you, Dover? Pray don't make anything of a toilet, Lady Ellington; it is the Highlands, you know. We went in to dinner because I felt sure you would prefer that we should. It is so much nicer to feel that one is keeping nobody waiting, is it not?"

There was only a small party in the house, so Lady Ellington found when she joined them in the dining-room. Mr. Osborne, whose brilliant sobriquet for Gladys has already sparkled on these pages, was there; he was a very wealthy man, who had married Lady Angela Harvey, the daughter of a Duke, and was one of the main props and pillars of English Protestantism. Lady Angela was there too, thin-lipped and political, sitting next Seymour Dennison, the Royal Academician, who had painted and exhibited so many miles of Sutherlandshire scenery that, were all the ordnance maps lost, it might almost have been possible to reconstruct the county again from his pictures without any fresh survey. His wife, of course, whom he had only lately married, was also of the party; Lady Dover had not previously met her, for she had lived in Florence, and though there was a certain risk about asking to the house someone who was really quite unknown, still to ask Mr. Dennison without his wife would have been to stigmatise her, which Lady Dover would never do without good reason. Harold Aintree, a first cousin of Lady Dover's, completed, with Gladys and her husband, the party of ten. He, too, was eminently in place, for he was a great traveller in out-of-the-way countries, which is always considered an enlightened pursuit. Moreover, you could read all his published accounts of them without having any sensibility or delicacy offended. Savage tribes, so his experiences showed, and Australian aborigines, had a true and unfailing sense of propriety.

Lady Ellington's place was next her host, and as she ate the grilse, Lord Dover told her about it. Gladys was his cousin, therefore he referred to her by her Christian name.

"Gladys caught that grilse only this afternoon," he said. "A beautifully fresh fish, is it not? Mr. Osborne calls her the fishmonger. Lady Fishmonger Ellington, was it not, Osborne?"

Mr. Osborne paused in his conversation with Mrs. Dennison to bow his acknowledgments.

"But Lady Ellington fishes too," he said. "We shall get into terrible confusion now."

"Ah, you must find another name for her," said Lady Dover. "Is it not a beautiful fish, Lady Ellington? The flesh is so firm. Dover says it could not have been up from the sea more than a day or two."

Mr. Osborne resumed his talk with Mrs. Dennison, whom he was questioning about the churches in Florence. Otherwise there was a moment's pause round the table, which was unfortunate, as she just then referred to the Catholic churches, meaning the Roman Catholic churches. She corrected her error, however, on seeing the questioning look in his face, and the general conversation was resumed.

"Yes, the sunset was one sheet of intolerable glory," said Seymour Dennison to his hostess, "and how little one expected that this rain was coming. What a wet drive Lady Ellington must have had."

"I did not see the sunset," said she. "I returned to write a few letters. You must describe it to us, Mr. Dennison, not in words but in colours. The sunsets here this year have been quite remarkable. They have been so very varied; no two alike, so far as I have seen."

Seymour Dennison was always in character as the poetical interpreter of Nature. His words, in fact, were generally as highly coloured as his canvases.

169

"And yet perhaps the finest sunsets one ever sees are at Hyde Park Corner," he said. "Is it not a wonderful thing how Nature takes the foul smoke of our cities, and by that alchemy of light transmutes them into those unimaginable spectacles which even the eye, much less the hand, cannot fully grasp and realise? Light! Where would the world be without light?"

Lord Ellington had a moment's spasmodic desire to answer "In the dark," but he checked it. It was as well he did.

"That dying cry of Goethe's is so wonderful, is it not?" said Lady Angela, turning to Harold Aintree, and picking up this thread. "'More light, more light,' you know."

Harold cleared his throat; he seldom spoke except in paragraphs.

"It is extraordinary how the most savage tribes have a deep sense of natural beauty," he said. "I remember entering a settlement in Zambesi at evening, and finding all the inhabitants sitting in rows watching the setting of the sun. It appears to be a religious ceremony, akin to some way to the sun-worship of the Parsees. Even the most rudimentary civilisation—this particular tribe of the Zambesi, I may remind you, are cannibals—show traces of some appreciation of the beauties of Nature. Indeed one almost thinks that perhaps civilisation obscures that appreciation. Else how do we in England consent to live in the sordid ugliness of the towns we build?"

He turned half-left as he spoke, to pick up Lady Ellington, so to speak, for Lord Dover had crossed over to Gladys, with whom he was again discussing the grilse she had been so fortunate as to catch that afternoon.

"Ah, but we don't all live in cities, Mr. Aintree," she said, "and I think that there is a great return to simplicity going on. Don't you remember last July how we all took to lentils and no hats? And think of Mr. Merivale, who lives in the New Forest, you know, and makes birds come and sit on his hand. We went down there, you know, Madge and I, and saw it all."

The simplification of life, therefore, took the place of sunsets, and spread slowly round the table, moving with a steady sort of current; there was nothing that flashed or sparkled, Mr. Osborne only suggesting that if we all went to live in the country it would become as bad as a town, and if we all lived on lentils, the price would go up so much that few could afford it. Lady Ellington, however, cleared those small matters up, gave it to be understood that Mr. Merivale owed a good deal to her suggestions, and rather congratulated herself on having got Madge's name introduced.

Dinner over, a variety of innocent pursuits occupied the party. Mr. Dennison, with a good deal of address, did some conjuring tricks (the same as he had done last night and the night before, and would do again next night and the night after), Lord Dover continued to discuss Gladys' grilse (it was such a fresh-run fish) with various members of the party, and at ten o'clock was held what was called the "council of war," though why "war" was not quite clear, since the purposes of it were wholly pacific, and merely consisted in the discussion of plans for the next day. Lord Ellington, it was settled, should try for a stag, Mr. Osborne and his host were to go grouse-shooting together, Mr. Dennison would be amply occupied in recording the upper beauties of the Glen—he had not as yet painted more than three-quarters of a mile of it—Lady Angela and Mrs. Dennison were to drive over and see some friends in the neighbourhood, while it was universally acclaimed that Lady Fishmonger Ellington should again exercise her remarkable skill on the river. And on old Lady Ellington's saying that she would like to fish too, Mr. Osborne rose to the occasion.

"We already have Lady Grilse Ellington," he said, "and I am sure to-morrow evening we shall have Lady Salmon Ellington."

This brought the council of war to a really epigrammatic ending, and Lady Dover rose with her customary speech.

"We all go to bed very early here, Lady Ellington," she said. "Being out all day in the fresh air makes one sleepy. What is the glass doing, Dover?"

"Going up a bit."

"Then let us hope you will have a fine day to-morrow for your painting, Mr. Dennison. I shall come up the Glen with you in the morning, if you will let me, and go down to the river after lunch to see what the fishmongers—I beg their pardon, it is Lady Salmon and Lady Grilse, is it not?—have done."

Before half-past ten therefore all the ladies were in their rooms, and since breakfast was not till a quarter to ten next morning, it might be hoped that they would all sleep off the effects of being out all day in the fresh air. And though Lady Ellington did not feel in the least inclined to go to her room, and almost everyone else would have sat up as long as she chose, obliging, if necessary, her hostess to sit up too, she never at Glen Callan found herself equal to proposing any other arrangements than those which were made for her, or indeed of criticising anything. For there was a deadly regularity about everything, against which it was useless to rebel, and to dream of suggesting anything was an unthinkable attitude to adopt. She knew, too, exactly what would happen now, just as she had known speeches about the barometer would precede their going upstairs. Lady Dover, since it was her first night, would come with her to her room, ask her if she had everything she wanted, poke the fire for her, and say, "Well, I am sure you must be tired after your journey. I will leave you to get a good rest. Breakfast at a quarter to ten, or would you sooner have it in your room?"

But Lady Ellington felt she would probably be equal to facing the world again after eleven hours of retirement, and said she would come down.

"It is a movable feast, dear," said Lady Dover, as she went out; "in fact, we do not think punctuality at all a virtue at breakfast."

And a small but certain suspicion darted into Lady Ellington's mind that her hostess had said exactly the same thing to her just a year ago, when she came to Glen Callan. She wondered how often she had said it since.

Breakfast was a very bright and cheerful meal at Glen Callan; everyone was refreshed by his long night after the day in the fresh air and ready for another one. Lady Grilse and Lady Salmon were already spoken of by the very clever names that Mr. Osborne had found for them, and he further seemed inclined to christen Lord Ellington as Lord Stag. But the

171

dreary amazement in that gentleman's face when Mr. Osborne made soundings on this point prevented its total success, though Dennison considered it excellent. He himself, though he had to walk but half a mile along a nearly level road to the particular point where he was painting, had so keen a sense of local colour, that, in deference to the fact that this road was in Scotland, he had put on knickerbockers, a Norfolk jacket, and thick shooting-boots. The Norfolk jacket also had a leather pad on the shoulder, so that the cloth should not be soiled by contact with possible oil on the barrels of his gun. But since he never carried nor had ever used a gun, this precaution was almost unnecessary. Still there is no harm in being prepared for any contingency, however unlikely.

The morning was cloudy but fine, and the clouds were high. In front of the windows of the dining-room the ground fell sharply away into the glen, through which brawled the coffee-coloured water of the river where the two ladies were to fish, and Mr. Dennison, as he walked about eating his porridge, a further recognition to the fact that this was Scotland, drew attention to the beautiful contrasts of green and russet in the glen. He also mislaid the spoon with which he had intended to eat his porridge, and after drawing attention to his loss, apparently drew the spoon out of Mr. Osborne's breast pocket. He was accustomed to be the life and soul of the party, and had equal command over the flowers of language and the easier feats of sleight of hand. The flowers of language were his next preoccupation, for Lady Dover had hoped that there would be enough sun for him to work at his picture.

"We landscape painters," he said, "are terribly at the mercy of the elements. We may perhaps half-grasp a conception, a cloudy effect, it may be, and then we are given a fortnight of bright and blazing sunshine. What are we to do? Begin another picture? Ah, that is to let the first conception fade. I spent a month once in Skye watching for an effect I had seen ten years before. Not a stroke of the brush did I make all that month; I waited. Then one morning it came."

He shrugged his shoulders.

"Quite a small picture," he said, "and I sold it for a song. But my reward was the fact that I had waited for it. That was my imperishable possession; my character, my artistic character, was at stake. And I won; yes, I won."

Lady Dover broke in upon the sympathetic pause.

"But a portrait-painter, Mr. Dennison," she said; "surely he may have to wait also for the same look to appear on the face of his sitter. Is not the sitter as fickle as the clouds or the sun?"

Dennison had finished his porridge, and was seated on Lady Dover's left. He drew with his long white forefinger a few imagined lines in the air.

"No, I don't think so," he said. "There are the features; the light can be adjusted. You have but to awake again the train of thought that was in the sitter's mind, and the expression, which after all is only a matter of line, becomes the same again. Look at Dundas's pictures, for instance. I do not deny their merit; but what is there? Five sweeps of the brush is the face, literally no more. A piece of mere scene-painting is the background, a bunch of bananas is the hand, I assure you, a bunch of bananas. That

172

would not be my scheme if I was a portrait painter. I should study my sitter till the very finger-nails were an integral part of the picture, so that the picture would be incomplete without them. Poor Dundas, I think we have heard the last of him. This terrible——"

The silence that succeeded this unfortunate speech was one that might, like darkness, be felt. Mr. Dennison, intoxicated by his own voice, had "forgotten." The silence made him remember. But the silence, though pregnant, was of almost infinitesimal duration, for Lord Dover immediately resorted to the grilse caught the day before, which was now kedgeree; his wife from the other end of the table, and without consultation, recommended Mr. Osborne to try it, and Lady Angela looked forward in anticipation to the lovely views that she and Mrs. Dennison were certain to enjoy during their drive. But this instinctive buzz to bury what had gone before died down, and the dead subject seemed like to have a disconcerting and resurging silence. But Lady Dover, whose mind was already made up on this subject, indicated her attitude. She turned to Lady Ellington, who sat three places from her, and in her quiet voice the social oracle thundered prophecy and promise—

"And how is dear Madge, Lady Salmon?" she said. "I wonder if we could induce her and Mr. Dundas to come for a week or two before we go south? It would be such a pleasure. She would enjoy these beautiful walks, I am sure, and Mr. Dundas must be so very hard-worked that I am certain a little holiday would do him good."

That was the pronunciamento for which Lady Ellington really had come here, weighing light all the discomfort of travel and the dulness of the days that she anticipated. It had been forced, squirted as it were, out of her hostess, but nobody had ever squirted out of Lady Dover anything insincere. She often, in fact, refrained from saying all she meant, but she never said what she did not mean. Her word was as good as the bond of anybody else's; it was trustworthy coinage, sterling in its own dominions. And Lady Ellington accepted it as such, not ringing it or testing it in any way. That it was given her was quite enough.

"I am sure Madge would love to come," she said, "if she can only tear"—she could not help hesitating a moment—"tear dear Evelyn away from his work. He is so busy; everybody wants to be painted by him. And I'm sure I don't wonder. His portrait of Madge! It is too extraordinary! You expect her to get down from the easel and say something characteristic. The hands, too, surely, Mr. Dennison, you don't think the hands are like bunches of bananas in Mr. Dundas's picture of my daughter?"

Mr. Dennison had not seen the picture; he hastened also to qualify what he had said before. The qualification did not fare quite so well at his hands as the missing spoon had done. That in itself was not extraordinary, since there was no comparison between the respective difficulties of effecting these two disappearances. But breakfast was practically over, and the need for beating a further retreat was thus reduced to an irreducible minimum.

The shooters and the stalker went their ways immediately, the motor-car was also soon round to convey Lady Angela and Mrs. Dennison to their friends, and it was not extraordinary that the artist did not join the remainder of the party on the terrace. Gladys also had gone to consult with the gillie on the question of flies, and thus in ten minutes Lady Dover and Lady Ellington were alone in their after-breakfast stroll. The latter, as usual, went straight to the point; she did not want to talk about salmon pools and rowan-berries or the prospects of slain stags; she had come here to find out what Lady Dover thought about Madge. For this purpose she called Lady Dover by her Christian name, as one has to begin some time. Her Christian name was Susan, a name inimical for confidences, but it could not be helped now.

"Oh, Susan," she said, "you don't mind my calling you that, do you, because I feel such friends with you. You have no idea how relieved I am. I wanted so much to know what you thought about poor Madge, and I should have found it so hard to begin, unless you had said what you did say at breakfast about asking them here. Of course it was all a terrible grief to me, you can well understand that."

"Yes, dear?" said Lady Dover interrogatively.

"I know you see what I mean. The marriage with Philip Home was so nice, so suitable, and it was all arranged. People stopped in London particularly for it."

Lady Dover's calm eyes surveyed the terrace, the glen, and lastly her companion.

"But surely that is rather a conventional view to take," she said. "What does a little inconvenience matter, if your daughter's happiness is secured? I am told they are devoted to each other."

Now Lady Ellington in her most wild and wayward dreams had never conceived it possible that she could be called, or remotely labelled, "conventional" by Susan. She had much to learn, however.

"I hope I am not a slave to convention, or anything of the sort," continued Lady Dover; "but if Madge really loved Mr. Dundas, why on earth should she not marry him? Suppose she had married Mr. Home, and found out afterwards she was not really fond of him? One does not like to contemplate such things; there is a certain suspicion of coarseness even in the thought. I do not know what the view of the world may be, for the view of the world concerns me very little, but I feel quite sure that a girl is right in obeying the dictates of her own heart."

Lady Ellington longed to contradict all this; it was not in the least in accord with what she felt, and what she felt she was accustomed to state. Thus the suppression of it was not easy.

"How lovely those lights on the hillside are," said Lady Dover, in parenthesis. "Mr. Dennison ought to see them before he settles on the subject of his next picture. Yes, about Madge. I don't know what other people think about it all, I only know what I think, and I am sure Dover agrees with me. It was a love match, was it not? What more do you want? Of course if Mr. Home had been a duke and Madge a girl without any position——"

"You mean it is just a question of degree?" asked Lady Ellington.

"Ah, my dear—er—Margaret," said Lady Dover, with a certain

174

intonation of relief, because she was sure that her excellent memory had not played her false, "everything is a question of degree; there is nothing in the world into which circumstances, mitigating or the reverse, do not enter. How beautiful the rowan-berries are, I wish Mr. Dennison could see them. They would work into his foreground so well. I must take him to the end of the terrace to-morrow. Yes; but the mitigating circumstances are here so strong. She threw over Mr. Home, who is charming—I met him twice last year at dinner somewhere, and we asked him to lunch, only he could not come—and has married a man who is charming also, with whom she fell in love. How vivid his portraits are, too; I am going to be painted by him next spring, if he can find time. Almost too vivid, perhaps; they seem to jump out on you. But that is my view about the whole question. Supposing she had married Mr. Home, and had fallen in love afterwards! That sort of tragedy is so dreadful; such extraordinary cleverness is required to avoid all the horror of publicity. I could never survive publicity."

"But there is publicity as it is," said Lady Ellington. "Poor Madge! What will people think of her? And of me?"

Lady Dover throughout this conversation had given justification after justification for the importance that Lady Ellington attached to her verdict. She gave more now.

"There is publicity, it is true," she said; "but no sense of respectability has been offended. Of her, they will think that she fell in love and followed her instincts. Of you, they will think that you tried, like an excellent mother, to secure an excellent match for your daughter, but that your daughter chose for herself."

Lady Dover's serene face grew a shade more shrewd.

"You see, she has not married Tom or Dick or James," she said. "Mr. Dundas, in fact, is a sufficiently important person. Was it that you meant, by the way, by saying it was a question of degree? I don't know what his income is; it may be precarious. But he has great talent. And talent happens to be rather fashionable. I daresay it is only a phase, but after all one wants, if the sacrifice of no principle is involved, to be abreast with the world."

Now Lady Ellington could not possibly have been called a conceited woman, and her conviction that she was herself pretty well abreast of the world was founded on sober experience. She was up to most things, in fact; the world, on the whole, did not worst her. Yet when Susan spoke of being abreast of the world, she was conscious that another plane altogether was indicated, a plane to which she had to struggle and aspire, whereas Susan moved quite easily and naturally on it. All the way from Golspie she had been labeling her hostess as conventional, but what if this conventionalism came out on the other side, so to speak, and was really the summit of worldly wisdom, a peak, not a mediocre plateau, where Susan and others walked gently about, as at some place of corrective waters, exchanging commonplaces. For Lady Dover, she was beginning to see, was not in the least conventional because it was the way of the world; she was conventional because she was made like that. It was the world, in fact, which was conventional because it was like Lady Dover, not Lady Dover who was conventional because she was like the world. Indeed she had spoken no more than the truth when she said the opinion of the world did not matter to her—it did not; she never had to take it into consideration, simply because it was quite certain to coincide with her own. And Lady Ellington found herself thinking that when Susan died her portrait ought really to be put in a stained glass window, a figure that should typify for all time the solid, respectable, virtuous aspects of the British aristocracy.

They walked in silence for a few moments, for there was really nothing more to say on the subject. Then Lady Ellington took Susan's arm and pressed it.

"It is a great, great relief to me to know you feel like that," she said, "and you have made my line with regard to Madge so clear. Poor Madge, I have been too hard on her, but the disappointment was so great. I could not help feeling for Philip, too."

"Of course one is always sorry for people in trouble," said Lady Dover, "particularly if it is not their fault. I will write to Madge this morning. And now, do you know, it is almost time you went off to the river. I insist on your being Lady Salmon by this evening. Mr. Osborne is so quick and clever, is he not?"

SEVENTEENTH

LADY DOVER put into instant execution her promise to ask Madge and her husband to come and stay, and half an hour later set off with Mr. Dennison up the glen to the scene of his picture; the "original," as she called it. As usual, in her interview with Lady Ellington she had behaved quite straightforwardly, and had expressed and acted on the view which she believed to be right, and though she could not help feeling that Lady Ellington had referred to her rather as an oracle, whose slightest word was a thing to be treasured up and reverently commented on, she was not naturally at all self-conscious, and did not dwell on the fact with any elation. Elation indeed she could not possibly have felt, since, had she been pressed to say how highly she valued Lady Ellington's opinion, she would have been forced to confess that, without wishing to be unkind, she did not value it at all. Secretly, indeed, her estimate was that poor Margaret wanted very much to be a woman of the world, and only succeeded in being a worldly woman; she schemed (she had no doubt schemed in the matter of Madge's marriage) and span threads in all directions, with the unfortunate result that she only succeeded in getting entangled in them herself. Lady Dover, on the other hand, never schemed at all; she walked calmly along a broad highroad and admired the flowers by the wayside. Consequently she was invariably free from preoccupations, and could talk with the artist about the exquisite lights and shadows on the hillside and the wonderful contrast of the purple heather against the golden gorse with sincerity and attention. It was quite possible also that they might see an eagle; one had been seen at the top of the glen several times that year.

Lady Ellington as she went down with Gladys to the river felt more herself than she had felt ever since that stormy interview with Madge in the New Forest. A sense of imperfect mastery had begun then, terminating, on Madge's visit to the studio, in a terribly certain conviction that she had no mastery at all. Madge, in fact, had made a fool of her, and her resentment at it was impotent. She felt, too, that the world very likely regarded her with a sort of amused pity, which was hard to bear. But she felt sure now after this interview that the world was going to forgive Madge and her husband, and welcome them to its midst. Her own course of conduct therefore was clear, she must quite certainly do the same, and if possible let it be understood that she had, though sorry for Philip, realised that this marriage was inevitable. Lady Dover had put this so plainly; how much better that their mutual love should be discovered before the irremediable mistake of Madge's marriage with Philip had been made. And since she was a woman who never wasted time or anything else, she began immediately to lay the foundations of this remarkably imaginative structure before Gladys.

"Poor Mr. Dennison," she said, "I was so sorry for him at breakfast when he said he thought we had heard the last of Evelyn. I am always sorry for people who put their foot in it. But I suppose that would be the middle-class view of poor Madge's marriage. It is easy to see that Mr. Dennison is not quite a gentleman."

This was so calm and glorious a disregard of all that she had previously said, thought, and felt, that the very completeness of it roused Gladys's admiration. Lady Ellington took her previous attitude off, like a pair of gloves, just threw it into the gutter, and walked on. Gladys knew it must have been Lady Dover's pronouncement that had caused this change, for she too was aware that the social Greenwich time was largely taken from Glen Callan, and had made a mental note, just as Madge's mother had done, that she must also alter her own time by this. It clearly would be too ridiculous if all London welcomed them back with open arms, and only Madge's family turned their backs on her. But she had a certain Puck-like sense of malice, particularly when she could exercise it on Lady Ellington, and she could not resist a little tap or two now.

"I am so glad you take it like that," she said, "and see it as Lady Dover does. At first, you know, I thought you were being too bitter about it, and really, to tell you the truth, I had no idea that you were taking Madge's part. Dear Madge; I hope they will ask her soon, while I am still here."

"Of course I was bitter about it at first," said Lady Ellington. "Who could help being, when all my plans were upset, and poor Philip Home was suffering too? I was more sorry for him than for anybody else. I had to tell him, you know, and had a terrible interview with him. But I soon saw that since Madge was not in love with him, but with Evelyn, it was a thousand times better that we should all suffer that purely temporary disturbance and worry than that she should be in the dreadfully false position of being married to one man while she was in love with another."

Gladys purred a rather feline approval.

"How glad dear Madge must have been when you told her how you felt," she said. "I wish I had been there when you made it up with her. Who is it who says something about the 'blessings on the falling out which all the more endears'; it must have been quite like that."

Lady Ellington met this as well as she could, though it was rather awkward.

"Yes, I think Madge will be perfectly happy," she said, "now she finds that everyone is quite as nice as ever to her."

"Dear Madge, I never felt different to her," said Gladys rather imprudently.

Lady Ellington jumped on to this with extraordinary quickness and precision.

"Ah, I am glad to know that," she said, "because I now also know that Lady Taverner must have simply invented a quantity of things that she said you had said to her about it. I felt sure you could not have been so unkind."

So the honours on the whole were pretty well divided; each of them saw through the other, and since each determined to write to Madge that night, it was highly likely that Madge would see through them both.

Mr. Osborne proved to be a true prophet, and it was indeed Lady Salmon and Lady Grilse who came back from the river about tea-time. He had the good luck to be in the hall when they returned, and preceded Lady Ellington to the drawing-room, where he threw open the door for her to enter in the manner of a butler, and announced loudly—

"Lady Salmon Ellington, my lady."

Lady Grilse also had vindicated her name again, and when after tea they played the game at which one person goes out of the room, and on return has to guess by mere "Yes" or "No" what has been thought of, Mr. Osborne, on learning that they had thought of fish, instantly guessed "Salmon," which proved to be right. Satisfactory reports also came from the grouse shooters; the two ladies had had a charming drive; Mr. Dennison had caught an effect of a highly pleasing kind, and though Lord Ellington had missed his stag, it was felt that Mr. Osborne was in tune with the general cheerfulness when he said that after all that was next best to hitting it. Indeed Mr. Osborne was in extremely fine form altogether, and Lady Dover, as she went upstairs with his wife at about half-past six, as it was refreshing after the day in the air to lie down for an hour or so before dinner, said that she knew no one so entertaining as her husband. Then, since Mrs. Dennison was with them, she added:

"And Mr. Dennison has promised to show us a new conjuring trick this evening. I can't think how he does them. So very clever. And what a resource in the evening; I am sure I should never be dull if he would conjure for me always after dinner."

It was during this last week of August, which saw this party at Glen Callan, that in point of chronology Philip broke down as recorded, and went to the Hermit in the New Forest. Madge and Evelyn, however, less lucky in the matter of locality, had to remain all the month in London, without any immediate prospect of getting away. That week at Le Touquet, with its motor-car, its suite of rooms, and Evelyn's serene and complete disregard of all questions connected however remotely with finance, had been somewhat alarmingly expensive, and his ill-judged selling out of his Metiekull shares when things were absolutely at their worst had not mended matters. He had taken Madge completely into his confidence, and as it was evidently likely that there would soon be an embarrassing lack of funds, she had insisted on their immediate return to London, where they would be anyhow rent free in Evelyn's house in the King's Road, and could, as he cheerfully suggested, live on lentils like the Hermit. But on arrival in London the hall table was discovered to be literally smothered in bills, chiefly "to account rendered," for Evelyn in the insouciance of the comfortable bachelor income which his pictures brought him in, had certainly for a year past thrown into the fire anything of a bill-nature. Nothing had ever been further from his thoughts than not to pay, but the knowledge that he could, by a strange but almost universal trait in human nature, had made him not bother to do so. But, now, however, by the converse of this law, which holds equally true, as soon as it was doubtful whether he could stand debt free, it became quite essential to his interior peace of mind that he should do so. This instinct appealed also to Madge, and after a dismal morning of adding up, the whole position was revealed. Every penny could be paid with the jetsam of Metiekull, and there was left over—his total assets except his hand and his eye—the sum of forty-three pounds. It was clearly necessary, therefore, to stop in London, to be extremely economical, and to hope that the autumn would bring sitters. Lady Taverner, at any rate, was assured, and Evelyn found himself thinking of that pink face and butter-coloured hair with almost affection.

The month was extremely hot, but of the stifling air, of the emptiness of town, of the economy that Madge insisted on being observed, what a game their love made! They were stranded on a desert island, so ran the silly tale that was made up from day to day, in the midst of the tropics. A huge town was (unexplainedly) there, in which they dwelt; but though cabs jingled about it, it was forbidden, as in an allegory, to get into a cab. A mile away there were restaurants, which both in a dreamlike fashion seemed to know; in these, too, it was forbidden to set foot, for a lion called Ellesdee guarded the doors. Ellesdee, who gradually grew more elaborate, also crouched on the tops of the cabs they would otherwise have driven in, and lay in wait at the main terminuses which would have taken them out of town. Ellesdee could assume various forms; sometimes he became quite little, and crouched behind a box of hot-house peaches, which would have been pleasant for dinner; at other times he was an apparently bland attendant at the door of theatres. He even, this was Madge's contribution, nearly prevented Evelyn buying a couple of very expensive brushes which he wanted, but impassioned argument on his part convinced her that it was not Ellesdee at all who had taken the form of the shopman, and consequently the brushes were bought. He certainly guarded the furniture

179

shops, where Evelyn was inclined to linger, and though he had an eye on what came in at the area gate, into the house itself he never penetrated. Nor was he to be found in Battersea Park, nor on the Embankment, where they used to walk in the cool of the evening.

But the Ellesdee who had been responsible for the disaster in Metiekull never showed his face. That had been a big and a dead loss, but Evelyn had shaken it off from his mind, just as some retriever puppy shakes off the water after a swim, dispersing it over yards of grass in a halo. And if Madge on the day when they sat on the sands at Paris-plage had had disquieting thoughts as to whether it was a man she had married or a mere boy, here at any rate was some consolation if it proved to be the latter. For Evelyn had certainly that divinest gift of youth in being able to utterly expunge from the present and from his view of the future all that had been unpleasant in the past. The moment a thing was done, if the result was not satisfactory, it ceased to be; if consequences called, as now they called, in the shape of rigid economies, he was simply not at home to them. The results he accepted with cheerful blandness, but he never went back to the cause. Whether it might or might not have been avoided no longer mattered, since it had not been avoided. The cause, however, was done with; it belonged to the mistlike texture of the past. Meantime his exuberant spirits made the very most of the present.

One afternoon some business had taken him towards the city, and he returned hot, dusty, but irresistibly buoyant shortly before dinner. Madge was sitting in the studio, where, with its north aspect, coolness was never wholly absent, and though her heart went out to meet even his step on the stairs, she looked suspiciously at a small parcel under his arm as he entered.

"Yes, champagne," he said. "One bottle, half for you and half for me. Oh, let me explain. I got a dividend this morning of eight shillings and sixpence from twenty-five shares in something which I had forgotten, and which had therefore ceased to exist. Oh, Madge, don't scream! What use is eight shillings? But we both want champagne, so its equivalent in champagne is of use. No, it's no use trying to make me feel sorry, because I'm not. I just had to. Oh, you darling!"

He sat down on the sofa by her.

"I'm hot, I know," he said, "but you might kiss just the end of my nose. I haven't seen you for five hours."

She kissed him.

"But you are simply abominable," she said.

"Yes, that probably is so. Another thing happened to-day, too. I saw Philip. He was driving to Waterloo. In a hansom. Luggage was behind with his servant in a cab. He didn't see me; at least if he did, he appeared not to."

Evelyn paused a moment.

"Poor devil!" he said. "I don't know how you feel, but I am awfully sorry for him. But how could I help it? Are you a fatalist, Madge?"

"If I am, what then?"

"Nothing; but you've got to listen to a little sermon, whether you are or not. It's dreadful about Philip; you see, he was my friend. But what else was to be done? Wasn't the whole thing inevitable? How could it have been otherwise but that you and I should be here?"

"Otherwise?" she said, "what otherwise was there? Yet—yet, oh, Evelyn, on what little accidents it all depended. The thunderstorm down in the New Forest, your atrocious——"

"What?"

"Your atrocious behaviour. And then that it was he who asked me to give you one more sitting, and that my mother should have opened my letter! Is life all accidents? Are you and I the prey of any future accidents? May we be marred and maimed by what is as fortuitous as all this?"

Evelyn shifted slightly in his seat. This summing up of the past was a thing he was not inclined to. It was summed up and finished with, except in so far as the present was the finished past. Why go over the accounts again? There was no doubt as to their correctness.

"I don't know whether it was all accidents," he said, "but if you begin to call things accidents, there is no stopping. If one thing is an accident, everything is. That I stayed at his house at Pangbourne when you were there you may call an accident. That we made friends there you will call an accident also, if you call the first an accident. And if you are consistent you will call the fact that we loved each other an accident. Only, if you call that an accident, you are using the word in a different sense to that which I use it in."

"Then nothing is an accident?" she asked.

"Yes, my buying this bottle of champagne was an accident, because I didn't mean to. But as it has happened, we may as well drink it."

But a sudden stab of disappointment somehow pierced Madge. She had been serious, and so to a certain point had he. But now, when their talk seemed to be becoming fruit-bearing, he could dismiss it all with a jest. Her wifehood, for a month or two ago she would have done likewise, had developed her in a way that marriage had not developed him. He was still the bright-eyed boy. She, on the other hand, was no longer a girl but a woman. All the sub-consciousness of this twanged in her answer.

"You are so undeveloped," she said suddenly.

But to his ears there was no reproach in this; it concerned the future, not the past. And his bright eyes but grew brighter.

"Surely," he said, "but the development is in your hands. And I lay it—whatever it is—at your feet."

That, too, Madge felt was so extraordinarily genuine; small as was the tribute, it could not be but graceful. Everywhere he was that, in no relation of life was he otherwise—the beautiful, undeveloped manhood put out buds everywhere, yet at present no bud was expanded into a flower. There was brilliant promise, no promise could be fairer or more sincere, for he was incapable of insincerity, yet it was the "imperishable child" with whose fate she had bound herself up. Everything was there, except one, and that was the man. His talent was brilliant, and she could not have parted with the constant companionship any more than she could have parted with the light of day, yet something was missing.

181

It was not less definite, this sense or quality which was missing in Evelyn, because it was indefinable; one could not know another person, whether man or woman, without knowing whether it was there or not, and indeed almost everybody was possessed of it. Philip had it to a notable degree—indeed it was that which, if she searched her heart, had in its extraordinary abundance in him made her originally accept the possibility of her becoming his wife. It had nothing to do with the ardour of love, since the man for whom she alone had experienced that had nothing of it. Nor was it brilliant in any way, since all that was his also. Only it was bed-rock; it was something quite secure and responsible, and willing to take all responsibility, and human. It co-existed with dulness, it existed in people who were frankly intolerable. It was probably bourgeois, but she felt the possibility, as yet far off, so far off that she would only strain her eyes if she tried to focus them on it, of its being necessary, just as food and drink were necessary. The little ghost at Le Touquet, in fact, had apparently begged its way across, and had established itself in the King's Road. But ghosts of this kind do not mind prosaic surroundings; the discerning reader will perceive they have no need of tapestry or panels, for they are concerned in no way with what is past and ancestral, but with what is alive and knitted into the fabric of the present.

But after thus dismissing the question of the accidents and essentials of life with this ill-timed little jest about the champagne, Evelyn quite suddenly returned to a matter as serious.

"You called me undeveloped just now," he said, "and I expect you are right in a way that you did not think. Tom Merivale told me once that I had not the rudiments of a conscience, and I have often thought of that, and believe it is quite true. That is where I am really undeveloped, and I expect it is that"—and his face lit up even more with this piece of intuition—"I expect it is that which you miss in me. He also said I had no depth. You miss that too, probably."

Evelyn announced these discoveries with a perfectly serene and unclouded air; perturbation that he was lacking in so large a piece of moral equipment as a conscience would do no manner of good; nor, because his wife missed it, would it help matters that he should mourn with her over his deficiency. But the unshadowed brightness of his face, his frank acceptance of this so genially and generously made, was something of a reproach to her. All the sunshine of his beautiful nature was hers, all the brilliance of his talent, his extraordinary personal charm, his blithe acquiescence in all that happened was hers, and yet she was discontent. And with a pang of self-reproach she contrasted all he gave her with what she had herself thought good enough to give to Philip when she promised to be his wife, affection, respect, esteem, just a platter of frigid odds and ends, compared to this great feast and glorious banquet of love.

But there was no doubt as to the accuracy of the diagnosis which Evelyn had made as to what she missed in him. He had risen from the sofa, and was standing in front of her, and at this she rose too, and laid her hands on his shoulder.

"Ah, I'm an ungrateful little brute," she said; "but I believe that is a woman's way. Whatever you give a woman, she always wants more, and

182

you—you, dear, whatever I give you, you always say you did not know so much was possible. So I confess, and am sorry."

He looked at her still smiling, but without speaking, and the warmth of her contrition cooled a little. He ought to have known, so she told herself, that what she had said was not very easy to say; he ought to have met the warmth of her amende with welcome and acceptance, and even acknowledgment of her generosity, for she had been generous.

"Well," she said at length, "have you nothing to say to that?"

He put his head a little on one side, as he did so often when he was painting.

"Yes, I was just arranging it in my head in beautiful language," he said, "but the beautiful language won't come, so you will have to hear it plain, not coloured. It's just this. I don't think one does any good by pulling oneself open to see what's inside—oh, yes, rosebud, that's part of the beautiful language—like a rosebud. One flowers best, I expect, by leaving oneself alone, by just living. Surely life is good enough! I suppose some people are naturally analytical, people who write books, for instance, about other people's moral insides. But I'm quite certain that I'm not like that. I paint pictures, you see, of other people's outsides. And if I went on painting your face for years, Madge, I should never get to the end of all it is, or all it is to me. Well, that's Evelyn Dundas: I beg to introduce him. And you are Evelyn Dundas, let me tell you. You are me; you can't get away from that. So don't make either the best or the worst of me; don't let us regard our relations like that. They are what they are, and want no interpretation or examination. Let them just burn, and not examine their light under a spectroscope. Dear me, there's more beautiful language. I apologise."

She could not help laughing at this conclusion; his earnestness, for he was absolutely earnest, was all of one piece with utter flippancy, and from one he passed to the other without break or transition. How that could be she did not know, only it was all he. And as far as any one person can convince any other, she was convinced. Indeed, it was tearing flowers open to behave and to think as she had been doing, and she answered him in his own manner.

"Take care of the habit of beautiful language, dear," she said. "It grows on you without your knowing it. And surely it's dinner time."

Evelyn cast a tragic glance round.

"Ah, there it is," he cried. "I really had completely forgotten—you needn't believe it unless you like—about the dividend we are going to drink. I suppose a little ice now wouldn't be possible? I would go and get it."

"Yes, but I don't officially know about it," said she.

Storms in the physical and material sense are variously supposed to have two diametrically opposite effects; they may be regarded as likely to clear the air, or, on the other hand, to cause a general unsettlement in the weather. And mental or spiritual storms can in the same way either be the precursors and causes of serene blue weather, or they can produce a disturbance of equilibria which is not easily or immediately adjusted again; the violent agitation sets everything shaking and jarring. And the worst of it is that there is no barometer known which will reliably predict which of these effects is likely to be produced. To speak of a thing, "to have it out" as the phrase goes, may get rid of it altogether; it may be pricked like a puff-ball and vanish in a little dust and smoke, leaving an empty bladder, and again "to have it out" may but emphasise and make its existence more real. The "having it out," in fact, is but a sort of preliminary examination, which proves whether there is something there or whether there is nothing.

This talk between Evelyn and his wife had its distinct analogy to a storm. Things had been gathering up—indeed they were clouds—in Madge's mind ever since Le Touquet, and though their bursting had been unaccompanied by rain or explosions, yet to-night they had been undeniably discharged, and it remained only to see whether the air should prove to have been cleared, or whether the disturbance had upset the moral atmosphere. Again, they had "had it out," she had indicated where her trouble lay, or rather he had laid an unerring finger on it, and as physician had said "Leave it alone; that is my suggestion. Don't let us hear any more about it." She fully intended to follow his advice, but half-consciously she made a reservation, for she knew that some time—next week, next month, next year—she must know that either he had been right, and that the trouble had vanished, or that he had been wrong and the trouble had grown worse. And so some secret sense of uncertainty and unsatisfiedness sat somewhere deep in the shadows of her heart. It did not often obtrude its presence, but she knew it was there.

On Evelyn, however, this same scene appeared to leave no trace of any kind—and, indeed, there was no reason why it should, because it had contained nothing that was new to him, and also because it had ended so thoroughly satisfactorily. Madge had agreed with him about the advisability of letting analysis alone for the future. He had, indeed, this evening indulged in a little, and he found that there was nothing in their mutual relations which he wanted altering, nothing which alteration would not have spoiled. Not for a moment did he say that there were not things in himself which he should have preferred vastly different, but with a certain good sense he considered that in shaping one's course in life one had to accept certain tendencies and limitations in oneself, and, having granted them, to do one's best. And he did not see that any perseverance or thought or pains on his part could create in him what Merivale had called a conscience. His life was honest, sober, and clean, not, it must be confessed, because morality indicated that it should be, but because his artistic sense would be hurt by its being other than that. It was sheer waste of time for him to sit down and think about duty, because it really meant nothing to him; he might as well have sat down and thought about Hebrew. But from the kindliness and warmth of his nature his conclusions as regards conduct were extraordinarily like those which the very finest sense of duty would have dictated. Yet now and then, as when he had said that he was sorry for Philip, but that nothing could have happened differently, though Madge in word agreed with him, yet she, with her fine feminine sense, knew that she agreed with him, but agreed somehow on a plane quite different from his. That nothing could have happened differently she knew in another way than his: deeply, fiercely, and whole-heartedly as he loved her. For all her

184

life up till now, her whole nature had lain dormant; it had awoke all at once, and awoke to find that one person only was there, even as Brunnhilde woke on the mountain top and saw Siegfried. That awakening had been long delayed, but when it came it was complete, like that thunder-clap when he had declared his love for her, it deafened and paralysed all other senses; there was only one thing in the world for her, and that was her love.

But to him—she could not help knowing this—his love for her had not been the blinding flash that awoke all his nature. He had loved before that, keen sensibilities had been his, the sensibilities that inspired his art and made it so extraordinarily vital. All his life a huge joy of life had inspired him; he had waved in the winds of human emotions, he brought to her a love which was new indeed, but one which was driven by an engine that drove other machines as well, his art, his joy of life, for instance. But all that she was, was this one thing; she had lain like a chrysalis hitherto, and the moth beautiful that came out with wings at first crumpled and quivering, but momentarily expanding in the sun, had till then lived in darkness, and the light it saw when it emerged from its cracked husk was the only light it had ever known. She did not compare the respective dimensions, so to speak, of the love of each of them for a moment—she believed that Evelyn loved her as completely as she loved him. But he loved other things as well; his art was a vital part of his life, while she had nothing but him. This was why, though he was so much more developed than she, she had spoken a sort of truth when she said he was undeveloped, for he did not love her to the exclusion of all else. She was not, and could not be, the only thing the world held for him.

In the same way also his sorrow for Philip's suffering was different from hers, for he, so it seemed to her, was sorry for Philip, as his nature would make it necessary for him to be sorry for anyone who had suffered great loss, for an artist who went blind, for a musician who went deaf, but had yet the other joys of life, with, in course of time, an increase in his other sensibilities as compensation to make his loss good. But she who had emerged from nothingness into the full blaze of this unconjectured noonday rated Philip's loss at what her own would have been. All had been taken from him, he was left in the original outer darkness which can only be estimated by those who have seen light, and not by the purblind creatures that have never left it. Philip, what must Philip's sufferings have been! Poor Philip, who was so kind, so likeable, so everything but loved by her. And it was she who had done this; she had brought a misery on him which she honestly gauged by the knowledge of what her misery would be if something happened which made Evelyn no longer love her.

She had carried the skeleton of these thoughts with her to bed that night, and she woke early to find that, as in the dry bones of Ezekiel's vision, they were beginning to knit themselves together, bone coming to his bone, and the flesh covering them. The pale dawn was beginning to peer into the windows, and the birds to tune up in broken chirrupings for the songs of the day. Had Philip woke like this, she wondered, during this hot August month that he, too, had spent in London? If so, what mitigation of his misery had he found? Not in his business, she could not believe that;

185

surely he must have taken to work as another man, unhappy but less manly, takes to a drug that deadens the power of sense. Surely that must be the explanation of his tireless industry in the city all this month, when others now went for holiday to moor and mountain. Oh, poor Philip! She had brought all this on him, too; she could have made him happy, she felt sure of that, had not soft, irresistible love made that gracious task impossible for her.

The room in spite of its open window was very hot, and she turned back the blanket quietly so as not to disturb Evelyn. He lay with his face turned towards her, in deep sleep, not dreamless, perhaps, because he smiled. Even in this wan morning light, when all vitality burns low, his face was radiant; no scruple, no pale doubt troubled his rest. He would wake to another day with the same welcome of "Good morning" for it as that with which he had said "Good night" to the last. His lips were closed, he breathed evenly and slowly through his nostrils, no sleep could have been more tranquil. It was just the sleep of a child tired with play, who would be recuperated on the morrow for another day of play.

Then she rose very quietly, and, opening the door with precaution, went into the bath-room. She was afraid that the splash of the water might rouse him, and put her sponge underneath the tap so that the sound was muffled, for she had the same womanly tenderness with regard to breaking his sleep as she had towards Philip. All suffering was sacred; even a broken hour of rest was a thing to be avoided. Then with infinite care she tip-toed back into their bedroom and dressed, but before she left it she looked at him once more. No, she had not aroused him, and no play of sub-conscious cerebration told him that she had gone; he slept on with the same tranquil sleep.

EIGHTEENTH

LADY DOVER'S letter to Madge was most elastic as regarded the date of their visit and thoroughly cordial, for she never did things by halves, and the welcome that would be given to her and Evelyn if he could possibly spare time to visit so remote a place was sincerity itself. About accepting it, she had her own view quite clearly formed, but her own pride, her pride, too, in her husband, prevented her from giving the slightest inkling of it to him. For she saw clearly that this visit was proposed by Lady Dover with the definite purpose of showing an act of friendliness after her marriage; it was clearly made with intention, and in her heart of hearts Madge was intensely grateful. To hint this, however, to Evelyn was impossible. But his frank eagerness to go made it unnecessary for her to consider any more the diplomatic reason for doing so.

"Oh, let's go," he said. "Surely Scotland is better than London. What

186

is there here? Just a stuffy town, and Battersea Park, and nothing whatever to do."

Madge knew that her own feeling of being hurt at this was unreasonable. This solitude of London had been unutterably dear to her, but she knew her own feeling to be unreasonable, since she never doubted—and rightly—how dear it had been to him. And why should he not want to be externally amused—to shoot, to fish, to do all those things that he delighted in? And echo answered "Why?"

It was at breakfast time that this letter arrived, and the bacon was undeniably less good than it would have been two days previously. Evelyn sniffed at it, and decided against it. But his sensitiveness to slightly passée bacon was sensitive to her feelings also.

"One doesn't want meat food in the summer," he said. "Tea and marmalade—how delicious!"

Madge handed him his tea.

"You dear," she said. "It is high, and it's my fault; I thought it would be good just for to-day. But it isn't. Oh, Evelyn, it was nice of you to pretend you didn't want any. But you can't act before me. I always know you. So give it up."

Evelyn gave a great shout of laughter.

"Madge and marmalade," he said. "That's good enough for me. In fact, I would leave out the marmalade if required. Oh, Madge, why can't you be serious and talk about this. By the way, I'll paint another sketch of you called 'Bad bacon'; the yearning face of the young wife. You are young, you know, and you are my wife. Don't chatter so, it confuses me. Now Lady Dover, if you will be silent one moment, lives at Golspie."

"That's where you are wrong," said Madge. "You have to go to Golspie before you begin."

"I don't want to begin. I want to get there. Don't you?"

Madge put on the woeful face that always introduced Ellesdee.

"I don't like the ticket man at King's Cross," she said. "I don't think he is what he seems."

Evelyn had eaten by this time all the crust off a Hovis loaf.

"More crust," he said. "There isn't any. Very good; marmalade in a spoon. But I won't distend my—my vie intérieure with crumb. About the ticket man. You are wrong if we are generous to Lady Dover with regard to the length of our visit. Why mince matters? Can we afford it? I say 'Yes.' Board wages for our enormous establishment here. Tickets for ourselves, third class—I wish there was a fourth or fifth—and what's the dem'd total, as Mr. Mantalini said. Besides these"—Evelyn waved his hand like a man commanding millions—"these are temporary economies. The pink and butter-coloured is going to visit these classic abodes in October, and if orders don't pour in like our own leaky roof, I'll eat all the gamboge in my paintbox. I can't say fairer. And as I don't possess gamboge," he added, "the bet finds no takers. I give you that information, for though I am poor, I am honest."

Evelyn proceeded to eat marmalade with a spoon.

"It will be very chic, if you come to think of it," he said. "Probably several ladies' maids and valets will arrive with their respective owners by the same train. You, Madge, will flirt with one or two of the valets, and I with several of the ladies' maids. The scene then is shifted to Golspie station. You squeeze the hands of the valets on the platform, and I gaze into the eyes of the ladies' maids. The sumptuous motor has come for Lady Dover's guests. We strive to subdue—quite ineffectually—our air of conscious superiority, and squeeze the hands of Dukes and Duchesses. Then they will know us in our true colours. Triumphal explosion of the motor-car. The valets and ladies' maids are saved. Hurrah for the lower classes! Another cup of tea, please. Right up to the top. And the point is the fare to Golspie. Arrived there, we shall have no more food and drink to buy."

The reasoning was inevitable; given that domestic economy could manage it, there was no reason that could reasonably indicate King's Road instead. Yet, even after the A.B.C. had added its voice to the overmastering argument, Madge hesitated. She could not quite see her husband among the surroundings that awaited her there. She had been there before, and knew. How would he and that particular milieu suit each other? All this was secondary to her original desire to go; her private, incommunicable feeling that such a visit would poser them—for she could not have been Lady Ellington's daughter so long without that point of view having soaked into her—was paramount, but the other was there, and the complication in her mind was that though she wished, taking the reasons all round, to leave this hot house which still was intertwined with exquisite and undying memories, she could not see how Evelyn should wish to leave this, not having her own worldly reasons for going to Golspie, without a pang. But since the question of whether economy would allow had been decided in favour of going, there was certainly no more to be said, and, so she told herself, no more to be thought.

But, since the logical conclusion is the one conclusion in the world that is absolutely without effect as regards results, she continued to think. For the ordinary mind is not in the least reasonable; it would cease to be reasonable the moment it was, and take its place among fixed stars and other unattainable objects. Logic, reason, are perhaps the most ineffective of human motives; they may be appealed to as a last resort; but if there is any impulse still alive, it, and not logic, will be seized on as a ground for action. Hence the divine uncertainty of human affairs. If the world was ruled by reason it would become duller than a week-old newspaper. But it is the fact that every human soul is so impredicable that lends the zest to existence. Finding out, in fact, not knowledge, is the spring that makes life fascinating. Whenever the element of certainty enters, it is the death's head at the feast. Nobody cares for the feast any more. The champagne is flat.

So to Golspie they went, and Evelyn's prophecy as regards the journey was sufficiently fulfilled to make anybody believe that there must have been something in it. He, at any rate, before they arrived at even Inverness, was engaged in conversation with an agreeable female opposite, a conversation which was not, however, so engrossing but that he could observe with secret glee the fact that Madge was reading the Scotsman, provided for her by an equally agreeable young man, who sat opposite, and hoped that his cigarette would not be disagreeable. Then, luck was really on his side that day, important people stepped out of first-class carriages at Golspie, and, by the usages of this cruel world, these acquaintances so pleasantly begun were rudely interrupted. A cart waited for their travelling companions, and the swift motor received them and the strangers, before whom their own travelling acquaintances were but dust and ashes.

It was, in fact, but a short week after Lady Ellington's arrival at Glen Callan that her daughter and son-in-law got there, and though she would, as previously arranged, have gone on to her next house the day before their arrival, she put off her departure for two days in order to have the pleasure of seeing them. The party, in fact, was unaltered, and so was their way of life; Mr. Osborne's flow of humour showed no signs of running dry, nor was the blank amazement with which Lord Ellington regarded him in the least abated. Mr. Dennison was getting steadily on towards the completion of his panorama of Sutherland, and Lady Dover found fresh lights and shadows on the purple heather every day.

Lady Ellington had carefully considered what her exact attitude towards Madge and her husband should be, and had come to the most sensible conclusion about it. Since the world had made up its mind to welcome them, and to draw a wet sponge over the past, it was clear that unless she wished to make an exception of herself, and not do in Rome what Rome did, she must extend to them not merely the welcome of the world, but the welcome of a mother also. And it was decidedly the best plan to make this thorough; astonished as Madge might be, it was better to astonish her than the world, and neither in public nor in private should she hear one word of reproach nor an uncordial accent. Lady Ellington had no desire to see private talks with her daughter; in fact, she meant rather to avoid them; but her whole policy was to accept what had happened, and welcome Madge in the flesh with the same unreservedness as she had shown in the letter she had written her a week ago, urging her to accept Lady Dover's invitation. She was determined, in fact (now that Lady Dover had shown the way), to make the best of it, and, instead of bitterly counting up (and mentally sending the bill in to Madge) all that would have been at her command, had not the speculation with regard to Madge's marriage failed, to make the most of the assets that remained to her. And the more she thought of them, unattractive as they had seemed at first, the more they seemed to her to have a promising air. Philip was immensely wealthy, and Evelyn was poor, that was unfortunately undeniable; but Evelyn—regarding him as a property—had certainly prospects which Philip had not, and though nothing could quite make up, to her mind, for the loss of much tangible wealth, yet Evelyn with his brilliant gifts might easily be a rich man, while even now he was a much more rising figure socially than the other. People talked about him, admired his cleverness and charm, asked to be introduced to him. All these merits, it is true, she had not seen in those days at Pangbourne, when she looked upon him merely as an impossible young artist, but since that impossible young artist had become an inevitable son-in-law, it was wise to take him into account. So her welcome to both was going to be unreserved.

They arrived, just as Lady Ellington had arrived, after the rest of the party had gone in to dinner, and their host and hostess came out into the hall as usual to meet them. Madge, it must be confessed, had gone through a bad quarter of an hour of anticipatory shyness as they got near; but this on arrival she found to have been a superfluous piece of self-inflicted discomfort, for Lady Dover was absolutely natural, and all that was required of her was that she should be natural too.

"Ah, dear Madge," she said, "how nice to see you and Mr. Dundas. And we have such a surprise for you; your mother is here still. We persuaded her to delay her departure a couple of days in order just to have a glimpse of you. We call her Lady Salmon, and are eating a fish she caught only this afternoon."

She turned to welcome her other guests, when Lady Ellington also followed her from the dining-room.

"My dearest Madge," she cried, kissing her, "this is too delightful. How well you are looking. But did you only wear this thin cloak for your drive; surely that was rash? How are you, dear Evelyn? This is nice. I could not help coming out of dinner to have a glimpse of you. You have brought no maid, Madge?"

"Dear mother, I haven't got one to bring."

"No? Evelyn, she must have a maid. But Parkins, of course, shall attend to you here. Now you must go and dress."

That her mother was still in the house had been absolutely a surprise to Madge, but her welcome fully endorsed the cordiality of her letter. She had not seen her since that afternoon in July when she had come to Evelyn's studio, and whatever had caused this complete and radical change she was grateful to it. It, too, bore its meaning as clearly stamped as did Lady Dover's greeting; whatever had happened, had happened but the past was over.

Everyone in the house, indeed taking the time from their hostess, welcomed them with a very special cordiality. Lady Dover, in her quiet, neat way, had dropped, casually enough, but letting the point of her observations be fully seen, little remarks to most members of her party on the very great pleasure she anticipated from the visit of the Dundases. They were both so charming, it was no wonder that everyone liked them. The meaning of this was explicit enough, and put without any hint of patronising, or, indeed, of doing a kindness; and though Lady Ellington had reflected that people followed Lady Dover's lead just because she was ordinary and they were ordinary, it might be questioned whether she herself could have given the lead so gently, for it hardly appeared a lead at all, or so successfully, for everybody followed it. From the fragments of Lady Dover's ordinary conversation already indicated, it may not unfairly be gathered that she perhaps lacked brilliance in her talk, and was not possessed of any particular intellectual distinction. But after all, the hardest art to practise is the art of living according to one's tastes, a thing which she certainly succeeded admirably in doing, and the hardest medium to work in, more difficult by far than metal or marble or oils, is men and women. But her manipulation of them was masterly, and, to crown it, she did not seem to manipulate at all.

In this instance, certainly, the subtlest diplomatist could not with all his scheming have produced a more complete result. Mr. Dennison, as has been seen, had on the tip of his tongue a conclusion disparaging in the highest degree to Evelyn and his art. Gladys Ellington had let things even more bitter pass the tip of her tongue, Madge's mother had felt not so long ago that the shipwreck was total, and that there was no salvage. Yet Lady Dover, with just a little repetition of the same sentence or two, had swept all these things away, as a broom with a couple of strokes demolishes all the weavings of spiders, and through the unobscured windows the sun again shines. In fact the volte-face of Society had been begun at any rate with immense precision and certainty; on the word of Lady Dover, who was in command, this particular company had turned right about with the instantaneousness which is the instinct of a well-drilled troop.

In effect the whole social balance of power was changed from the moment of their appearance. Evelyn, as natural in his way, but that a more vivacious one, than Lady Dover, gave a brilliant sketch of their arrival—third class—at Golspie Station, and the adjustment of social distinction consequent. Also, he had prophesied it, Madge would bear him out in that, and he reproduced admirably Madge's face from behind the Scotsman which had been so kindly lent her. Mr. Osborne made one attempt to reconstitute himself the life and soul of the party when he addressed Gladys as Lady Grilse, and unfolded to Madge, who sat next him, the history of that remarkable piece of wit, meaning to follow it up by the sequel (sequels were usually disappointing, but this was an agreeable exception) of the true circumstances under which her mother had been called Lady Salmon. But Madge had cut the sequel short, without any ironical purpose, but simply because she wanted to listen to and contradict the libels Evelyn was telling of her conduct on the opposite side of the table.

"How very amusing," she said. "You called her Lady Grilse (I see, do I not), because she had caught one. Evelyn, I said nothing of the kind; I only said that I rather liked the smell of a cigarette."

But her quite literal and correct explanation of Mr. Osborne's joke was fatal to the joke; it was a pricked bladder, it would never be repeated any more.

Then came the deposition of the Royal Academician. Mr. Dennison had finished his picture of the upper glen only that afternoon, and the occasion was therefore solemn. So was he.

"Yes, Lady Dover," he was saying, "I only touched the canvas a dozen times to-day, yet I have done, as I said, a full day's work. C'est le dernier pas qui coûte; it is on those last touches that the whole thing depends. I knew when I went out this morning that I had not got what I meant; I knew, too, that it was nearly there, and it is that "nearly" that is yet so far. There was the shadow of a cloud, if you remember, over the bank of gorse."

"Oh, I thought that shadow was quite perfect," said Lady Dover. "I hope you have not touched it."

"It has gone," said Mr. Dennison, as if announcing the death of a near relation who had left him money, for though his voice was mournful, there was a hint of something comfortable coming. "Gone. I saw I could not do it so as to make it true."

He looked up at this tragic announcement and caught Evelyn's eye.

"Mr. Dundas, I am sure, will bear me out," he said. "We poor artists are bound, however it limits us, to put down only what we know is true. We are not poets but chroniclers."

"Oh, Evelyn, and you've been telling such lies about me," said Madge, from the other side.

"Chroniclers," resumed Mr. Dennison. "When we feel sure we are right we record our impression. But unless that certainty of vision comes to us, we must be honest, we must not attempt a vague impression merely. Is it not so?"

Evelyn's face looked extraordinarily vital and boyish as he leaned forward.

"Oh, I don't agree in the least," he said. "I think we always ought to try to record just those suggestions—those vaguenesses—which you say you leave out. Look at 'La Gioconda.' What did Andrea mean us to think about that sphinx? I don't know, nor do you. And, what is more certain than even that, nor did he know. Did he mean what Walter Pater said he meant? It again is quite certain he did not. No, I think every picture ought to ask an unanswerable riddle, any picture, that is to say, which is a picture at all, a riddle like 'Which came first, the hen or the egg?' Surely anything obvious is not worth painting at all."

Mr. Dennison had clearly not thought of things in this light. It was not thus that the ordnance map of Sutherland would be made.

"An amusing paradox," he said. "Nobody is to know anything about a picture, especially the man who painted it. Is that correct?"

His tone had something slightly nettled about it, and Evelyn's imperturbable good humour and gaiety might perhaps represent the indifference of the nettles towards the hand they had stung.

"Yes, just that," he said. "Take any of the arts. Surely it is because a play has a hundred interpretations that it is worth seeing, and because a hundred different people will experience a hundred different emotions that an opera is worth listening to. And the very fact that when we hear 'The jolly roast beef of old England' we are all irresistibly reminded of the jolly roast beef of old England shows that it is a bad tune."

Mr. Dennison waved his hand in a sketchy manner.

"I have not the pleasure of knowing that tune," he said; "but when I paint the upper glen here, I mean it to produce in all beholders that perception of its particular and individual beauty which was mine when I painted it. And when you exercise your art, your exquisite art, over a portrait, you, I imagine, mean to make the result produce in all beholders the beauty you saw yourself."

Evelyn laughed.

"Oh, dear, no," he said. "You see, I so often see no beauty in my sitters, because most people are so very plain. But I believe that the finest portraits of all are those which, when you look at them, make you feel as you would feel if you were on intimate terms and in the presence of the people they represent. Besides, people are so often quite unlike their faces; in that case you have to paint not what their faces are like but what they are like."

Mr. Dennison's tone was rising a little; that impressive baritone could never be shrill, but it was as if he wanted to be a tenor.

"Ah, that explains a great deal," he said; "it explains why sometimes I find your portraits wholly unlike the people they represent. And the conclusion is that if I knew them better, I should find them more like."

"That is exactly what I mean," said Evelyn.

But here Lady Dover broke in.

"You must have some great talks, Mr. Dundas," she said, "with Mr. Dennison; it is so interesting to hear different points of view. One cannot really grasp a question, can one, unless one hears both sides of it. I think Lady Ellington has finished. Let us go."

But the verdict over this little passage of arms was unanimous; Mr. Dennison was no longer in anyone's mind the pope and fountain-head of all art and all criticism thereon. His impressiveness had in the last ten minutes fallen into the disrepute of pomposity, his grave pronouncements were all discredited; a far more attractive gospel had been enunciated, far more attractive, too, was this new evangelist. And as Lady Dover passed him on the way out she had one more word.

"That is a delightful doctrine, Mr. Dundas," she said. "You must really do a portrait of yourself, and if we think it is unlike, the remedy will be that we must see more of you."

Evelyn drew his chair next to the Academician; he had heard the rise of voice and seen the symptoms of perturbation, to produce which there was nothing further from his intention.

"I'm afraid I talk awful rot," he said, with the most disarming frankness.

Now Mr. Dennison was conscious of having been rather rude and ruffled, he was also conscious that Evelyn's temper had been calmer than the moon. He felt, too, the charm of this confession, which was so evidently not premeditated but natural.

"But that does not diminish my pleasure in meeting you, Mr. Dundas," he said.

Afterwards the same triumphant march continued. Mr. Dennison even showed to Madge how a couple of his most astounding conjuring tricks were done, and Lady Ellington talked to her son-in-law in a corner about Madge, until the council of war summoned them to debate. Then, when it was decided that Madge should join the fishmongers on the river, Mr. Osborne instantly suggested that she would be Mrs. Sea-Trout, and though a cavilling mind might find in this but a futile attempt to establish himself once more as the life and soul of the party, it was not indeed so, but meant merely as a compliment, a tribute to Madge. Then, when the council of war was over, more remarkable things happened, for the whole party played Dumb-Crambo till long after half-past ten, quite forgetful, apparently, how important it was to get a good rest after all the day spent

193

in the open air. How such a subversion of general usage occurred no one knew, but certainly there was something in Evelyn which conduced to silly gaiety. And nobody was a whit the worse for it, while the effects of the moon-light on the hills opposite, which had nightly been the admiration of the whole party, went totally unheeded, and all the exquisite lights and shadows, the subtlety of which it had become the office of Mr. Dennison to point out and Lady Dover to appreciate, might never have been in view at all.

Lady Ellington went with Madge to her room when the women retired; she had not really meant to do so, but Lady Dover's "Good night" had made this necessary.

"Dear Madge," she had said, "I know your mother will want to talk to you, so I shall not come to see you to your room. I hope you have everything you want. Breakfast at a quarter to ten, or would you rather have it in your room after your journey? We have been so late to-night too. How excellent Mr. Dundas's last charade was. Only Mr. Dennison guessed. Good night, dear."

Lady Ellington was thus, so to speak, forced into Madge's room; she carried with her her glass of hot water, she carried also, which was even more warming, the memory of the undisguised welcome that not only Madge but the impossible artist had received. She almost, in fact, reconsidered her valuation of wealth; had Philip Home appeared in Evelyn's place this evening, she knew quite well he would not have been able to stir the deadly gentility of this house half so well as the impossible artist. He could not have piped so as to make them dance, yet this, this key to the sort of set which she knew really mattered most, the solid, stolid, respectable upper class, had been just rats to his piping. His natural enjoyment, his animal spirits, to put that influence at its lowest, had simply played the deuce with the traditions of the house, where she herself never ventured to lift her voice in opposition or amendment to what was suggested. But Evelyn's "Oh, let's have one more Dumb-Crambo" had revised the laws of the Medes and Persians, and another they had. Even at the formal council of war he had refused to say what he would like to do to-morrow, a thing absolutely unprecedented.

"Oh, may I go and shoot if it is fine," he had said, "and do nothing at all if it is wet? Don't you hate shooting, Lord Dover, if your barrels are covered with rain? And birds look so awfully far away in the rain. But I should love to shoot in any case," he added. "My goodness, Madge, think of the King's Road and the 'buses."

Yet all this revolt against the established laws, so Lady Ellington felt, had somehow not transgressed those laws of propriety which she was so careful about here. Evelyn, from ignorance, no doubt, rode rough-shod, and no one resented his trespasses. Even Lord Dover had been stirred into speech, a thing he did not usually indulge in except on the subject of the grouse that had been shot and the fish that had been killed that day.

"My dear boy," he said, "you shall do exactly what you like to-morrow. There is a rod for you on the river, or we should like another gun on the moor. Tell us at breakfast."

194

All this Lady Ellington took up to Madge's room with her hot water; that Lady Dover would be as good as her word, and that, having asked these two to Glen Callan, would give them a genuine welcome, she had never doubted, but what was surprising she was the extreme personal success of her once better-forgotten son-in-law. This stronghold and central fortress of what was correct and proper had received him as if he was almost a new incarnation of what was correct and proper, or if that was putting it too strongly, at any rate as if no question of his correctness and propriety had ever arisen. Surprising though it was, it was wholly satisfactory.

"We are so late, dear Madge," she said, "that I can only stop a minute. Has it not been a delightful evening?"

The desire to say something salutary struggled long in her mind. She wanted so much to indicate that it was for the sake of her feelings, even in consequence of her own intervention, that so charming a welcome had been extended to Madge and her husband. And to be quite truthful, it was not the instinct for truth that prevented her, but the quite certain knowledge that Madge would not stand anything that suggested a hint of patronisation. Besides the house was Lady Dover's, that person who, as Lady Ellington was beginning to learn, was natural because she happened to be natural, and was quite truthful, not because this was a subtler sort of diplomacy. That naked dagger of truth was an implement that required a deal of mail-coat to ward off. Any moment Lady Dover might wreck any scheming policy with one candid word, and the corresponding surprise and candour of her eyes. But the welcome had been so warm that Madge could not but be warmed by it, even to the point of confession.

"Oh, mother," she said, "I have been disquieting myself in vain. All this last month I have been wondering secretly whether people were going to be horrid to us. How senseless it all was! I have been thinking all sorts of things."

She put down her candle and drew a couple of chairs to the fire.

"I have had all sorts of thoughts," she said. "You see, you did not write to me. I thought you might—well, might have washed your hands of me. I thought that people like Lady Dover would think I had been heartless and Evelyn worse than heartless. I was hopelessly wrong; everybody is as nice as possible. But, heavens, how I have eaten my heart out over that all this month in London!"

She poked the fire with a certain viciousness, feeling that she pricked these bubbles of senseless fear as she pricked the bubbling gas of the burning coal.

"All in vain," she said; "I have been making myself—no, not miserable, because I can't be otherwise than happy, but disquieted with all sorts of foundationless fears. I thought people would disregard—yes, it is that—would disregard Evelyn and me; would talk of the fine day instead. And then, you see, Evelyn would also have nothing to do, nobody would want to be painted by him. We should be miserably poor; he would have to paint all sorts of things he had no taste for just to get a guinea or two and keep the pot boiling. Ah, I shouldn't have minded that—the poverty, I

195

mean—but what I should mind would be that he should have to work at what he felt was not worth working at. Don't you see?"

Never perhaps before had Madge so given herself away to her mother. Lady Ellington's system had been to snip off all awkward shoots, and train the plant, so to speak, in such a way as should make it most suitable as a table ornament. The table for which it was destined, it need hardly be remarked, was an opulent table. There was to be no wasting of sweetness on the desert air; Mayfair was to inhale its full odour. And as things now stood, the destination of this flower was as likely to be Mayfair as ever. Lady Ellington respected success, nobody more so, nor was there anything she respected so much, and on a rapid review of the evening, the success she felt inclined to respect most was that of her impossible son-in-law. If a plebiscite for popularity had knocked at the doors of the occupied bedrooms, she had no doubt as to the result of the election. There was nothing left for her but to retract, wholly and entirely, all her own resentment and rage at the marriage. And since this had to be done, it was better done at once.

"Dearest Madge," she said, "how foolish of you to make yourself miserable! Of course at first I was vexed and troubled at it all, and I was, and am still, very sorry for Philip. But though I did wish that certain things had not happened, and that others had—I mean I wish that you had been in love with Philip, for I am sure you would have been very happy, yet since it was not to be so, and since you fell in love with Evelyn, what other issue could I have desired?"

Suddenly, quick as a lizard popping out and in again of some hole in the wall, there flashed through Madge's mind the impression—"I don't believe that." She could not be held responsible for it, for it was not a thought she consciously entertained. It just put its head out and said "Here I am." What, however, mattered more was that this was her mother's avowed declaration now; these were the colours anyhow she intended to sail under. She had been launched anew, so to speak, with regard to her attitude towards her daughter, and Lady Dover had christened her, and broken a bottle of wine over her for good luck.

But having made her declaration, Lady Ellington thought she had better be moving. From a child Madge had been blessed with a memory of hideous exactitude, which enabled her, if she choose, to recall conversations with the most convincing verbal accuracy, and Lady Ellington did not feel equal, off-hand, to explaining some of those flower-like phrases which had, she felt certain, fallen from her in her interview with Madge after the thunderstorm in the New Forest, if perchance the fragrance of them might conceivably still linger in her daughter's mind. Nor did she wish to be reminded, however remotely (and as she thought of this she made the greater speed) of the letter from Madge to Evelyn which had lain in the hall one afternoon as she came in, with regard to which her maternal instinct had prompted her to take so strong a line. So she again referred to the lateness of the hour, "all owing to those amusing games," and took the rest of her hot water to finish in her own room.

But she need not have been afraid; nothing was further from

196

Madge's intention than to speak of such things, and though she could not help knowing that she did not believe what her mother had said, she deliberately turned her mind away, and so far from exercising her memory over the grounds of her disbelief, she put it all away from her thoughts. Such generosity was easy, her present great happiness made it that.

She felt in no mood to go to bed, even after the night she had spent in the train, and from the thought of the vain disquietude she had felt about how people would behave to them, she passed in thought to another disquietude that she told herself was as likely to be as vain as that. For what was the sense of measuring and gauging and taking soundings into the manner of Evelyn's love for her, and comparing it unfavourably, to tell the truth, with hers for him? For she knew quite well, the whole fibre of her being knew, that in so far as he was complete at all, his love for her was complete; there were no reservations in it; he loved her with all his soul and strength. Yet when the best thing in the world was given her, here she was turning it over, and wondering, so to speak, if the ticket to show its price was still on it, and if it was decipherable! It is ill to look thus at any gift, but when that gift is the gift of love, which is without money and without price, such a deed is little short, so she told herself now, of a desecration.

The next day bore out the reliability of Lord Dover's aneroid, and there was no fear of Evelyn finding rain-drops on his gun-barrel. The Honourable Company of Fishmongers—Mr. Osborne was at it again—went to the river, Mr. Dennison to a further point of view up the glen, and the shooters to the moor. They started a little before the party for the river, and Madge saw them off at the door. They were to shoot over a beat of moor not far from the house, which would bring them close to the river by lunch-time, and it was arranged that both parties should lunch together. Gladys started with them, for she was going to fish up the river from the lower reaches; Lady Ellington and Madge would begin on opposite sides at the top. This would bring them all together about two o'clock at what was called the Bridge-pool, where Madge, fishing on this side, would cross, meeting Lady Ellington and Gladys, who would have worked up from below, while the shooters converged on them from the moor.

It would indeed have been a sad heart that did not rejoice on such a morning, while to the happy the cup must overflow. There had been a slight touch of early frost in the night, which, as Madge skirted the river bank, which was still in shadow, lay now in thick, diamond drops on the grass, ready when the sun touched it to hover for a moment in wisps of thin mist, and then to be drawn up into the sparkle of the day. Swift and strong and coffee-coloured at her feet the splendid river roared on its way, full of breakers and billows at the head of the pools, and calming down into broad, smooth surfaces before it quickened again into the woven ropes of water down which the river climbed to the next pool. Every pool, too, was a mystery, for who knew what silver-mailed monster might not be oaring his way about with flicks of the spade-like tail that clove the waters and sent him arrow-like up the stream? The mystery of it all, the romance of the gaudy fly thrown into this seething tumult of foam and breaker, its circling

197

journey (followed by eager eye and beating heart) that might at any moment be interrupted by a swirl of waters unaccounted for by the stream, and perhaps the sight of a fin or a silver side; then a sudden check, the feeling of weight, the nodding of the tapering rod in assent, and the shrill scream of the reel—all this, all the possibility of every moment, the excitement and tension, all added effervescence to the vivid happiness that filled Madge and inspired all she did with a sort of rapture.

So step by step she made her way down the first pool; the broken water at the head gave no reply to the casting of the fly upon the waters, and with a little more line, and still a little more line as the pool grew broader, she went down to the tail. There, far out in mid-stream, was a big submerged rock, with a triangle of quiet water below it, and more line and more line went out before she could reach it. Then—oh, moment of joy!—the fly popped down on the far side of the rock, and with entrancing little jerks and oscillations of the rod, she drew it across the backwater. And then—she felt as if it must be so—the dark stream was severed, a fin cut the surface, the rod nodded, bent to a curve, with an accelerating whizz-z-z out ran the line, and a happy fishmonger looked anxiously, rapturously at her gillie.

A couple of hours later Madge had come to within a hundred yards of the Bridge-pool, her fish secure in the creel, and her aspirations for it reaching, somewhat sanguinely as she knew, as high as sixteen pounds. The Bridge-pool itself was this morning part of Lady Ellington's water, for on Madge's side it ran swirling and boiling round a great cliff of nearly precipitous rock, some fifty feet high, over which she had to pass before getting to the skeleton wire bridge which crossed the river just below the pool. She could see her mother half-way down the pool already, and called to her, but her voice was drowned by the hoarse bass of the stream as it plunged from rapid to rapid into the head of the pool below, and after trying in vain to make her hear, and communicate the glorious tidings of the fish, Madge followed her gillie up the steep, rocky pass which led over this cliff. As she mounted the stony stair, steep and lichen-ridden, the voice of the water that had been in her ears all morning, and rang there still like the tones of some secret, familiar friend, grew momently more faint, but another voice, the voice of the sunny noon, as friendly as the other, took its place, and grew more intense as the first faded. From the shadow and coolness and water-voices she emerged into the windy sunlight of the moor; bees buzzed hotly in the heather, making the thin, springlike stems of the ling quiver and nod beneath their honey-laden alightings, swallows and martins chided shrilly as they passed, and peewits cried that note which is sad or triumphant according to the mood of the hearer. Then as she gained the top of this rocky bastion, sounds more indicative of human presences were in the air, the report of a gun came from not far off, and immediately afterwards a string of shots. Though she had killed her salmon with such gusto only an hour or two before, Madge could not help a secret little joy at the thought that probably this particular grouse had run the gauntlet of all the guns and had escaped again for another spell of wild life on the heather. Then, following the gillie's finger, she saw not half a mile away the shooting party, who were also approaching the general rendez-vous with the same coincident punctuality as she, while a quarter of a mile further down from this point of vantage she could see Gladys coming up. The shooters were walking in line across a very steep piece of brae that declined towards the river, three of them, but with the gillies and dog-men seeming quite a party. The hillside was covered with heather, and sown with great grey boulders.

Madge was a few minutes before the others; Gladys had still several hundred yards to go before she reached the bridge which was now but thirty yards off, while Lady Ellington had still the cream of the Bridge-pool in front of her, and she sat down on a big rock at the top of the cliff while the rest of the party converged. At this distance it was impossible to make out the identity of the shooters; they were but little grey blots on the hillside, but every now and then the muffled report of a shot or of two or three shots reached her, and though she had felt glad that one grouse had perhaps escaped the death-tubes, yet she felt glad another way that they seemed to be having good sport. Then her mind and her eye wandered; she looked up the glen down which she had come; she saw the river sparkling a mile away in torrent of sun-enlightened foam; above her climbed the heathery hill, crowned with the larches of the plantation round the house itself, and from the house the gleam of a vane caught her eye. Beside her sat the brown-bearded gillie, in restful Scotch silence, ready and courteous to reply should she speak to him, but silent till that happened. And "pop-pop" went the guns from the hillside opposite.

Suddenly he got up, looking across no longer vaguely, but with focussed eyes, and she turned. The little grey specks of men were closer, and it was possible now to see that there was some commotion among them. From the right a little grey speck was running down hill; from the left another was running up. And that was all.

Madge watched for a moment or two, still full of sunny thoughts. Then from the point of convergence of the little grey specks one started running towards the bridge by which she would cross. At that, faint as reflected starlight, an impulse of alarm came to her. But it was so slight that no trace of it appeared in her voice.

"What is happening, do you think?" she asked the gillie.

But the courteous Scotsman did not reply; he gazed a moment longer, and then ran down the steep descent to the bridge. And in Madge the faint feeling of alarm grew stronger, though no less indefinable, as she looked at the leaping little grey speck growing every moment larger. At last she saw who it was; it was Mr. Osborne jumping and running for all he was worth. At that she followed her gillie, and hurried after him across the wire bridge. And as if a drum had beat to arms, legions of fears no longer indefinable leaped into her brain in hideous tumult.

A hundred yards ahead her gillie had met the running figure, and in a moment he had slung off the creel and started to run towards her, leaving Mr. Osborne to drop down, as if exhausted, in the heather.

"What is it?" she cried as he approached.

"An accident, ma'am," he said. "I don't know what."

199

Madge did not delay him, but went on towards Mr. Osborne. As she got near he sprang up from his seat.

"Ah, my dear Mrs. Dundas," he said; "don't go—don't go!"

His panting breath made him pause a moment, but he looked at her face of agony and apprehension, and, clenching his hands, went on.

"No, not killed; there is nobody dead. But there has been an accident, a ricochet off one of those rocks. Someone has been—yes, my poor, dear lady, it is your husband. But don't go; it is terrible."

But before he could say more to stop her she had passed him, and was running up the hill.

NINETEENTH

SINCE the moment when the ice had been broken between Philip and Tom Merivale, and, what was perhaps more vital, since that terrible ice round Philip's heart had begun to thaw, talk between them, till then so scanty and superficial, had taken a plunge into the depths of things, into those cool, wavering obscurities that lie round the springs of life and death. And the import of this was perhaps no less weighty to the Hermit than it was to Philip; never before had he unveiled, not his mystery, but his exceeding simplicity, to another, except in so far as half-laughing paradox and the apparent marvel of the nightingale that sat on his hand and sang could be considered as unveiling. But he was very conscious in himself, with that premonition that birds and beasts, and all the living things, that have not had their natural instincts blunted for generations by indoor and artificial life, possess, that something critical was at hand. What that was he could not guess, and, indeed, refrained from trying to do so. But for months now he had waited for some revelation, as a neophyte waits for a further initiation. As far as he could tell he knew all the secrets of that antechamber in which he waited. Up to a certain point his knowledge was complete and consolidated; the joy of animate nature was utterly his, no thrush or scudding blackbird knew better than he the joy that comes from the mere fact of life and air and food and sleep and drink, of which every moment brings its own reward. To none, too, could he have stated this so easily as to his old friend, and the very fact that Philip was but now just beginning to emerge from black and bitter waters, made his understanding of it more piercing. It was the fresh, vital air to a man who has sunk and nearly been drowned in a pool, from the depths of which he has but just had strength to struggle, and lie with eyes but half open and mouth that could only just drink in the freshness of the day God made. And it was this very sunlight and freshness of air which penetrated to those other depths which were the springs of life and death. From the bitter depth of his own hell Philip had swum up into life, and yet as he went up he was getting down, by the same movement, into other depths; but these were cool, and no blackness mingled with their veiled obscurities.

Early September this year in the New Forest had harked back to June. After that day or two of storm and hot rain, the weather had cleared again, and a week of golden hours, golden with the sun by day and with the myriad shining of the stars by night, made one almost believe that time had stopped, or that its incessant wheel had begun to run back to the clean and early days of the world. That moment which had come to Philip, when the outpouring of his bitterness and resentment were stayed, was an epoch to him, which ranked by itself. It drew away from his other days and deeds, it was a leaven that worked incessantly, clouds cleared, Marah itself began to grow sweet, and splash by splash pieces of his bitterness dropped like stones into that sea of forgetfulness and forgiveness which, before any soul is complete and ready to stand before God, must spread from pole to pole. The determination to forget in most cases, as here, sets the tides on the flow; forgiveness, the higher quality, is often the natural sequel. Yet to forget a grudge is to have forgiven it, while forgiveness may be a hard, metallic thing—the best perhaps of which we are capable—but it will not grow soft until forgetfulness has come as well. The cause for the grudge must cease to exist in the mind before the grudge can be wholly forgiven. Poor Philip was not near that yet, but still bits of the grudge kept falling into the sea of forgetfulness as from the stalactitic roof of a cavern. Some dropped on the beach merely, and were still hard and unabsorbed, but others fell fair, and a dead splash was the end of them.

These tranquil golden days helped it all; while the huge beeches grew slim and straight against the sky, while the warm, wholesome air was an anæsthetic to his pain, and while above all this serene, joyous youth, a patent, undeniable proof of the practical power of inward happiness, was with him, it became daily more impossible to nurse and cherish any bitterness, however well nourished.

Philip had been here now nearly three weeks, and for the last ten days he had lived completely cut off from any world but this. Telegrams and communications at first had followed him from the City, but times were quiet, and he had entrusted his junior partner with all power to act in his absence, saying also that he felt sure that no business need be referred to him. He wanted a month's complete rest, and if any news or call for a decision came to him he would disregard it. He was to be considered as at sea; nothing must reach him. Also he had begged Tom Merivale not to take in any daily paper on his account; he was at sea—that was exactly it— without the disadvantage of having to sleep in a berth and use a quarter-deck for exercise. But on this transitory planet an end to all things comes sooner or later, even when those things are as imperishable as golden days. And, physically and spiritually, the end was very near.

They had dined one night as usual on the verandah, but for the first time for ten days the wonderful twilight of stars was quenched, and a thick blanket of cloud again overset the sky, and the heat of the evening portended thunder. A week before this Merivale had told his friend of that thunderstorm when Madge had been here with Evelyn, and had confessed

201

to passive complicity in their love. Philip had not resented this either openly or secretly; Merivale had not encouraged it; he had, so he thought to himself, but seen that it was inevitable. And to-night the thunderous air brought up the previous storm to the Hermit's mind.

"The traces of that are cleared away," he said. "The tree that was struck is firewood in the wood-shed now. But there is a wound; the senseless fire came down from Heaven; it killed a beautiful living thing, that tree."

They had finished dinner, and Philip turned his chair sideways to the table.

"Yes, and where is the compensation?" he said. "Surely that is needless suffering and needless death."

"Ah, I don't believe that. You and I say it is needless, because we cannot see what life is born from it. Your suffering, my dear fellow, you thought that gratuitous, like a lightning flash, but it isn't; you know that now."

This had so often been mentioned between them that Philip did not wince at it.

"I take it on trust only," he said, "but the proof will come when, because of what has happened to me, I am kinder, more indulgent to others. If it has taught me that it is all good, but at present no test has come. I have but lived here with you."

He paused a moment.

"And I must soon get back," he said. "Your métier is here, but mine isn't. This is your life, it has been my rest and my healing and my hospital. But when one is well, one has to go back again. Oh, I know that, I feel it in my bones. This has been given me in order that I may make my life again. With it behind me I have to go—I should be a coward if I did not; I should tacitly imply that I 'gave up' if I did not face things again."

He drew his chair a little closer to his friend.

"Tom, you have saved me," he said, "but my salvation has to be proved. It is all right for you to stop here, that I utterly believe, but I believe as utterly that it is not for me. I must go back, and be decent, and not be bitter. I must continue my normal life, I must play Halma with my mother, and slang the gardeners if they are lazy. Now, dear old chap, since my time here will be short, I want to talk to you about your affairs. Or rather I want you to talk about them. I want to grasp as clearly as I can any point of view which is not my own. That will help me to understand the—the damnable muddle the world generally has got into. It's all wrong; I can see that. Nobody goes straight for his aim. We all—you don't—we all compromise, because other people compromise. Now I don't want to do that any more. I want to see my aim, and go straight for it. So tell me yours, and let me criticise. Any point of view that is quite clear helps one to believe that there are other points of view as clear, if one could but see them."

A tired light came over the sky, as if drowsy eyelids had winked. Through the clouds the reflection of distant lightning illuminated the garden for a moment. There was a gap in the trees by the stream, where the stricken tree had stood, but of its corpse nothing remained; it had all been cut up and taken to make firewood for the winter. But a hot air blew, and in the bushes those strange, unaccountable noises of creaking twigs sounded insistently loud.

"Ah, you know my gospel well enough," said Merivale. "The joy of life; the joy inherent in the fact of life. I have really nothing more to tell you of it—from living here with me you know it all. And you have to peel life like an orange, to simplify it, to take the rind of unnecessary things off, before you can really taste it."

"Well, speak to me of your fear then."

"I have no fear."

He smiled with the convincing, boyish smile, that is pure happiness.

"Oh, lots of things may happen," he said, "but I assure you that I don't fear them. At least, I don't fear them with my reason. I feel convinced—and that is a lot to say—that my general scheme of life was right for me. Was? And will be. The future holds no more terrors than the past. Indeed the two terms, which sound so opposite to most people, are really one. Past or future, it is I. I have pursued the joys of life, not beastly, sensual joys, for never have I had part in them, but the clean, vital joy of living. And you tell me, as Evelyn has told me, that there are vital pains of living, as clean and as essential as those joys. Well, let them come. I am ready. They can come to-night if they choose. Ah, the huge Bogey of pain and sorrow may come and lie on my chest, like a nightmare. But my point is this——"

He paused a moment.

"If that is to be, if that is essential," he said, "I give it the same welcome as I have ever given to joy. It may frighten me out of existence, because the body is a poor sort of thing, and an ounce of lead or less will kill it, or, what is worse, deprive it of sight or hearing. But whatever can happen cannot hurt me, this me. Do you tell me that a rifle bullet, or a hangman's noose can kill me? And can a frightful revelation of all the sorrow of the world, and its pain, and its terror, and its preying, the one creature on another, touch my belief that life is triumphant, and that joy is triumphant over pain? Oh, I can believe most things, but not that. Should that come, I daresay my stupid flesh would shrink, shrink till it died if you like. But me? How does it touch me?"

He looked round with a sudden startled air, even as the words were on his lips.

"Tramp, tramp," he said, "there is a skipping and jumping in the bushes. I saw a frightful big goat on the ridge to-day, and it followed me, butting and sparring. I could almost think it had got into the garden. There is a sort of goaty smell, too. Well, it can't reach me in the hammock. Ah, there is lightning again: there is going to be a storm to-night."

"Sleep indoors," said Philip quietly. He was quiet, for fear of his nerves. But Tom laughed.

"I should rather say to you 'Sleep outside,'" he said. "If the lightning makes another shot here, it will certainly shoot at the highest thing, and the house is much higher than my hammock."

He looked at him a moment in silence, with the pity that is akin not to contempt, but to love.

"Ah, you are afraid of fear," he said. "That is one degree worse than anything we need be afraid of. It is of our own making, too. We dress up Fear like a turnip-ghost and then scream with terror at it. Or, don't you remember as a child making faces at yourself in a looking-glass till you were so frightened you could scarcely move? That is what most of us do all our lives."

Again, and rather more vividly, a blink of lightning was reflected in the clouds, and from far off the thunder muttered sleepily.

"So when I go," asked Philip, "I can think of you as being as happy and fearless—as certain of yourself and the scheme of the world as ever?"

Merivale smiled.

"Yes, assuredly you can do that," he said, "and though I do not like to hear you talk of going, of course I know you must. If you stopped here you would get bored and fidgetty. You have not at present because you have been getting well, and in convalescence all conditions, so long as one is allowed to stop still, are delightful. But your place, your work is not here. I feel that as strongly as you. You have the harder part; you have to go back and sort the grains of gold from the great lumps of worthless alloy, and distinguish many things that glitter from the royal metal. However, you know all that as well as I do."

He leaned forward over the table, and looked very earnestly at Philip.

"Think of me always as happy," he said, "and think of me as of a man who is waiting in an antechamber, waiting to be summoned to a great Presence. At least that is how I feel myself, how strongly and certainly I cannot explain to you. Here am I in this beautiful and wonderful antechamber, the world which I love so, in which I have passed days and months of such extraordinary happiness. But at one end of the antechamber there is a curtain drawn, and behind that is the Presence. Soon I think it will be drawn back and I shall see what is behind it. I think it will be drawn soon, for—all this imagery is so clumsy for what is so simple—for lately the curtain has been stirred, so it seems to me, from the other side: it has been jerked so that often I have thought that each moment it was to be drawn away, whereas till lately it has always hung in heavy, motionless folds. And I am waiting in front of it, conscious still—oh, so fully conscious—of all the beautiful things I have loved, but looking at them no longer, for I can look nowhere but at the curtain which stirs and is twitched as if someone is on the point of drawing it back."

He paused a moment, but did not take his eyes off Philip, but continued looking at him very gravely, very affectionately.

"Of course I cannot help guessing what lies behind," he said, "and conjecturing and reasoning. It may be several things; at least it may appear under several forms, but of this I am certain, that it is God. And will there be a blinding flash of joy, which shows me that even the sorrow and the death which is everywhere is no less part of perfection than the joy and the life? Even now, as you know, in my puny little attempts to be happy in the

204

way that Nature is happy, youth has come back to me in some extraordinary manner, and when I see what I shall see, will immortal life, lived here and now, be my portion? I don't know; I think it quite possible. And if that is so, if that is the initiation—ah, my God! that impulse of joy which I shall receive will spread from me like the circles in a pool when a stone is thrown into it."

He paused again, his smooth brown hands trembling a little.

"The Pan-pipes, too," he said—"they are never silent now: I hear them all the time, and I take that to mean that I am at last never unconscious of the hymn of life. I heard them at first, you know, just in snatches and broken stanzas, when I could screw myself up to the realisation of the song without end and without words that goes up from the earth day and night. Where does it come from? As I told Evelyn, I neither know nor care. Perhaps my brain conceives it, and sends the message to my ears, but it is really simpler to suppose that I hear it, just as you hear my voice talking to you now. For there is no question as to the fact of its existence; the hymn of praise does go on forever. So, perhaps, in my small way, I am complete, so to speak, with regard to that. Then—then there is another thing that may be behind the curtain. It may be that I shall be shown, and if I am shown this, it must be right and necessary—all the sorrow and pain and death that is in the world. I have turned my back on it; I have said it was not for me. But perhaps it will have to be for me. And that—to use a convenient phrase—will be to see Pan."

He paused on the word, then shook his hair back from his forehead, and got up.

"And now I have told you all," he said.

Philip got up, too, feeling somehow as if he had been mesmerised. He could remember all that Merivale had said; it was strangely vivid, but it had a dreamlike vividness about it; the fabric, the texture, the colour of it, for all its vividness, was unreal somehow, unearthly. But as to the reality of it and the truth of it, no question entered his head. He had never heard anything, no commonplace story or chronicle of indubitable events which was less fantastic. He looked out in silence a moment over the garden, and though half an hour ago he had been vaguely frightened at the thought of the mysterious and occult powers that keep watch over the world, yet now when they had been spoken of with such frankness, so that they seemed doubly as real as they had before, he was frightened no longer. It was, indeed, as Merivale had said; he had been afraid of fear.

It was already very late, and after a few trivial words he went indoors to go up to bed. As he got to the bottom of the stairs he looked back once, and saw his friend standing still on the verandah, with his face towards him. And as Philip turned, Merivale, standing under the lamp in his white shirt and flannels, with collar unfastened at the neck and sleeves rolled up to the elbow, smiled and nodded to him.

"Good night!" he said; "sleep well. I think you are learning how to do that again."

Philip began undressing as soon as he got to his room, feeling unaccountably tired and weary. His servant slept in a room just opposite him, and he hesitated for a moment as to whether he should tell him not to call him in the morning till he rang, for he had that heaviness of head which only satiety of sleep entirely removes. But it was already late, and the man had probably been in bed and asleep for some time. So he closed his door, drew the blind down over his window, and put out his light. His brain, for all the vividness of that evening's talk, seemed absolutely numb and empty, as if all memory were dead, and he fell asleep instantly.

He slept heavily for several hours, and then external sounds began to mingle themselves with his dreams, and he thought he was in a large, empty, brown-coloured hall lit by dim windows very high up, through which a faint, tired light was peering. But now and again the squares of these windows would be lit up for a moment vividly from outside, and as often as this happened some low, heavy, tremulous sound echoed in the vault above him like a bass bourdon note. He was conscious, too, that many unseen presences surrounded him; the hall was thick with them, and they were all saying: "Hush-sh-sh!" A sense of deadly oppression and coming calamity filled him, he was waiting for something, not knowing what it was. Then the coils of sleep began to be more loosened, and before long he awoke. His room looked out over the garden, and the "Hush-sh-sh" was but the rain that fell heavily on to the shrubs below his window. Then the light and the tremulous note were explained too, for suddenly the window started into brightness, and a couple of seconds after a sonorous roll of thunder followed. But the uneasiness of the dream had not passed: he still felt frightfully apprehensive. All desire for sleep, however, had left him, and for some half hour, perhaps, he lay still, listening to the windless rain, for the night was so still that his blind hung over the open window without tapping or stirring. Then with curious abruptness the rain ceased altogether and there was dead silence.

Then suddenly a frightful cry rent and shattered the stillness, and from outside a screaming, strangled voice called:

"Oh, my God!" it yelled. "Oh, Christ!"

For one moment Philip lay in the grip and paralysis of mortal fear, but the next he broke through it, and sprang out of bed, and, not pausing to light a candle, stumbled to the door. At the same moment his servant's door flew open, and he came out with a white, scared face. He carried a lighted candle.

"It was from the garden, sir," he said. "It was Mr. Merivale's voice."

Philip did not answer, but went quickly downstairs, followed by the man. The door into the verandah stood open, as usual, and he hurried out. There on the table were the cloth and the remains of dessert; his chair stood where he had sat all evening; Merivale's was pushed sideways. The moon was somewhere risen behind the clouds, for thick as they were, the darkness was not near pitch, and followed by the servant, the light of whose candle tossed weird, misshapen shadows about, Philip set his teeth and went down towards where the hammock was slung in which Merivale usually slept.

That strange, pungent smell, which he had noticed more than once before, was heavy in the air, and infinitely stronger and more biting than it had been. And for one moment his flesh crept so that he stopped, waiting for the man to come up with the light. He could not face what might be there alone.

A few yards further on they came in sight of the hammock. Something white, a flannelled figure, glimmered there, but, like some strange, irregular blot, something black concealed most of the occupant. Then that black thing, whatever it was, suddenly skipped into the air and ran with dreadful frolicsome leaps and bounds and tappings on the brick path of the pergola, down to the far end of the garden, where they lost sight of it. Then they came to the hammock.

Merivale was sitting up in it, bunched up together with his head drawn back, as if avoiding some deadly contact. His lips were drawn back from his teeth, so that the gums showed, his eyes were wide-open, and terror incarnate sat there, and the pupils were contracted to a pin-point as if focussed on something but an inch or two from him. He was not dead, for his chest heaved with dreadful spasms of breathing, and Philip took him up and carried him away from that haunted place into the house, laying him on a rug in the passage.

But before they had got him there the breathing had ceased, the mouth and the eyes had closed, and what they looked on was just the figure of a boy whose mouth smiled, and who was sunk in happy, dreamless sleep.

There was nothing to be done. Philip knew that, but he sent his servant off at once to fetch a doctor from Brockenhurst, while he waited and watched by Merivale or what had been he. All terror and shrinking had utterly passed from that face, and Philip himself, in spite of the frightful, inexplicable thing that had happened, was not frightened either, but sat by him, feeling curiously calm and serene, hardly conscious even of sorrow or regret. Nor did he fear any incomer from the garden. For the curtain had been drawn, and the dead man had felt so sure that whatever form the revelation was to take, it would be God, that the assurance of his belief filled and quieted the man who watched by him.

His shirt was open at the neck, as Philip had seen him last, standing below the lamp on the verandah, and his sleeves were rolled back to above the elbow. And as Philip looked, he saw slowly appearing on the skin of his chest and the sunburnt arms curious marks, which became gradually clearer and more defined, marks pointed at one end, the print of some animal's hoofs, as if a monstrous goat had leaped and danced on him.

It was a week later, and Philip was seated alone with his mother in the small drawing-room of his house at Pangbourne which they generally used if there was no one with them. He had arrived home only just before dinner that night, and when it was over he had talked long to her, describing all that had happened during his stay with Merivale, all that had culminated in that night of terror about which even now he could hardly speak. The story had been a long one, sometimes he spoke freely, at other points there were silences, for the words would not come, and his choking throat and trembling lips had to be controlled before he could find utterance. For it concerned not Merivale only; and, indeed, friend of his heart as he had been, one who could never be replaced, Philip could scarcely think of his death as sad.

"For though," he said, "just for that moment when he cried on God's name and on the name of Christ, when that terror, whatever it was, came close to him, the flesh was weak, yet I know he was not afraid. He had told me so: his spirit was not afraid. And he so longed to see the curtain drawn."

The joy of getting Philip back again, the joy, too, of knowing that that black crust of hate and despair no longer shut him off from her, was so great, that Mrs. Home hardly regarded the anxiety she would otherwise have felt. For she had never seen Philip like this; what had happened had stirred him to the depths of his soul. Even the sudden and dreadful death of so old a friend she could not have imagined would have affected him so.

"Philip, dear," she said, "you are terribly excited and overwrought. Get yourself more in control, my darling."

He was quiet for a moment, and even lit a cigarette, but he threw it away again immediately.

"Ah, mother, when I have finished you will see," he said. "Let me go on."

He paused a moment, and the soft stroking of her hand on his calmed him.

"It was just dawn when Flynn came back with the doctor," he said; "a clear, dewy dawn, the sort of dawn Tom loved. The doctor needed but one glance, one touch. Then he said: 'Yes, he has been dead for more than an hour.' So I suppose I had sat there as long as that; I did not think it had been more than a minute or two. Then his eye fell on those marks and bruises I told you of, and he looked at them. He undressed him a little further: there were more of them. I needn't go into that, but you know what the surface of a lane looks like when a flock of sheep has passed?—it was like that.

"All this, of course, came out at the inquest, where I told all I knew, and Flynn corroborated it. I saw also what Tom had told me that afternoon, how a huge goat had sparred and gambolled round him as he came home across the forest. And the verdict, as you say, perhaps, was brought in, in accordance with that. The world will be quite satisfied. I am satisfied, too, but not in that way."

He was silent again a moment, and then went on.

"It all hangs together," he said; "the dear Hermit was not as all of us are: he could talk to birds and beasts, and the very peace of God encompassed him. He knew, in a way we don't, that all-embracing fatherhood. I learned slowly, these weeks I was with him, what the truth of that was to him. And he used often to speak, as you know, of the grim side of Nature, of the cruelty and death, which he had turned his face from, which he called Pan, who, as the myths have it, appeared in form like a goat, to see whom was death. We had been talking of it that night, we both heard curious tramplings in the bushes, and the pungent smell of a goat. Every sensible person, considering, too, that he had seen a big goat that afternoon, would come to the conclusion that, somehow or other the brute

208

had found its way into the garden, and had sprung on him like a wild beast, and trampled him. Then, too, he was thinking about Pan; he might have imagined when the goat appeared, that this was what he in those imaginings, if you like, which were as real to him as the sun and moon, believed to be Pan, and that he died of fright. The jury took the view that some wild goat was the cause of his death: I daresay fifty juries would have done the same. But if you ask me whether I believe that a goat, a flesh and blood goat, killed him, why I laugh at you. For what goat was that? Who saw the goat except the Hermit?"

He paused again, and looked up at his mother with sudden solicitude.

"Ah, dear, you are crying," he said. "Shall I not go on?"

Again that gentle, loving stroking of his hand began.

"Ah, my son," she said.

Philip kissed the hand that stroked his. These lines were easy to read between.

But if he had more to tell his mother, she had something also to tell him that he did not know yet.

"You see, I saw such strange and impossible things there," he went on, "that nothing seems strange nor impossible. It was like an allegory: Tom himself was an allegory. The birds came to his bidding, the shy creatures of the forest were his friends. It was no miracle: it was but what we all could do, if we realised what he realised, and knew as he knew the brotherhood of all that lives. He put into practice the theory of Darwinism that no one in theory denies. The living things were his brothers and his cousins: they knew it, too. But from one huge fact, the fact of sorrow and pain, he turned aside, and, so I believe, it all came to him in a flash, making him perfect. And it came in material form, at least it was so material that it could bruise his flesh. It seems cruel; but—oh, mother, if you had seen his face afterwards, you would have known that the hand that made him suffer comforted him when he had learned what the suffering had to teach him. It could have been done, I must suppose, in no other way."

Then for a little the strong man was very weak, and he broke down and wept. But one who weeps while eyes so tender watch, weeps tears that are not bitter, or at least are sweetened, each one, as it falls. Then again he went on: much as he had told, there was all to tell yet, yet that all was but short—a few words were sufficient.

"And so my lesson came home to me," he said. "A month ago I said, as you know, 'I will hate, I will injure.' A fortnight ago I said, 'What good is that?' But now, when poor Tom, who was all kind and all gentle, had to be taught like that, with those battering hoofs, that pain must be and that one must accept it and sorrow, and not leave them out of life, now I say, 'Can I help? May not I bear a little of it?'"

He got up.

"You don't know me," he said. "I don't know myself. But I suppose this is how such a thing comes to one. I have been in an outer darkness: I have been black and bitter and all my life before that I was hard. That, I suppose, was needful for me. I don't think I am going to be a prig, but if that is so, perhaps it doesn't much matter. But I do know this, that I am sorry for poor things."

Mrs. Home said nothing for the moment; then she turned her eyes away as she spoke.

"You have not heard then, dear?" she said.

"I have heard nothing."

"It was in the paper this evening," she said. "I know no more than that. Evelyn was shot in the face yesterday."

Then her voice quivered.

"They think he will live," she said. "But they know he will be blind. Oh, Philip, think of Evelyn blind!"

TWENTIETH

THE room where Madge had talked with her mother on the evening of her first day at Glen Callan was darkened, and only a faint, muffled light came in through the blinded windows. The clean, neat apparatus of nursing was there, a fire burned on the hearth, by which Madge sat, and on the bed lay a figure, the face of which was swathed in bandages. The whole of the upper part of it was thus covered, only the chin and mouth appeared, and round the mouth was the three days' beard of a young man.

It was a little after midday; the nurse had gone to her lunch, and had told Madge to ring for her if she wanted her. It was not the least likely: all was going as well as it apparently could, but while Evelyn was still feverish it was necessary to be on the guard for any one of a myriad dangers that might threaten him. There was the danger of blood-poisoning; there were the after-effects of the shock; other things also were possible. Madge had not inquired into it all; she knew only what it was right for her to know if she was in charge of the sick-room for an hour or two. If he got very restless, if he came to himself—for he was kept drowsy with drugs—and complained of pain, she was to ring the bell. But the nurse did not think that there was any real likelihood of any of these things happening.

They had carried him back over the wire bridge, above which the accident had happened, and now for nearly forty-eight hours he had lain where he lay now. By great good luck a surgeon of eminent skill had been staying in a house not very far off, and he had come over at once, in answer to this call, and done what had to be done. Madge had seen him afterwards, and very quietly, as Evelyn's wife, had asked to be told, frankly and fully, what had been necessary. Sir Francis Egmont, whose surgical skill was only equalled by his human kindness, had told her all.

"He won't die, my dear lady," he had said. "I feel sure of that. He will get over it, and live to be strong again. But—yes, you must be brave about it, and more than that, you must help him to be brave, poor fellow."

This happened in the sitting-room adjoining. Sir Francis took a turn up and down before he went on. Then he sat in a chair just opposite Madge, and took her hands in his. And his grey eyes looked at her from under the eyebrows, which were grey also.

"Yes, you have got to make him brave," he repeated, "and there is your work cut out for you in the world. You are young and strong, and your youth and strength have got their mission now. Don't label me an old preacher; old I am, but I don't preach, Mrs. Dundas, unless I am sure of my audience. And I am sure of you. Your husband will get well. But his face will be terribly disfigured. That must be. That could not be helped. And there is another thing. He will be blind. Yes, yes, take the truth of that now, for it is you who have to enable him to bear it. Blind! Ah, my dear girl—I call you that: you are so young, and I am so sorry!"

How it had happened hardly interested her. They had been walking in line, it appeared, on the steep hill-side, where she had seen them as she sat on the top of the cliff above the Bridge-pool. Then a hare had got up, and Lord Ellington had fired. The shot struck a rock not far in front, and of the whole charge some ten pellets had ricocheted back and hit Evelyn in the face. One eye was destroyed, the other was so injured that it had been found impossible to save it; other pellets had lodged in his face. All this— the manner of the accident—did not matter to Madge: the thing had happened, it was only wonderful that he was alive.

But the operation—what it was Madge did not inquire, for it would do no good—had satisfied the surgeon. He could not have expected better results, he would not have predicted results so good. With the unhesitating obedience to duty, which is the motto and watchword of his profession, he had stopped in Lady Dover's house, waiting till he could without misgiving or fear of after-results, leave the case. All yesterday he had been in and out of the sick-room, he had slept in the dressing-room last night, and had only left an hour or two before, when he could put his patient into the skilled hands of the nurse who had come from Inverness. He was a kind, shy man, and fumbled dreadfully in his pockets as Lady Dover saw him off.

"You will do me a great service, Lady Dover," he had said, "if you will convey somehow to Mrs. Dundas that her debt to me, whatever it is, is discharged. Discharged it is; to see a woman being brave is sufficient. Besides, I am on my holiday: I could not think of taking a fee. So if so absurd a notion occurs to her—ah, the motor is ready, I see, but if so absurd a thing occurs—you, my dear lady, will please exercise your tact, you will let her be under no obligation, please. A Daimler surely—beautiful machines, are they not—yes, just a little tact—I was in the house or something—I am sure you will manage it—besides, on my holiday. Yes, good-bye, good-bye. I think I have told the nurse everything, and the doctor from Inverness—dear me, his name has gone again, whom I am very pleased to have met, is, I am sure, most reliable. God bless my soul, poor Dundas, a rising painter too; well, I'm no judge. But it is pitiful, isn't it? Of course, if I am wanted again, I'll step over at once: Brora, you know, it's no trouble at all. And the poor fellow, too, who caused this accident; I'm sorry for him, too—nobody's fault. But tell him we'll pull Mr. Dundas

211

through—oh, yes, we'll pull him through, and there's Braill's system and all afterwards. A brave woman, you know, Mrs. Dundas is; does one good, that sort of woman. Very brave. She'll need to be, poor thing, too. Good-bye, good-bye."

But Evelyn lay still, and there was no need for Madge to ring for the nurse. Sometimes he shifted his head from side to side, and occasionally he put a hand up to the bandage that covered his face, with little moans and sighs below his breath. Madge had been warned to be on the alert for this, and very gently, as often as he did this, she would take the feeble, wandering fingers in hers and lay his arm back again on the blanket. It was something even to have that to do, the slightest, most trivial act, was a relief from absolute inaction. Yet all the time she dreaded with ever-increasing shrinking of the heart the hour when she should have to act indeed, when her husband would come to, and begin to ask questions. No one but she, she was determined, should answer them; it was she who would tell him all that he had yet to learn. Would it kill him, she wondered, when he knew? Would he die simply because life was no longer desirable or possible? Blind! Madge could not fully grasp that herself yet, but she felt she must realise it, she must make haste to realise it before she was called upon to tell him. Lady Dover, her mother, Sir Francis, had all urged her to let him be told by someone else; but Madge would not hear of it; some wifely instinct was stronger than any reason that could be suggested.

There was another thing which she shrank from, too, though in part that would be spared Evelyn, the disfigurement about which Sir Francis had spoken. He had told her it would be terrible, and she had to get used to that in anticipation, so that when she saw it, she should not shrink, or let Evelyn guess. He would not be able to see it himself; as far as that went, it was merciful. All that splendid beauty, which she loved so, the brightness and the sunshine of his face, she would never see again. A few details about that the surgeon had told her; it was horrible. Her love for him, her love for his beauty were inseparable; she could not disentangle them, the latter was part of the whole. Yet though she knew that it was gone, it was impossible to imagine that the whole was diminished, though a part of it was withdrawn. But she had been warned how terrible the change would be, and what if involuntarily, without power of control, her flesh recoiled, her nerves shrank from him? Yet that was the one thing that must not be; all that she could do for him was to make him know and feel that in every way the completeness of her love for him was undiminished, and only that pity, the broad, sweet shining of pity, framed it as with a halo. She knew that this was true essentially and fundamentally, but she had to make it true not only in principle, but in the conduct of the little trivial deeds of life. She must act up to it always; his closeness, his bodily presence, must not be one whit less physically dear to her.

Blind! Ah, if she only could take that and bear it for him, how vastly easier even to her personally than that it should be borne by him! For it was from that, from the exquisite pleasures of the eye, that as from a fountain his gaiety, his joy of life, chiefly sprang. Of the five senses that one was to him more than all the rest put together; of the five chords that bound him to life and made the material world real the strongest had been severed, and the others in comparison were but as frayed strings. Any other loss would have been trivial compared with this, and how doubly, trebly trivial would the same loss have been to her. But that it should come to him! How could he bear it?

There was nothing to be reasoned about in all this: she had but to let thoughts like these just go round and round in her head, till she got more used to them. Round and round they went, yet at each recurrence each seemed not a whit less unendurable. She tried to imagine herself telling him; she went even over forms of words, choosing the speech that should tell it him most gently, and even while she spoke should make him, force him, to feel that by the very fact of her love the burden and the misery of it all was more hers to bear than his. Yet what were words, this mere formula, "It hurts me more than you?" That did not make it hurt him less. A pain that is shared by another is not diminished; there is double the pain to bear, a dreadful automatic multiplication of it alone takes place. It was all too crushingly recent yet for poor Madge to refrain from such a conclusion; it seemed to her as yet that this was a dark place into which the light of sympathy could not penetrate. She herself certainly was at present beyond its range; the kindness, the deep pity, which all felt for her did not reach her yet.

The nurse returned from her dinner, and with her came the Inverness doctor, a kind, rugged man. Bandages had to be changed, and fresh dressings to be put on, and Madge left the room for this, for she had been told that if she saw his face now she would be needlessly shocked. When the wounds healed, it would not be nearly so bad. So, though she would really have preferred to know worse than the worst, she yielded to this.

Madge went downstairs while this was going on, and found Lady Dover waiting in the hall. The rest of the party had all left yesterday, and though Lady Ellington had offered, and, indeed, really wished to remain, Madge had persuaded her to go; for the girl, out of the range of sympathy and pity at present, found the consolation that Lady Ellington tried to administer like a series of sharp raps on a sore place. Also Madge could not help reading into it a sort of tacit reproach for her having married him. The accident, indeed, seemed to have stained backwards in Lady Ellington's mind, and to have re-endowed the marriage itself with disaster.

But Lady Dover's touch was very different to her mother's; indeed it was because it did not seem to be a "touch" at all that Madge unconsciously answered to it.

"Ah, there you are, dear," she said; "I was expecting you. Will you not get on your hat, and come out for a little? It will do you good to get the air, and it is a lovely afternoon. I have never seen the lights and shadows more exquisite."

It was this that poor Madge wanted, though she did not know she wanted it, just the cool spring water, the wholesome white bread of a kind, natural woman. Sympathy was no good to her yet, consolation could not touch her, but just the quiet, patient kindness was bearable, it made the

213

moment bearable from its very restfulness; the lights and the shadows were still there, Lady Dover still talked of them, and though she did not know it, it was this very fact that other lives went on as usual that secretly brought a certain comfort to Madge.

"Yes, I will come out," she said; "but I don't want a hat. I cannot go far, though."

"No, we will just take a turn or two up and down the terrace. We get the sun there, and it is sheltered from the wind, which is rather cold to-day."

Simple and unsophisticated as the spell was, if spell indeed there was, it worked magically on the poor girl, and for a little while that dreadful round of the impossible images which formed the panorama of her future ceased to turn in her head. Had Lady Dover's tone suggested sympathy, or, which would have been worse, spoken of the healing power of time, Madge could not have spoken. But now, when that incessant procession of the unthinkable future was stayed, she could focus her mind for a little on a practical question which must soon arise, and on which she wanted advice.

"I want your counsel," she said. "They are going to give Evelyn, the doctor told me, no more drugs, and by this evening he will be himself again, fully conscious. Now, unless I deceive him, unless I tell him that he is being kept for the present in absolute darkness, he must find out that—that he is blind. Soon, anyhow, he must know it. Is it any use, do you think, putting it off?"

Lady Dover did not, as Madge's mother would certainly have done, squeeze her hand and utter words of sympathy. She did not even look at Madge, but with those clear, level eyes looked straight in front of her while she considered this. Her first instinct was, as would have been the instinct of everyone, to say something sympathetic, but her wisdom—the existence of which Lady Ellington really did not believe in—gave her better counsel. For to be natural is not synonymous with doing the first thing that happens to come into one's head.

"That must be partly for Dr. Inglis to decide," she said; "but if he sanctions it, I should certainly say that you had better tell him at once. I think people get used to things better and more gradually while they are still weak and perhaps suffering, though Dr. Inglis said he thought he would have no pain, whereas the same thing is a greater shock if one is well; it hits harder then. He perhaps will half-guess for himself, too; all that would torture him. To know the worst, I think, is not so bad as to fear the worst."

They had reached the end of the terrace and looked out over the river a couple of hundred feet below. Just opposite them was the Bridge-pool, beyond which rose the steep moorland. Ever since it had happened, Madge had given no outward sign of her helpless, devouring anguish; she had been perfectly composed; there had been no tears, no raving cries. But now she turned quickly away.

"I can't bear to look at it," she said. "There was a piece of white heather, too, where he fell."

Lady Dover's sweet, rather Quakerish face did not change at all, her quiet wisdom still held sway.

"We are wrong, I think," she said, "to associate material things with great grief. One cannot always wholly help it, but I think one should try to discourage it in oneself. I remember so well walking on this terrace, Madge, just after my mother died. It was a day rather like this; there were the same exquisite lights on the hills. And I remember I tried consciously to dissociate them from my own grief. I think it was wise. I would do it again, at least, which, in one's own case, comes to the same thing."

She paused a moment; there was one thing she wanted to say, and she believed it might do Madge good to have it said. Deep and overwhelming as her grief was, Lady Dover knew well that anything that took her mind off herself was salutary.

"But sometimes, on the other hand," she went on, "we ought to remember those people who have been most associated with it. It does not do any good to anyone to shudder at the heather. But I think, dear, it would be kind if you just wrote a line to Lord Ellington. I think you have forgotten him, and what he must feel."

For the moment she doubted if she had done wisely, so bitter was Madge's reply.

"Ah, I can never forgive him!" she cried. "To think that but for him——" And she broke off with quivering lip.

Lady Dover did not reply at once, but the doubt did not gain ground.

"I think, dear, that that is better unsaid," she replied at length. "You do not really mean it either; your best self does not mean it."

Again she paused, for she did not think very quickly.

"And this, too," she said, "you must consider. How can you help Mr. Dundas not to feel bitter and resentful, for he has more direct cause to feel it than you, if you have that sort of thought in your heart? You will be unable to help him, in the one way in which you perhaps can, if you feel like that. Also, dear, supposing any one of us, Dover, I, Mr. Osborne, had to become either Mr. Dundas or Lord Ellington, do you think any of us could hesitate a moment? Do you not see that of all the people who have been made miserable by this terrible accident, which of them must be the most miserable?"

Then came the second outward sign from Madge. She took Lady Dover's hand in both of hers.

"Don't judge me too hardly," she said. "I spoke very hastily, very wrongly. I have been thinking of my own misery too much; I have not thought enough about poor Evelyn. But I did not know there was such sorrow in the world."

Lady Dover looked at her a moment, and drew her gently to a seat behind some bushes. And her own pretty, neat face was suddenly puckered up.

"Oh, Madge," she said, "just let yourself go for ten minutes, and cry, my dear, sob your heart out, as they say. Have a good cry, dear; it will do you good. It is not cowardly, that—it helps one, it softens one, and it makes one braver perhaps afterwards. Yes, dear, let it come."

And then the fountain of tears was unloosed, and those sobs, those deep sobs which come from the heart of living and suffering men and women, and are a sign and a proof, as it were, of their humanity, poured out. Madge had surrendered, she had ceased to hold herself aloof; brave she had been before, but brave in a sort of impenetrable armour of her own reserve. But now she cast it aside, and the womanhood which her love for Evelyn had begun to wake in her, came to itself and its own, more heroic than it had been before, because the armour was cast aside, and she stood defenceless, but fearless.

Before she went up again to Evelyn's room she wrote:

My Dear Ellington,
    I had no opportunity of speaking to you——

Then her pen paused; that was not quite honest, and she began again:

> I ought to have just seen you before you went yesterday, and I must ask your pardon that I did not. I just want to say this, that I am more sorry for you than I can possibly tell you, and I ask you to say to yourself, and to keep on saying to yourself, that it was in no way your fault. Also perhaps you may like to know how entirely I recognise that, and so, I know, will he.
>
> You will wish, of course, to hear about him. He is going on very well, though up to now they have kept him under morphia. He will be quite blind, though. We must all try to make that affliction as light as possible for him. And I want so much to make you promise not to blame yourself. Please don't; there is no blame. It was outside the control of any of us.
>
> I will write again and tell you how he gets on.—Your affectionate cousin,
>
>   Madge Dundas.

Evelyn's room looked out on to the terrace, away from the direction of the wind, and the nurse had just gone to the window to open it further, for the room, warmed by the afternoon sun, was growing rather hot. But just then he stirred with a more direct and conscious movement than he had yet made, half-sat up in bed, and with both hands suddenly felt at the bandages that swathed the upper part of his face. Then he spoke in those quick, staccato tones that were so characteristic.

"What has happened?" he said. "Where am I? What's going on? Why can't I see? Madge——" And then he stopped suddenly.

She bit her lip for a moment, and just paused, summoning up her strength to bear what she knew was coming. Then she went quickly to the bedside and took his hand away from his face.

"Yes, dearest, I am here," she said. "Lie quiet, won't you, and we will talk."

The nurse had come back from the window, and also stood by the bed. Madge spoke to her quickly and low.

216

"Leave us, please, nurse," she said. "We have got to talk privately. I will call you if I want you."

She left the room; Evelyn had instinctively answered to Madge's voice, and had sunk back again on his pillows, and slowly in the long silence that followed, his mind began piecing things together, burrowing, groping, feeling for the things that had made their mark on his brain, but were remembered at present only dimly. The remembrance of some shock came first to him, and some sudden, stinging pain; next the smell of heather, warm and fragrant, and another bitter-tasting smell, the smell of blood. He put out his hand, and felt fumblingly over the clothes.

"Madge, are you still there?" he said quickly.

She took his hand.

"Yes, dear, sitting by you," she said. "I shall always be here whenever you want me."

Then came the staccato voice again.

"But why can't I see you?" he asked. "What's this over my face?"

Again she gently pulled back his other hand, which was feeling the bandages with quick, hovering movements like the antennæ of some insect.

"You were hurt, dear, you know," she said. "They had to bandage your face, over your forehead and your eyes."

Again there was silence; his mind was beginning to move more quickly, remembrance was pouring in from all sides.

"It was at Glen—Glen something, where we came by a night train, and you flirted with a valet," he said.

"Yes, dear, Glen Callan," said Madge quietly. But her eyes yearned and devoured him: all her heart was ready now, when the time came, to spring towards him, enfolding him with love.

But his voice was fretful rather and irritable, from shock and suffering.

"Yes, Glen Callan, of course," he said. "I said Glen Callan, didn't I? We are there, still, I suppose. Yes? And you went fishing in the morning, and I went shooting. Shooting?" he repeated.

All that Madge had ever felt before in her life grew dim in the intensity of this. The moment was close now, but somehow she no longer feared it. Fear could not live in these high altitudes: it died like some fever-germ.

"Yes, dear, you went shooting," she said. "We were to meet at lunch, you know. But just before lunch there was an accident. You were shot, shot in the face."

His hands grew restless again, and he shifted backwards and forwards in bed.

"Ah, yes," he said, "that is just what I could not remember. I was shot—yes, yes: I remember how it stung, but it didn't hurt very much. Then I fell down in the heather: I can't think why, but I stumbled—I couldn't see. I was bleeding, too; the heather was warm and sweet-smelling, but there was blood, too, that tasted so horrible—like—like blood, there is nothing—all over my face. And then—well, what then?"

217

"We brought you back, dear," said she, "and you had an operation. They had to extract the shot. It was all done very satisfactorily: you are going on very well."

Then all the nervous trembling in Evelyn's hands and the quick twitching of his body ceased, and he lay quite still a moment, gathering himself together to hear.

"Madge," he said, speaking more slowly, "will you please tell me all? I don't think you have told me all yet. I want to hear it, for I feel there is more yet. I was shot: that is all I know, and am lying here with a bandaged face. Well?"

Madge's voice did not falter; that love and pity which possessed her had for this moment anyhow complete mastery over the frailness and cowardice of the mere flesh. She just took hold of both his hands, clasping them tightly in her's, and spoke.

"You were shot all over the upper part of your face," she said. "You-"

But he interrupted her.

"Who shot me?" he asked.

"Guy Ellington," she said. "The shot ricocheted off a rock and hit you. It was not his fault."

"By Gad, poor devil!" said Evelyn.

"Yes, dear; I wrote to him just now, saying just that, how sorry I was for him and how sorry you would be when you knew. You—you were shot very badly, dear Evelyn. You were shot in the eyes, in both eyes——"

Again there was silence. Then he spoke hoarsely:

"Do you mean that, all that?" he said.

"Yes, dear; all that. And I had better say it. You are blind, Evelyn."

Then deep down from the very heart of her came the next words which spoke themselves.

"I wish I could have died instead," she said.

He lay long absolutely motionless; there was no quiver of any kind on the corners of his mouth to show that he even understood. But she knew he understood, it was because he understood that he lay like that.

At last he spoke again, and the sorrow and anguish in his voice was still comfort to her beyond all price.

"So I shall never see you again," he said.

Then she bent over the bed, and kissed him on the mouth.

"But never have I been so utterly yours as I am now!" she said, her voice still strong and unwavering. "And, oh, how it fed my heart to know what your first thought was, my darling. I think it would have broken if it had been anything else!"

TWENTY-FIRST

AFTER dinner that night, before she went to bed, Madge looked into Evelyn's room several times and spoke to him gently. But on all these occasions he was lying quite still and he did not answer her; so, thinking he was asleep, she eventually retired to her own room just opposite, and went to bed. For the last two nights she had scarcely closed her eyes, but now, with the intense relief of knowing that Evelyn knew, of feeling, too, that he was bearing it with such wonderful quietness and composure, she fell asleep at once and slept long and well.

But her husband had not been asleep any of those times that she went into the room. He had never felt more awake in his life. But he had not answered her, because he had felt that he must be alone: just now nobody, not even she, could come near to him, for he had to go into the secret place of his soul, where only he himself might come. And as at the moment of death not even a man's nearest and dearest, she with whom he has been one flesh, may take a single step with the soul on its passage, but it has to go absolutely alone, so now none could go with Evelyn; for in these hours he had to die to practically all, Madge alone excepted, which the word "life" connoted to him. And having done that, he had to begin, to start living again. There Madge could help him, but for this death, this realisation of what had happened, this summing up of all that had been cut off, he had to be alone.

There was no comfort for him anywhere: nor at any future time could comfort come. There would be no "getting used" to it, every moment, every hour, that passed would but put another spadeful of earth on his coffin. There was no more night and morning for him. Sunset and sunrise spilt like crimson flames along the sky existed no more: the green light below forest trees was dead, the clusters of purple clematis in his unfinished picture had grown black, there was neither green nor red nor any colour left, it was all black. The forms of everything had gone, too; it was as if the world had been some exquisite piece of modelling clay, and that some gigantic hand had closed on it, reducing it to a shapeless lump: neither shape nor colour existed any more. People had gone, too, faces and eyes and limbs, the gentle swelling of a woman's breast, outline and profile and the warm, radiant tint of youth were gone, there was nothing left except voices. And voices without the sight of the mouth that spoke, of the shades of expression playing over the face, would be without significance: they would be dim and meaningless, they would not reach him in this desert of utter loneliness, where he would dwell forever out of sight of everything. And that was not all; that was not half. Of the world there was nothing left but voices, and of him what was left? Was he only a voice, too?

He was blind, that is to say, his eyes must have been practically destroyed. And the bandages extended, so he could feel, right up to his hair, and down to his upper lip. There were other injuries as well, then. What were they? How complete was the wreck? Above all, did Madge

219

know, had she seen? If ever love had vibrated in a voice, it had in her's, but did she know, or had she only seen these bandages?

With his frightfully sensitive artistic nature, this seemed to cut deeper than anything, this thought that he was disfigured; horrible to look on, an offence to the eye of day and to the light of the sun, and—to the sight of her he loved. He would be pitied, too; and even as man and woman turned away from the sight of him they would be sorry for him, and the thought of pity was like a file on his flesh. Would it not have been better if the shot had gone a little deeper yet? His maimed, disfigured body would then have been decently hidden away and covered by the kind, cool earth, he would not have to walk the earth to be stared at—to be turned from.

His nurse not long before had made her last visit for the night, and, seeing him lying so still supposed, like Madge, that he was asleep, and had gone back to the dressing-room next door, to go to bed herself. His progress during the day had been most satisfactory, the feverishness had almost gone, and the doctor, when the wounds were dressed that afternoon, had been amazed to see how rapidly and well the processes of healing were going on. Certainly there was no lack of vitality or recuperative power in his patient, nor in the keenness and utter despair of his mental suffering was vitality absent. That same vitality coloured and suffused that; he saw it all with the hideous vividness of an imaginative nature. Doubt and uncertainty, however, here were worse than the worst that the truth could hold for him, and he called to the nurse, who came at once.

"What is it, Mr. Dundas?" she asked. "I hoped you were asleep. You are not in pain?"

"No, not in pain. But I can't sleep. I want to ask you two or three questions. Pray answer them: I sha'n't sleep till you do."

She did not speak, half-guessing what was coming.

"I want to know this, first of all," he said, speaking quite quietly. "What shall I look like when these things are healed, when the bandages come off?"

Nurse James was essentially a truthful woman, but she did not hesitate about her reply. There are times when no decent person would hesitate about telling a lie, the bigger the better. She laughed.

"Well, I never!" she said. "And have you brought me from my bed just to ask that! I never heard such a thing. Why, you will look as you always have looked, Mr. Dundas, but your eyelids will be shut."

The good, kind woman suddenly felt that the ease with which all this came to her was almost appalling. She was a glorious liar, and had never known it till now.

"Why, bless you," she went on, "your wife was in here when your face was dressed to-day, and—you were still under morphia, you know, and did not know she was there—and she said to Dr. Inglis: 'Why, he only looks as if he was asleep.'"

"She has seen me, then?" asked Evelyn eagerly. "She has seen my face?"

"Why, of course, and she bent and kissed it, just as your wife should do. There's a brave woman now. Is that all, sir?"

220

Evelyn gave one great sigh of relief.

"Yes, nurse," he said. "I am sorry I disturbed you. Yet I assure you it was worth while. I can't tell you how you have relieved me. I thought—oh, my God! it is not hell after all."

She arranged the bedclothes about him, and though she had been so glib, she could not now speak at once.

"There, then; you'll go to sleep, won't you, now you know that," she said. "But to think of you worrying here all these hours!"

Madge was, of course, told by Nurse James what happened before she saw Evelyn again, for that diplomatist came to her room very early next morning, and informed her of it all. She acquiesced in it, as she would have acquiesced in anything that in the opinion of nurse or doctor conduced to his recovery, and for the next day or two his progress was speedy and uninterrupted. He had faced the first shock, that he was blind, with a courage that was really heroic, and except for that hour when he held himself in front of it, purposing and meaning to realise once and for all exactly what it implied, he exercised wonderful self-control in not letting himself brood over it. This was the easier because that second fear, the roots of which went so much deeper than the other, had proved to be groundless. Terrible as was his plight, the knowledge that it might have been so much more terrible was ever in his mind, casting its light into the places that he had thought were of an impenetrable darkness.

But in this balance and adjustment of the human soul to the anguish with which circumstance and fate visit it, the mechanism of its infliction is wonderfully contrived, so that it shall not snap under the strain. The Angel of Pain, we must suppose, sits by, with the screws and levers of the rack under its control; it loosens one, as Evelyn's dread about disfigurement had been loosened for the present at any rate, since it was, perhaps, more than he could stand (and the Angel of Pain, with the relentless hands but the tender eye and pitying mouth, had not finished with him yet) but it tightens another; the fact of his blindness had been screwed down very tight. Then as the racked sinews and tortured nerves began to writhe and agonise less, another little torture was added. It was but a small thing compared to the others, and though it had been there all the time, neither Madge nor he had noticed it at first. But now when he was weary with pain, it was like a fly that kept buzzing and settling on his face, while his hands were bound, so that he could not brush it off. It had seemed but fear of the imagination at first, but gradually to both of them, as he recovered so well, and the future as well as the present began to make itself felt again, it became terribly real. It was simply this: What was to happen to them? How among other things were their doctor's and nurse's bills to be paid? And how, after that, were they going to live?

For several days each suffered the buzzing, flittings and alightings of this without speaking of it to the other, since each believed that the other had not yet thought of it. But one afternoon they had been talking of that hot August month in London, with their childish tales of Ellesdee, and the curious fact that if you only make a game out of a privation, the privation ceases and the game becomes entrancingly real. Evelyn had laughed over this.

221

"We shall have heaps of games in the future," he had said unthinkingly, and stopped rather abruptly. In the silence that followed he heard Madge just stir in her chair; an assent had dropped from her lips, but she had said no more, and it was clear to them both that their thoughts had met. Then Evelyn spoke.

"Madge, has it ever occurred to you what we are going to do?" he said. "How we are going to live, I mean?"

"Yes, dear, I have thought about it a good deal. I didn't speak of it, since I hoped you wouldn't begin to think about it yet."

"There were forty-three pounds?" he said; "from which you have to subtract our railway fares."

"Yes, dear," she said almost inaudibly.

The Angel of Pain turned that screw a little more. They could bear a little more of that.

"There is an unfinished portrait of Lady Taverner," said he. "There is the finished portrait of you. But even if we sold those, what next, what afterwards?"

"Ah, there is no necessity to think about it," said Madge quickly. "Of course mother will help us. She will do what she can. And Guy Ellington, of course——"

"We shall have to live on their alms, you mean?" said he with a sudden dreadful bitterness. "On the pity of others? They can't do it, besides. They can't support us. And even if they could, how could we accept it?"

His hand, with the rapid, hovering movement so characteristic of the blind, felt over the bedclothes and found hers. He was acquiring this blind touch with extraordinary rapidity.

"Madge, do you hate me for having married you?" he asked. "Would it have been better for you if we had never seen each other? Here are you, tied—eternally tied—to a beggar and a cripple, half a man with half a face!"

For one moment she winced at the thought of that which she did not yet know. Supposing it was very terrible, supposing she cried out at it? But she recovered herself at once.

"I bless God every day for your love, dear," she said.

He was silent after this a little, his fingers playing over hers.

"I am getting blind man's hands already," he said. "I can feel which your rings are. There, that is the wedding-ring, that is easy, and the one with sapphires in it. No, it can't be that, there are four stones in this, and there are only three sapphires. Ah, that is the ruby ring; do you remember how you scolded me for giving it you? Then on the next finger one pearl: that is easy. Then the first finger, no rings there, but—yes, at that knuckle the little scar that runs up halfway to the next knuckle, where you cut your finger to the bone when you were a girl over the broken glass."

Madge felt herself suddenly turn white and cold. He had felt the little scar on her finger with absolute accuracy, tracing it from where it started to where it finished. And if he could do this with so little a scar, what of other scars that would be within reach of his hands always? He would find them out, too; he would guess; all their attempts at concealment from him of what his injuries really were would be futile. He must come to know.

But he was busy just now on the exploration of his powers of touch. It was a new game; already touch was beginning to be a new thing to him, and whereas he had regarded his hands hitherto as holders to grasp other things, prehensile endings to the arms merely, he was now beginning to find out new powers in the soft-tipped fingers. He was like a child which has hitherto regarded its legs merely as agreeable though silent play-fellows, who begins to see that a hitherto undreamed-of power of locomotion resides in them.

This was fascinating to Evelyn; for the moment there was a sudden hope springing up. It was like a message of relief coming to a beleaguered garrison.

"Why, if I can do this already," he said, "who knows what it may not grow to? Madge, I am sure I could not have felt so much before—before it happened. Quick, give me something, and I will tell you what it is. What if the form and the shape of things has not been annihilated for me?"

And so this game, for so it was, began to interest him. For him, since some measure of the excitement, the chance, the experimentalism of life, had begun to come back, the Angel of Pain relaxed the screws a little, yet her hands did not altogether leave them. But poor Madge! The Angel of the relentless hands and tender face looked gravely on her. She had to bear very much, and bear it with a smiling face and cheerful voice, fetching books for Evelyn to identify, and small objects from his dressing-case and what-not. The screws were turned rather smartly for her; it was inevitable that he should before very long identify his own face, identify the damage there. She herself had not done so yet, but awfully as she had feared that for herself, she now feared it more for him. He was building so much, she knew that, on a place where no foundation was possible. It would all sink into the mire and clay. He would learn, as she would have to learn, how dreadful that was: his sensitive, hovering fingers with their light touch and constructive imagination would build up and realise by degrees. He would know that the worst fear of all was fulfilled.

That view of his, which Madge knew so well he would take when he learned, one way or another, of the wreck that had come to his face, might or might not be a shallow view, but that view he would assuredly take, and construe her love for him into mere pity and forbearance. She did not love him for his face—he would not say that—but his face was part of him, and if that was spoiled, so surely was part of her love spoiled. Body and soul she had loved him, but how could a woman love a sightless, scarred thing? He would grant, no doubt, that her love for him went further than that which was now hideous, but would she, to put it from her own point of view, have scarred and hacked and blinded her own face, and gone back to him who saw, in perfect confidence that his love for her would be undiminished and undeterred, knowing that it lay too deep for any such superficial maiming to injure? She knew well she would not, for love, however spiritual, includes the body as well as the spirit, and however fine, cannot but take the body as the outward and visible sign of the beloved

223

soul, its expression and aura. And how could he to whom the surface of beauty and loveliness had been by profession such a study and worship, still think, whatever her asseverations to the contrary, that her love for him was as complete as it had been? And, to get nearer the truth, would not he be right? She did not know about that yet; she had not seen. At present she could not think of his face as other than it had been; all she knew was that, in spite of herself, she dreaded with her whole soul the removal of those bandages. What if she shrank and winced at the sight? Those slim, delicate fingers of the Angel of Pain tightened the screw, and the kind eyes looked at her, seeing how she bore it. If there was a terrible moment coming for Evelyn when his fingers, which were now to be to him his eyes, told him what he looked like, there was a moment, a double moment, coming for her. She had first to control herself, to make him believe, whatever she saw, that she saw no difference; nothing that made her love one jot less urgent and insistent; she had also, with a feigned conviction that had got to convince him, to assure him that his fingers were at fault, that there was no scar where he said there was a scar, that there was no empty hole.... That she knew. What she did not know was how to face it all.

At present, anyhow, by a great effort, she put off the moment which she foresaw must come. He could not remain indefinitely ignorant, his own hands must some day inform him. But just now he was eager and interested in this new game. By a splendid effort of vitality and will, he had pushed into the background the fact of his blindness: he had put it for the time being, anyhow, among the inevitable and accepted facts of life, while he had filled his foreground with the fact that he had eyes in his fingers. How glorious that bit of bravery was she knew well, for he was so brave that just now he was not even acting; he genuinely looked forward to the future, not without hope. At her bidding he had left the grinding difficulties of the future alone, he had left the question of the stark fact as to how they were to live, he had left also the fact of his own supreme deprivation, and with a splendid effort he looked on the possibilities that might lie in front of them, not on the limitations, cramping and binding, that certainly lay there.

"Yes, all those things are easy," he said; "of course I can tell a toothpick and a sovereign-case, that is a mere effort of memory. But let's go on, if you are not tired of it. You see, dear, you've got to educate me now; I am just a child again, learning a new set of letters. Now give me really new letters."

Now Lady Dover a day before, in her quiet way, had telegraphed to London for a couple of packs of blind cards. They had the index in raised cardboard in the corner, and had arrived this morning. She had put them in the dressing-room adjoining his bedroom, and had just mentioned it to Madge, in the way that, had she been a stranger in the house, she might have mentioned where the bath-room was.

"Mr. Dundas is so eager and alive," she had said, "that I thought, dear Madge, that he might like to begin any moment to accustom himself a little, poor fellow, to his new circumstances. So you will find a couple of packs of raised cards, I think they call them, in the dressing-room. I thought he might perhaps feel inclined to experiment with them."

So Madge fetched them now, and a couple of minutes afterwards she and Evelyn were deep in a game of picquet. His childish pleasure in "new things" stood him in good stead now; he got as excited as a schoolboy over the riddle of what his hand contained. Again and again he fingered the raised index in the corner, with sudden bursts of triumph when he solved it to his own satisfaction.

"Ah, I used to call you slow at picquet, Madge," he cried, "but you can't retaliate. How very good for you! If you call me slow, I shall merely throw the cards away and burst into tears. Seven or nine, which on earth is it? Don't look and tell me. I trust you not to look."

But he soon got tired, and it is doubtful whether Madge was not more tired than he. When he waited long, feeling with those thin finger tips at the index, it was bad enough for her; but it was worse when he felt the card right almost immediately, and almost laughed with pleasure at his newly-acquired quickness—he, who used to be so quick! And all the time the certainty of the moment that was coming when he should learn all that had happened darkened her with an amazement of pity. What would he feel when he knew that? And what would she feel? And how, if that was very bad, would she have power to conceal it, so that he should believe, so that she could force him to believe that it was not there?

Two mornings after Madge slept on very late; but before she came down she had been in to see Evelyn, and subsequently had a talk to the nurse, who told her that Dr. Inglis had already seen her husband, and that he intended to take the bandages off his eyes that day. The wounds had healed in a manner almost marvellous, and they would now be the better for the air and light. And though Madge as she went downstairs felt that only thankfulness ought to be in her heart, she felt that she carried some sort of death-warrant in her pocket.

The post had just come in, and as she entered the breakfast-room, from which Lord Dover had already gone, but where his wife still waited for Madge, ready to make fresh tea on her entry, she found a letter by her plate directed in a handwriting that was very familiar to her. She wanted to open it at once, but instead she pushed it aside.

"What a glorious morning, dear Madge," said Lady Dover. "Dr. Inglis has already made me his morning report. He has no further anxiety, I think, at all. I am so glad."

She herself had a pile of letters, of which she had opened only about half, but abandoned them entirely to talk to Madge, and make her tea. But the sight of all those letters, somehow, diverted Madge's attention from her own, and a sudden thought struck her, which was new.

"Lady Dover," she said abruptly, "I believe you have been putting all manner of visitors off because of poor Evelyn."

Lady Dover looked up in gentle, clear-eyed acquiescence.

"Why, my dear, it was most important he should be quite quiet," she said.

Madge arrested the hand that was pouring out her tea.

"Ah, you dear," she said, "and all these days I never thought of it, or thanked you."

The spout of the teapot poured a clear amber stream on to the table-cloth.

"And I have spilt the tea, too," said Madge. "But I do thank you, and—and I am frightened!"

"There is nothing wrong?"

"No; but they are going to take the bandages off, and what shall I see? Will you be there, too, and help me not to mind if it is dreadful? You see—you see, I suppose I loved his face as well, why not, and if all that is terribly changed.... They have told me it will be. And he must not guess that I mind, that I even see it is different. And when his hands tell him what has happened, as they will, I must still convince him somehow that to me there is no difference. Oh, I want help!" she cried. "Indeed it is not only for me, I want it for him—I must convince him that it does not matter."

But at this point Lady Dover failed a little. She was not, in spite of her obvious kindness and sympathy, quite human enough to go to the depths that Madge's gropings reached blind hands to. The trials and difficulties that came within her ken, the loss of someone loved, the parching of love in what had been a fountain, she could have understood, but the fear of a maimed face affecting love she could not quite grasp. Her idea of love may perhaps have been spiritually finer, it may also perhaps have not been adequately human.

There was a pause, anyhow, and since nothing but immediate and spontaneous reply was conceivable from Madge's point of view, she took up her letter again.

"This, too," she said, "it is from Philip."

But to that Lady Dover responded instantly.

"Then, dear, you will want to read it alone," she said. "And if you can tell me about it afterwards, and if I can be of any use, advising or suggesting, you will come to me, will you not? But, dear Madge, he would not write unless he had something very particular to say, and, personally, whenever I see a letter that may be very private, I always keep it till I am alone. So let me leave you alone, dear. I see they have brought in a fresh hot dish for you of some sort, and I have just made the tea. I shall be in my room."

Here again tact played a great part; she did not look at Madge, either inviting or repelling confidence. And without the least suspicion of hurry or of lingering she left the room, with her pile of letters, opened and unopened.

Madge waited a minute or two. Then with a sudden mechanical series of movements, she tore open the envelope, took out Philip's letter, and read it. It was dated from Pangbourne.

My Dearest Madge,

I have every right to say that, and you must not mind. I heard only last night of the terrible thing that has happened to Evelyn, and unless I am stopped by a telegram from you or Lady Dover I shall come up to Glen Callan at once to see if I can be of any use. You will want somebody, anyhow, to look after you both

226

when you move. I write to Lady Dover by the same post; she will receive my letter at the time you receive this. She will not mind my proposing myself—in fact she has asked me to before now.

I have just come here from the New Forest: you will not have heard what has happened. Tom Merivale is dead, the Hermit, you know. I will tell you about it all when we meet; now I can only say that the sorrows of the world were, I believe, suddenly revealed to him, and he died of it. And some of the sorrows of the world, you poor dear, have been revealed to Evelyn and you, and perhaps to me. Only we have got to live and not die.

And before we meet I want very sincerely and humbly to ask your pardon for all the hard things I have thought and said and done. Please try to grant it me before you see me, so that I know that it is implied in your handshake.

So unless you stop me you will see me on the evening of the day on which you get this, and before then I want you to grant me a further favour. You must accept, please, tacitly and without any word on the subject, just the little material assistance that I can give you and him. In other words, do not let any material anxiety increase or aggravate what you two have to endure, and which no one can help you about. Only where you can be helped, accept such help, and let the privilege of helping you be mine. In doing this you will be helping me more than I can say: you will be helping me to learn the lesson of the sorrows of the world, which, as I now know, we must all learn. And I am,—Your loving friend,

Philip Home.

P.S.—I express myself badly; but I think you can easily understand what I mean. Just read my letter straightforwardly, I mean all I have said, and I think I have said all I mean. How fully my mother endorses it all, I need not tell you. She says (she has just read it) that it is too business-like. Well, I'm a business man, but her criticism encourages me to think that it is clear.

Madge read this through once without comprehension: the predominant feeling in her mind was that it was some kind stranger who was writing to her; she did not know the man. Yet even as she read there were things very familiar to her: Philip somehow was in it all. Then at the second reading the simplicity and clearness of it—that which Mrs. Home had called business-like—made itself felt, and it was Philip, after all, the potential Philip. But some immense change had happened, yet immense though it was, she saw now it was no stranger who had written it, but he himself, only—only he had learned something, as he said.

But how his begging for her forgiveness cut her to the heart! That he should do this, while it was she whose part it was, only she had not been woman enough. She had been sorry—God knows she had been sorry for him, and sorry for her own part in the catastrophe of July. But she had known it was inevitable, she could not have married him, she could not have done otherwise than marry Evelyn, and it was perhaps this sense that she was but a tool in the hands of the irresistible law which had excused her to herself, so that she had said almost that it was the Power that made them all three what they were that had done this. And thus her human pity and sorrow had been veiled. But now that veil was plucked aside; whatever great and inexorable laws ruled feeling and action, nothing could alter the fact that here was she, unhappy and sick at heart, and that another man, who loved her, unhappy, too, was man enough to forget his own unhappiness, to forget, too, that it was she who, willing or unwilling, had brought it on him, and let himself be guided only by the divine and human impulse of Pity, so that he desired nothing in the world more than to be allowed to help her.

Yet how bitter it was, somehow, that it should be he of all men in the world who should offer to help. And his offer was so humble, yet so assured, it was made so simply, and yet—here was Philip's hand again—so authoritatively. "You will want someone with you to look after you...." That was Philip, too, and though it was all bitter, what unspeakable comfort it was to feel that somebody strong and tender was waiting to take care of them, only asking to be allowed to take care of them. In spite of Lady Dover and all her kindness, Madge felt so lonely: no one could understand that so well as Philip, who had felt lonely, too.

And Tom Merivale was dead! Ah, what was happening to the world? Was happiness being slowly withdrawn from it, leaving misery only there? It seemed indeed as if sorrow, like some dreadful initiation, had to be submitted to by everyone, even those who appeared to have been born in the royal purple of happiness. How much had come into her own immediate circle in so short a time! To Merivale it had come in so blinding and overwhelming a flood that it had killed him who had radiated happiness. To Evelyn, it had come, blinding, also, and that cruel stroke, more cruel because it was so illogical, like the blasting of the tree by lightning down in the Forest, had stricken her, too, and had not perhaps dealt its worst blow yet. It had come to Philip through her in a way perhaps not less illogical. For it was not in her to control love or not to love; her meeting with Evelyn, her loving him, was as much an accident as the descent of the lightning-flash or the scattering of the lead pellets. Yet Philip had not died, and though he might have said that his life was wrecked, that all that remained for him was hatred and despair, he had struggled to shore, he stood there now strong and unembittered, and held out his hands to her. He had learned something it seemed from these accidents. He had learned, perhaps, not to call them accidents. Was he right? Were these vague lines part of a pattern, of a design so huge that she could not yet see it was a design at all?

Madge had forgotten about her breakfast; it lay still untasted, while she mused with wide eyes. And as this struck her, she stood up and pushed her plate from her. Greatly as she had grown in human strength and tenderness, since that day so few weeks ago, when she had promised to marry Philip, she felt now suddenly like a little child, who wanted to be led. There were dark places, she knew, before her. She must try not to be frightened, she must realise that there was nothing to be frightened about. And thus, feebly, hesitatingly, she put out her hand.

TWENTY-SECOND

EVELYN woke that morning out of one of those cruel, dreamless sleeps that seem for a little while on waking to have expunged all memory, and he lay a few minutes conscious vaguely of something a little wrong, but for the moment not knowing where he was, and not caring to make the effort to guess. Then suddenly, like the stroke of a black wing across the sky, memory came home for the day. Whenever he woke in the hereafter he would awake to that, to his maimed, ruined life. The knowledge of it was more unbearable to-day than it had been yesterday; to-morrow it would be worse; it would keep growing worse.

Then out of that utter darkness there grew a little light. It might have been even more desperate—how was that? Then he remembered Madge. She had seen, and the worst of all that he had imagined was not true.

This morning he felt within himself a sudden accession of strength; his long sleep-acting with his extraordinary recuperative powers, had set fresh tides of vitality on the flow. Something had happened lately which in spite of all, interested him—ah, yes, the gradual compensating sensitiveness in his hands. He had played a whole partie of picquet with Madge, using those cards with raised indexes. The partie had only taken an hour—not bad for a beginning; to-day perhaps he would be a little quicker. To-day also these bandages that worried him with their close-clinging, sticky feeling would be removed, and with regard to them he could not help half-thinking that when they were gone, some light, however dim, must reach him. Surely the blackness would become a sort of grey. It was unreasonable, he knew well, but he could not help feeling that it must be so. But the fact that he thought about the picquet he had played and the greater celerity with which he was going to play it, even the idea, which he himself knew to be purely imaginary, that he would not feel so terribly alone and in the dark when these bandages were removed, all pointed one way: he looked, or tried to look, forward instead of brooding backwards. And in such matters, as indeed in all others, the will is the deed, provided only that the will be undivided. So for the time the utter blackness of his waking moments was gone, the tiny things of life, as well as life's ultimate possibilities, still retained their interest, and while he waited for his breakfast, he kept feeling with his nimble, hovering hands at all objects within reach: the woolliness of the blankets, the cool texture of the sheets,

229

a certain slipperiness of counterpane, which eventually he determined to be silk-covered. Then there was wall-paper above his head; there was a pattern on that, and with both hands he traced his way up the slight raising of the design, stopping often, visualising to himself what the picture of the course of his fingers would be like.... There was a spray of some sort; it branched to the left and ended in narrow, slender leaves. On the right it went higher before it branched; there were leaves there, too, and above again there started a stem like the one he had traced a minute before. Yes; it repeated here, for first to the left went out a thinner stem with narrow leaves; then again to the right it branched, and narrow leaves forked out from it. He had seen it, of course, before, on the evening he arrived here, but he could not remember it from that.... Thin stem and narrow leaves— ah, a Morris paper of willow twigs! But the feeling fingers had given it him; without this exploration he could not have known it.

This was an enormous advance, and, without pause, for he instinctively knew the step that came through the dressing-room adjoining, he called out:

"Oh, Madge, such a discovery!" he cried. "Blanket here, sheet here, a coverlet with silk on the top, and the paper—it is a Morris willow paper. I found that out. And I want breakfast."

Yet somehow Madge's heart sank at his elation. The Evelyn who spoke was the old Evelyn: it was in such a voice and with such joy of discovery that he had told her at Pangbourne how the purple of the clematis would heighten the value of the pink and butter-haired Jewess who sat in the centre. There was just the same triumphant ring about it. And as such it was unnatural; she feared he was recovering too quickly: for this elation there would be a corresponding depression. It was too sudden to satisfy her. All this was instantaneous and instinctive; she feared really without knowing she feared. But she had come prepared for the further development of his newly-awakened interest in the senses that resided in fingers, and had brought with her some small objects of baffling shape. She had, too, in her hand Philip's letter.

The first two or three were easy to him. A knife certainly, but a knife with no edge to it. And of this he talked.

"Dessert knife," he said. "No, not dessert knife, because the blade of a dessert knife would, anyhow, be as cold as the handle, even if both were made of metal. And the blade of this is warmer than the handle. Oh, shade of Sherlock Holmes! Cold handle, warmer blade. Oh, Madge, how easy. Paper-knife of course; silver handle, ivory cutter. Ask another."

"I haven't asked how you are yet," said she.

"Quite well. And I want breakfast. I say, Madge, do you know just for the moment, I don't mind being blind. You see there's a new sense to cultivate. I always love experiments. Ah, damn it, there's no colour left. But there is shape; somehow, I feel there's a lot to learn in shape. There's warmth, too; of course I knew that ivory was warmer—less cold than metal, but now I have found it true without help. Give me another."

This time it was an absurd Dutch cow, spindle-legged and huge of body and head, a cream-jug cow, into which the cream was put via an aperture in the back, on which sat a gigantic fly, and from which, via the mouth, it was conveyed to tart. This was puzzling, and he thought aloud over it.

"Four legs," he said, "as thin as a stag's. So where's the head? That won't do; horn each side, and—good Lord! what's this on the middle of the back? It's movable, too. Shall I break anything?"

"Not if you are not violent."

"Well, a big head with a switch-horn, and a mouth, why it's from ear to ear. And a lid on the abortion's back. Tail—is it a tail; oh, yes, it must be, it comes from there—curled up till it nearly reaches the hole in the back."

He paused a moment, feeling it with nimble fingers, and though Madge could not see his forehead, she knew from his mouth that he was frowning. Then it came to him.

"Dutch cow," he cried. "There's an insect, a fly, I should think, sitting on the hole at its back, where you put the cream in. And it comes out of its mouth, you know. Looks rather as if it was being sick."

Madge's letter slipped to the ground as she applauded this.

"Give me that letter," he said. "I'll tell you whom it is from. Oh, there's nurse; is it breakfast? I am so hungry. I'll tell you about the letter afterwards."

Then for a moment he was silent, and his mouth grew grave. He had insisted late the evening before on being shaved, and the smooth chin, the smooth upper lip, were clean below the white bandages. The nurse had been confederate to this.

"You see, the bandages are coming off to-morrow," he had said, "and Madge would hate to see me with this awful stubble. Sometimes, nurse, I usen't to shave before breakfast, and she always cut me—figuratively, you know—till I did. You'll find a razor about somewhere. Clip it first, please."

So to-day he had cleanness of lip and chin, and now when the breakfast was being brought in, Madge drew her thumb and fourth finger down from his cheek to meet and pinch his chin.

"You were afraid I should cut you," she said gently.

"Yes, so I got shaved by nurse. Ah, Madge, sit on the bed, just there, and see me have breakfast. Have you had yours, by-the-way?"

Madge recalled the events of the morning.

"I don't think I have," she said.

"Then may we have another cup, nurse?" said he. "Oh, it's bacon, I can smell bacon. Now, Madge, I'm boss of this show. You may think you were going to feed me; not at all—I'm going to feed you. How elusive bacon is. Are you sure the plate is there? Oh, I felt it, then."

Here the nurse intervened, but with laughter.

"Oh, Mr. Dundas, do lie quiet, and we will give you your breakfast. Yes, another cup. I'll send for one. But your bed will be 'all over' bacon."

Madge made a negative sign to her. "There, you've got a piece," she said. "Raise it slowly, you clumsy boy! That's right; now wait. Your hand is really very steady. There!"

And she slipped it off the fork into her mouth.

"Oh, Madge," he cried, "how greedy! I thought I was going to get it.

And I can't manage everything. I'll give you bacon if you'll give me toast and butter."

So she buttered the toast, and they ate it like children, bite and bite about, and Evelyn chivied bacon round the plate, and fed now himself and now her. The extra cup lingered on its way, and one cup did for them, and all this to Madge was a sort of rehearsal of what would be. And it was a rehearsal of the best possible. For what if his gaiety, his interest in this new game was but a last flare-up? He could not feel this childish excitement in the entrancing sport of feeding each other, always. Besides, even if he did, she herself did not know all yet. What horror perhaps awaited her under the bandages of that swathed face? Tender and womanly and loving as she was, she could not help wondering as to that. She had put up her hand for guidance and leading; she wanted nothing else. But she wanted to be led very strongly, very firmly.

Then when breakfast was done, Evelyn went straight back to this identification game. A match-box was easy, because of its rough sides, a cigarette could not be a pencil, because of its smell. "And——"

"Oh, the letter!" he said.

"Dear, it's quite impossible," said Madge. "I'll tell you whom it is from with pleasure; in fact I meant to talk to you about it. I brought it up here for that purpose, to read it to you——"

But he interrupted again, rather peevishly.

"Ah, that's finished then," he said, dropping the envelope.

"What nonsense; you can't guess," said she.

"It's no question of guessing. You brought a letter in with you, and didn't mention it. You knew I shouldn't—see. You were meaning to talk about it afterwards. Well, it's either the Hermit or Philip. Besides, if the Hermit wrote to you, you would have told me. No, it's Philip."

This was no more than ordinary reason could have done.

"What does he say?" asked Evelyn in a harsh, dry tone. "Does he say he is very sorry, and it serves us right? That is the correct attitude, I should think."

Madge put a cigarette in his lips.

"Won't you smoke?" she asked.

"No, it doesn't taste. It's like smoking in a tunnel. About Philip now?"

"He doesn't take the correct attitude," said she. "If he had, how could I have wanted to talk to you about him? He wants to help us, Evelyn. And he will arrive here to-night, unless we stop him on his way at Inverness or Golspie."

The corners of his mouth were compressed; she knew he was frowning.

"Philip?" he said. "That isn't Philip."

"It wasn't perhaps," said Madge, "but it is, I think. Things have happened—Mr. Merivale is dead. Philip was there."

"Dead?" he asked.

"Yes; I only know about it from Philip. Oh, yes, you have guessed right. I can only tell you what he said. Mr. Merivale died because—because

232

sorrow, pain were revealed to him. He died very suddenly—that I gather, and he died terribly, somehow. I know no more than what I tell you."

Evelyn was silent a little.

"Yet he was the happiest man I ever saw," he said. "I used to feel like a convict in chains beside him. What does it all mean? Have we all got to suffer in proportion——"

Again he broke off.

"And Philip is coming here?" he asked. Then his voice got suddenly shriller and more staccato. "I won't see him!" he cried. "He has come to gloat over me. My God, is it not enough——"

Madge laid her two hands on his chest, pressing him gently down again.

"No, my darling," she said, "he will not come for that."

"Well, then, to make love to you again," he cried. "He knows I am a cripple, a blind man, a blot on the earth!"

Madge gave a great sigh.

"Ah, why say things you don't mean?" she said. "And why make those dagger-thrusts at me, that cannot touch me? No, don't go on. Be silent, dear, or else beg my pardon, and his. I am sorry I should have to ask that, but you have said what is abominable! Oh, I don't want words. Just nod your head, my darling, and that will mean it is said. But for the sake of love, I must have that token."

"Why does he come here, then?" he asked.

Madge could not reply for the moment; she felt so sick at heart and helpless. She had fancied, poor thing, that she had catalogued, so to speak, all the troubles and difficulties which Evelyn had to face, which she had to face with him, but here was a fresh one, that attitude of suspicion which besets those who have a sense missing, and who imagine that even those whom they love and trust most may be taking advantage of their defect. Had he been able to see her face, the absolute frankness of her expression, the candour of her eyes would have made it impossible that the merest shadow of suspicion should have crossed his mind, that peevish cry "he has come to gloat over me or to make love to you," could not have crossed his lips, for there would have been no impulse in his mind which could determine the words. Yet they had been spoken by him, fretfully, irritably, all but causelessly.

But cause there had been, and that cause was an instinct to ascribe the worst motive to the action of others instead of assuming the best. That was to be a foe to him more bitter and relentless than his sightlessness; even that which his bandages concealed would not draw so deeply on the healthful spring of kindly sanity which alone can carry a man smiling and indulgent through the frets of the world.

But for the present Madge restored his balance.

"Oh, Evelyn," she said, "don't disappoint me, dear, or make yourself bitter. You have been so brave and so splendid. Philip is coming here—or proposes to come because—he is sorry for you, because in spite of the injury we did him he still loves me—why not? But when you ask if he is coming to make love to me, then, dear, you let something which is not

233

yourself speak for you. You utter counterfeit coin. It rings false. Besides, you have not heard his letter yet; I will read it you. And then you shall take back what you said, but did not mean to say."

She read it through, every word.

"And now, dear?" she said.

But the corners of his mouth were tremulous, and that was enough; she knew well why he could not speak. So she kissed him again, and no more was said.

Lady Dover usually came up to see Evelyn after breakfast, and thus it was quite natural that she should be there when Dr. Inglis made his morning visit. She had already asked him whether she might be there when the bandages were removed, and so, when he came in now, she said:

"We are going to make quite a little festival of congratulation this morning, Mr. Dundas—that is to say, if you and Dr. Inglis will allow me to stop and see how wonderfully Sir Francis' surgery and Dr. Inglis' doctoring have succeeded."

So while this was going on, she and Madge sat in the window, looking out on to the broad sunny day. The bracken on the hillsides was already beginning to turn colour, and Lady Dover said in a low voice, for fear Evelyn should hear, and be wounded, that the gold of the sunlight striking the gold of the bracken made each appear more golden. There was time, indeed, for a good deal of leisurely art-criticism of this nature, for the unswathing of his face, the gentle withdrawal of the lint dressings from the healed wounds took time, and more than once the nurse went out to get more water for the sponging away of the gum of plaster. For Dr. Inglis, kind man of silent sympathy as he was, knew well what this moment must inevitably be to Madge—knew the torture of suspense in which she must be awaiting the sight of her husband's face. Brave as he well knew her to be, he knew also that she would have here to summon her bravery to her aid; and he wanted to make it as easy for her as he could, and thus took great pains to render the sight as little painful as might be. But he could do so little; whatever sponging and smoothing was possible, it still was so small a salvage. For the shot had struck him sideways, ricocheting off the rock, and on his forehead there was a long wound, healed indeed as well as it would ever be healed, but the outer skin had been destroyed, and it showed a long, pink line, as if perhaps some corrosive match had been struck on it. Another such went across the right cheek, another had crossed the left eyebrow, leaving a little hairless lane between the two severed sides of it. One eyelid had been struck and torn before the pellet did its deadlier work, and the other, though intact and drawn down over the hole of the eye-socket, was not like the eyelid of a man whose eyes were closed in rest or sleep, swelling gently over the eyeball and lying on the lower lashes; it hung straight, like the blind of a window, for there was nothing beneath to cause its curvature.

His kind, twinkle-eyed Scotch face had grown grave over his operations, but he guessed what the suspense to Madge was, and rightly decided that nothing could be gained by lengthening it. Then he completed the shaving operations which the nurse had begun the evening before to the uncovered part of the face, and brushed into order his thick brown hair. Finally he adjusted a pair of large dark spectacles. Evelyn demurred at this.

"What is that for?" he asked.

"Ah, that is necessary," said the doctor; "we have to protect the—the place of the worst injury. You will always have to wear them, I am afraid. And now I think we are ready."

Madge got up from the window-seat. Though she had wished Lady Dover to be there, at this moment she cared not one farthing who was there or who was not. It was only she and Evelyn who mattered; Piccadilly might have buzzed round them, and she would have been unconscious of the crowd.

And she looked—she saw——

For one moment she stood there facing him, her breath suspended, only conscious of some deep-seated terror and dismay, and her face grew white. Once she tried to speak and could not, for she knew that some dreadful exclamation alone could pass her lips. Lady Dover had got up, too, and stood by her; she looked not at Evelyn at all, but at Madge, and before the pause had grown appreciable she whispered to her—

"Say anything. Don't be a coward."

It was therefore as well that Lady Dover had come with her, otherwise anything might have happened, Madge might have screamed almost, or she might have left the room without saying a word, so dreadful was the shock. But Lady Dover's words were a lash to her, and the power of making an effort came back.

"Ah, dearest Evelyn," she said, "how nice to see your face again."

For a moment the tremor in her voice, the imminent sob in her throat, all but mastered her. Yet all this week he had been so brave, and for very shame she could not but put on the semblance of bravery and try to infuse her speech with a grain of courage.

"It is good, it is good to see you," she said, and the first physical horror began to fade a little as her love, that eternal, abiding principle, slid out from under the paralysis of the other. "All those bandages gone, all the plaster and lint gone. You look yourself, do you know, too—just, just yourself."

She turned an appealing eye on Lady Dover; that was unnecessary, because she was quite prepared to speak as soon as Madge stopped.

"I must congratulate you too, Mr. Dundas," she said in her neat, precise tones. "Why, you look, as Madge said, quite natural; does he not, Madge? And really I think dark spectacles are rather becoming. I shall get some myself."

Evelyn had not spoken yet; but reasonably or not, for he had been quite unreasonably suspicious once before that morning, he thought he detected some insincerity in these protestations. And with one quick movement of his hand he took the spectacles off.

"Are they really becoming?" he asked. "Or do you like me better without, Madge?"

Again she saw, and, with a movement uncontrollable, she hid her own eyes for a moment. But Lady Dover again came to the rescue.

235

"Ah, Doctor Inglis won't allow that, Mr. Dundas," she said.

But Evelyn still held them away from his face. Brutal as it all was, the thing had to be gone through once, and it was on the whole better to do it now.

"Ah, I asked Madge," he said quietly.

As he spoke, with his other hand he let his fingers dwell with that firm yet fluttering movement over his eyes. That straight, drawn-down lid was visualised by him, that tear in the other eyelid was visualised also. Then the hovering finger-tips traced the course of the pellet through the eyebrow, and felt, like a dog nosing a hot scent, the course of the scar where another had crossed his forehead. To that constructive touch the truth was becoming hideously plain. And deliberately, as he felt and traced, he set himself to believe the worst. He sat as judge to weigh the evidence of his fingers as they bore witness to the state of this wrecked face of his. Again and again, in days past, he had said, and meant also, that he did not wish to go below the surface of things; the eyebrow, the curve of the mouth, the light of the eye itself, as he had said to the Hermit, were enough for him, there was symbol enough there. And since this choice was so instinctive and natural to himself, it was not possible to him to dissociate others from it, and as, with terrible certainty, he framed to himself what he looked like, he put himself into Madge's place, and seeing with her eyes, framed also the conclusion which he believed to be inevitable. Yet she had seen him before, the nurse had told him so, and after that he had heard with ears that somehow seemed quickened in their sense even as touch was, the authentic ring of love in her voice. Or had he been deceived in that?

But thought, like the electric current through wires, travels many miles in an interval that is not appreciably greater than that which it takes to go a yard or two, and the rapid brushing of his fingers over his face had been almost as speedy. So when Madge answered (her thought too had gone far) he was not conscious that there had been a pause. She had complete command of her voice now.

"How can anybody be so silly?" she said. "I like you best without spectacles, dear, but as you have to wear them, there's the end of it. And"— she was embarked on a big lie, and did not mind—"you look so much better than you did when I saw you a week ago when your face was being dressed, that I should scarcely recognise you. At least I feel now as if I should scarcely have recognised you then; now there is no need for recognition. Put them on again, Evelyn; there is a strong light."

She gave a little gasp at the end of this. Lady Dover heard it, and laid a quick hand of sympathy on her shoulder. But Evelyn did not; for the present he was convinced, and that conviction, like some burst of sudden sound, shut out all other impressions.

"Here we are, then," he said. "This is the new me; positively the first appearance. A favourable reception was accorded by a sympathetic audience. And now—are you still there, Dr. Inglis?—what manner of reason is there that I should not get up?"

"You want to?" he asked.

"Why, certainly."

"Then, there is an excellent reason why you should. When my patients want to do a thing it is an indication, generally correct, that it is good for them. Yes, get up by all means."

Again the boyish delight in the new game took possession of Evelyn; yet that delight, and the pity of it, stabbed Madge like a sword.

"And let me do it myself," he cried. "Let my clothes be put by my bed, let my bath be put there, and let me be left quite alone. Madge, I bet you I shall be dressed in an hour. And the parting in my hair will be straight," he added excitedly.

This also was agreed to, with the provision that if he felt faint or tired during these operations he was at once to desist, and lie down again and ring his bell. The nurse busied herself with the preparations for this great event, and the other three went out together.

Dr. Inglis paused in the corridor outside the room.

"Mrs. Dundas," he said, "you have got to keep that up, you know. You did it well, and I don't think you ought to have done differently. Come, come, we shall have you fainting next."

Poor Madge had been utterly overwrought by this scene, and indeed as the doctor spoke she swayed and staggered where she stood. But they got her to a chair, in which she sat silent with closed eyes for a minute or so. Then she looked up at him.

"Shall I get used to it?" she asked. "Please tell me if there is a reasonable chance of that?"

"Certainly there is—we will come down in a minute, Lady Dover, if you will go on—yes, certainly, there is much more than a chance. You will get used to it. I did not know, by the way, that your husband had been told you had seen him before; but that does not matter now. But it is idle to pretend that you will get used to it at once. You won't, you can't. You will have to be patient, and all the time you must keep the strictest guard on yourself, to prevent the least suspicion getting to his mind that you are shocked by his appearance. He knows, poor fellow, more or less what he looks like. The curious blind sense of touch is developing in him with extraordinary rapidity. But you convinced him just now—his whole face flushed—that you don't mind. You must keep that up, otherwise no one can say what may happen."

"What do you mean?" asked she, still rather faintly.

"Just that. His hold on life is strong enough, quite strong enough, but it comes to him now mainly through one channel. That is you."

The rather cruel abruptness of this was intentional and well calculated. It did not dismay Madge, but just braced her. She got up from the chair.

"That will be all right, then," she said.

"I am sure it will. But as I shall go away to-day, I want to say a little more to you. His recovery, his recuperative power, is excellent, but there is one thing which I do not altogether like. His moods vary with great rapidity and great intensity. No doubt that was always so to some extent with him."

"Yes," said Madge eagerly, "it is just that which is so like him. Surely that is all for the good, that he should be so like himself?"

"Yes, within limits. But, as I need not tell you, he has been through a frightful shock, not only physical but mental, and quiet is the best restorative of all. Keep him amused and interested in things as much as you can; but also, as far as you can, keep him from feeling extravagantly. His mental barometer is jumping up and down; in proportion as it goes unnaturally high, so it will also go unnaturally low. That is frightfully tiring; it is to the mind what fever, a temperature that jumps about, is to the body."

He paused a moment.

"Of course I know the difficulties," he went on. "It is no use saying 'Be tranquil,' but you can certainly induce tranquility in him by being tranquil yourself, by surrounding him with tranquility. Keep his spirits level by keeping your own level. It won't be easy. Now, if you are quite yourself again, shall we join Lady Dover?"

Evelyn spent several hours that afternoon downstairs, but the excitement of coming down for the first time tired him, and before Philip's arrival he had gone up to bed again. All day, too, to Madge's great disquietude, his spirits had been jumping up and down; at one time he would go on with the identification game with the most absorbed enthusiasm; then again, even in the middle of it, he would suddenly stop.

"Oh, it's no use," he said. "Why, it takes me half an hour to find out what is on that table, and it would take me a week to find out what the room was like. Take me on to the terrace, will you, Madge, and let me walk up and down a bit."

This had been medically permitted, and with his arm in hers they strolled up and down in the warm sunlight. Evelyn sniffed the fresh air with extraordinary gusto.

"Ah, that's good," he said; "it is warm, yet it has got the touch of autumn in it. What sort of a day is it, Madge? Is it a blue day or a yellow day?

"Well, the sky is blue——" she began.

"Yes, I didn't suppose it was yellow," said he. "But what's the rest? Is the air between us and the hills yellow or blue? Oh, Lord, what would I not give for one more sight of it! I would look so carefully just this once. Tell me about it, dear."

So Madge, as well as she could, tried to make him see with her eyes. She told him of the brown, foam-flecked stream that wound and crawled in the shadowed gully below them, of the steep hillside opposite, that climbed out of the darkness into the broad, big sunlight of the afternoon, of the feathery birch trees, just beginning to turn yellow, that fringed the moor, of the bracken, a tone deeper in gold, of the warm greyness of the bare hill above, with its corries lying in shadow, and its topmost serrated outline cutting the sky with so clear and well-defined a line that the sky itself looked as if it was applique, fitted on to it. Away to the left was a pine wood, almost black as contrasted with the golden of the bracken, but the red trunks of the trees burned like flames in it. Beyond that again lay the

238

big purple stretches of heather over which ran the riband of the road to Golspie. Then in the immediate foreground there was a clump of rowan trees, covered with red berries; they found but a precarious footing, so steeply did the ground plunge towards the river; but halfway down there was a broad, almost level plateau, across which flowed the burn. It was covered with grass and low bushes, bog-myrtle, she thought, and a big flock of sheep were feeding there. The shepherd had just sent the collie to fetch them up, and the running dog was like a yellow streak across the green.

Evelyn gave a great sigh.

"Thanks, dear," he said. "Now shall we go in? Somehow, I don't think I can stand any more just yet. I suppose one will get more used to it. Ah, how unfair, how damnably unfair!" he cried suddenly. "Why should I be robbed like this? I wish to God I had been born blind, so that I could never know how much I miss. But to give me sight, to give me a glimpse of the world, just to take it away again! How can that be just? And I did like it so. It was all so pleasant!"

Never before had Madge so felt the utter uselessness of words. How could words be made to reach him? Yet how, again, could the yearning of her whole soul to console and comfort him fail to reach him? What she said she hardly knew; she was but conscious of the outpourings of herself in pity and love. She held that poor blind head in her hands, she kissed the mouth, she kissed the scars, she pushed up the dark spectacles and kissed the dear, empty eyelids, and all the horror that had involuntarily made her shudder when first she saw his face was gone, melted, vanished. For it had been but a superficial thing, as little her true self, as little to be taken as an index of what her heart felt, as the sudden shudder of goose-flesh, and just now at any rate it was swept away. That she would feel it again, often and often, she did not doubt, but of that she took no heed whatever. This—this pity and love—which had come upon her like a flash of revelation—was her true and her best self, and though again and again she might fall back from it, her flesh wincing and being afraid, yet there would be always the memory of this moment to guide and direct her. There would be difficult times; the whole of the rest of her life would be difficult, but it no longer presented the appearance of impossibility. And how full and dear to her heart was Evelyn's response.

"Oh, Madge," he said, "the worst of all was the thought that you would shrink from me. I minded that so much more than anything. I should not have reproached you, I don't think I should have done that even to myself, after guessing, as I have guessed, what I must be like, for I should have understood. But what I don't understand is how it is you do not shrink. I don't want to understand, either; it is quite enough for me that it is so. And when I am cross, as I shall be, and despondent, as I shall be, and odious, try to remember what I have said to you now. I want to be remembered by that."

So that was his best moment, too.

Philip arrived by the dinner train that night with a couple of other guests, and when the rest of them went up at the usual early hour, to get a good night after the journey of the day in the fresh air, he and Madge lingered behind, for naturally he wanted to learn about Evelyn and also about her. Both also perhaps felt that it was inevitable that they should have one talk together; it could hardly have been otherwise.

It began abruptly enough. As soon as the door was shut behind the last of the outgoers she came towards him with hands outstretched.

"I know you don't want me to say 'thank you,' Philip," she said, "but I can't help it. I can't tell you how deeply I thank you."

He held her hands for a moment, pressing them closely, and smiling at her.

"It is said, then. You mustn't say it twice, you know. That is vain repetition, and we have so much to say to each other that we have no time for that. I also must say once that I thank you for letting me do what I can. It would have been easier for you to have refused my help and to have refused to see me. Also it would have been more conventional. Now, about that there is just one word more to be said, and it is this. You told me once you looked upon me as an elder brother. Well, you have got to do it again. I'm going to manage for you. You have got, you and Evelyn, to do as I tell you in practical matters, because I'm practical and you are not."

A great lump rose in Madge's throat. These days had tired her so; it was such an unutterable relief to have anything taken off her hands, to feel that the almost intolerable weight of the future was being shared by another. But for the moment she could not speak, and but just nodded to him.

"Now, I am the bearer of a message first of all," he said, "and the message is from my mother. She wants you both—in fact, she insists on your coming down to Pangbourne for—for a period which she says had better be left indefinite. London, she truly says, is dust and ashes in September. It really would be the best plan, so will you join with me in persuading Evelyn, if persuasion is necessary?"

"Ah, Philip," she said, "you cut me to the heart. And—and this makes it worse, that I accept your generosity for Evelyn's sake. It is that which—which is so ruthless."

Philip's lip quivered a moment, but he went on bravely.

"Well, as an elder brother I recommend it, too," he said; "for it is just that I want to be to you, dear. Ah, do you think I don't guess?"

Madge got up, and drew a chair close to him.

"Tell me about yourself, if it does not hurt you to talk of that," she said.

"No, I want you to know what has happened to me," he said; "both because I have to ask your forgiveness for certain things——"

"Ah, don't, don't!" said she.

"Yes, you will see, and because perhaps what I have been through may help you. Well, Madge, I have been through deep waters, and waters as bitter as they were deep. For that month while I was in London I hated you and I hated him with such intensity that I think, but for the very hard work I did, I must have gone mad. And I think the only pleasure I felt was when I was the cause—indirectly anyhow—of his losing a large sum of money. I could have saved him that if I chose, but I did not choose. I must speak of that afterwards. But I loved you all the time I hated you, Madge, if you can understand that. All that was base and hard in me loathed you, because you had made me suffer; but there was something below, a very little thing, like a lump of leaven perhaps which still loved you, my infinitesimal better self. But all the time in London I did not know there was in me anything better than this worst.

"Then one morning I fainted, and they told me to ease off. So I went down into the country and stayed with the Hermit, who, I think, lived the happiest life that was ever lived on this earth. It was the contrast between him and me perhaps that first suggested to me whether it was worth while to hate, as I was hating, for that as far as I know was the beginning of what happened afterwards. It made me also throw away something I had bought in order to kill myself—never mind that. Then one night he talked about pain, on which he had turned his back, and told me that though he could not understand how or why it was necessary, it perhaps might be, and that he was willing himself, if so, to face anything that might be in store for him. And then, I must suppose that little lump of leaven began to work, because that night—we had talked also about free will—I asked myself if I chose, deliberately chose, to be bitter and hating. And I found I did not.

"It was not long after that—a week, I suppose—that the end came. By then I knew but this for certain, that I was not deliberately hard any longer. It was the contemplation of happiness and serenity that had produced that; I had begun also not to stare at a blank wall that had seemed to face me, but to say to myself that there was no wall except that of my own making. Do you know Watts' picture of Hope? Of course you do. Well, I thought all my strings were broken, but they were not. There was just one left. But that I knew must inevitably break if I continued to be black and bitter. My bitterness had corroded it already."

Philip paused a moment.

"I am jawing dreadfully about myself," he said.

"Go on," said she.

"Tom died in the night. I don't want to tell you that in detail, but he died because he saw or thought he saw some revelation of the pain and sorrow of the world. Whether he imagined it or not, and whether what I thought I saw was imagination only, I don't really care. He was sleeping in a hammock out of doors, and suddenly his cry rent the night. He called on God and on Christ. And when I went out I thought I saw a shadow like some dreadful goat skip from him. And he was dead.

"Now, how one learns anything I don't know. But what I learned was pity for sorrow. And so, dear Madge, I am here."

Again her hand sought his. "Oh, Philip, Philip," she said. "What can I say to you? How could I guess what love was till I felt it? Ah, I don't say that in excuse—you know that."

"No, dear. It is no question of excuses, of course. And I have only told you all this that you may never need to look for any, and that you may understand that I am sorry for having been so bitter. And if you forgive that"—and the pressure of her hand answered him—"let us leave the past

241

forever behind us, and look forward only. But it was better to have talked of it just once, so that we may dismiss it. Now, tell me about Evelyn."

To Philip somehow she could pour out her heart in a way she could scarcely have done to anyone else, for the knowledge of what he had been through and of the bitterness from which he had emerged so unembittered threw open the golden gates of sympathy, and she spoke without reserve. She told him of the myriad dangers and difficulties that faced them, of the loss Evelyn had sustained which she could not yet estimate, which he, too, was only just beginning to realise, and which for a long time yet to come must daily grow more real to him. She spoke quite frankly, yet never without the utter sinking of herself, which is love, of his moods and transitions from boyish cheerfulness to a sort of dumb despair. She spoke finally of her first mortal horror when she saw his face, and her dread lest that should suddenly overmaster her, so that she should shrink from him and he should see it.

"But it is he," she said, "whom I tremble for. He can stand it to-day, he will be able to stand it to-morrow, and for a week perhaps, or a month. But will it get easier for him to bear or more difficult? He can't stand much more. He will break."

"Ah, you mustn't think about that," said Philip. "It is no use adding up the sorrow and the pain that may be in front of one. One is meant just to bear the burden of the moment, and, God knows, it is heavy enough for you and him. Face difficulties as they arise, Madge, don't make a sum of them and say the total is intolerable."

He paused a moment.

"And let me bear all that you can shift on to me," he said. "Because otherwise, you see, my coming here will be purposeless. And I hate, being a practical person, doing useless things."

TWENTY-THIRD

IT was a dismally wet afternoon some weeks later, and Evelyn was sitting in one of the deep window-seats in the drawing-room of Philip's house above Pangbourne, which looked out on to the terrace, where only six months ago the nightingale had sat and sung on Tom Merivale's finger. Below, communicating with the upper terrace by a flight of stone steps, was the bedless square of grass, below again the rose garden, from which the ground went steeply down to the river. He had occupied himself with closing the shutters of this row of windows, one of which, reaching down to the ground, communicated with the terrace, and, not satisfied with this, he had drawn the curtains over them, leaving the room in darkness. The window-seats were well cushioned, and having arrived at the last, he slipped between the curtains he had drawn and curled himself up in it.

During this last month he had made, so everybody said, extraordinary progress; he could already read a little, fast enough, that is to say, to enable him to remember the sentences he spelled out with his fingers in the raised type; he could remember the cards in his hand sufficiently to enable him to play a game of bridge, and with a stick to feel his way he could walk alone. But none, except he, knew the dreadful progress which despair had made in his mind. He had begun to be able once to look forward, to frame the future; but now the future was unframeable, he was only able just to bear the present moment. Soon that might be unbearable, too.

For a week now this dull weight, starting from a definite moment, had been gaining on him, for a week ago he had gone with Philip to the lodge, and the four-year-old child of the lodge-keeper had come out with his father. Evelyn, sitting down and waiting while Philip spoke to him, had called the child, who toddled up to him, and then, when he got close, burst into shrieks of frightened dismay. Evelyn had understood, and he said nothing about it to anyone. But he put the fact away in his mind, and when he was alone he took it out and looked at it.

At this moment he was alone in the house. Mrs. Home was spending a few days in London, Philip would soon be due by the evening train, and Madge was out, doing some small businesses in Pangbourne. She had been unwilling to leave him, but he had made it unmistakably and ill-temperedly clear he would sooner be left. He thought with a dull wonder at himself of the fact that he could have been cross with her. It had happened often before, and in spite of its recurrence he never got used to it. It always seemed strange to him. And with a wonder that was almost incredulous, he thought how he had behaved to her to-day. For she had come to him with a word which a man can only hear once, to whisper which a woman nestles close to him, pouring out her very soul in the joy of knowing that she will some day put into his arms her first-born child. That Madge had told him, but he felt nothing; it did not reach him, neither joy for her nor for himself seemed any longer capable of being felt, and he had said only, "I shall never see it." He was thinking about that now, if this leaden contemplation of facts could be called thought, of that and of the child that had cried when it saw his face. Over that face he passed his sensitive fingers.

"I'm sure I don't wonder," he said to himself.

The door opened once as he lay in this window-seat, and correctly and mechanically he pictured what was going on. Only one person entered; that he could tell by the footfalls, and that one person whistled gently to himself. He paused by the table, then went to the door again, and again re-entered and paused by another. Then he poked the fire and swept up the grate. Clearly the footman making the room ready, and he banged the door as he went out.

Now if that child had cried at the sight of his face, what must it be to others? Surely they would cry too if they obeyed their natural impulse, either cry or turn away, in pity, no doubt, but also in repulsion. It must be an effort to everybody to look at him, to be with him. And Madge was with him so much; she kissed him, she let him kiss her; she was his wife, the wife of this man with the nightmare face at which a child cried out as if it saw bogey. Philip had been quick and ready on that occasion, had said the child was teething, and wrung corroboration from the father. But he had answered, "Yes, it teethes when it sees me," and Philip was not ready enough for that.

The crying child explained other things too; for Mrs. Home had cried when she saw him; he could hear from her voice that she was crying, there were sobs in it. He had thought then that it was from pity merely and sympathy, but he told himself now that it was not so; she cried from horror at him. All his life he had hated ugly things, and now it would be hard to match himself in that abhorred category.

The very kindness, too, and pity which he knew surrounded him were scarcely more bearable. He did not want to be pitied, he would sooner be left to drag out a lonely, shunned life than to be surrounded with pity; while with regard to kindness, the knowledge that he and Madge were frankly living on Philip became harder every day to swallow. Philip certainly had done all he could to minimise the burden of that; he had, soi-disant, bought the unfinished picture of himself, declaring that no finished picture could possibly be so like him; he had bought, too, after argument, the picture of Madge. The proceeds he had invested for Evelyn, promising since he had advised him so ill before to take greater care this time, and twice during this last month he had reported substantial profits from the investments he had made for him, so that if he insisted, as he did insist, on paying the bills for his nurse and doctor, he still could run up to London whenever he pleased if Pangbourne bored him. With luck, too, and care his investments would grow fatter yet.

On this occasion Evelyn had broken out.

"Ah, I can't stand it," he cried. "I can't go on living here, Madge and I, indefinitely. Yes, I know how kind you are, both you and your mother, and how you would be pleased—really pleased—for us to stop forever, but can't you see how impossible it is for me to accept your hospitality like that? I must, I simply must, pay my way, earn something, work and get tired, if only for the distraction of it. A barrel-organ, now. 'Totally blind. Ky-ind Gentleman!' That would be more self-respecting than to sit here and do nothing. It's better to beg in the streets than to accept alms without begging for them. That's why the poor have such a horror of the workhouse. They would sooner be cold and hungry, and so would I."

He was silent a moment after this.

"I suppose I needn't have said all that," he observed drearily. "However, it doesn't much matter what I say."

Philip had a horror of improving the occasion, but he could hardly let such a chance of a word in season slip. He was, too, keenly wounded by this.

"You don't recollect, my dear fellow," he said, "that we are all doing our best, and that it is hard not to be hurt by words like those."

"Oh, for God's sake don't preach," cried Evelyn.

Philip flushed for a moment rather angrily, but re-collected himself.

"Indeed, I hope not," he said with a laugh. "Now are you ready to give me my revenge at picquet?"

It was quite dark behind the curtains, though to Evelyn, who lay there, whatever the light was, it would have been dark in any case, and in a grosser darkness than that, a darkness of despair unilluminable by any sun, he pondered these things, his own helplessness, his blindness, the horror of his own face, and the dead weight of his indebtedness to Philip, the one man in all the world whose charity, from the very nature of things, was most unbearable. Together, poor fellow they formed a blank wall which it seemed hopeless to try to scale; indeed, he no longer really wanted to scale it, he only wanted to be allowed to sit down and have not only sight, but hearing and feeling and taste and smell closed forever, for death was surely a thing far less bitter than this living death in life. He could no longer now look forward to the future at all; it required all his energies to get through the hour that was present, without some breakdown; decent behaviour for the moment, when he was with any of the others, was the utmost he was capable of, and even of that he often felt incapable. And his energies, such as they were, were gradually failing before the hourly task. He was in no sense beginning ever so slightly to get used to it all, and the trials of each day, so far from making the trials of the next more easy to contemplate or to bear, only weakened his powers of bearing them. It was all so hopeless; for him hope was dead, and the last chord of her lyre had snapped.

But he did not feel this dully and vaguely; the very vividness and alertness of his nature which had made life so passionately sweet to him before made his hopelessness just as passionately felt now. He, too, like Tom Merivale, but with less of set purpose and more of instinct in his choice, had been in love with life, and that fire which had gone out had left not mere grey ash, but something burningly cold, and life was now as actively terrible to him as it had once been lovely.

There was the muffled sound of talking in the hall, and next moment the steps of two people entered, and Madge spoke. The other step went on towards the fireplace.

"Evelyn not here?" she said. "I suppose he's gone to the library for tea."

Then Philip's voice spoke.

"How has he been to-day?"

"Ah, so bad, poor darling!" she said. "Sometimes I almost despair, Philip; if it wasn't for you I know I should. Of course he tries all he can, but it seems almost as if his powers of trying were failing. It makes me utterly miserable to think of him."

Evelyn did not move nor reveal his presence in any way. He felt as if the speaker was but being the echo of his own thoughts. Philip said something sympathetic in tone, but he did not catch that; he wanted only to hear how far Madge agreed with himself.

"And I dread his suspecting more," she went on. "I so often see him feeling his face, as if trying to picture it to himself more clearly. And if for a moment I should break down and let him know—ah, I can't talk of it. Let us go to the library and see if he is there."

Her voice choked a little over this; then without more words they passed out of the drawing-room again, and Evelyn felt as if something had snapped in his brain. He almost wondered that they had not heard it.

As soon as the door had closed behind them he got swiftly and quietly up from his seat and felt his way to the centre window, which opened on to the terrace. He undid the shutters of it, stepped out, and closed it behind him. He was hardly conscious of any motive in his action— he certainly had no plan as to what he should do next. One overwhelming fact had become a certainty to him, the fact contained in Madge's last sentence, and he knew nothing more than that he must go away somewhere, lose himself somehow, do anything rather than go back to her, to be pitied, to be secretly shuddered at, to be a daily, hourly fear to her. Indeed, he would never look upon their child.

It was a cold, windless evening, and the rain descended in a steady downpour, hissing on to the shrubs, while the gutters of the house gurgled and chuckled. But louder than the rain and more sonorous was the great rush and roar of the river below, as it poured seawards, swollen to a torrent of flood from these persistent rains. And something in the strength and glory of that deep voice called to him; he must go down to the river, for it had something to say to him. Yet it was not the river that called to him, but in some mysterious way Tom Merivale, whose jovial, deep voice was shouting to him to come with the authenticity of actual hallucination. He hardly knew which it was; he knew only that he could never go back to the house he had just left, and that something called, with promise in its voice of life, real life, or of death and deliverance, he knew not which.

He had no stick to guide him, but without hesitation he crossed the gravel of the terrace, and felt his way along the wall of it to where a stone vase stood at the top of the steps leading to the lawn below. A purple clematis twined round it; he had made a study of it for a picture last summer. Then came the twelve steps, the shuffling across the soaked grass of the lawn, and a further flight of twelve steps into the rose garden.

But at the thought of deliverance of some kind so close to him, so that he need no more now think of "to-morrow and to-morrow," and all the impossible to-morrows, his poor tired brain cleared, his myriad troubles and sorrows seemed to roll away from him, for though the bitterness of death was not past, the bitterness of life, in comparison to which the other was sweet, was over. So with unclouded mind and soul, which no longer rebelled and resented, he thought quietly, as he felt his way across the rose garden, and struck the steep path leading to the river, of all the past.

How wonderful and beautiful life had been; since his earliest boyish recollections, how full of surprising joys! Health and vigour had been his, a clean, wholesome life, the power of loving this exquisite world, an artistic gift that had made a daily Paradise, and, above all, love itself, and the fulfilment of love. Then had come a crash, a break, but how short had been these weeks in comparison of the rest. If this was the pain with which he had to make payment for all his joy, how cheap, to look at it fairly, had joy been. Now that he knew that was the full payment that would be demanded for the joy he had received in such unstinted abundance, he no longer complained, it was only while the payment seemed to be going to be charged him indefinitely, every day for years to come, that he had rebelled and owned himself bankrupt. The one eternal necessity of life, which, the moment it ceases to brace begins to paralyse, had passed from him, the necessity of going on always, every day and hour, having to meet one difficulty after another, and without hope of getting any respite, so long as life lasts. For now he knew that some end was very near.

He paused a moment to brush his dripping hair back from his face, wondering in a sort of vague, uninterested manner whether something had actually cracked in his brain, whether he had gone mad, or so the world could call it. But whatever had cracked, it had been the tension of it which all these weeks had caused his misery, and in this exquisite moment of peace that had suddenly come to him he almost laughed aloud for the unspeakable relief which the cessation of pain had brought. He felt that up till now his mental eyes had been as blind as his physical ones, that the blows that had been dealt him had been dealt from the dark, so that he could not guess who wielded the whip. But now they had ceased, and the clouds of darkness were rolled away, and there sat there One with a face full of infinite compassion, and since none but He was there, it must have been He, or some ministering angel of pain, who at his bidding had chastised him thus. Then Evelyn felt as if he had asked permission of Him to go on, for the river—or Tom's voice—still hailed him joyously; and since it was allowed, still without intention, without definite thought of any kind, he went on his way, with shuffling steps indeed that stumbled over the gravel of the path, but with a great, serene light shining on him.

He had by now come close to the edge of the river, and the rain for the moment had ceased, so that he could hear the suck and gurgle of the hurrying flood-water, which whispered and chuckled to itself. But this rapturous noise of swift-flowing water sounded but faintly, for a hundred yards below was the weir. All the sluices were raised, and tons of water momently plunged through the openings, bellowing with a great hoarse laugh of ecstasy as they fell into the pool below. It was to that place, somewhere in the middle of the narrow pathway of planks that he was called; it was from there, where he would be surrounded on all sides with the noise of waters, that the voice of Tom, that faithful lover of water, called him. That somehow, and he did not question how or why, was his goal, nor did he know whether life or death awaited him there; only there was going to be reconcilement in some manner.

He had been there many times before; he had been there, indeed, only yesterday to listen to the splendid tumult of water. But to-day its voice was redoubled, and he could feel the mist from the plunging stream wet on his face as he went slowly and cautiously out over the wet planks. Louder and more triumphantly every moment the voice of the river—or was it Tom laughing with open mouth, as he used to laugh when he swam in the garden pool below his cottage?—called to him. On both sides, before and behind, he was surrounded by the joyous riot of waters, that filled and possessed his brain till his whole consciousness was flooded with it till his voice too had to join in it. So he raised his arms, spreading them out to the night, and threw back his head with a great shout of ecstatic rapture. And as he did this his foot slipped on the wet planks, and he fell into the roaring, rushing pool below. So the great Mother took him back to herself.

EPILOGUE

IT was just a year later, a warm, mellow afternoon of mid-October. For the last few nights there had been an early autumn frost, though the days were almost like a return of summer, and the beech-wood below Philip's house at Pangbourne was just beginning to don its russet livery. The frost, too, had made its mark on blackened dahlias, but the chrysanthemums were still gorgeous. And on the terrace were walking two figures, both dressed in black, one tall, who strolled beside the other, Madge and Mrs. Home. The latter was still as like a Dresden shepherdess as ever in the pretty china delicacy of her face, but Madge had changed somewhat. Trouble had written its unmistakable signs on her face, but tenderness had been at work there, too, and though her eyes were sad, yet with the sadness was mingled something so sweet and gentle that no one who loved her would have wished that the sadness should not be there, if the other had come hand-in-hand with it. And it was hand-in-hand that they had come during the last eighteen months of her life, which had been to her of such infinitely greater import than all the years that had gone before.

"Yes, it is even as I tell you," she was saying. "I never think of Evelyn as blind. I think of him—well, a good deal, but he always comes back to me, not as he was in those last weeks, but in those first few weeks before, bright-eyed—you know how bright his eyes were—and full of a sort of boyish joy at this jolly world. No, I scarcely feel sad when I think of him. He was fragile; he would have broken if he had had to bear more. And I think God knew that, and spared him by letting him die."

She walked on a little without speaking. Mrs. Home's hand on her arm pressed its sympathy, but she said nothing.

"I have been allowed to forget, too," Madge went on, "or to remember it only as a nightmare from which I awoke, the way I shrank from him, and I only wonder now whether, if he had lived, I should have got used to it. Ah, surely it must have been in a dream only that I shrank from him."

"Yes, dear, it was only that," said Mrs. Home. "At least, no one knew. You behaved so that no one guessed."

"Philip knew. If it had not been for him during those months I think I should have gone mad. And for the second time he kept me—it is hardly an exaggeration—kept me sane when baby died."

Mrs. Home, when she had anything important and difficult to say, often gave out little twittering, mouse-like noises before she could manage to speak. Madge knew this, and thus, hearing them now, waited for her to overcome her embarrassment.

"And is there no hope for Philip, dear?" she asked at length.

Madge had rather expected this was coming, but her answer gave her less embarrassment than the question had caused his mother.

"I owe Philip everything," she said, "and though I don't suppose I can ever love again in the way that I have loved, still—you know once I told him quite truthfully that I would give him all that I was capable of. You see, I did not know then what love meant. That was a niggardly gift to offer him. And now again I can give him—oh, so gratefully—all I am capable of. It is, I hope, not quite such a mean thing as it was. I think——"

Madge paused a moment.

"I think sorrow has made me a little more worthy of him," she went on. "It has made me a little more like a woman. So if he cares still——"

"Ah, my dear, you say 'still.' Why, day by day he loves you more."

Madge looked at Mrs. Home a moment in silence, and the sadness of her eyes was melted into pure tenderness.

"You are sure?" she said.

"He will tell you better than I."

Madge gave a long sigh, then let her gaze wander down the steep path to the river, which crossed the weir and formed a short cut through the fields of Pangbourne. The sun, which was near to its setting, dazzled her a little, and she put up her hand to shade her eyes.

"Ah, that is he coming up the path," she said. "He must have caught the earlier train. Shall we go to meet him?"

"You go, dear," said Mrs. Home. "I will wait for you here."

www.ingramcontent.com/pod-product-compliance
Lightning Source LLC
Chambersburg PA
CBHW011940260626
47157CB00018B/3264